Carol McGrath is the author of ~~~~~ series *The Rose Trilogy*.

Born in Northern Ireland, sh~~~~~ at a young age, when exploring lo~~~~~ digs. While completing a degree~~~~~ by the strong women who were s~~~~~ ~~~~~ ~~~~~, and was inspired to start exploring their lives. Her first novel, *The Handfasted Wife*, was shortlisted for the Romantic Novelists' Association Awards, and *Mistress Cromwell* was widely praised as a timely feminist retelling of Tudor court life. Her novels are known for their intricacy, depth of research and powerful stories.

Praise for *The Rose Trilogy*

'Powerful, gripping and beautifully told. A historical novel that will resonate with the #MeToo generation. Carol McGrath bewitched me with her immaculate research, vivid characters and complex tale of politics, power and love. I could smell the secrets and taste the fear that stalked King Henry's court. Clever, intimate and full of intrigue, I loved it' **Kate Furnivall**

'Fascinating . . . Brings to life one of the most determined and remarkable queens of the medieval world' **K. J. Maitland**

'A very well-researched tale of a fascinating period'
Joanna Courtney

'Completely engrossed me from the start . . . A wonderful read'
Nicola Cornick

'Temptation for any fan of scheming behind the arras and swooning courtly love!' **Joanna Hickson**

By Carol McGrath

The Stolen Crown

The Rose Trilogy

The Silken Rose
The Damask Rose
The Stone Rose

Mistress Cromwell

Daughters of Hastings Trilogy

The Betrothed Sister
The Swan-Daughter
The Handfasted Wife

THE
STOLEN
CROWN

CAROL McGRATH

ACCENT

First published in 2023 by Headline Accent
An imprint of HEADLINE PUBLISHING GROUP

1

Cataloguing in Publication Data is available from the British Library

ISBN 978 1 4722 9734 1

Maps and family tree by Kieron Grearson

Typeset in 10.5/13pt Bembo Std by Jouve (UK), Milton Keynes

Printed and bound in Great Britain by Clays Ltd, Elcograf S.p.A.

HEADLINE PUBLISHING GROUP
An Hachette UK Company
Carmelite House
50 Victoria Embankment
London
EC4Y 0DZ

www.headline.co.uk
www.hachette.co.uk

For Patrick, my greatest knight

TABLE 1 The English succession

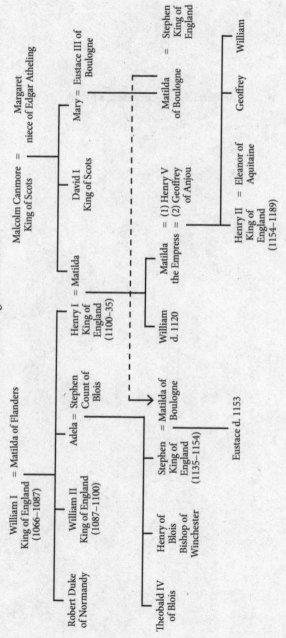

Map 1 England in the twelfth century

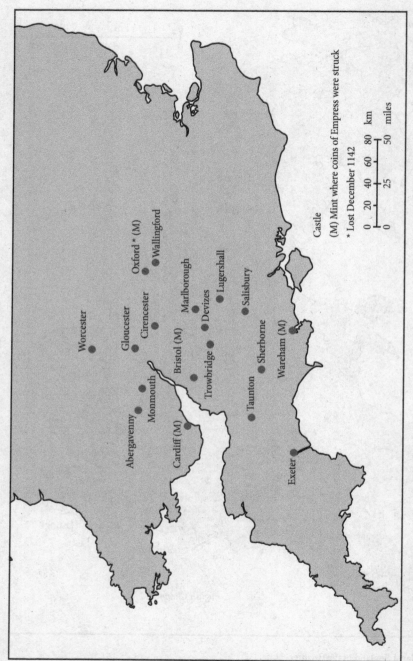

Map 2 Principal castles held for Empress Matilda

Worcester

Gloucester
Cirencester

Oxford * (M)
Wallingford

Marlborough
Bristol (M)
Devizes
Lugershall

Monmouth
Trowbridge
Salisbury

Abergavenny

Cardiff (M)
Taunton
Sherborne

Wareham (M)

Exeter

Castle

(M) Mint where coins of Empress were struck

* Lost December 1142

| 0 | 20 | 40 | 60 | 80 | km |
| 0 | | 25 | | 50 | miles |

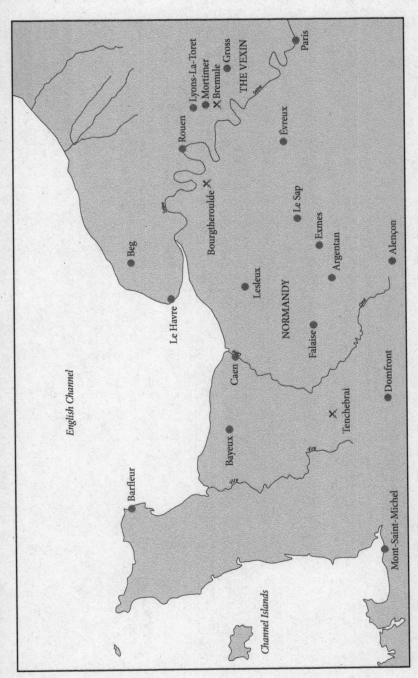

Map 3 Normandy in the twelfth century

'Glistering', by Edwin Stockdale

Oxford Castle, December 1142

> Ice and snow have caught the castle millstream.
> Maude is ready, pulls on her ermine cloak,
> slips from Saint George's Tower, lets herself out
> of the postern gate. Against the hollows of drifting snow
> she is invisible, an artic fox.
>
> Looking back, she can't see the coral rag stone
> concealed in frost. The water's voice is deadened
> with ice. Maude picks her way down the frozen tributary
> to the Thames. Her feet are frigid: she no longer knows
> if she is creeping past Stephen's lines.
>
> The watch's shouts echo in the blizzard.
> Maude trudges on unseen.

My thanks to Edwin for this lovely poem.

Part One

Chapter One

Windsor Castle
January 1127

Windsor Castle's great hall doors flew open to admit the Archbishops of Canterbury and York. The neatly tonsured pair swept in from the snow, followed by a retinue of abbots and bishops. Ordered to attend King Henry's Christmas court, they crowded into the tall, hammer-beamed hall. A blaze in the central hearth briefly flared up from the draught, before crackling and dying down as the doors closed behind the last abbot, aging William Godemon of Gloucester Abbey, who tapped his way forward, leaning heavily on a stick. The nobles – fashionably clad in the finest of woollen gowns, embroidered long-toed shoes and fur-lined mantles pinned with ostentatious jewels – moved aside to allow the clergy to gather closer to the fire.

Maud sat proudly by her father on the dais, her face immobile and chin held high. She rarely smiled in public. She had, after all, been Empress of Germany and Queen of the Romans until her much-loved husband's death a few years earlier, when her papa, the first King Henry had recalled her to England. She had willingly agreed to a return, knowing that he hoped to declare her as his heir. An empress ranked more highly than a queen, naturally, but Maud and Emperor Heinrich V had been childless. Now that there was a new emperor in Germany, she could not pass up the opportunity to rule England and Normandy as a queen in her own right. It was far preferable to settling for a lesser role in the German court or, worse, a new marriage in that land where she had lived from the age of eight.

3

Maud knew that England's clergy and barons had been summoned to Windsor over Christmas to recognise her as her father's heir, because the widowed young Empress was her father's only living legitimate child. It was not, of course, that King Henry did not have other children. He had sired nineteen in all, born to his many mistresses, most of them raised together as faithful subjects and half-siblings at his court. Maud's mother, the Princess Edith of Scotland, known as Queen Matilda of England, had accepted them all, considering her marital duty done once she had provided Henry with a son and a daughter. But, seventeen years ago, William, Maud's brother, had drowned on a vessel called the *White Ship*, whilst departing Boulogne. His death had broken her father's heart. And, although King Henry had remarried following his first wife's death, this union had not produced children in five years of marriage. Surprising, Maud mused, as he had many children with his mistresses.

Queen Adeliza, Empress Maud's golden-headed young stepmother, smiled serenely upon the enormous crowd as Maud idly watched her. It was an unusual gathering of both priests and nobles, Maud concluded, her blue eyes moving past Adeliza to take in the crammed hall. She hoped she looked as regal, to them, as the jewelled gold band on her head. Her glossy black plait, adorned with golden bindings, lay over her right breast, reaching down to her magnificent belt studded with sapphires and pearls. A delicate cream silk veil framed her handsome face.

The faces at the back of the crowd blurred into a sea of pale ovals, too far away for Maud's short-sighted eyes to reach. She blinked, focused hard and studied the countenances of the bishops who knelt before her instead, ready to take the succession oath demanded by her father. On bended knee, they would recognise her, a woman, as King Henry's heir and as their liege lady, after his death. Yet, even raised above the peerage and the bishops as she was today, she was not precisely sure whether this meant she was to be a queen in her own right, a queen consort or a queen mother. Her father had been deliberately vague on this point. Ideally, she suspected, he would like her to provide him with a grandson before his death. But, to her mind, the oath's wording lacked a certain clarity. After all, she had experience ruling alongside Heinrich, Emperor of the Germans and the Holy Roman Empire. She knew she could command a populace as well as any prince. Maud wriggled slightly and scratched her wrist in impatience. She wondered, as the interminable oath-taking slowly began, how many of these nobles and bishops truly meant their oath and how many did not.

The order of oath-taking was masterfully directed by Roger of Salisbury, an efficient and popular bishop with sharp eyes, tall and thin as a willow reed. First of all, the archbishops swore allegiance to her, followed by the bishops, who also proceeded without complaint. Only Salisbury himself dared to express a caveat, declaring that, if the lady – meaning Maud herself, she realised with a shock – was to remarry abroad, then they, the clergy, must be consulted. King Henry looked at the Bishop with thunderous eyes under his grey, bushy brows. With an impatient flick of his hand, he summoned him to come closer.

When Bishop Roger had slowly mounted the dais and bent his head close to the King's ear to hear better, Henry muttered something incomprehensible to them all. Maud strained hard to hear his words – but then, with a nod, the elegant Bishop Roger was turning and floating down the dais steps as if he walked on air. He returned to his place at the front of the queue of bishops. In a clear voice, he took the oath.

Maud swallowed and swore under her breath. She would not share her throne or her bed with any man unless he was one of her own choosing. The remaining bishops successively took the oath, and then her uncle, King David of Scotland, who took precedence over the English nobles, swore next. He was followed by her cousin, flaxen-haired, pleasant-mannered Stephen of Blois, who swore in a reedy yet confident voice, his pale head dipped so that she could not see his face. There was something hooded about Stephen's usually open demeanour today. Did she sense reluctance about that stocky young man who had grown up in her father's court and was married to the icy heiress, Matilda of Boulogne? He was a grandchild of

5

William, the Norman Conqueror, just like Maud herself. And yet she, Maud reassured herself, a ghost of a frown darkening her brow, was daughter of the King, whilst Stephen was only the son of Adela, William's daughter. He was the heir to Blois, a wealthy land across the Narrow Sea. Wealthy, but paltry in comparison to a throne.

As Stephen straightened up from taking his oath, his clear blue eyes met Maud's at last, for a second, and she caught his bland smile; but then he was stepping back and her favourite half-brother, dark-eyed, bear-like Robert of Gloucester, was stepping forward and swearing in his gruff voice, his face open, whereas Stephen's had been closed. Maud began to relax again, but momentarily. Gazing down the hall at the gathered assembly, she heard a snatch of some complaining voice.

'It is a disgrace,' Abbot Anselm of Bury St Edmunds was saying. 'The nobility should never be given precedence over the abbots.'

Could a cleric put a stop to the oath-taking?

'Father!' she hissed, again leaning towards her father. 'Do you hear Abbot Anselm?'

He had, because Henry lifted his hand and roared at the abbots who were shoving past the peers of the land. 'What is done cannot be undone. Cease complaining about who takes precedence and get in line. The other earls first and then you abbots!'

Maud breathed more easily after that, though her father's stern words taught her a valuable lesson. The silly fracas indicated that keeping order amongst upstart abbots and vain, competing nobles might require firmness – even ruthlessness – once she was their queen.

It was Brien Fitz Count's turn. Her heart fluttered as he bowed his dark tousled curls and, rising, smiled at her, his black eyes dancing, giving her renewed courage. Brien had been her dearest friend at court since she was a child, and, since she had returned to England, she had found herself looking for him more and more often. She knew that Brien would be as fiercely loyal to her as he was to her father. If she was indeed crowned England's Queen and Duchess of Normandy following her father's death, Count Brien and her

half-brother, Robert, were more than equal to the task of supporting her rule. Papa, she noted, looked in superb health today, his grey
hair neatly curled, his short beard trimmed and his eyesight as keen
as ever, missing nothing, even though he was into his fifth decade.
This first Henry had reigned for a quarter century and more. There
would be plenty of time for him to instruct her about the particular
ways of ruling his kingdom.

As the afternoon light faded and sconces were lit, the oath-taking
drew to a close. Tonight, they would dine with the great men of
England, on the understanding that, for now, the succession was
settled.

'You are every inch a future queen and my daughter,' her father
said, with warmth in his voice. 'I'm proud of you.' He thought for a
moment, glanced sideways at Adeliza. 'And now, my beautiful
Queen, we must turn our attention to finding her a husband, so that
she may give me a grandson.'

Adeliza inclined her head in agreement, but Maud's heartbeat
quickened. Clasping her hands in her lap, her whole body was rigid
with indignation. For she had been married to the great Emperor of
Germany and Rome for thirteen years, and had learned much about
leadership. She simply did not need a husband chosen for her, from
within this kingdom or from any kingdom beyond the Narrow Sea.
In fact, she had already rejected many suitors since her return to
England and she would continue to do so.

And yet . . . glancing along the supper table to where Brien Fitz
Count was seated beside her brother Robert, she reflected that
someone similar might persuade her otherwise, but she knew of no
one similar. Count Brien himself was taken to husband already by
the heiress Tilda of Wallingford. That lady, mused Maud, was a
woman as wealthy as the richest bishop or noble in the land, but she
was far too old to give her handsome husband children, and much
too interested in managing her own vast land holdings to accompany Brien to court. Tilda was, Maud thought, a somewhat dour if
self-possessed woman, as pleased with herself as a cat that had just

snatched a fish from an abbey pond. Roger of Salisbury had warned against a foreign marriage, and who was more English than Brien? Maud flexed her fingers beneath her long sleeves. Marriages – particularly if there was no issue – could be annulled.

Supper dishes were pushed aside and tankards were refilled. Count Brien stood, stretched and approached Henry's chair. Maud felt a ghost of a smile tugging at the corners of her otherwise purposefully serious mouth. Brien loved fashionable garments for his court appearances and today he was dressed in crimson damask with scalloped gold borders, his long tunic narrow to show off his fine figure, split at each side, revealing hose of deep blue. She noted on his feet a pair of beautiful embroidered shoes that slightly curled up above his toes, like little gold and red snakes.

When the King gave him a nod, Brien clapped his hands, and, at this signal, a group of minstrels tripped into the centre of the hall from behind an arras. They played carols on various instruments and a young girl with flowing fair hair began to sing in a pure and clear voice, the notes dropping like pearls from her mouth. The ballad told of the adventures of a pair of swans that magically changed into a prince and princess who long, long ago ruled over a very ancient kingdom of the Celts. The guests were hypnotised by the beauty of her voice and the exquisite accompaniment of harp, triangle and a citole, played by two equally fair-haired young boys.

Maud slipped her hand to her belt and loosened her coin purse. Gesturing to a page, she instructed him to take it to Count Brien, that he might, on her behalf, reward the girl with the sweet voice and her family of musicians. Count Brien grinned and nodded to Maud on receipt of the gift. She felt colour rise up her throat at his smile.

'I am tired tonight and I think we can respectably leave the company now,' Adeliza said a little later, with a delicate yawn, quickly masking it with her ringed fingers. There would be other entertainments that night. A juggler was already tossing coloured balls into the air. Cups were being refilled. But Maud was content to leave too.

Outside, snow appeared to hover in the air. Maud and Adeliza drew their mantles closer against the shock of the cold night after the heat in the hall. With a rustle of silks, they entered into a chilly outer passage, which led to the royal bower hall and, beyond that, into the peace and quiet of Queen Adeliza's apartments.

'They'll drink and toast far into the morning,' Adeliza remarked as they hurried along the stone passageway. 'Tomorrow, there'll be an afternoon's entertainment with carolling for Epiphany. We'll need our rest.'

Maud was not listening because her attention had wandered. 'Look!' She stopped and peered through an open archway into a garden. 'Snow. It makes this palace look so peaceful.'

Adeliza crossed herself. 'By Saint Romanus, it *is* beautiful.' She stood so close that Maud could feel her stepmother's warm breath on her cheek. 'And let us pray this land remains so,' Adeliza whispered into the night.

Maud knew why Adeliza spoke as she did, because everything could change in a moment. The barons would attack each other's castles in a trice if there was not a firm hand at the helm. What will I inherit if they start fighting with each other over lands and castles? she wondered, with a shudder, as she followed Adeliza into the bower.

Before Maud drifted into sleep that night, she uneasily recalled her father's words: *We must find her a husband.*

'Papa, try as you may, you'll find me unwilling.' Maud thumped her pillow mutinously, causing a rip and scattering a snowstorm of duck feathers. She brushed them away. 'You cannot force me.'

Chapter Two

The New Forest
June 1128

Maud seethed at her father's insistence that Geoffrey of Anjou would make her a suitable husband.

'Geoffrey of Anjou cannot have seen more than fifteen summers,' she argued. Why would she wed a fifteen-year-old boy when she had been previously married to one of the greatest men in Christendom? She had travelled to Italy – to Rome itself – with Heinrich, and had ruled for him in his absence. Known as 'the good Matilda' throughout the Holy Roman Empire, she had earned great respect. And, one day, she would rule over England and Normandy. That mere boy, Geoffrey of Anjou, was not her equal in any way. She had been offered better matches in Germany after Heinrich's untimely death and had declined all suitors. Besides . . . A dark-haired, wickedly smiling face swam into her mind. She comforted herself by thinking the bishops would not like the match any more than she did. But, for all her fiery determination not to be forced into a marriage not of her choosing, her father, she knew, would not be gainsaid.

And she was proved right. She had voiced her objections, but her father tried over and over throughout March, April and May to persuade her there was an unprecedented threat to their territory of Normandy. It came from William Clito, who was closely allied to Louis, the King of France.

'Only marriage to the youth can avert this danger,' Henry had told Maud during Pentecost at Winchester. They sat at the high table, presiding over the Pentecost feast, enjoying the late spring sunlight reflecting off their golden dishes as they feasted on roasted swan; all were perfectly content until King Henry raised the difficult subject of marriage.

Winchester was one of Maud's favourite castles, one which held the royal treasury. It boasted a gleaming stone keep, a clean and spacious courtyard, a sweet-smelling pleasant garden she could access through a side door from the great hall, and stout, crenellated high walls. Some of the newly added chamber windows were glazed with pale green glass and the hall itself contained two rows of pillars painted with acanthus tendrils and flowers. There was a great central fireplace, and tapestries depicting hunts hung from the walls. Maud enjoyed this castle's convenience to both town and markets, as it was situated close to Winchester's West Gate, through which she could ride with her ladies, dogs and falcons out into the woods beyond the bustling town. Winchester was as ancient as the royal bones held in caskets within its cathedral. Today was spoiled. A shadow was cast over her happiness.

'His lands of Anjou can protect Normandy's southern border,' her father was saying as he lifted a morsel of swan flesh with his stubby fingers.

'I see,' she said, but she didn't.

Later, sitting before the flickering light of the fire in King Henry's private rooms, Maud searched for excuses not to agree. 'Geoffrey is too young,' she said. 'His rank is too inferior to my own. I still mourn Heinrich.'

But Henry countered her arguments at every turn. In March, King Louis had created William Clito the Count of Flanders, and the latter was now married into the Capet royal family, having been given the Queen of France's kinswoman to wife. With the only sure, safe, loyal region on Normandy's borders being the county of Blois, held by her cousin Stephen and his wife Matilda of Boulogne, her father argued endlessly that it was her duty to ensure Normandy's protection by agreeing to this awful marriage.

'A pawn in the game of kings. Such is a princess's fate,' Maud muttered angrily to herself later, in bed, spilling more feathers from her pillow every time she thumped it.

Adeliza was, of course, tasked with persuading Maud that it was the right thing to do and that it was her duty to agree to this marriage. 'The right thing to do?' she stormed at her stepmother, despite her affection for her. 'It is not the right thing for me.'

After Pentecost, the royal family spent June at Henry's favourite hunting lodge near Broceste, in the depths of the king's New Forest. On the morning following their arrival, Henry, Adeliza and Maud privately broke their fast in the great chamber above the hall. Outside, the stamping and snorting of horses reached up through the opened shutters. Maud planned to ride that morning, hunting small birds with her own personal guard protecting her. She hoped the subject of her marriage would – if not forgotten – be set aside for the moment.

But Geoffrey of Anjou was not forgotten – far from it. As soon as she sat down to break her fast, her mind set upon hunting in the forest that day, her father set a soft roll spread with honey onto his plate, puffed his scarlet wool-covered chest out and pounced, repeating his arguments yet again. 'This union will secure Normandy from France and Clito. We lost Anjou's support when your brother drowned, and his widow, young Geoffrey's sister, passed from my control. Your marriage—'

'Papa, I pray you, I do not wish to discuss this today. I have other plans this morning.'

Henry pushed his tankard of watered ale aside and brushed crumbs from his tunic. 'Enough. I require you to be ready to travel to Rouen within a week's space, Maud. You will be betrothed to Geoffrey as soon as he travels with his father, Count Baldwin, into Normandy. Let this be an end to your objections.'

Turning to her father, she lifted a hand to cup her ear and said angrily, 'Don't you hear them, Papa? My knights have saddled up and are waiting for me out there.' She waved her hand impatiently towards the sounds filtering through the window. 'It's a glorious morning, the sky so blue. Not a cloud to disturb it. I promised them we would fly our falcons.'

Henry rose and thrust his bare head out of the opened window. He grunted and, after drawing his neck inside again, turned to her. 'If you have promised to go on a hunt, Maud, ride out into the woods today, but take care. My dear brother, Rufus, was killed in that forest.'

Maud suppressed a shiver; heirs to the throne were never safe.

'Make sure Drogo guards you with diligence,' Henry added.

'Indeed, Papa, he will.'

Tall, powerful and quick-thinking, hawk-eyed Drogo had been in command of her personal guard since she was twelve years old. He was devoted to her and had accompanied her when she returned to her father's court. She determined that, if there was no alternative and she had to travel to meet Geoffrey of Anjou in Rouen, Drogo would command her household knights.

'We won't stray from the bridleways, Papa. The mounts sorely need exercise.' It was a lame excuse, because her knights were perfectly capable of exercising their horses without her, but Maud loved to ride and was an accomplished horsewoman. She even wore a divided *bliaut*, a variation on that full-skirted gown, created especially for her comfort whilst hunting. Otherwise, she rode side-saddle.

'And your women?' Henry said, frowning. 'I trust they will be in attendance?'

She knew there was no chance of slipping away without a few of her ladies keeping her company. 'Of course, Papa. Those who ride well are accompanying us today.'

Henry growled, 'Return prepared to understand that our crossing to Normandy is an urgent matter.' He knit his brows and his irritation with her showed in his steely gaze. 'We leave within the month. Your brother, Robert of Gloucester, is strengthening our castle walls in the south, but it is *not* enough.'

Maud remained unimpressed by her father's harsh tones. 'Well, a curse on Clito,' she said forcefully.

Adeliza, ever gracious, tried to diffuse the uncomfortable atmosphere with a smile and a dulcet tone as sweet as the honey dripping from her dainty spoon. 'Enjoy your ride, Maud, but please return to the bower before Vespers. Bishop Roger has come over from Salisbury and he is officiating this afternoon. We want him on our side.'

'Of course,' Maud said, slightly inclining her head. She knew full well that the elegant Bishop Roger was unlikely to agree to an objectionable foreign marriage, and that, if Lady Fortune smiled on her, the Bishop could delay the sea journey to Normandy. He might even ferment a rejection of this whole marriage plan amongst the nobility and clergy.

'On the contrary, he does not need to know,' Henry said quickly, firmly putting an end to her hopes of help from that quarter. He glared at his wife. 'Do not mention the betrothal plan to the Bishop, Adeliza. This is best kept within the family.' He looked sharply from wife to daughter. 'See it remains so, both of you.'

Maud bowed her head low and made her escape, her thoughts in turmoil. If her father found her disobeying this command of silence on the matter, he might send her to a convent. He alone could disinherit her, and make someone else his heir, like her strong brother, Robert, or the bland Stephen of Blois.

In high dudgeon, she flew down the narrow outer staircase and swept through the side entrance into the manor's hall, where she summoned her three patiently waiting ladies to accompany her on her ride. Waving her hand at a band of servitors, she told them to hurry up, carry out refreshments and load these onto a wagon. There would be no return until Maud heard the Vespers bells ring out. Straight-backed and head held high, she marched from the busy hall into the courtyard, where her guards waited with their commander, a giant of a man, his long white hair tied with a cord behind his neck. This was Drogo. On seeing him, Maud smiled at last. Argos, her small black stallion, was already saddled up. She reached into a secret purse inside her woollen mantle and withdrew an apple. The horse nuzzled her hand and began to munch. Assisted by Drogo – she did not consider she needed his help, but occasionally liked him to think she did – she mounted the horse, taking her small peregrine falcon, Lady Blisset, onto her leather glove. Jangling her reins, impatient to escape the tensions within the manor over the brat from Anjou, she gave her mount's flanks a nudge with her boots. Moments later, they were out of the gateway, cantering along a wide, leafy trackway deep into the sunlit forest.

After a pleasant morning watching Lady Blisset taking down thrushes or rooting around verges for rabbits, Maud called a halt. They had reached a leafy glade off the main track, where the June sunshine filtered through the tree canopy. In the distance, a church bell from a woodland hamlet rang out the hour of Sext. Now was a sensible time to rest and this glade would be perfect for their outdoor picnic. After the ladies dismounted and the knights set up a camp, her falconer tempted Lady Blisset into a large, strongly woven cage of willow struts by dangling a dead mouse. There, together with the other fowling birds, she was fed treats of chicken livers and more dead mice.

'Lady Blisset is so graceful,' Maud remarked to Drogo whilst they drank watered ale and munched cold pies. 'Did you see her dive that last time?'

Drogo replied in his throaty Alsace accent, 'She is the swiftest falcon of the whole cast of them.'

'Papa knows a good peregrine. Pity all his gifts to me are not as welcome.'

But Drogo was not listening. His head jerked around on his thick neck and she realised her quip had passed him by.

'My lady, I hear horses.' Drogo had turned his watchful eyes toward the pathway. He jumped to his feet and scrambled up the high bank to see who was approaching. A heartbeat later, he called down, 'There is company coming towards us.' His knights were alert, positioning themselves protectively in a circle around the ladies, bows raised and arrows set. Then Drogo shouted, 'By the saints, I believe it is Count Brien.' He signalled to his men to lower their bows. Moments later, a laughing Brien Fitz Count, wearing a jaunty green cap with a pheasant's feather, rode into their camp, followed by a rattling open-topped wagon on which were riding three fair-haired children and an assortment of oddly-shaped instruments, a hobby horse and what looked like puppetry.

Astonished, Maud rose to her feet and dusted herself down, heart still thudding. She raised a quizzical eyebrow as he approached. Why was Brien pursuing her into the woods? After the Easter court at Winchester, he had returned to the dowdy Countess Tilda.

Brien dismounted and bowed to her, and, as she rose from a curtsey, she noted his soft red leather riding boots with slightly pointed toes. She smiled to herself. Brien was nothing if not vain, even in the woods.

He bowed to her ladies – one by one, clearly ready to charm by referring to each by her name – Dame Margarete, Ladies Lenora, Anna and Mary. 'I see I surprise you.' Her women were fluttering their eyelashes at Brien's boldness and seemed even more delighted when the handsome count indicated the rickety wagon, which was rolling dangerously close to their lady.

'Halt!' he raised a gloved hand and called to the lad holding a horse's reins. Turning back, he said, 'I arrived at the castle earlier and heard you were hunting. I thought you might enjoy an afternoon's entertainment.' He laughed, tossed back his shoulder-length dark curls, whistled and indicated that the cart should position itself in the centre of the open grassy circle. It disgorged the little group of musicians Maud had watched at Christmastide. To her delight, she recognised the young girl who sang like an angel. Seeing her in daylight, Maud thought her to be around fourteen or fifteen summers old, with her two brothers perhaps a few years younger. But were they siblings? Looking at them now, Maud saw that the girl was fairer than both boys.

'May they play for you, my lady?' Count Brien said to Maud.

'It would be a waste of your effort in bringing them here if they did not,' she said with a smile. After the arguments with her papa, Count Brien was just the light-hearted tonic she needed.

He stood back proudly, his legs akimbo and his arms folded under his light woollen and – she observed – silk-bordered mantle. The little troupe gathered before a stand of beech trees and lifted their various instruments. They began to play a number of country tunes. The girl, strands of golden hair escaping below a simple linen coif, sang a duet with one of the boys, a simple song about summer, love, flowers, birds and creatures of the wood. Maud listened intently. Her ladies and knights sat or leaned against trees, clearly enjoying Count Brien's mischievous surprise. The canopy of trees allowed shafts of soft sunshine to percolate through their leaves, dappling the forest floor, and the sky peeped through, as blue as the bluebells that carpeted the woodland. It was a scene from a romance, Maud mused.

'Come,' Brien said, reaching out his hand to her. 'Maud, I must speak with you privately.'

So that was it. Maud rose unwillingly, wondering what he had been charged to say, because now she began to suspect there was more to his appearance in the woods today than a sudden desire to entertain her. She could see through this ploy. Her wily, determined father must have sent for him – no wonder he had so easily agreed to her hunt that morning. This conversation would be about Geoffrey of Anjou and her imminent voyage over the Narrow Sea to Normandy.

When Drogo rose to follow her onto a woodland track, she signalled to him to stay at a distance. 'Drogo, we will not move out of your sight,' she called back over her shoulder as she strode off towards a distant beech tree to listen to what Brien had to say. The three mummers were setting up a play involving the hobby horse, an angel and a devil. 'Well?' she said. 'Have you come because my father sends you?'

'Drogo is watchful,' Brien remarked, not responding to her question. She would warrant her father *had* sent him to waylay her and encourage his ridiculous marriage plan.

'As he should be,' she said tartly.

Brien spread his cloak over a log and bade her sit, which she did, becoming disturbingly aware of his warmth and the almond scent of the oil he used to tame his curls. But she pushed away these thoughts; he was here to speak to her of Geoffrey of Anjou. 'Do these entertainers accompany you everywhere? You didn't bring them to court at Easter.'

'Countess Tilda had company,' Brien said, and Maud's heart gave a small pang at Tilda's name. 'They entertained her guests. The girl's name is Alice; she occasionally comes to the castle and helps in the still room, though she lives with the parents of these boys on a farm upriver from us. She can juggle, manipulate puppets and she sings with their troupe. The whole family are entertainers and, at my request a half dozen years ago, they took Alice in, nurtured and adopted her.' He lowered his voice. 'Alice, you see, is a by-blow of some cousin of Tilda's. She was brought to the castle by a priest as a tiny child. Tilda refused to raise her in the castle —'

Dour Tilda, thought Maud, immediately feeling a rush of warmth towards the fair-haired child.

'— so I found the child a home. These players are useful to me, Maud. Since they travel about the countryside from castle to castle, they can gather news.'

'Useful indeed, I imagine, picking up news. What a peculiar arrangement. So why have you brought them here today? Did my father send you after me?'

'Indeed, but I thought to bring you the musicians as a surprise.' He drew a long intake of breath. His dark eyes became as serious as deep woodland pools. 'I have not come to speak of mumming today, my lady. I come to speak of the Anjou marriage proposal.'

Maud froze, and in that moment she hated him. He was her father's weapon, because Henry had guessed she would listen to Brien Fitz Count.

'Maud, you need to listen to reason. It is important for the safety of the realms you will one day inherit that you agree to this marriage. England and Normandy must be protected and, with France looking for the best opportunity to isolate Normandy, a renewed alliance with Anjou is as important as it was when your brother married Geoffrey's sister all those years ago, before they all drowned. We need Anjou as a buffer kingdom between Normandy and France. You need Anjou. Clito is angling to attack Normandy, now he has Flanders through marriage and France is his ally.' He folded his arms over his chest. 'Your brother, Robert of Gloucester, waits to greet you in Rouen.'

Maud buried her head in her hands. 'You are pushing me into this, Brien,' she said accusingly. 'Geoffrey of Anjou is an absolute nobody. His father is only a count . . .'

'Ah, but so am I!' A smile played upon Brien's lips. 'You can make him somebody.'

'And I am an empress,' she wailed. 'One day, I shall be a queen. Why would I marry Geoffrey of Anjou? Besides, he is eleven years younger than me. His father won't die for years.'

'Why? Because Robert of Gloucester is struggling to hold the Norman border. With Anjou on side, the task will be easier. Besides, Geoffrey's father, Faulk, plans to marry Melisande, Baldwin of Jerusalem's heir . . . and one day they will rule over the Holy Land. You *will* be Countess of Anjou, because Faulk will hand over Anjou to Geoffrey.'

'And that boy intends to acquire both England and Normandy – as my husband.'

'No, Maud, you know that would be unacceptable to our barons. But, don't you see, a son could rule England, with you as our queen regent.'

'I *do* see, only too well. I see that I am my father's pawn,' she snapped.

He reached out and momentarily touched her cheek so lightly, it felt as if she were being caressed by passing dandelion fluff.

'Believe me, Maud, the marriage will be advantageous to you. As for Geoffrey of Anjou, he will wed both wisdom and beauty. He will pursue you like a puppy, listen eagerly to your wise advice, and share your interest in both falconry and in the gathering up of libraries. Your father will never allow him to take advantage of your position. You will be queen. He would be only a consort.'

'So, I am to be a queen mother until a possible heir comes of age?' She thought aloud for a moment. Birds rustled above in the trees. She could hear the players begin their performance with the clashing of cymbals and a drum roll. Brien sat silently, waiting for her response.

Finally, she said, 'I will marry Geoffrey of Anjou. I have no choice, since it appears an alternative could be the convent.' She fixed him with a stern glance. 'Apparently, it is all arranged, but, Brien, be aware I will not be manipulated further. I am an empress, not a countess. You all know this and you'll all refer to me as such.' She kept her voice cold.

'So be it, Maud,' he said with a grin and flash of his teeth. 'You're making the right decision. If Clito and France made a serious bid for Normandy, England would be next, and you might indeed find yourself seeking refuge within convent walls, regardless.' He rose and helped her to her feet. 'And so, the play is waiting. Alice has another song for you – one telling of knights and queens.'

'Alice appears to have an endless repertoire concerning knightly courage and love.'

'Only in song. Alice not only sings, but she has a clever way with herbs in the still room. She makes creams to ease aches and simples to ease the feeling of discontent.'

He was humouring her. 'Does she, indeed? I would she made a potion to discourage manipulation.' He had no response. She shook off his helping hand and walked gracefully before him, back to her ladies and the play.

Chapter Three

Normandy and Anjou
1128–9

Maud saw Geoffrey of Anjou for the first time at her betrothal ceremony, which was held in Rouen, one of the largest and richest cities in Normandy. The betrothal was kept secret, as King Henry had planned, from Roger of Salisbury and the other awkward clergy. Henry sent Count Brien ahead, with Maud, intending to travel to the city of Rouen later with Adeliza. Maud and her ladies crossed the Narrow Sea to Le Havre, at the mouth of the River Seine, in Normandy. From there, they rode along by the curving river, their sumpter horses and wagons laden with Maud's new wardrobe of samite and damask gowns, her ladies' travelling boxes, silver and gold plate and tapestries, her precious jewel caskets and her even more precious reliquary that contained a finger bone belonging to Saint James of Compostella. The sea had been calm, the crossing smooth and the sun shone every day, but nothing, not even Count Brien's company, could make this journey to a marriage she did not desire in any way pleasurable.

Maud had fond memories of Normandy. Her grandfather, William I, had left the duchy to his eldest son, Duke Robert, father of the very fat, greedy William Clito. Her father, the first King Henry, had seized Normandy from his brother, as compensation for having paid off Duke Robert's Crusade debts. For years now, King Henry had ruled Normandy and England both. Duke Robert had been kept captive for nearly twenty years, in honourable confinement in England, until his death.

As well as a stout stone castle, there was a ducal palace situated within Rouen's city walls. This palace was built over three levels, with a cavernous undercroft, where, as a child, Maud had loved to play hide-and-seek games with her companions. The rambling timber palace had a busy courtyard, herb gardens, an orchard that ran down to the river wall, a chapel and a substantial wooden palisade. The bower hall and Maud's own apartment always felt airy. She enjoyed listening to the blacksmiths' hammers, the clucking of hens, a crowing rooster and the mingling townspeople, the sounds of which drifted daily over the palisade and up into her chambers. She settled into the palace, recollecting happier times, and tried not to agonise about her imminent betrothal.

Too soon, Geoffrey of Anjou arrived with his father and was lodged in the draughty castle, chill even in summer. As Maud prepared to meet them in the palace hall, Count Brien quietly said to her, 'Maud, we cannot change now what is. It may not be the future you wanted, but it is necessary to protect your throne from the locusts, should your father die.'

She scowled at the Count and said, most ungraciously, with a grim countenance, 'If I must. No, it is not the future I desired.' She sought his dark eyes, but he looked away.

'You must be kinder in your thoughts, Maud,' he said, turning back to her.

She swallowed her bile and was polite to the ungainly, golden youth during their brief pre-betrothal encounter.

When, some weeks later, her father and stepmother arrived, just in time for the betrothal ceremony, Maud grudgingly admitted to Adeliza that Geoffrey of Anjou was a handsome youth – if colt-like, with narrow shoulders. His beautiful reddish-gold hair was artfully curled below his chin. An exceptionally pretty face was surprisingly unblemished, since many boys of his age were blighted with wens. A long noble nose and wide-set impish green eyes made up for his lack of inches. He was scarcely taller than she was, certainly not the height of Brien Fitz Count, and he was absolutely dwarfed by her brother Robert. Despite Geoffrey's good looks, it was quickly obvious that his father, Faulk, doted on and spoilt the youth; there was an arrogance to the set of his shoulders.

Maud knew she was herself attractive. Her polished-metal mirror reflected a pair of deep blue eyes and silky black hair. Today, for the betrothal ceremony, her slim figure was gowned in burgundy sarsenet hemmed with cloth of gold, and she sensed from the eyes that followed her every gesture that many nobles admired her. Yet Geoffrey himself hardly glanced at her throughout the ritual and ignored her at the celebration feast held later that afternoon, mixing only with his company of lads, and flirting openly with their pretty sisters and cousins. She bristled at his rude behaviour.

After the feast, acrobats and Count Brien's troupe of actors performed songs, feats and balancing acts. Maud glowered at Geoffrey's party from her place beside Adeliza. Once Alice began to sing ballads, her temper was a little soothed, but she was aware, peeping across at Geoffrey, that his eyes followed the willowy girl's every movement. Admittedly, Alice was more his age than Maud was.

It was a very hot, still July day and, after her performance, Alice departed the hall quickly, possibly in need of the privy or to take the air out in the garden. Geoffrey rose too and, leaving his companions, appeared to be treading in the girl's footsteps. Maud, somewhat suspicious, signalled to Drogo. A heartbeat later, she stood and slipped away, with Drogo following her like one of her faithful greyhounds. Queen Adeliza, unaware of any emerging drama, continued to watch the juggler throw golden balls into the air.

As Maud walked into the arched corridor outside, she heard raised voices, followed by a cry. Quickening her pace, she hurried further along the passageway towards the sound's source, and saw Geoffrey pushing the girl, at the point of his dagger, into one of the passageway arches that opened onto a garden courtyard.

Glancing back over her shoulder, she called out in a voice loud enough for Geoffrey as well as Drogo to hear: 'I fear my betrothed is sorely in need of a lesson in manners.' She kept her rising temper under control as she increased her step, drawing closer to Geoffrey, this time shouting, 'Unhand the girl at once, or you will answer to Brien Fitz Count, her master!'

Geoffrey turned towards Maud with a face so shocked by her presence it could have preceded a paroxysm of his heart. Ignoring him, she reached out her hand to Alice. The girl's blue eyes were frightened, like those of a startled woodland creature, and her mouth was opening into another scream. Geoffrey shoved his dagger into his belt and glared at Maud. He was clearly in his cups; his face was as red as a blood orange and his hands were shaking.

'I meant no harm to the girl,' he slurred. 'But she is rather beautiful,' he added.

Drogo stepped forward clutching the hilt of his sword. He glowered down at Geoffrey from his great height.

Maud ignored Geoffrey and turned to the girl, feeling something new – an uncharacteristic rush of protectiveness towards this young woman who was her dearest friend Count Brien's charge. 'Come, sit with me and Queen Adeliza. You will be safe with us,' she said calmly. And, taking the girl's hand, she led Alice – who was pale as a sheet of linen – back to the feast.

Heads turned when they entered the hall – among them, Brien Fitz Count's – with raised brows and surprised eyes. As she ushered Alice to a place amongst her ladies, she also observed Geoffrey's stumbling return to the hall. His companions glowered at her, as if reading her lips when she whispered to Queen Adeliza, 'Count Geoffrey is not to be trusted.'

'What?' Adeliza gasped, shocked.

Brien glanced from Maud to Geoffrey, and then towards the still-silent Alice, who was evidently in some kind of shocked state. Maud shook her head, trying to warn him not to make a fuss.

Adeliza leaned across Alice towards Maud. 'What has he done?'

'Not now – later. But I wish to retire. I have been insulted by that boy.' She looked over at her betrothed with distain and turned to Alice. 'Before I depart, Alice, I shall ask Count Brien to see to your protection.'

'Thank you, my lady,' the girl said timidly.

24

'Ah,' said Adeliza, her forehead wrinkled into a frown. 'Geoffrey has much to learn about chivalry before he is knighted. I can see now the kind of base creature that boy is. Maud, Alice is safe with me. Take your women and leave. I shall see that Count Faulk knows how his son has behaved, and I shall ensure that Count Brien protects her.'

'Thank you, my lady.' Alice's eyes filled with tears of gratitude.

Brien was already approaching them. He bowed to Maud and Adeliza and held out his hand, clearly intending to escort Alice back to her brothers, and his knights.

'She is untouched by that ignoramus, just a little shocked,' Maud murmured, trying to swallow back her anger at her betrothed's uncouth and insulting behaviour.

'Thank you, my lady. It *was* Geoffrey, wasn't it? I saw you return with Alice and Drogo. A moment passed and Geoffrey also reappeared.'

She nodded. Alice, who had recovered somewhat, spoke quietly: 'Count Brien, my lady saved me.'

Brien said in a gentle voice, 'Young Geoffrey will not dare accost you again. I shall ensure that Dame Margo watches over you, day and night.'

'Dame Margo – who is she?' asked Maud.

'A trustworthy member of my household who travels with us and looks after my linen and such.'

Maud stood. She was no longer shaking with anger and humiliation, but inside she was still furious. As she signalled to her ladies, she could not help glancing over at Geoffrey, who was slumped drunkenly among a pile of half-empty goblets and chicken bones. He was like a spoilt child who considered it his right to take by force that not willingly given.

King Henry spent much time with Count Faulk in Angers Castle in Anjou whilst Maud remained in Rouen, a city with a castle dwelling which she very much liked because of its spacious chambers, internal staircases, the fireplace in its great hall, its pleasant gardens and the hunting opportunities in the woods close by. Their wedding took place thirteen months later, in Le Mans, not far to the south, after the unpleasant Geoffrey had been knighted by Henry and created Count of Anjou by his father. Faulk was anxious to depart for Jerusalem and marriage to Queen Melisande. Maud would now become the Countess of Anjou.

'No, I shall remain Empress,' she said with firmness to Adeliza in the marriage chamber, just as she had to Count Brien a year earlier.

'Geoffrey seems subdued, older, and more sensible than at your betrothal. He has behaved charmingly today,' Adeliza remarked, as she tidied Maud's hair, which, for her wedding, she had worn loose (as demanded by tradition), with only a jewelled chaplet to hold it in place. Her cloth-of-gold wedding gown had been whisked away, and she was glad, for she never wished to see it again.

Maud snorted. 'He was clearly intent on accosting Count Brien's performer last July. That's the kind of selfish, cruel creature my new husband is – a thick-skinned, obnoxious, preening youth. If he forces himself on me –' she turned, paused and flashed her ocean-deep eyes up at Adeliza – 'I'll have a dagger waiting under my pillow.'

'No, no, Maud, this is nonsense. Henry says he has behaved impeccably these last months and he will make you a handsome, devoted consort.' Adeliza drew breath and added, more gently, 'You *do* understand, Maud, you will have to give him the marriage debt. He is, after all, your husband.' She resumed her brushing of Maud's long silky hair in silence, as two attendant ladies turned the bed's coverlet down and scattered rose petals onto the bed linen. One lady made sure there was food and drink in a cupboard and others set wine and goblets on a low table close to the bed. Moments later, Adeliza stood back and surveyed her stepdaughter as Maud rose from the stool, dressed in her delicately embroidered linen shift.

'Maud, you look so beautiful. He will never be able to resist you. No daggers, because if your father were to hear of such a thing there would be the devil to pay. Geoffrey never so much as glanced at the girl when the mummers put on their play this afternoon.'

'Without doubt, he was warned off. He might not dare to pursue Alice again, but there will be others, Adeliza. My father kept many beautiful mistresses.'

Adeliza set the hairbrush down, leaned close to Maud's ear and said, in a voice so low that the women flitting around the chamber could not hear her, 'Those times are over. My lord has had no mistresses of late. It is for you and Geoffrey to make an heir now. And I believe God will smile upon you both.'

So, that was the way of it. For some reason, her father could not have children with Adeliza – but why? Was it Adeliza who was barren, or was her father now incompetent?

Before she could ask, a great noise and clashing of cymbals drifted up from below, drawing closer and closer. The groom's companions were coming to her chamber, and too soon for her comfort. She did not feel prepared for this. Though Heinrich had married her when she was twelve, he was considerate and had waited several more years for her to mature. They had been good friends first and she had respected and trusted him with all her heart. Their coupling had been gentle and loving. Now, Maud steeled herself to face the husband she still considered loathsome. The tinkling of bells, a slow light beat on drums and the strumming of stringed instruments sounded from the outer passageway. Adeliza and her women ushered Maud over to the bed, where she sat up against the pillows, her hands demurely folded, resigned and awaiting her fate. Steeling herself to do her duty, she prayed that Geoffrey would go away as soon as he spilled his seed into her. Could she dismiss him from her bed? The pleasing thought flitted across her mind.

A great crowd entered her chamber and pushed Geoffrey forwards. He climbed onto the bed beside her without looking at her. Tears pricked the back of her eyes. Her father wished her well. The officiating Bishop of Le Mans blessed the bed and, before she could cry out *Don't leave me!* the company, including Adeliza and their women, slipped from the chamber. Though she could hear Geoffrey's breathing, she had never felt so alone.

Good manners seemed to desert the young imp once the company

27

had departed. He wouldn't even meet her eyes, which hurt her pride, nor did he speak, except to say, 'Lady, neither you nor I want this marriage, but *they* want it.' He glanced towards the door and added, in a contemptuous tone, 'I am going to lift your night rail, wife, and we shall see.'

Though humiliated, she dutifully lay back against the pillows, feeling like a corpse. His breath smelled of too much wine. And he was awkward. For a few moments, he felt her body, then grunted that she was much too old for him. She lay back unresisting as the ignorant fifteen-year-old mounted her, fumbled about and speedily pumped on top of her. Something was not right. His member had briefly hardened, but she realised that, after panting for a few moments, he had lost his seed, though not inside her. Disgusted, she felt his sticky stream pour down her thighs. She gasped and moment-arily felt sorry for him, but remained silent.

'As you can see, we are not well matched,' he grunted – again, his tone sarcastic.

'Apparently not,' she said, with equal sarcasm.

Abruptly, he turned onto his right side, his back to her, and imme-diately fell into a deep, drunken sleep. She rearranged her night rail and turned onto her left side, equally pointedly. She felt puzzled. If this was always to be the way of it, and he could not make her preg-nant, the marriage would have no point other than to prevent incursion into Normandy. Perhaps she could seek an annulment.

Days after their wedding, Maud, Geoffrey and Adeliza rode south to Angers whilst Henry was overseeing business in his Norman demesne. The great Angers castle was of a wooden construction, freshly whitewashed, and it gleamed in the sunlight as their party approached. The town nestled around its castle, a collection of two-storey houses clearly belonging to affluent merchants and minor nobles. Adeliza, Maud and their women settled into an apartment with small chambers and a narrow bower hall that smelled stale, felt gloomy and was dimly lit by oil-filled terracotta lamps and a few sconces on the walls, and heated with charcoal braziers – altogether less pleasant than her chambers in Rouen. Maud walked the length of the bower hall, touching a large harp, trailing her fingers along a tapestry depicting the Wedding at Cana, lifting baskets filled with embroidery threads and peering into them. She stopped to glare at a loom set in a window recess. I will not pass my days here weaving, stitching and sewing garments for the poor, she thought rebelliously. Rouen is by far the pleasanter city with a palace and a castle. Aloud, she said, 'There will be improvements made here. I am used to better.'

'I am sure Geoffrey will not object,' was Adeliza's diplomatic response.

Weeks passed. Geoffrey occasionally visited her chamber, where the awkward fumbling, followed by embarrassment continued. She confided in no one at first, except once to Adeliza as they played a game of merills in the bower hall.

Adeliza was sympathetic, but said, 'He is simply overwhelmed by your beauty. All will come right in time. He is young, and young men have little self-control.'

'He does not attract me and I do not attract him.'

'Marriages are not made for love, though you may come to like Geoffrey, trust him and develop mutual respect for each other. This way lies a sound marriage. Love can be fleeting. Give him time, Maud. You will get with child and then all will change.'

Maud twisted her face into an expression of what she hoped was scorn rather than fear. 'I am not hopeful of that outcome. And he is a vain youth, far below my rank,' she said – and moved her merills counter into a position that outmanoeuvred Adeliza.

Only too soon, Adeliza returned to Rouen. Geoffrey's father set off for Jerusalem and his wedding to Melisande. They never expected to see him again and the leave-taking between Geoffrey and Faulk was filled with sorrow. Geoffrey sulked for weeks and never came near her, not even to visit. She suspected he had a woman somewhere, perhaps in a hunting lodge, since he often rode out with his own companions. She tried not to care, but her pride was further wounded. They had only been married three months and soon it would be Christmas.

That autumn, to her relief, William Clito died on campaign after being wounded in battle. A serious threat to her succession rights and to Normandy's safety had been removed by that quick sword strike. The marriage that had appeared so essential seemed far less important with Clito's demise. She and Geoffrey rarely conversed other than to wish each other good morrow or good afternoon. They sat together in chapel and at communal dinners in the hall; otherwise, by day, Geoffrey was ever seeking escape from her, hurrying out to the stables or to play dice with his vile teenaged companions, to practise sword fighting or to hunt in the woods surrounding the castle, without ever asking her if she wished to accompany him.

He still occasionally visited her chamber, but when they attempted to sleep together it was always a disaster. Maud's fury with him grew and grew. She did not *want* to keep calm with him. Why should she? She was an empress.

'My father expects us to give him grandchildren, Geoffrey,' she said one night, lying flat on her back, bolstered by pillows. 'Do I need to ask a wise woman for a potion to slip into your wine?'

'What a suggestion! I am beginning to think you must be barren, Maud,' he replied nastily. 'You never had a child with the Emperor.'

'You will never find out, if you are not able to penetrate me.'

His voice was peevish. 'You don't inspire me. You are far too old. Any child from your womb will be unwholesome and doomed.'

'How dare you! I am only twenty-seven summers old. Clearly, *you* do not want children.'

Geoffrey's face was purple with rage.

'No, do not argue,' she continued. 'You want my titles. You want my castles – and, if my father dies, you want my throne.' She paused, then accused, 'A throne for *you* and not for a boy child.'

He spat out his next words. 'Actually, I want none of you, Maud. I have two pretty children already. Ask anyone in the castle.' He gave a hysterical laugh. 'You are a shrew. The fault is clearly none of mine.'

Maud reared up indignantly. Geoffrey seemed to vault from the bed in his eagerness to get away from her.

'What?' she said, her voice rising as her own temper took her over. 'You tell me you are raising illegitimate brats? Not inside this castle, surely? If so, I order you to remove them. Who is the mother?' Her resolve to remain superior and calm was quickly dissolving on hearing this information. Even if it were untrue, he had grievously insulted her.

'It's no more than your own father has done,' he reminded her, pushing one foot into his expensive reindeer-leather slipper. 'Their mother is none of your affair. She is safe from you, for I warrant you are a witch. You glower all the time. You cause your servants to quake if they make mistakes. You . . . would cast a spell against her if I told you – and you might, anyway.'

'Get out of my chamber, you pup!' Maud could hear herself shouting. 'Never address me in such a tone again. I am an empress and far, far above you. My father was a fool to wed me to an imp from Anjou. You . . . you are nothing.'

Geoffrey began to head for the door, tugging a robe over his nightgown. Maud reached for the cup of wine placed on a table close to her bed, lifted it and hurled it as hard as she could. The cup's rim caught his ear, dropping to the floor with a crash, spilling red wine over his costly slippers and into the floor straw. Her hands flew to her mouth; his flew to the wound on his ear. A drop of blood dripped from the small cut and she laughed hysterically.

Grabbing a towel from the top of a nearby chest, he held it to his ear, turned and groaned as the red splash of blood widened into a deep crimson bruise spreading through the pale linen. 'You will pay for this, you shrew!' he shouted back at her, his face almost as red as the blood. He flung open the door and rushed out.

Maud found herself still giddy with laughter. Perhaps I am going mad, she thought. I have to get away before he destroys me, or I him. He will be unforgiving, so I must be too.

Geoffrey galloped away the very next day and stayed beyond Angers's walls for several weeks. Since it was a husband's right to claim his wife's property, Maud brooded about what Geoffrey's rights would be if her father died. Her lowly and inadequate husband had wed into the purple, but she, in turn, had grown even more determined to guard what was hers. If Geoffrey was unable to have a child with her, she would insist that the marriage be annulled. Biting her lip, she brooded over the difficult problem when in chapel or whilst perusing a favourite book of legends. She suspected this would be no simple task. The nobility of Anjou would say it was her fault.

She tried to enjoy embroidery, which was not, in truth, a favourite pastime, though she was as good at it as she was everything she put her mind to – except getting with child. Much as she loathed him, she felt Geoffrey's rejection of her was a slur on her femininity and she grew increasingly unhappy. To distract herself from her misery, she worked on the large frame set up in the bower, where her ladies were stitching an altar cloth depicting Noah's Ark. She felt marooned herself, caught in the midst of a flood much deeper than any deluge Noah had experienced. She was, quite simply, trapped. Angrily, she tugged her needle through a woodland creature, imagining it was Geoffrey every time she stabbed the fabric. She had selected black silk to create its bulging eyes. The effect on the white stoat was grotesque and it pleased her to think Geoffrey was too.

By Advent, Geoffrey had returned, but, detesting the very sight of him, she bolted her door every evening. When Geoffrey demanded to enter, she reminded him that the Church forbade carnal relations during the season. They stopped speaking to each other entirely. She made fun of Geoffrey to her own women, referring to him as *the imp*, not bothering to conceal her dislike for her husband. She was too proud to ask sexual advice – even discreetly – from her older women, though she did wonder if she should seek out a love potion for Geoffrey – and, perhaps, one for herself. When Adeliza wrote to her of everyday life at the English court, she wept into her pillow at night; she missed the warmth of her father's household. But she replied to her stepmother without confiding her problems, preferring instead to speak of books she had collected and the tapestry she was stitching. She was an empress and a queen in waiting. It was hard not to sound resentful.

After a bleak, not very festive Christmas, Geoffrey disappeared again, this time to Le Mans. Perhaps that was where his mistress was dwelling, because, although Geoffrey flirted openly and even charmingly with the wives and sisters of his friends, there was no evidence of his lover living in the castle at Angers.

In June, Maud received a curt message from Geoffrey demanding that the castle be made ready for his return. She sighed, but ordered a welcome feast to be prepared for him. It was a pleasing event, held on midsummer's night, outside on the swathe within the castle walls. Musicians played, and tables groaned with food and endless flasks of wine. That night, Geoffrey thumped on her bolted door until she opened it. After sending her attendants away, he demanded, as she'd feared, his conjugal rights. Again, it was a disaster, and he spilled his seed on the linen sheets. Tossing aside the coverlet, she slid down from the bed. She poured herself a cup of wine without offering him any.

Glancing back up at the high bed, observing that he lay drunkenly against the pillows, she said quietly, 'Marrying you was a huge mistake, Geoffrey. Marriage may not be for love, but it *is* for the begetting of heirs, and –' she paused – 'you are a waste of my time.'

He looked at her from under darkened brows. 'And you mine, particularly since your father has not even released the major part of your dowry, including the castle of Argentan, and those other fortresses on the borders with Normandy that he promised me.'

'Why should he give you anything more, when *you* cannot observe the bond of marriage, and when you treat me, an *empress* –' she emphasised the word – 'as you do, with such contempt?'

'*Empress* – that is nonsense. You are a countess, though you persist in alienating my barons with your rejection of my title. They feel they owe you no loyalty.' He snorted. 'You never had a child with your Emperor either.' This often-repeated accusation infuriated her. It was not her fault. Heinrich had never been able to father a child.

'Return to your father,' Geoffrey was saying. 'I hear he is in Rouen again. I do not desire you to wife, you . . . you scold.' He swung his legs over the other side of the great bed and, gathering up his scattered clothing, he made to leave the chamber, all the time letting her hear his muttering – 'Witch, harpy, drab.'

She drew herself up to her full height and stiffened her spine. Raising her cup, she said, 'It will be a pleasure for me to leave Anjou, a true pleasure. I loathe it here. Even the air reeks.'

He had reached the arched doorway, but turned, shouting furiously, 'Begone, then, harridan! Get out of my lands by the week's end! Go back to your father, and do not return without my castles.'

'I won't return at all,' she said contemptuously, and drank back her wine. 'Never.' She threw the emptied cup across the wide bed at the dreadful youth's retreating back. It missed him this time.

He laughed drunkenly and left, clutching most of his clothing childishly in his arms. As his parting shot, he shouted over his shoulder, 'The marriage can be annulled.'

He would not get the better of her. Her resolve not to let him hardened. She *herself* would seek an annulment.

On the calends of July, a few days later, Maud ordered her baggage to be loaded onto sumpter horses and into carts. Every hanging she had brought to her wedding, every linen sheet and embroidered coverlet was laid with lavender into her coffers. Every silver plate and every favourite reliquary from her private chapel was packed up and sent ahead to the castle in Rouen. Even the Noah's Ark embroidery would leave Angers, although not only her English and German ladies had worked on it. She bade the castle cooks and servitors farewell. During Geoffrey's absences she had, to her credit, won their hearts with her ability to organise the castle's domestic staff efficiently. She had made sure her steward saw that all floor straw was regularly changed and the hall smelled sweet. She had ordered the walls of her own chambers and others to be freshly whitewashed and painted with hunting scenes. Domesticity did not come naturally to Maud. She resented it, but considered that she had succeeded in managing everyone who served her according to her high standards, and she always refused to be gainsaid. Those who had directly attended her stood weeping in the courtyard as she departed. They had come to admire and respect her, even if Geoffrey did not.

As Maud proudly rode side-saddle out of the castle yards, dressed in beautiful silk robes for all to note and appreciate, she sat erect on her mare, Juno, hoping never to see Angers or Geoffrey again. And, to her relief, he was nowhere visible as she departed. When she reached Rouen a week later, she discovered that her father, Adeliza and their court had only a week before sailed for England. There was no further decision to make. The city of Rouen was her home and she would stay there as long as she pleased. When she recovered her temper, which could still boil over like a cauldron of unattended pottage, she would write to her father explaining her actions. Geoffrey, after all, had *sent* her away, and, though she was glad of it, no blame lay with her.

Chapter Four

Shillingford
September 1131

Alice longed to work on the new costumes whilst there was still strong morning light pouring in through un-shuttered windows. Her working day began with stitching their few precious seed pearls onto the lady puppet's gown. Someone was going to interrupt. She sighed. The gown would get finished eventually. Glancing up, she heard the door latch lifting, and Dame Margo, to whom Alice had become close since Empress Maud's betrothal, rustled into the farm dwelling's hall, setting down her basket and sweeping off bits of straw from her gown and cloak with an impatient hand. Alice greeted the older woman warmly, bidding her sit by the window and rising to offer her some buttermilk. As Alice poured the milk from the jug into her cup, Dame Margo explained that she had taken a castle boat upriver from Wallingford – the fastness where Count Brien and Countess Tilda lived – to Shillingford.

The dwelling where Alice lived was historically called Shillingford Farm, but most people referred to it as Snowdrop Farm because in mid-winter its orchard and swathe were carpeted with the creamy flowers, bright against the earthy-coloured trunks of apple trees. Alice was brought to Wallingford Castle soon after her mother died, and she had never known her own birth date. She had been brought up in a nunnery, and was aware that she was the illegitimate daughter of a distant cousin of Countess Tilda's, who had requested that his wealthy relative take Alice into her castle after her mother died. Countess Tilda had passed on responsibility for finding a foster home for the girl to her new young husband, Brien Fitz Count. Within weeks, Brien, who enjoyed poetry and song, discovered that the child had a clear voice, and so he found a talented musical family amongst his wife's tenants, dwelling on a farm north of the castle, close to the river, where they grew crops such as oats and barley and needed more land.

Ingrid and Walt now ran Snowdrop Farm, but they had been part-time musicians and performers, and had three young sons who, even at a young age, used to tumble and sing in Tilda's hall. In return for taking Alice in, Brien had offered them some land and money for improvements to the rundown farm house, which at the time was a rundown hall house. Alice had been warmly welcomed by Ingrid and Walt, and was happily adopted into the family. There were no daughters, but the three sons of Ingrid and Walt were all talented musicians, mimics and actors. These days, Ingrid and Walt could not leave the farm, especially at harvest time, so Alice and her brothers would, when Count Brien wanted, travel with him to entertain at other castles in the land. They had animals to keep – cows, a pig and a small flock of sheep, as well as six hens, a goat called Periwinkle and two shaggy sheepdogs. As well as their fields and an orchard, they cultivated a vegetable plot and herb garden, which Alice loved and she was often in the still room making tinctures and creams.

Alice showed increasing talent for singing as she grew up. She had a beautiful voice, learning songs from the musical family with ease, and she could even mimic voices. Unlike other girls around Shillingford, she had been able to travel. It was such a pleasant and exciting life. Alice could not imagine any other and, as she neared marriageable age, she decided to remain free, not saddled with a husband she did not love. Her visit to Anjou for Empress Matilda's wedding, and the behaviour of Count Geoffrey and the oafs who were his friends, convinced her to avoid wedlock until she found someone she loved. The powerful, blue-eyed Empress, whose kindness had left a deep impression on young Alice, could not have a happy marriage married to such a creature as Count Geoffrey. *She* would never be forced into a marriage without love.

It was pleasant to see Dame Margo again, that morning. As Alice put the finishing touches to the puppet's gown, they chatted about the castle and the fact that Countess Tilda was much in London, these days. Finally, Alice said, 'Dame Ingrid and our maid are gathering apples in the orchard. Would you like me to send for her, Dame Margo?'

'In a moment.' Dame Margo took another sip of her buttermilk, lifted her wicker basket onto the worktable and took out a linen-wrapped parcel. 'I have something for you, my dear. For your name day this year, let us say.'

Alice laughed. 'I suppose, since I know it not, September is as good a month as any for a name day. It has moved right around the calendar.' Last year, they had chosen to celebrate it as a spring event, and, in the previous year, her fourteenth birthday had fallen during Christmastide.

Dame Margo laughed, shrugged and continued, 'I believe Count Brien chose the gift himself. Unwrap it.' It was a rough linen parcel, but Alice suspected there would be an item of great beauty inside.

Excited to discover what it was this time, she fumbled with the cord fastenings and eventually untied the knot. She let out a squeal of delight. Inside lay a gown of pure cornflower-blue linen, her favourite colour. The fashionable Brien often sent clothing or trinkets – he had made a pet of her, and it was necessary for her to make a favourable impression when he wanted her to impress his friends and guests – but none had been as beautiful as this was. She held it up. It would fit perfectly. But why had Count Brien himself ordered it to be made now? There could only be one reason. He wanted her to perform for a particularly wealthy family, within a great castle.

Dame Margo lifted up her triple chins and, obviously reading the question in Alice's eyes, said, with a sense of importance and pride in her tone, 'Count Brien has requested you to accompany us to Northampton for the King's council on the eighth day of this month. All the greatest earls and clergy in the land will be present. It's a great honour, my dear, and you must bring one of the musicians to accompany you. One of the fine young men is enough this time. Count Brien knows that a farm is busy at harvest time.'

'Much of the harvest is already gathered in, this year. We employed extra hands, scythes and gleaners.' Alice felt her excitement rising again. 'Am I to sing for the King again? For it's been so long since I sang at the Empress's betrothal.'

'Yes, indeed, at all their feasts,' Dame Margo said, with a twinkling smile.

'Oh dear, I need to think about this. What shall I sing?'

'No need to worry, Alice. You have a lovely voice and anything you sing will sound as sweet as the nightingale's song.' Dame Margo took another sip of her buttermilk. 'Songs appropriate for the season, and you can sing in French or English, or both.'

Occasionally Alice sang in both languages, and she was proud that she could sing in Latin too, if so requested. After all, she had been taught to read by nuns before she came to live on Snowdrop Farm. She considered, her heart beating fast. She would sing in Latin, this time. That would impress any bishops who might be there. She would choose something of a religious nature first, and then a song in French for the court. Just as she was about to voice her ideas, Dame Ingrid, an energetic, petite woman of middling years, and her maid Bessie bustled into the hall carrying baskets of apples.

'Bessie, take these out to the kitchen,' she urged the maid.

Espying the visitor seated on a bench with a cup raised to her lips, Ingrid called out, 'Why, good day to you, Dame Margo. What causes you to come to us today?' Dabbing her perspiring forehead with a linen cloth she had tugged from her belt, she gasped, 'Forgive me. It is hot enough to burn the wimple off the Virgin Mary today. Did you come all the way from Wallingford this morning?' Before Dame Margo could reply, Ingrid's eyes lit on the new gown laid across the workbench. 'Ah, you have come for Alice, is it? So, she will sing again?'

'Indeed, Ingrid.' Dame Margo lowered her voice and said, in a confidential tone, 'Indeed, indeed, Alice is to sing for the King again.' She glanced down at the puppet on its long stick, lying neatly beside the gown. 'And perhaps she can organise a puppet show for the Empress Maud, who is also in Northampton. The King's council is meeting again this month.'

'I heard the Empress had returned to England. News travels even as far as Shillingford. Oh dear, no, I cannot spare all our sons – not all three of them at harvest time,' Ingrid said slowly. She furrowed her brow and shook her head. 'We have to gather in more crops yet, and there's the barley strip we must bring in for the Countess too.'

Margo raised a finger. 'Just one lad is enough. Count Brien suggests that your middle son – Xander, is it? – could accompany Alice on the harp. And we saw him with those puppets in the castle at Christmastide. He has a rare talent for those voices of knights and angels and wicked counts. A true mimic, he is.'

'I suppose Walter will be able to spare Xander to play for our King. But when?'

'The eighth day of September.' With a sense of urgency, Margo added, 'We must depart for Northampton on the morrow to be there in good time. I am charged with bringing them both back to Wallingford with me today. Samuel, the castle boatman, is waiting by the jetty.'

'Ah, dearie me! Poor Samuel must be parched, on a day like today. A boy will fetch him and I'll send him out to the kitchen for some ale, then a bowl of pottage and a trencher of gravy and meats. You'll sup with us, Margo?'

'I thank you kindly, if you'll have me . . . as long as we are able to return before night falls.'

'It can be ready forthwith. The cook has made a salmon pie for us, and I know you like it well . . .'

'Best pastry coffin north of Wallingford,' laughed Margo, and she drained her cup. 'That *will* be a treat.'

Bessie was already busily setting up trestles for the midday meal. A boy was sent to fetch the ferryman and, on cue, Walter and the boys hurried into the hall from the fields. All four of them greeted Dame Margo warmly. Within the hour, they were devouring the salmon pie, beef, saladings and bread with cheese. There was an apple pie, too. As she cut into it, Ingrid said, 'Bessie will fetch you another apple pie for the Countess. I baked half a dozen, two days ago.' She turned to Alice. 'Now, my young lady, you fetch your travelling coffer and –' she turned to Xander – 'you do likewise, Xander. Pack your best tunic, the one of burgundy scarlet. It's an honour – a true honour, indeed – to perform for our King.' She grinned the width of her broad, pleasant face and, with a plump hand, tucked a strand of greying hair back into the band of her wimple. 'Fetch your harp and pack the puppets carefully.'

Xander was a lanky youth at sixteen, awkward except when performing. He had fair hair, like his mother's before the grey crept onto her head, and, when he smiled, his soft brown eyes looked like treacle marked with streaks of honey. He had not stopped growing yet, but it looked as if he would be as tall as his father when he did; although he took after Walter in stature, Xander had not inherited his silent temperament, loving to chatter. The family called him their jackdaw. Walt stood up and said, ''Tis a great honour, and, since much of the grain has gone to the miller down river already, we can spare Xander. And our Alice – guard her well for us, Dame Margo.'

Walter, Alice realised, was recollecting how she had near been assaulted when she played for Lady Maud across the Narrow Sea – though, no doubt, Walter knew from Count Brien how the Empress had rescued her from unwanted attentions.

'I shall guard her as I would my own,' said the widow firmly. She patted Alice's arm fondly.

'In that case, may God bless your journeys,' Walter said, and sank his narrow frame back down onto the bench again.

Alice, her curiosity getting the better of her, remarked, 'I heard that Lady Maud has not been living with Count Geoffrey for two whole years.'

Margo replied – a second too quickly, Alice thought – 'Ah, well, there's a reason for that: she's been learning how to rule the kingdom under her father's guidance. The council are meeting to decide when she will return to Anjou. She'll be Queen of England one day.' Dame Margo was dissembling, realised Alice. There was a tightness about the widow's lips and mouth; she would clearly not say anything more on the subject.

Distraction was provided by Xander clumsily emerging from their musical storeroom behind the hall, shouldering his harp. Then he and Walt began to set the puppets into a small oak coffer, side by side, ready for travel, Xander chattering away with excitement. Alice hurried off to her chamber above the hall and packed her necessary clothing into her small leather travelling coffer. She slung a scrip over her shoulder and glanced around to make sure she had forgotten nothing. At the last moment, she snatched up a chain with a cross and fastened it over her head. God would protect her.

As they stepped from the farmhouse, the afternoon light was edging towards dusk. A church bell from a nearby village began to peal out the hour for Vespers. After crossing the doorstep, Dame Margo turned to her hosts. 'We'll be at the castle by nightfall. I give you my thanks; it has been a very pleasant afternoon.'

In addition to the large apple 'coffin', Dame Ingrid made the ferryman carry a bag of new wool for the women of the castle to spin. Ingrid and Dame Margo always had much to speak about concerning weaving, spinning and baking pies, and this afternoon had been no exception, but no further information about Queen Adeliza and Countess Maud had been forthcoming, which made Alice more than usually curious. She would listen to the conversations of others as they journeyed to Northampton and perhaps learn if the Countess had left the Count for good.

'God keep you and your sons,' Dame Margo said, on parting with Walt and Ingrid. 'And may Godwin's future happiness be assured.'

Godwin, Xander's nineteen-year-old brother, was betrothed to Annie, the blacksmith's daughter. It would be a winter wedding. Although Godwin would one day inherit the farm, the young couple were to have a new dwelling of their own, beyond the orchard, which Count Brien intended as a wedding gift. Alice was glad the couple were moving, because she, Xander and their youngest brother, thirteen-year-old Pipkin – little Pipkin – had no liking for Godwin's sharp-tongued, supercilious betrothed, Annie. They secretly referred to her as 'Saint Anna'.

Alice made sure the box of puppets, their theatre, the bound sheaf of play stories and the viol, harp and flute were all stowed carefully on the skiff. That done, she turned to Xander and whispered, 'I want nothing to do with Saint Anna – or no more than is necessary.'

Northampton Castle
September 1131

The long journey to Northampton, through woodland and across harvested fields, passed pleasantly. Alice rode a white palfrey alongside Dame Margo on her grey one, whilst Xander drove the cart containing their puppets and instruments. A small guard accompanied them, flying Count Brien's colours – an embroidered pennant, half blue and half gold – but no outlaws threatened their journey. On the day following their arrival at Northampton Castle, Xander played the harp whilst Alice sang beautifully. The bishops present remarked approvingly on her ability to sing in Latin when she performed an *Ave Maria* for them. A few days later, she was asked to organise a puppet show.

A page led Alice, Xander and Dame Margo into the garden where they were to perform. The sheltered, turfed garden lay beneath a very high wooden keep. Margo pointed to the outside staircase that led up to the Queen's apartment on the – Alice counted – second level. With a wave of her hand, Dame Margo indicated a high arched doorway. 'The Queen, Countess Maud and their attendants will descend after dinner. By then, you must be ready to perform, so rehearse whilst you can. Meanwhile, I shall run along to the kitchens –' her plump hand gestured towards a door by the herbal – 'and fetch ale, bread and cheese – if there's any to be had, with so many others needing feeding today.'

'Indeed, we do need to practise, Xander,' Alice said anxiously. Her belly felt as if tumbling balls were bobbing around it, so nervous was she. But she forgot her concerns as they erected the puppet theatre and she leafed for the hundredth time through the codex containing their stories.

'I think they might enjoy *The Lady, the Angel and the Devil*. The devil teases and tempts the lady, taking on various disguises. Yes, Xander, this one. You can be the devil and –' she lifted up a handsome-headed puppet on a long stick, dressed in silk robes – 'this is Sir Moth, who tempts the lady with fine jewels. Use that tiny necklace, there. Can you get the puppet to dangle it in front of her?'

Xander lifted the puppet, placing the beads on its hand, where it hooked easily between fingers and thumb, and waved it about.

'And I am Lady Desire, so I shall play the puppet I made a costume for last week.' She lifted the lady up, gently touching the seed pearls decorating her gown. 'I can be the angel using my other hand.' The angel puppet was dressed in a diaphanous white gown and matching wings. Glancing around the garden, where benches had already been set up under an open-sided pavilion, she remarked, 'The mulberry tree will have to serve as our background. Pity it's not Eve's apple tree.' She peered about, as if one might mysteriously appear in the garden. 'We could have put on the performance in the orchard.'

'They'll want it to be convenient.'

'Yes, it would have meant leaving the bailey, and the branches in an orchard might impede their view, anyway.'

For a while, they rehearsed, ducking down behind the puppet theatre, mimicking voices, trying out scene changes and manipulating their characters, until Alice leaned back against the mulberry tree, satisfied. 'If we need a second story –' she leafed through the collection of plays again – 'we can do *Jonah and the Whale*. The whale is in the puppet box, as is Jonah. We've done it so often that we don't even need to practise. But, once you have played the flute and I have sung, it could be time for Vespers. We may not have time.'

At that very moment, Dame Margo returned carrying a basket of provisions, which they fell on gratefully, seated on the ground in the shade of the leafy tree.

'I am dining in the hall with Count Brien's retainers,' Dame

Margo announced, proudly puffing out her chest at this. It was clearly an honour. 'I could not resist watching you both from the staircase. The play is entertaining and quite convincing, but the devil's head might terrify the women – though the angel looks serene enough.'

'I doubt they will be too frightened,' Alice demurred, as she ate. 'It is not our intention to scare, but to amuse. Anyway, Lady Maud is most courageous.' She did not believe the puppet to be terrifying, but she was polite to Dame Margo anyway.

Dame Margo placed her hands on her wide waist and nodded at the basket she had carried out. 'Well, finish up your dinner. It's all you'll get until supper. It could be a long afternoon, and –' she drew her hand over her brow – 'hotter than a cooking cauldron, despite the shade erected over those benches.' With those words, she waddled back towards the kitchens.

They were fishing about the remaining contents of Dame Margo's basket, and Xander had just fetched out a chicken leg, when Alice's ears pricked up. Voices drifted down the staircase. Glancing upwards, Alice saw Queen Adeliza and Lady Maud descending the stairs, unaccompanied. 'Not already,' Alice said, scrabbling to pack away the remains of their dinner, including Xander's chicken treat. He let out a howl of protest.

'Shush, Xander.' She peered around the side of the puppet theatre. 'Ah, they just seem to be taking the air. The hall must be uncomfortably hot.' She produced Xander's chicken leg again and he snatched it from her.

'And noisy,' whispered Xander, in-between chews. 'It must be loud up there, with so many people dining together.'

She nodded. Looking around the side of the theatre again, she said, 'Hush, now, Xander, let me hear what the Queen and Lady Maud are saying.'

Xander flashed her a mischievous look, grinned, and then, acting the fool, stuffed into his mouth the linen cloth they used to clean the puppet heads, pretending to silence himself. Then he removed it to finish eating.

Alice listened carefully, protected from sight by the foliage of the mulberry tree. For a moment, Queen Adeliza and Lady Maud walked the paths of the herbal, releasing the heady scent of camomile as they trod; no wonder camomile was often scattered amongst floor straw indoors. After a while, the Queen sank onto a turf bench not far from their tree and Lady Maud joined her. Now they were closer, Alice could make out what they were saying.

'I cannot return to Anjou,' Lady Maud was saying. 'I really can't.'

'But the council insists. Geoffrey has written to request you go back to him, and he is deeply sorry, Maud, for any part he played in your quarrel. And so they have voted that you must return.'

'It was not just *one* quarrel.'

'Maybe so, but he promises to treat you with honour, and he is, after all, your husband, Maud.'

Maud snorted.

'He's older, now. More mature.'

Lady Maud frowned. 'He wants my crown, Adeliza.'

'Henry did not ask them all to swear loyalty to Geoffrey of Anjou, but solely to you.' She paused. 'And Henry will not release your castles on Normandy's border yet. Geoffrey has to prove himself deserving of them.'

Maud's voice sank into despondency. 'That is no help. Geoffrey will never cease to badger me over my castles, which are part of my dowry.' There was silence until she sighed and said, 'When I return, because I suppose I really have no choice, I trust he will be a proper husband to me – in every way.'

Alice stifled a gasp with her fist. What did *that* mean?

'There won't be occasion to find out, if you do not return,' Queen Adeliza was saying.

'If he does not consummate the marriage, I can request an annulment and be free of him.' Maud drew breath and gave a rueful laugh. 'I have often thought Geoffrey may need a love potion to help him.'

'I hope you have not suggested that? It might enrage him, and insult his manhood.'

'Of course not, I have only hinted.'

46

It was Adeliza's turn to chuckle. 'And your father, too, for that matter; let us say . . .' She lowered her voice and Alice strained her ears to hear. Maud had a shocked look on her countenance.

'He is not young anymore,' Queen Adeliza continued, 'and, if we cannot accomplish what is necessary to beget children, there won't be any – so all rests on your shoulders, if Henry's line is to continue.' Before Maud could respond to this comment, Queen Adeliza ran on, 'But, you know, it's not the same for a young man. Count Geoffrey just needs to grow up. He was sixteen when you parted . . . just a boy—'

'That *boy* sent me away,' Maud interrupted.

'Well, he has changed his mind. He is all of nineteen, now, and you are his lawful wife. When he sees you, he will not resist your elegance and charm, and you really are very beautiful.'

Alice found herself nodding. Lady Maud *was* beautiful. If only she could serve her in some way. She recollected Count Geoffrey and found she was shaking her head. As Dame Margo would say, quoting a favourite homily, *You cannot teach an old hound new tricks.* Count Geoffrey was no doubt still unreformed.

'He says I am proud and overbearing, not soft and gentle, as a woman ought to be,' Lady Maud was saying, with a flash of scorn.

'As well he finds you so. After all, one day, you will be a queen.'

It seemed as if Maud was looking straight at her, so Alice ducked behind the tree. Xander's mouth was just opening in a yawn. Alice swiftly leaned over and silenced him. When she glanced up again, Adeliza and Maud were strolling back to the stairway. Alice realised that soon they would collect their ladies and return to the garden.

'Xander,' she said, 'play your flute the moment you see them coming out again. It won't be long. The hall has quietened since they came down here.'

That night, as she lay on her pallet beside Dame Margo, Alice revisited the afternoon in her head. The puppets had been a huge success. And not just the ladies, but a chamberlain and several bishops and nobles came to watch as well. Alice and Xander had performed both

47

plays and, when she emerged at the end to bow, and Xander played his flute again, she realised that, clothed in her new gown, she looked as well dressed as any of Lady Maud's own attendants. Queen Adeliza applauded vigorously and Lady Maud sent them a purse of silver pennies.

'You must visit us in Anjou when Count Brien comes, you and all your troupe,' Lady Maud said graciously to Alice, before she and Queen Adeliza departed the garden, adding, 'And Count Brien must lend you and your brother to me, too, when I am at court.'

A moment later, they were gone, and tomorrow Count Brien was sending Alice and Xander back to Wallingford with Dame Margo. Alice speculated on what Godwin would say about their adventure. He would be full of praise, especially as they were bringing Ingrid and Walt their earnings. She smiled to herself. Saint Anna would tumble off her plinth with envy.

The midnight Angelus rang out. Somewhere in the orchard, an owl hooted. As Alice turned on her side and prepared for sleep, Countess Maud's words in the garden teased her thoughts. Could the youth who had attempted to take her own honour actually be unable to do the deed? And that talk of potions! Her eyes flicked open wider. Today had proved that she was sharp-eared and excellent at listening, unseen, to the conversations between others – discovering their secrets. For a heartbeat, she watched a moonbeam slide in through the window. She knew how to guard secrets too.

Chapter Five

Anjou
1131–4

When Maud reluctantly returned to Geoffrey, life in Anjou was very different from that hideous year following her wedding.

Geoffrey had indeed grown up; he was better behaved and more attractive in every way. Not only was he more mature, he was now admired as a warrior who would not hesitate to ride out and hunt down rebels. Maud suspected advisors had taken him to task, for he welcomed her with fanfares and feasting. He was attentive. He had her apartment in the castle of Le Mans decorated with tasteful wall paintings of hunting scenes, woodland birds and flowers. He ordered new tiled floors and introduced Oriental rugs. She was given a new silk mattress stuffed with thousands and thousands of goose feathers. To her delight, the window in her chamber had been glazed with pale green glass, and she enjoyed opening it outwards and closing it again with the latch. Below the pale glazed window, a bench had been purposely placed so she could enjoy the view of distant orchards. It was covered with silken cushions embroidered with Geoffrey's arms – red lions looking as if they intended to leap from their long kite-shaped shields. A small altar, with a statue placed upon it of the Virgin clad in blue robes, stood discreetly in an alcove, whilst, opposite, a door led into a garderobe that smelled sweetly of lavender and was large enough to contain a rail on which to hang gowns, since moths never entered that place.

Geoffrey greeted her, the first night he visited her in this luxurious chamber, with a sincere declaration of affection, if not love. 'Let us not quarrel again, Maud. I am sorry for any injury I have done you,' the handsome nineteen-year-old said, tears brimming in his eyes, as they stood in their night rails beside her bed.

'I am sure we shall quarrel often,' she replied haughtily, one hand smoothing her new embroidered coverlet. Then she added, admittedly with reluctance, 'But I regret the insults I levelled at you.'

Geoffrey pulled her into his arms. He was not overly tall, and could never physically intimidate her, but he was handsomer than ever and, when he kissed her, she felt her mouth opening and, within a heartbeat, she was returning his kiss.

'How could I not have seen it before? Maud – you are beautiful.' He took her by the arms and held her away from him.

She could feel his strength. 'Do you know, Geoffrey, you are developing a true warrior's physique.'

With his face set into the serious countenance of an older man, he said, 'And you are clever. Together, we can be formidable. Normandy is at peace as long as your father lives, but, Maud, when he dies, even though they have promised you the succession, there could be unrest in Normandy on my borders. Believe me when I tell you I am constantly quelling rebellions in Anjou.'

'I understand this could be so, but my father will rule for many years yet.' She paused, then added, 'I need a son. That would silence opposition to my future queenship.'

Geoffrey winked at her and grinned. 'So, let us put my new physique to good use, Maud.'

Before she could protest, he had lifted her onto the bed. Within minutes, she had lost her chemise and he his braies. A long drawn-out breath passed and they were comfortably entwined within each other's loins.

Later, as she drowsed, she suddenly thought she heard Count Brien's laugh, and awoke with a shock. It was night; moonlight cast shadows in the dark room. She listened, heart beating, and heard a dog bark. It was only a dog; Brien was far away in England, perhaps sleeping beside Tilda – he was ever-faithful to his wife.

She rolled over and looked at the sleeping shape of Geoffrey beside her. He was now clearly determined to become her lover, but, she wondered, unable to shake her sense of Brien, could he ever become her friend?

Weeks passed without the tempestuous quarrels of the past. Life grew pleasant, if not perfect. She still resented being married to a mere count, but she found herself mellowing towards Geoffrey and he towards her, though she still suspected he had mistresses tucked away in various of the castles she was never invited to visit.

She became pregnant within a year. Her withdrawal from court life, the birth, recovery and churching all occurred in the castle of Le Mans and its cathedral. Her first son, Hal, named for her father, Henry, entered the world on a blustery March day, bellowing and kicking. He was a beautiful, strong, healthy baby, and she was in love with him.

When he visited Le Mans that April for little Hal's christening, her doting father arrived with gifts, including a silver rattle and a small carved image of Saint Julian, who was to be Hal's protector and was the patron saint of the Le Mans Cathedral. Maud ordered a richly embroidered and jewelled pall for the cathedral's Saint Julian, because she was so grateful to be delivered of a healthy son.

Baby Hal crawled over the floor tiles. Although it was October, the weather was unseasonably mild and her window was open. After a short time crawling and shaking his silver rattle, the baby grew hungry and began to scream. Maud summoned his wet nurse.

'He knows his mind,' Maud said as the wet nurse hurried over.

'Nothing wrong with Hal's appetite,' the wet nurse said as she undid her bodice. Within a quarter hour of the candle clock, Hal was satiated and sound asleep, his downy red head comfortably leaning against his nurse's bosom.

'He looks rather like his father, don't you think?' Maud said to sloe-eyed Lenora, her senior lady, a wealthy widow a little older than she was, who had determined never to remarry. Lenora, beset by suitors, would send replies to them all, stating that her service was to Lady Maud, never to a husband. Maud appreciated her loyalty – though, if Lenora took a vow of chastity, as some widows did, she hoped she would remain by her side for many more years and not enter a convent as a long-term guest.

Lenora shifted her linen-clad posterior on the bench, set aside her sewing and watched the child for a while before remarking, 'Henry certainly has his father's red hair. Oh dear, he will possess a fiery temperament.' She studied the sleeping child in his nurse's arms. 'And he is sturdy, just like his grandsire.' She pointed at his legs. 'Looking at those, I would say he will be very strong . . . but he's stubborn too, determined to get what he wants, even if only a silver rattle. My lady, one day, he will be a great king.'

'May the Madonna bless him,' Maud said, laughing. 'I never thought I could be maternal, Lenora, but this son proves me wrong.' She turned to the nurse. 'Put Henry in his cradle and summon the rocker.'

The nurse nodded and hurried the child away, carrying him gently against her shoulder so as not to awaken him.

When she was sure she had departed, Maud picked up a piece of sewing and said quietly to Lenora, whilst one hand moved protectively to her midriff, 'To my surprise, I find myself looking forward to giving birth again. If only I did not feel so wretchedly sick.' She made a neat stitch and abandoned her work.

Lenora set her own stitching aside with a look of concern on her brow. 'I shall request another tisane for you and we should close the window shutters.'

'Later, perhaps. Let's enjoy the sunshine, for now. It's not yet chill.'

'A mantle, just in case.' Lenora, ever diligent, hurriedly fetched a warm, prettily patterned shawl from the coffer and placed it around Maud's shoulders. 'There, that's better,' she said, and sank onto a bench again, where she picked up the shirt she had been working on, one of a half dozen for the poor who dwelled in leaky cottages beyond the castle, making careful stitches on the coarse fabric, so tiny they were hardly visible.

Maud glanced admiringly at Lenora's work and then down at the shirt she was embroidering for little Henry. He was growing quickly. Her work was not nearly as perfect as Lenora's. She dropped it into her lap. 'You know, I've been thinking, Lenora, my father is in Rouen this winter and I long to see him and Adeliza. He intends passing a whole year in Normandy, keeping order there. And, after all, Rouen's castle keep is much more comfortable than Le Mons or even Angers, with its lovely gardens. All my favoured abbeys lie nearby and I love the palace too. Do you know, the Rouen keep now has fireplaces and there's glass in all of the royal apartment's windows, not just one or two. There have been many renovations made there since my wedding to Geoffrey.'

'I remember.' Lenora sighed and shook her long dark plait. 'It is a beautiful castle, my lady. I liked the gardens. Reminds me of Burgos.' Lenora had been raised in Spain and often spoke of its comfortable palaces.

'Well, yes, and I am considering birthing my next child in Rouen. If I travel there in spring, will you accompany me?'

Without hesitation, her lady said, 'Certainly I shall, my lady. As if I would not! I would not miss attending the birth of your child for a bag of silver.'

'Then it is settled. We shall pass spring and summer in Normandy.' Lenora smiled and said, 'I think all your ladies will want to come.'

'Then all shall,' Maud said, glad she had made this decision.

Geoffrey could hardly object. It would surely be in his interests, since, without doubt, he would press her to insist her father release the Norman castles he had agreed in her dowry settlement. She said aloud, 'Don't say anything to my women or anyone yet, not until after Christmastide.'

Lenora placed a finger on her lips and shook her head. Removing her finger, she said, 'Silent as the grave.'

Christmastide passed and, by January, Maud was entering her fifth month. Snowstorms blew about the courtyard. The women felt trapped inside the draughty castle at Angers and, despite tisanes and massages, Maud's feet were swollen and she felt unwell. Letters were carried by messengers to the English court. Arrangements were discreetly made in Rouen for her confinement.

February was no better, for it was damp and chill. She had not yet told Geoffrey of her plans to travel, since he was so often away from their castle of Angers. But finally, on a March afternoon following a dinner she could hardly stomach, her little creamy-coloured greyhound pup trailing her, she found her husband in the great chamber behind the hall where he did general business, consulted with dignitaries and had his scribes write letters. When she swept in, feeling uncomfortably cumbersome, he glanced up from studying a map of Anjou's borders, alone for once, and she was grateful for this fact, since there were no stewards or priests to overhear what she had to say.

'What brings you in here, Maud? You should be resting.' He rolled up the map and secured it with a cord. 'At least, whilst you are here, be seated by the brazier. Here, take my chair.' He politely did not say it was more suitable for her than the smaller, armed chair to the other side, but he did look at her enormity as if it was the first time he had noticed. She eased herself into the great chair, the pup curling by her feet, chewing at the chair leg. Geoffrey stepped forward, as if to kick it away, but she lifted a hand and he clearly thought better of it, retreating a few paces. He leaned against the table and asked again, 'What occasions this visit, Maud? Are you in need of anything I can help with? You appeared well at dinner . . . though you left without eating much. Is all well with our son?'

So, he had at least noticed that she had not eaten, she thought to herself.

'Henry is quite well, Geoffrey, but I am not. Even so, I shall survive.' She stroked her long black plait, as if the action was a comfort. 'I am making arrangements to travel to Rouen, because I wish to have our second child in Normandy. I have written to my father, and Adeliza is as delighted as he is . . . She knows of reliable midwives and doctors.'

His mouth opened and closed. He shook his gold-red curls dramatically and finally declared, 'By the rood, you have decided all this without consulting me, your lord and husband.'

'You are rarely here *to* consult, husband.' She let her tongue dwell overly on the word *husband* this time and added, 'I am informing you now. My doctors tell me the child will be born at Pentecost. And so . . . I wish to spend spring and the summer recovering in Rouen.'

Geoffrey balled his hands into tight fists. He banged one down on the table, making her heart jump like a pair of dice tossed about a gaming board. The little dog let out a bark. 'You should have conferred with me.' He glared at her and snorted, 'Well, I won't forbid you, but, when you see your father, you will request the castles promised to us by him, do you hear?'

She raised her head and lifted her chin at his hectoring tone. 'I have made our request before, but my father says he cannot let them go just yet. He will, when the time is right.'

'Does he think I'll sell them off to France? He plays with us, Maud!'

'I shall ask again.' It would have to do. By right, they were her dowry and her papa was unreasonable.

These Norman border castles remained a sore issue between herself and Geoffrey, particularly because the barons and clergy of England had not extended any oath of fealty to Geoffrey, even though they were the same prelates who had insisted she return to her husband three years previously, to beget an heir for the English throne. They accepted Geoffrey as her husband, but they would never accept him as their king. Their loyalty was exclusively to her and any heirs she produced, but never to Geoffrey himself.

He shrugged. 'Go and arrange your travel. Take that pup out of here before he soils the straw. Well, I must get on with attending to business in Anjou.'

'Will you join me in Rouen? I wish to bring Hal to see his grandsire too.'

'No, Hal remains here with me and his nurses. You will be confined, in any case.' He folded his sarcenet-clad arms over his breast. He repeated, 'My son and heir will not travel to Rouen.'

This was a bitter disappointment and she felt anger boil up inside her. How dare Geoffrey make this decision? Yet she knew it was best to keep the peace between them, so she conceded. 'As you wish, Geoffrey.' Nonetheless, she determined that, as soon as her second child was born and she could travel, she would return to Anjou.

Clearly relenting his hastiness, Geoffrey came around his desk to her side, leaned down and lifted her hand, saying, 'I shall bring Henry with me to Rouen to see the new child and escort you back here, once you have been churched.' He dropped a kiss on her forehead. 'I have a pressing meeting this afternoon with the castle steward. When do you intend travelling?'

'By this week's end.'

'I have to visit one of my knights this week, but I'll return to wish you Godspeed.'

Although he lifted her hand and dropped a perfunctory kiss on it, she noted he could not get away quickly enough. His business with a knight was more likely with a lady, perhaps even the knight's wife. Well, it was an unspoken arrangement between them. The best she could hope for from her marriage was a truce with Geoffrey, a political alliance with Anjou and the cradle filled with male heirs. She sighed. Such was a woman's lot.

With a flurry of his voluminous woollen mantle, her handsome, strong-willed, possibly devious husband was gone. She, too, departed for her bower, the faithful pup trailing behind her. She turned her thoughts to packing.

After discovering Lady Lenora bent over a coffer instructing one of her junior ladies to place lavender amongst the Empress's linen, she called her away from the task.

'We are departing on Friday. Organise our packing. And choose six reliable, sensible ladies to accompany us.'

'So at last Lord Geoffrey knows you wish to have the child in Rouen?'

'Indeed, and now I am going to rest. Take this pup. Send Doctor Ignatius to me, and my priest. They are travelling to Rouen as well. And find Drogo, too. Tell him we are travelling on Friday. He'll be in the hall.'

★

Five days later, she was lying against woollen cushions within a carriage, wrapped in a blanket, her feet raised and both a midwife and Lenora watching over her. Other carriages followed with her ladies selected by Lenora, as well as her servants. Sumpter carts trailed behind and Drogo still commanded her knights.

She shed tears on leaving little Hal. 'I shall be home before we know it. Anyway, when your brother or sister enters the world, you shall come to Rouen.' Hal was not listening. A tabby cat had crossed the yard and that was much more interesting. Geoffrey descended the steps from the hall at that very moment. On seeing his father, Hal's attention shifted from the cat and he reached his arms up to Geoffrey. His father swept him from his nurse and, encouraged by his adoring father, the child waved Maud's cavalcade farewell.

She remarked acidly to Lenora, as the carriage jolted and they were moving forwards, 'Geoffrey loves his son.' To herself, she added, Even if he has a paucity of love for me.

Rouen Castle
Pentecost 1134

Robert, Earl of Gloucester, Maud's much-loved half-brother and loyalist servant, his skin as weathered and leathery as his well-worn boots, impatiently shook his bridle reins and twisted his head around, intending to chivvy his wife Mabel forward. She had paused to adjust her position in her saddle, and was, in fact, only a few yards behind.

They had been on the road since Prime and were in a hurry to reach Rouen's castle before nightfall. It's not so far from Caen to Rouen, he thought, his anxiety palpable, his large hands gripping his reins more tightly. Mabel quickly caught up and soon they were riding, side by side, along a forest path.

'Robert,' Mabel said, 'she will survive. I am sure of it. Your sister is determined and she is tough. Just remember all she has experienced: reigning as an empress, her husband's long slow death from a tumour, ruling for the Emperor, and then marriage to that boy, leaving him, returning to a loveless marriage because your father ordered it, and now a terrible childbirth.' She swept a hand towards the trees. 'Maud is as strong as that oak tree. Your sister is no feeble woman. She will recover with renewed strength. You will see.'

The generally optimistic Robert turned his head with sadness in his bearing. 'I pray to God and all his angels for her recovery.' In his heart, he was afraid for his sister. His father, the King, had summoned them to her bedside. Maud was dying. The Archbishop of Rouen Cathedral intended to give Maud the last rites. She wished, Henry had written, to be laid to rest in the abbey she loved most – the Abbey of Bec.

He wrote that Maud's priests claimed God was calling her to him. It was a miracle the child, another boy, had survived his long and terrible birth.

They fell silent and all Robert could hear was the clip-clop of their guards' mounts, occasional neighing and a rustling of creatures in the hedgerows, but, for most of the journey, he was locked inside his own thoughts and memories. Occasionally, he felt a tear roll down his cheek. He loved his younger half-sister dearly.

Hours later, when their party rode through the gates of the castle, he felt hollow at heart. The bustle of busy life continued within the bailey. Yet, somewhere deep inside the castle's keep, his sister's life-blood was draining away.

King Henry had been watching for them. They had no sooner dismounted than he swept down the steps to them, his crimson robe flowing behind him.

'Robert, my son.' Henry greeted him with an embrace, tears rolling down his aging, purple-veined cheeks. 'And Lady Mabel – this is, indeed, a sad occasion. The doctors say they have done all they can. It was a brutal birth. The child lay awkwardly in her womb and it was a slow and difficult task to manipulate him out.' He wiped away his tears with his sleeve as he led them into the hall. 'My son, it's in God's hands, now, whether she lives or dies. I prayed for my daughter to live and the child to die, but God does not accept bargains.'

Mabel asked, 'How is the baby?'

'A strong healthy boy. His name is Geoffrey, for his father.'

'May we see Maud?'

'After her husband has a little time with her, then you may have yours.'

Robert looked past his father, having noted Adeliza entering the hall from behind an arras. She greeted them both warmly, took Mabel's hands and said, 'Come to my solar, Mabel, and take refreshment. Leave Robert with Henry. They will send for us soon. Prayers are to be said for Maud in the chapel.'

'You must tell me everything, Adeliza,' Mabel said quietly. 'I have given birth many times. All may appear worse than it is.'

Adeliza shook her head. 'Too much blood lost. After you have rested, you can meet baby Geoffrey.'

Robert noted Adeliza's pale drawn face and that her sorrowful violet eyes were full of tears.

A little later, Robert joined Mabel in a nursery chamber, where the baby was peacefully asleep in his cradle. Henry promised to summon them to Maud's bedside within an hour by the candle clock.

'Come aside,' Mabel whispered.

Robert felt her hand take his own. They moved to the alcove by a window. 'What is it, Mabel?' he said gravely.

'Apparently Maud was cut to ease the birth and had a great loss of blood, and now she has a fever. Doctors insisted on bleeding her, but I have suggested they make wafers of mugwort, sage, pennyroyal and willow weed. And they *must* persuade her to eat these. I have advised they mix clay with vinegar and make a plaster to lay over her liver. Adeliza says she has bleeds from the nose, but such a plaster can be placed on the forehead too. It will ease the bleeding. I have seen it work before.'

Robert looked at his wife with hope in his eyes. 'Henry says the Archbishop is speaking of last rites.'

'Prayer alone will not save Maud. There is more they can do, but they must not bleed her again.'

Robert nodded. He glanced towards the doorway, where a page stood diffidently to usher them to Maud's bedside. They followed the liveried boy along a corridor and up a curling stairway to the birthing chamber, where Maud had been secluded for over a month. Her room was hushed. It smelled of frankincense, like a church. Robert stared at his sister. Maud was asleep. Count Geoffrey nodded at Robert, who thought his brother-in-law had aged considerably. He had been with Maud all day.

Robert leaned down and whispered into Geoffrey's ear, 'Go and take refreshment now, while we are here. Mabel has a suggestion for the midwife.' He glanced to the corner bench, where a midwife was sitting with a small piece of sewing. 'Little Henry – how is he?'

'Robust. He is with Lady Lenora, whom he adores.'

Robert placed his hands on Geoffrey's shoulders. 'Take heart, brother,' he said softly. 'We are all in God's hands. The Archbishop would do better to pray for her recovery, not convince her she is dying.'

He watched Mabel speaking in a soft voice to the midwife. Adeliza slipped into the chamber along with a maidservant and a doctor, who carried a silver dish with the clay plasters.

'When Maud awakens, we shall persuade her to eat the wafers,' he explained to Geoffrey. 'There will be prayers chanted in the chapel this evening, for her recovery – again.'

Either Mabel's remedy worked or God was with Maud. Robert remained at his sister's side for days as she began to slowly recover. Mabel insisted she sipped broth. She forbade any bleeding and she – sensibly, Robert decided – banished all talk of death or final rites. Geoffrey carried Maud's Madonna statue closer to her bed, so she could see the Lady Mary when she opened her eyes. He placed beside her a reliquary box Maud loved, as it contained Saint James's finger bone.

'Thank you,' Maud said, on seeing her favoured saint and the precious reliquary. Later, she spoke in a whisper: 'I believe I am not for God's Kingdom – or the Devil's – after all.' She had grown strong enough to hold her father's mottled hand as she spoke. Looking over at Geoffrey's face, she said, 'This means I am meant for my own kingdom, and the ruling of England. Send for my baby, husband. I wish to see him.'

Earl Robert and Lady Mabel departed from Rouen on a sunny July day, feeling more light-hearted than on their previous journey, for Maud had made a miraculous recovery. As they rode by fields full of grain, Robert grinned and remarked to his wife, 'You helped her to heal, my love.'

'Not entirely. The doctors were bleeding a woman who had already lost too much blood, foolishly thinking to relieve Countess Maud of ill humours. She has two healthy sons. Geoffrey is as proud as the lion he truly wishes he was.'

Robert found himself laughing heartily at the image of Geoffrey as a lion. 'He does have a lion's mane, curled to the very bottom of his neck, and his hair is golden red. The sons look like they'll take after him. Did you note a covering of red fluff on the baby's head? And, Mabel, never let Maud hear you call her Countess, because she calls herself Empress. And, if our father dies, though I pray not for years yet, she will be Queen of England and Normandy's Duchess, not a mere countess.'

'How did you find Geoffrey?'

'Geoffrey is not an imp lacking manners anymore. He is maturing. They seem to rub along together, though there is not much love between them. He will make a good warrior. Pity he seems to be more interested in Normandy than England. Geoffrey does not wish to be a male consort and he is insisting my father releases the Norman castles promised to him. You know my father. He keeps everyone waiting and he won't make an exception for Geoffrey . . . or for Maud, for that matter.'

They rode on in comfortable silence for a while, until Mabel noticed a pair of swans on the river as they were crossing. The elegant creatures and their offspring were just disappearing below the bridge. She slowed down to look at the glide of cygnets following their parents beneath the stone arch, appearing again on the other side.

'They have quite a family,' Robert remarked. 'Swans mate for life.'

'Yes,' said Mabel. 'It's a pity Adeliza and Henry have no children, despite her being by his side whenever he travels.' After a hesitant moment, she added, in a lower voice, 'Did you notice how that knight, William d'Aubigny, looks at the Queen? If he could fall on his sword in her service, he would.'

Robert could not resist another hearty laugh. He leaned towards her and responded with, 'Good that she has an admirer, as long as he keeps his distance. Look at how my father was cock of the walk for decades. Our Queen is beautiful and young. Fortunately, she is also devoted to my father. It is indeed sad there are no children. There are murmurings it is a fault on the distaff side, but I do wonder. My father long ago renounced all mistresses, and now he is aging.' With one hand, he made the sign of the cross in the air. 'But may good King Henry live for many a year more. He might still make Adeliza pregnant. Who knows! What man could resist such a beautiful woman?'

Mabel grimaced, then tilted her nose into the air. She was clearly not encouraging this talk of beautiful queens. He smiled at her and drew his mount even closer to his wife's. 'Fortunately, I have a lovely wife of my own. There has been none other for me in many a long year, and never will be.' He meant it. He had strayed once, acknowledged his son of long ago by a mistress and promised God and himself he would never betray the wife he later married.

Chapter Six

Normandy
November and December 1135

How quickly fortune's wheel turns. Earl Robert turned this thoughts over and over, his heart saddened because King Henry was ill and hope for a recovery was fading. On a sullen Monday in November, the King had left off his recent campaigning and chased a stag through the forest of Lyons-la-Forêt. Henry had planned a whole week of hunting, but it was not to be. That Monday evening, he'd fallen so ill, he was incapacitated for days. A dish of eels was the culprit. Even though he loved the delicacy, it always seemed to disagree with him. As the King sickened, Robert did not hesitate to send out messengers for doctors from Caen. Without delay, a band of physicians rode out to the hunting lodge, where, serious-faced, they gathered around Henry's bedside, shaking their greying heads. One consulted the stars, another suggested bleeding the King to allow the bad humours to escape, and the third, the most senior, despaired of the King's recovery.

Four days later, Robert despaired too, because the King's condition had worsened almost until death.

The hunting lodge, usually a place of merrymaking and relaxation, grew hushed and sombre. A discreet retinue of nobles and priests, led by Earl Robert, kept a constant vigil by the King's bedside. Queen Adeliza wept, wrung her hands and prayed for a miraculous recovery, alongside her ladies, in the lodge's Madonna chapel.

On Friday evening, the King's doctors requested a final private conversation with Earl Robert, withdrawing from the King's side to seclude themselves in a closet beyond his bedchamber. Robert studied the collection of grim faces with dread, because he knew that there was no hope of any miraculous recovery – and it did not seem as though Maud's claim would be easy to launch, when she was so far away and still weakened from successive childbirths.

They gathered in a glum huddle, close to the window, so as not to be overheard by certain others. Robert particularly feared the old and powerful knight, William de Warenne, a man built large and muscled, though today clad in a heavy, dark woollen mantle. His jowly, ruddy face, although slightly turned Robert's way, was as ever closed. His eyes were so heavy-lidded, it was difficult to read his true thoughts. Robert knew none now in attendance to the King were true supporters of Maud, particularly since disturbances invoked by Maud's husband were rife around the Norman borderlands in which they all owned castles, estates and trading interests.

Robert patiently waited, though the three doctors each seemed reluctant to be first to speak. At length, he barked, 'Well, speak up! Spit out the worst.' They should have saved his father. 'Come on, one of you must know the way of it. Any chance my father can survive this?' He knew it was hopeless. And most likely they feared he would accuse them of incompetence.

Two of the physicians looked down at their feet. The senior of the trinity, the one with a long white beard similar to the Noah painted on the wall behind Robert, said hesitantly, 'It is time, my lord Robert, to send to Rouen for the Archbishop.' Further moments of hesitation passed until the sad-faced doctor whispered, 'Alas, the King's time is nigh. Death comes for us all, and he has been weakened by his recent campaign. King Henry needed rest, not fighting and sieges. He has near enough seventy years.' The physician made the sign of the cross with a wavering hand. 'My lord Earl Robert, G-God –' he began to stutter – 'G-God decides—'

'God decides what?' Robert interjected. 'Speak!'

'When every man meets his heavenly Father, my lord – even princes.'

Silence. The air stirred and candles flickered in their sconces.

Beyond the shuttered windows, the late November evening settled frosty and bitterly chill. Robert pulled his warm, woollen cloak closer. He felt a tear roll down his cheek and, to disguise his sorrow, he opened a window shutter and peered out at the eerie ethereal moonlight bathing the world beyond in a ghostly blue light. When he turned back and refastened the shutter, it seemed to him as if all three physicians were frozen into a waxen tableau, trapped within a single moment of time. Robert knew he would never forget this moment as long as he lived.

The Archbishop of Rouen must be fetched out to the hunting lodge at once. He said, 'I shall send for him tonight. It's only a half day's ride; he will arrive by dawn.'

'What about the King's daughter?' the white-beard asked in a gentle tone.

Maud was in Angers, a week's ride away. Even if she could travel, she would never reach the King in time. That year, she had quarrelled bitterly with their father over the border castles, which Henry had flatly refused to release into her and Geoffrey's custody, and in response the aging King had spent months patrolling and strengthening them all, especially that of Argentan. There had been some sharp skirmishes with his son-in-law, Geoffrey. If Robert had feared it would end badly for Maud and her bellicose husband, now he was sure of it. There would be great unrest once Henry died, and Maud, who was again with child and very unwell, he had heard, might never secure her inheritance. Yet, he could understand why Maud, the mother of two little boys, was planning for her sons' future. This had united Maud and Geoffrey, the husband she had once despised. Earl Robert shook his head and said, 'We cannot fetch the Empress Maud in time. Anjou is too distant.'

The long-faced doctors looked to the side door in concert, and Robert was aware of a leather curtain separating. A heartbeat later, Queen Adeliza swept in, attended by two darkly-gowned women. Her usually animated eyes were red-veined with weeping.

'I told my lord not to eat the eels.' Pale-faced, Adeliza, standing by the glowing brazier, said softly, 'I said, "Send them away." Eels

65

and lampreys have always disagreed with him.' She wiped tears from her eyes with her long, embroidered sleeve. 'We all tried to stop him, but Henry would never take advice.'

The chief physician raised his bowed head. 'Your Grace, regrettably the King enjoyed that particular dish too much. I, myself, told him long ago never to touch them.'

Robert sighed, 'If only we could throw away the candle clock and turn back time.' He felt his stomach churning with the scant meal of gruel he had eaten earlier. 'My Queen, we can only look to the future. With your agreement, I am sending for the Archbishop.' He gestured towards the rheumy-eyed, bearded doctors, and the senior amongst them said, 'The King has only days left in this world.'

Robert snapped at him, 'That is clear. All must be prepared, as our Lord God commands, for my father's entry into Heaven's eternal embrace.'

Tears coursed down Adeliza's cheeks. She brushed these away and said, 'As you think best, Robert.' Her voice was choked and he laid a comforting hand on her arm.

'It is God's will, my Queen,' he said softly.

The doctors bowed and discreetly withdrew, leaving Adeliza and Robert to their privacy. Her women huddled together in an alcove, their hands folded in prayer, silently weeping.

Adeliza echoed what Robert had been thinking: 'Maud – she should be here with her father. There will be the succession to consider. There's unrest already and there will be more soon. The barons will fight over the succession, no matter what they swore. Maud must return to us.'

'Ah, Adeliza, as you know well, my sister has not ventured to Rouen for months. She and Geoffrey are united in their determination to take over the border castles.' He frowned. 'Maud is like an unruly sparrowhawk. When meat is offered and then taken away or hidden, she grows keener to acquire what she feels is hers by right. And Geoffrey is determined to take them by stealth or by force, or both.'

Adeliza's brow creased with concern. 'Henry has always considered he should spin out the affairs of everyone, grip within his own hands and keep those such as Count Geoffrey hanging on in hope.' She drew a jagged breath. 'Robert, I sent a letter to Angers as soon as Henry sickened and her response was tart: "My father has abandoned me."'

Robert leaned back against the wall and stiffened his resolve not to make matters worse by sending riders for his sister. 'They are as stubborn as each other,' he muttered. 'The earls may not accept an Angevin ruling beside my sister, certainly not Geoffrey. I must try to ensure their son, Henry, is named our next king.' He paused. 'And that, Adeliza, will be no easy matter.' He thought for a few moments. 'I wonder if the King is strong enough to enlighten us as to his wishes. Only he can dismiss the earls' loyalty to the oath they made, and only he can insist upon them observing it.'

Adeliza raised an eyebrow. 'And you, Robert? What do you want?'

'A peaceful and honourable succession, as I pray the King also wishes.'

The Archbishop and his retainers rode into the courtyard on the following afternoon, just as the sun was bleeding into a red and yellow fuzzy circle over the western oaks. The prelate of Rouen entered the King's bedchamber and remained closeted there whilst the candle burned away the hours and the forest chapel rang out the passing of Masses, calling all to prayers for their dying ruler's gentle passing.

Knowing that there were things he must enquire of his father, Robert replaced the Archbishop at his bedside. Henry lay on his back, his head gently propped up by pillows; his once stocky frame was a diminished mound under a golden-threaded coverlet; his pale eyes were open and serene. He had received absolution and extreme unction. Kneeling by his side, Robert leaned down towards the King and said softly, 'Papa, you have made your peace with our heavenly Father. But what are your wishes for the kingdom? We must be assured of peace after you . . .'

Henry stuttered, 'D–die, you mean. S–say it, my son. Spit out what you m-must say.' There was a pause as Henry drew a shallow breath. 'I have had sixty and seven good years . . . peace for much of that time, in England . . . at least.' In a feebler voice, he murmured, 'My daughter is not with us. I hear . . . another child. Easier than last time, I pray to God. She does not lack . . . courage . . . even if she *is* listening to the Angevin pup.' The King's difficult breathing became like the restless wind soughing through the forest trees outside. Logs placed on the large brazier warming the chamber hissed. Candles shone dimly from sconces. The bedchamber felt muted and shad-owed. The many nobles and priests gathered by Henry's bed, respectfully a few paces behind Robert, were silent as woodland phantoms, all trying hard to catch hold of the King's words. Robert shuddered. His father's death was nigh. What he must say to the dying man, his own father, was difficult.

'My father,' Earl Robert tried again. 'We must be sure of the succession.'

Other figures edged closer.

Henry raised his left hand and motioned Robert to lean down. He appeared to become lucid. 'All my lands, both sides of the sea . . . go to my daughter . . . in lawful succession . . . in keeping for my grandson . . . mine own namesake, who will on his majority inherit all my kingdoms.'

Although Henry tried harder to breathe, it seemed to Robert that his breath grew shallower.

'Take your time, father.'

Henry gripped hold of his hand with surprising strength for someone so old and ill. In a whisper, close to Robert's ear, he said, 'The Anjou brat does not inherit my kingdoms. He does not rule for my grandson, nor will he rule alongside my daughter. Tell them *all* this.' Henry, whose head had risen as he spoke, uttered a croak-ing dry cough and fell back against his pillows, closing his eyes. Of a sudden, Henry's eyes flicked open again. He said, loud enough so they all heard him, 'Do not abandon me, my son . . . and I would have an oath from you all, my old companions . . . that you will watch over my corpse until you have delivered me on my last journey . . . to my abbey at Reading, over the sea. Do you hear me, my son?'

'I understand.' Robert had heard it told that his grandfather, the first William, great conqueror of England, had been robbed, bundled into a coffin too small for his great frame, deserted and disrespected on burial.

One by one, the gathered knights all knelt – with reluctance, Robert thought – as each obeyed and took the oath. There was William de Warenne, Rotrou of Mortagne, who was a mild-mannered little man, and the identical Beaumont twins – the Earl of Leicester (also a Robert) and Waleran of Meulan – and every one of them was slow to kneel, but especially, it seemed, De Warenne. They bade their King farewell and swore to accompany his bier to Rouen and stay with his coffin until it could cross the sea to England.

'Now, send my . . . Adeliza . . . to me,' were the King's whispered final words to Robert.

Heads bowed, their eyes brimming tears, one by one, his favoured and loyal lords kissed the King's brow and slowly departed the chamber.

After Henry had passed away and Robert had tearfully closed his father's eyes, the King's body was transported to Rouen Cathedral. During the shortening, stormy days of early December, he sat with other earls by a fireside in the draughty castle at Rouen, waiting for word of a fair wind to blow them over the Narrow Sea to England. He sent messengers to Maud to inform her that her father had died. She never came. The Anglo-Norman earls conferred together. Lesser nobles arrived in Rouen from all over the duchy; none of them wanted Maud to rule them. This presented Robert with a dilemma, because already news had seeped into Rouen Castle that there was increased unrest on the border between Normandy and Anjou. Geoffrey was on the move again to Argentan, with Maud riding by his side. Those who had sworn loyalty to Maud on at least two occasions in past years considered themselves free of the oath they had taken.

The aged warrior, William de Warenne, represented thoughts held by others when he said at a meeting in Robert's chamber, 'Empress Maud has her hands full. She is with child and she's not here. If Normandy is restless, England will follow. We need a strong ruler at the helm, a warrior – and certainly not Count Geoffrey of Anjou.'

Robert held back, determined to not invite quarrels at such a sensitive time, not with Henry's coffin awaiting a fair wind for England. Carefully measuring his words, he said, 'The King wanted Maud's son to inherit. The realm should be granted to him.'

'A mere child,' William de Warenne sneered in an outraged tone. 'Never. How can he rule our lands?'

'No female succession either,' Waleran of Meulan said, as he swept close to the firelight with a swirl of blue woollen mantle – one that Robert observed was ostentatiously decorated with a golden border, lined with squirrel fur and pinned with a large brooch fashioned as a cross within a gold circle, studded with rubies.

His less vocal twin brother, the Earl of Leicester, nodded. 'It is most unwise.' Leicester's own mantle was of brown worsted – sensible, considered Robert, for the season, given the mud and dirt in the floor straw and in the courtyard beyond the hall – though his imposing height and his closed, hatchet-faced countenance mirrored that of his twin. Robert noted warily the twins' small penetrative and round glittering eyes. He had long marked them as a formidable pair. I can't tell those two apart, he thought to himself. A fair listener, he paid close attention to what was being said by all the nobles present, but it was obvious this pair did not have a shred of loyalty to Maud, or, for that matter, to the dead King's beloved little grandson.

The first twin, Waleran, added, breaking into Earl Robert's thoughts, 'I hold the greatest number of lands in Normandy of us all. I refuse to kneel to either the Empress or to Geoffrey of Anjou – but, Robert, especially to him.' He snorted and his deep-set eyes narrowed. 'The King forced that oath upon us. It cannot hold any strength, now the land is restless and nobles are arming. And the Church will never uphold it.'

Leicester nodded, his pale face identical even in expression to that of his twin. 'It will be years before the child can rule.'

There was a short, pregnant silence. Did any of them dare propose an alternative, Robert thought? Before he could speak – and, hopefully, quash this – Leicester spoke again. 'Offer the throne to Count Theobald of Blois. After all, he is the dead King's own nephew and rightfully his heir.'

Robert opened his mouth to say this was untrue, but, at that exact moment – another he would never, ever forget – there was a banging at the hall door. Pages ran to unlatch it. 'No!' shouted Robert. 'Steward Gilbert, look through the peephole first.'

Gilbert, a stately, plump little man, stretched up, slid back a square-shaped hatch set into the great oak door and set an eye to it. Swift as a dancer, despite being rather rotund, he spun around and announced, 'Anjou colours, master. A messenger.'

'Let him in,' said the elderly William de Warenne, rudely speaking for Robert, his hand moving away from his sword hilt.

Steward Gilbert shifted his eyes from De Warenne to Earl Robert, ignoring De Warenne and politely waiting until his master spoke.

'Aye, open the door, Master Gilbert, slide the bolt,' called Robert, wondering whether the messenger came from Count Geoffrey or his sister.

The steward nodded to his lads to heft up the iron latch. Moments later, the door swung open and in swept the messenger, his mantle displaying Count Geoffrey's badge, embroidered with golden lions.

'I come from Argentan, my lord. Empress Maud ordered me to inform you, my lords . . .' There was a slight hesitation.

'Spit it out, man!' Waleran grunted, narrowing his narrow eyes further.

The messenger dropped to his knees and folded his hands as in prayer. Nervously looking up, he said, 'The Lady Maud and Count Geoffrey have taken over the border castles.'

'Those she has a God-given right to,' Robert said in a firm, quiet voice, turning to his companions. 'They are, as you know well, her dowry fortresses.'

The messenger nodded. 'And the Empress requests I inform you that Marshal Wigan of Argentan has received her as his liege lady. She now has possession of Argentan and Domfront. Count Geoffrey has occupied others. He intends, she ordered me to report, to recover the inheritance belonging to his wife and sons. The Empress also stakes her claim to the crown of England. She expects you all to come to her at Argentan with your oaths of homage.'

There was a gasp. 'Does she indeed?' Waleran's voice cut through the smoky air of the hall. He glanced about. 'I don't see her,' he laughed. 'If she really wanted the throne, she would be here.'

'Sires, I am only the messenger.'

In a kindly voice, Robert addressed his steward: 'Take the Empress's man out to the kitchens, Steward Gilbert. See he is watered and fed whilst we decide if there is a reply for my sister.'

After the messenger had gone from the hall, Waleran gave a cynical laugh and said, without hesitation, 'Now, we *must* offer the succession to Theobald of Blois. He will keep the Anjou faction in check.'

'A sound choice,' his brother, Leicester, agreed, raising his stubby hand. 'We must be reasonable and sensible. A woman cannot hold power. *That* woman is as difficult and stubborn as her father – and, worse, moody – and she's no warrior, as he was.'

Robert frowned. How could he oppose them? These were the strongest and wealthiest of the Anglo-Norman lords. He needed time to consider.

De Warenne remained thoughtful, stroking his short grey beard. Waleran jumped with agility to his feet. 'Earl Robert, mark you this, a woman cannot don armour or ride at the head of an army. The King of France will see her weakness in an instant, and her fragility born of her ancestress Eve. He'll encroach on our Norman borderlands, mark my word.'

His twin added, with a sly look in his narrow glinting grey eyes, 'We'll see how long the Empress keeps hold of those castles.'

Robert cradled his head in his hands. What to do? He was loath to turn from Maud, to whom he had pledged allegiance. She could

72

be a great ruler if they all supported her, but, without their support, she was a chicken in the coop, ready to be pounced on by a court of foxes. Would the barons be loyal to her? Would the Church? Would the Pope? It was as clear as the crystal encasing a reliquary how the King of France would manipulate the Pope, his own ally, to favour the House of Blois. Robert had promised his father he would see that the child, Henry, inherited the throne. Geoffrey of Anjou ruling for his son would be distasteful to many, himself included. The others would not hesitate to revolt. He glanced from one to the other. He folded his hands and composed his face. 'Let us see what Count Theobald of Blois has to say,' he said quietly. 'Let us send for him.' No response followed, so he said firmly, 'I shall send the Empress's messenger back to Argentan, informing my sister we are considering the succession question.'

'And do not overlook our request to Count Theobald,' Waleran insisted, drawing his pebble eyes into slits. He was sly, thought Robert.

De Warenne and his sons did not accompany the funeral procession to the port at Caen, whence its entourage would sail to England. He said he had business in the City of London and would try to get a crossing further north, at Wissant. It might be days yet before they could sail over the stormy sea. They waited for Theobald of Blois, the newly proposed heir, to respond to Earl Robert's messenger. Another week passed and at last Count Theobald came to them, the bearer of surprising news. The tall, elegant and mild-natured Count arrived with a bevy of serious-minded courtiers, and he at once stated that England's throne was unavailable. It had already been seized by his brother, Stephen.

Stephen. Robert remembered the bland, amenable young man who had sworn before him, in front of Maud, so long ago.

Once the Beaumont brothers had listened to the Count's surprising news, they made their decision to support Stephen. Robert, unhappy as he was about this outcome, gathered the many other Anglo-Norman nobles in the great hall of the castle in Caen for a meeting. Robert gravely surveyed them all from the dais. He felt a sense of expectancy hum about the hall. Below the dais, he watched groups of noblemen in various long colourful fur-lined woollen cloaks, chain mail and leather riding mantles, conferring excitedly together in hushed voices. They seemed aware that a decision had been made. Some may even have had their own sources, since he suspected they were already conscious of what he was about to announce. It was not the decision he favoured, but, to avoid a civil war at a very difficult time, he had decided on a pragmatic approach. His steward, Gilbert, banged his staff on the floor. Conversation stopped and the nobles looked expectantly towards Robert, who stood up, flanked by Leicester and Waleran, the Beaumont twins, and Count Theobald.

'My lords,' Robert began in a clear voice. 'Stephen of Blois, Count Theobald's younger brother, as you all know, was much loved by King Henry, his uncle. Many of you were raised with my cousin Stephen, and learned the etiquette of knighthood and to fight alongside Stephen at my father's court.' He paused and surveyed their now anxious faces. 'Stephen was lately in Rouen himself with the King, but he then returned to Boulogne, to his young family and to the Lady Matilda, his wife.' Robert drew breath. The expectant air grew stiller. He tried hard not to give way to the fury he felt rising in his heart, the churning of his stomach and a sense of futility because no English earl wanted Maud as Queen. He began to speak, measuring his words out with care: 'On the third day of this month, Stephen of Blois crossed to Kent from Wissant. At first, my Kentish castles closed their gates to him, but Count Theobald, here, reports his brother continued to London and was welcomed there. The City merchants and magnates have adopted his cause and have accorded him the title of King. Stephen of Blois will be crowned England's King. God bless us all.'

There was a resounding cheer. The only man present who did not cheer was Theobald of Blois himself, who must have been astounded that his popular and affable younger brother had stolen a march on him. The Beaumont twins wore their usual identical smiles on their

74

narrow faces. As the cheers died down and the Beaumont brothers stepped from the dais to join the throng that called excitedly in favour of *King* Stephen, Earl Robert gently offered Count Theobald hospitality away from the baying pack of gilded nobles. Theobald inclined his head in agreement and Robert wasted no time ushering him to the passage behind the screens of the dais. He led Theobald to a narrow wooden staircase that rose up through the floors above the great hall. As they mounted the stairs, Theobald whispered into his ear, 'I wish my brother well, but I fear he has taken a poisoned chalice. And I can see that you, Earl Robert, have no choice but to support him.'

'Theo, what do *you* intend?' Robert said, as they climbed further up the keep's zigzagging internal stairway.

'First, I'll relinquish my custodianship of the Norman Castle of Falaise,' he chuckled, 'but not before I pay it a special visit first. Stephen will not have its treasures.' They hesitated on the last stairway as Theobald said, 'What will Maud do?'

Robert turned about to face him. He could not disguise the sadness in his voice as he replied, 'Maud has not come to Rouen or Caen. She's with child again and intent on securing her Anjou marriage inheritance, as well as our homage.'

'Ah,' said Theobald. 'It's not over yet.

'It has not even begun,' replied Robert. 'I gave my sister my oath, but I will lose everything if I pursue her cause now – my castles, my lands, my own children's inheritance, my family's safety – and, in truth, my heart craves peace.' He drew a long slow breath that made his chest ache more than it did already, let it out slowly and added, 'King Stephen will take my homage too.'

He knew he must not reveal his true thoughts to Theobald, though much of what he had said was honest. Now was the moment for pragmatism. Robert had never liked Stephen of Blois. He considered him spoilt, weak and easily influenced. He doubted King Stephen would, in fact, be able to preserve England's peace. Deeply buried inside Robert's heart, his own true loyalty lay with Maud's son, three-year-old Henry. He had made a promise to his dying father, and one day, he prayed, the cub would grow into a lion, and he could honour that promise.

They had reached the doorway to Robert's private apartment, two rooms separated by a heavy woollen hanging. As if he sensed much would remain unsaid, Theobald laid a hand on Robert's woollen sleeve. 'Play a cautious game, my friend. You have too much to lose and, as you say, a young family to protect.' Theobald removed his carefully manicured fingers and, in the light cast by a wall sconce, Robert noted a bemused smile hover at the edges of Theobald's mouth. The Count then added, 'I wonder what King David of the Scots will do. After all, he owes Maud his loyalty and he was devoted to his sister, her mother.'

'A good question. Stephen will try to win King David over to his cause.'

Was Theobald of Blois on an emotional fishing trip? Robert's stomach churned as he poured them both goblets of ruby-red wine, thinking again about his red-headed three-year-old nephew. He stiffened his resolve. For now, he must plough a middle course and not encourage dissent against the Count of Blois' younger brother, though he suspected he could one day face a battle with Stephen involving his child nephew, perhaps one contained within a longer war.

The King's corpse would rest in the cathedral in Caen, awaiting passage to England. Robert would send his father to be laid to rest with proper respect in the abbey he had so loved, at Reading. This was one oath Robert would not break. As for the other, only time and God's will would tell.

Chapter Seven

Angers
July 1139

Four years passed during which Geoffrey harassed Normandy, which had belonged to the English crown, until he was beaten back by King Stephen, who was settled on Maud's English throne and determined to retain Normandy as well. Maud and Geoffrey were united in their fury at how easily the English earls and barons had accepted Stephen as their king, yet she had recently heard of discontent amongst a number of English nobles. Her brother Robert and Brien Fitz Count had reluctantly supported Stephen at first, but she had received letters from them – and many of England's clergy – complaining that Stephen was a weak king, who favoured his own friends and dispossessed others – loyal to him, but less favoured – of their lands. In addition, he threatened some of England's greatest bishops, who owned castles and private armies.

In the Castle of Angers, Maud drummed her fingers on her desk, rereading a letter which she already knew by heart. It was from her dear brother, Robert, informing her that he was coming to Angers to discuss her return to England. If she agreed with Robert's plans and prepared to fight for her crown, her sons would remain in Geoffrey's household, which worried her. She must decide, and soon, because Robert was expected later that morning.

Robert had now renounced any loyalty to Stephen. She rose, and began to prowl about the castle's great chambers, hands clasped beneath her chin, thinking furiously. On whom could she also depend for support? Her thoughts turned to the brave and loyal Baron Baldwin.

When Baron Baldwin was not confirmed as possessor of his lands in Devon and the Isle of Wight, he had decided to seize Exeter, threatening fire and sword against any who did not yield to him. Within a month, King Stephen, Maud had heard, arrived with a mercenary force, mostly composed of hated Flemings, and, with Exeter declaring for Stephen, the courageous piratical Baldwin and his beautiful wife had no option but to retreat to safety inside Exeter's castle.

Besieged, they ran out of water and used huge amounts of wine from the castle stores instead, both for cooking and drinking. Stephen launched torches over the walls and set the castle's wooden storehouses on fire. Maud had shed tears when she heard how the Baron's pretty wife, whom she liked, was so desperate that she had fled the castle, emaciated and barefoot, with her hair loose, pleading for mercy and fair terms of surrender.

Once Stephen had broken the siege, he exiled Baron Baldwin. Further unrest had occurred elsewhere in England, weakening Stephen, and this, mused Maud, as she considered her dilemma, was undoubtedly God's will. She wished she could spit on this upstart King and his wife, Matilda of Boulogne, whom she had never liked. It was Matilda, she was sure, who wielded the power behind Stephen. She was an ambitious and ruthless woman, and though – with her flaxen hair and plain face – she seemed demure, she was poisonous.

Maud stopped pacing and watched a yellow and black spotted butterfly bat fragile wings against the shutters. For a moment, she contemplated how this little captive would have only a single day of precious life to live. She pushed the shutters further open to reveal a summer morning of blue skies and racing puffy clouds, then gently lifted the butterfly. With the creature enclosed within her palms, she reached out and freed it, wondering if it could survive in the herb garden below, where all kinds of dangers lay in wait.

A rap on the stout outer door reminded her she had sent for the cook, having previously given instructions for a birthday subtlety – a marzipan cake, fashioned like a castle. Not only was Robert expected that morning, but it was also her youngest son William's third name day.

Momentarily, she glanced through a second window, into the courtyard, where William was seated on his birthday gift – a shaggy little white pony called Blanche. Henry was leading his brother. Geoffrey watched proudly over his eldest and youngest sons. His namesake was being educated in Saumur, and might, with a sound education, enter the Church and one day become a bishop.

'Empress, you sent for me?' the rotund, smiling cook stood in the doorway.

She spun around to greet him. 'Is all ready, Master Marchand? The strawberry syllabubs, the chicken pasties, the gingerbread – and you haven't forgotten the shields with gold and red lions for the subtlety?'

'The trestles will be ready by noon and laden as you have ordered.'

'Very good, Marchand,' she said. 'And Mistress Alice, Master Pipkin and Master Xander are setting up their puppet show in the garden?' Robert had previously visited her at Christmas, escorting the mummers to entertain them for the season. They had remained with her since.

'All is in hand. Steward Albert is helping them set up, and he will greet Earl Robert when he arrives and direct his knights to their quarters.'

She nodded. 'Thank you, Master Marchand. Return to your kitchen –' she smiled – 'and the syllabubs.'

Returning to her desk, Maud opened a casket which contained correspondence sent from England during the past three and a half years. Selecting a number of letters, she decided she would read them again. Perhaps she had missed something previously, and looking through them did make her long to claim her crown.

The trail of messages she had received from England since the second year of Stephen's reign chronicled the new King's declining popularity. Firstly, she lifted up a letter from Adeliza. As she unfolded it, the parchment released a scatter of faded rose petals. Maud smiled reminiscently. Adeliza had a great love of roses, and often dried them to enjoy during winter.

After her husband's death, Adeliza had initially dwelt in Wilton Abbey, and wool merchants from the town had carried her correspondence to Anjou. Picking up a silver pointer, Maud slowly began to read the words her stepmother had written, two years earlier.

Wilton, February, in the year of our Lord 1137, the second of Stephen's reign.

I have passed more than a year within the shelter of the abbey at Wilton. I am truly sorry for what has passed . . .

Maud could not blame Adeliza for wanting a peaceful life – who would not? But Adeliza had broken her oath to recognise Maud as Queen. She had betrayed her deceased husband.

I am most happy to learn that you have given birth to a third healthy son. Had he lived, the King, your father, would have been proud of baby William. I send you, as is the tradition, an engraved silver spoon to mark his name day.

Before you judge me, Maud, remember I am a widow, and powerless, and not only did all the nobility and clergy press for Stephen's coronation, but his claim was recognised by Pope Innocent. Matilda of Boulogne has been crowned Queen. She is stalwart in support of her husband . . .

Maud's hand hovered over her inkpot. She badly wanted to throw it at the wall, but clutched her hands together in an attempt to resist the urge. Matilda was no rightful queen. Maud had almost burned this letter when she first read it . . .

Robert has passed much time in Normandy, as you know. There is no love lost between Robert and the King. Stephen, I suspect, is wary of your brother. Count Brien remains quietly at Wallingford. On occasion, he visits court dressed more handsomely than any other knight

*present. So must I, to attend Queen Matilda. Do not be angry, Maud,
I have no choice . . .*

Maud clenched her hands until her knuckles grew white. Yes,
you did have a choice, Adeliza – you could have left England and
come to me. She unclenched her fingers and read on.

*. . . Brien never brings the mummers we so enjoyed to Stephen's court.
They perform elsewhere. But the girl, Alice, came to sing for the ladies
of Wilton on May Day. She remains unwed, saying, if asked, that she
does not want a husband . . .*

Maud smiled at this, because she had noted one of her own young
household knights, the eldest son of a wealthy landowner, watching
Alice with longing. The young man was called Sir Jacques. It would
be a good union for Alice; Maud would bless such a union, if it ever
came to pass.

Then she opened a more recent letter from Adeliza.

*I have been smiled upon by the knight, William d'Aubigny, who is one
of King Stephen's advisors. He is a gentle knight, who shares my interest in gathering libraries into my castles . . .*

Enough! Adeliza, it seemed, *was* Stephen's creature now. Maud
swiftly refolded Adeliza's letters and swept the crumbling rose petals
onto the floor straw. She placed the letters back into her cedar-wood
casket. There was no need to remind herself that Adeliza had married a gentle knight who supported Stephen, and that they now lived
in Adeliza's castle of Arundel. She had given birth to a healthy
daughter and, like the singer, the baby's name was Alice.

Then Maud opened her most precious letter. This one, from
Count Brien, had not contained flowers, but he *had* written her an
enigmatic verse – an old riddle – which, now, as she reread it, began
to take on new significance. Her eyes flicked down the letter to the
end to the verse, which read:

From the trunk of a willow and the scrapped hide of a cow
I am made
Suffering the fierce savagery of war
I with my own body always save my bearer's body
Unless death takes the man's life
What fierce soldier endures such a fate?
Or receives so many deadly wounds in war?

'A shield,' Maud said aloud, smiling fondly. 'Dear Brien, the time may yet come when you must be my shield,' she whispered into the warm air. 'Do you have the courage to fight for me?' She sighed, for she was not really sure of Brien's skills in battle. He was no true warrior, like Robert or John Fitz Gilbert, the tough Marshal of England. But, if it came to a trap or an attack on her person, Count Brien would guard her with his life. Of this she was convinced.

She glanced down again and returned to the beginning:

Maud, my childhood friend and dearest companion, I send you this letter with a trustworthy wine merchant and shall be brief. Your brother, Robert of Gloucester, has your interests in his heart. What I am about to relate concerns him. On Easter Day, Earl Robert crossed to Normandy intending to support the King. No sooner had he arrived in Rouen than he discovered a conspiracy against his person instigated by the commander, William of Ypres, a Fleming and as ugly a creature as any devil who walked this earth. How Robert heard of King Stephen's plans to destroy him, I know not.

Stephen has had his eye on appropriating Earl Robert's castles in Normandy and in England, especially his fortress of Bristol. I heard the King would offer Robert friendship to his face, but vilify him in his absence. King Stephen has tried to deprive the Earl of such portions of his estates as he can grab, having wasted much of your father's treasure on siege weapons and warfare against the Welsh and the Scots. Earl Robert intends renouncing his oath to the King, which pray God he will have done by the time the merchant delivers my letter to you.

As for the rest, it contained pleasantries and good wishes for her health and that of her sons.

After Christmas, her brother had returned to England and had held out against Stephen in Bristol. Later, Robert Lovell had resisted at Castle Carey, Ralph Payel had held Dudley, Robert of Lincoln had stood against Stephen at Wareham and William Fitz Allan had resisted the King at Shrewsbury. Could she count on these nobles?

Finally, Maud picked up the letter Robert had sent her a month previously.

Pentecost, in the year of our Lord 1139

Maud, much loved sister.

Such illegal acts have occurred in England as you would scarcely countenance. King Stephen continues to demand castles and to covet estates from the nobles. He illegally aspired to a kingdom and now acts contrary to his coronation oath and the law. He has taken my possessions, including my castle of Leeds, and his captain has laid to waste lands around Bristol, causing hardship and famine. He has imprisoned courtiers who were once loyal to our father. He fears you will return and that the clergy will support you. As you know, Theobald of Bec, your favourite abbey, has been created Archbishop of Canterbury.

Maud clicked her tongue against her teeth as she read on.

On his return from the campaign in Scotland, the King held a conference with the clergy in Oxford. He arrested Bishop Roger, friend and advisor to our father. Then he took Bishop Roger's nephew, Alexander of Lincoln, prisoner and arrested the Bishop of Ely. His excuse is the unrest between his knights and those of Bishop Roger concerning their accommodation in Oxford. His real reason is that he has lost the bishops' trust in his kingship. He intimidated the bishops, starving them until they gave him the keys to their castles. He claims he found money belonging to him by rights in Bishop Roger's castle of Sherborn. The King's brother, Henry of Winchester, who is the papal legate, has called a council at Winchester to resolve the dispute between Bishop

Roger and the King. I shall report its outcome and support for your
return, in person, as soon as I can safely make arrangements to cross
the sea.
   R.

Maud added this letter to the others, rose and moved to the window, this time looking towards the road that ribboned its way to the castle. In the distance, she could see the dust from the galloping hoofs of many horses, and fluttering pennants belonging to her brother. The courtyard below was quiet, now, apart from the odd servant crossing to and fro. Geoffrey must have taken the children to the mews. The chapel bell rang out the hour of Sext, its sound sharp, cutting through the warm summer air. Their Benedictine priest, his black robes flapping like a crow's wings, hurried through its oaken doors. How could she ever take back her throne and rule as her own father had wished? Stephen was by now too well established. It was an impossible task. The priest disappeared from view, just as she felt God had abandoned her. God had turned his back on her and allowed Stephen his claim and her kingdom. Their heavenly Father, whom she had loved with devotion all her life, clearly advocated that a king and not a queen should sit on England's throne. Sighing, she supposed she must attend Mass and give thanks for her son's birthday.

Just as Robert and his knights came thundering over the drawbridge, Maud was leading her ladies into the castle chapel.

The children adored Alice and Xander's puppet shows; and Geoffrey, Maud was relieved to note, always behaved respectfully and distantly towards Alice now, still unmarried though she was, despite being past her twentieth year and more. Why did she turn her back on suitors? Though, Maud had noted Alice's pretty blue eyes following one of the Angers household knights, the curly-haired Sir Jacques, a handsome fellow whose wife had sadly died in childbirth and who was much admired by her younger ladies.

The play that afternoon had entranced the little ones. It told of a princess imprisoned by a witch in a mighty tower. Her flaxen plaits were so long that a handsome prince was able to climb up her hair and rescue her. The marzipan subtlety that followed the performance was greeted with cries of delight. Robert had brought gifts of wooden swords and shields for Henry and William – young Geoffrey had not been able to come from Saumur to join the celebration – and he gave the delighted castle children small, gaily-painted balls fashioned from pigs' bladders. Maud was content – William's birthday celebration was a success.

Later, Robert sat with Maud and Geoffrey in the antechamber. Lifting his goblet, her brother drained his wine and sprang a huge surprise.

'I have heard from Adeliza. She is going to aid our efforts to reclaim your stolen crown, though she may not realise it yet.' He grinned and folded his arms.

'What?' said Maud, startled from her embroidery. 'I thought Adeliza had forgotten me.'

'Ah, well, here is the plan. When the time is right, she will welcome you to Arundel Castle as her guest, along with a small number of your household knights and ladies.' Robert smiled wryly. 'A social visit, of course.'

Maud's eyes widened. What did Robert mean by a 'social visit'?

'Adeliza's plan, or your plan for Adeliza, brother?' she said, adding quietly, 'Your plan for me.'

She had been almost ready to give up on England and her heritage there, but now Robert was giving her more hope than she had believed possible. Would she leave Anjou, after so many years? Leave Geoffrey, with whom she had finally reached a kind of peace – and leave her three sons?

'It is too late, Robert. I have three boys and my life is more settled now.'

Robert explained his thinking: 'You have Hal's future to consider, his inheritance, your father's wishes and your own right to England . . . and, indeed, Normandy. I shall accompany you.' He folded his arms and the look on his face was intractable. By God's

85

legs, her brother was determined. 'And a key part of the plan is that you bring the players with you. The young people who are from Brien's retinue – they already travel between castles, so their movements will not be suspicious, and Count Brien assures me they are loyal to him. Once in England, they will return to Wallingford, to alert Count Brien, who will advise others who might join your cause that you have landed.' He looked thoughtful. 'Stephen will have spies posted all along the coast and of course he will know soon enough if you return. The players are innocent young people. With luck, he is unaware of their existence. There is support for your cause, Maud. Already you have allies who are unhappy with Stephen.'

'Who?' She could not quite believe what she was hearing.

'I know we also have the support of Bishop Roger and the Archbishop of Canterbury—'

'Robert, do you truly believe this is the moment that I may take my throne back at last?' Maud interrupted. She glanced at Geoffrey, who had not so far interrupted Robert.

Geoffrey raised his eyebrows and scratched his head, looking at Robert studiously, but not without cynicism in his handsome eyes. At last, he said, 'Yes, tell us how. I do not believe it will be easy. Will Maud have enough knights at her disposal? Because it will take a great army to defeat Stephen – and a fortune to pay and feed them.' He shook his coppery mane. 'Before you ask me, Robert, my knights defend my own territories. I cannot risk France sneaking over my borders and I certainly cannot leave Anjou to fight in England.' He seemed deep in thought for a moment. Then, to Maud's surprise, he appeared to change tack, saying, with a belly laugh, 'Of course, with Stephen distracted, I could take Normandy at last.' He turned to Maud again. 'And, to be sure of that and of the loyalty of bishops and supporters, you will cross the Narrow Sea and show yourself. I doubt you will command them from Anjou.'

Robert smiled at the younger man. 'That is fair, Geoffrey, and it will strengthen Maud's campaign. Many English nobles, like myself, have lands in Normandy too. Firstly, we must make sure we can get Maud secretly into Arundel. They need to see her to believe in her, and to give her their obeisance and their loyalty. Then, once she is there, we will be able to bring others over to her cause and muster an army. The element of surprise and speed will give us an advantage. If we are successful, this could be ended within months – a year, at most.'

'But, if Adeliza's husband supports Stephen, can you trust her?' Maud asked in a concerned voice. Her quest could be over from the moment she landed. 'Can I not sail to Bristol?'

'Stephen has his eye on Bristol. He has already attempted to take it and failed. Arundel is the only safe entrance to England for you. The west, where most of your support is, will suggest to Stephen your intentions before we are ready. He is watching the coastline west of Arundel. We can make this landing work, and you can move west innocently to visit Reading, where your father lies, to kneel and pray by his grave, and to go to Wilton, to visit the nuns. Meantime, I can move west and work up support for you.' He lowered his voice. 'I hope to enlist assistance from the Bishop of Winchester and the clergy.'

'What? Stephen's brother?'

'Now is the moment. He is displeased with Stephen for his curtailing of Church power.'

Maud's eyebrows flew up. 'And so to Arundel. It is a quiet harbour.'

'Yes, and Adeliza will be told this is simply a social visit, not an invasion. She promised you help to return, but she might cry off at any moment, since her husband is Stephen's knight. You must correspond with her in an innocent manner. Send her the players as a mark of affection. Yes, send Alice, Pipkin and Xander ahead to Adeliza. They can return to Caen with me this week and continue to England with letters. I shall escort you to Arundel in September and remove myself to Bristol as soon as is possible. After all, my older boys and my daughters are still there. I must make sure of their safety.' He winked at Maud.

His plan for raising support was audacious, but it might work. At worst, she would have to return to Anjou after a supposed social visit to Arundel and her father's tomb at Reading Abbey.

'How long do we have?' Geoffrey said.

'Six weeks at most. There will be time for Maud to visit little Geoffrey.'

'No,' Maud said. Her mind was whirring. This had all come to her so quickly. But she had to put aside all sentiment and leave her sons behind – at least, for now – in order that their future be secured. 'My second son will come to me here, at Le Mans, and remain until I depart. After all, if this plan succeeds, I may not see my boys for some time . . . until I am Queen of England, at least.' Feeling almost frightened at the thought that what she had so long wanted was at last within her grasp, Maud lifted her chin. 'It is *my* crown and I shall, with God's blessing, own it.'

'As you wish, Maud, but try to curb your arrogance. It is unseemly,' Geoffrey said, his tone turning a little bitter, despite his earlier enthusiasm. 'I'll also be fighting for our sons' inheritance in Normandy.'

Maud noted how her husband's blue eyes glittered like an icy pond in winter. Geoffrey was set on conquering Normandy. He had no interest in England, nor had he much empathy for her own claim. It was all about the boys' inheritance in Normandy and Anjou. She wanted to spit the words out at him that he only thought her arrogant because she was a woman. He was still jealous of her independent spirit. Maud locked her protests within her heart. To respond in anger was beneath her dignity, at that moment. She would prove her worth to him. She would prove it to them all. She lifted her head higher and studied her reliable warrior brother. If Robert believed he was doing this for six-year-old Henry's sake, he could think again. The crown of England was rightfully hers, and not her son's. She would be Queen of England, not merely a regent for Henry, with her power weakened and her actions directed by a child's group of councillors.

Part Two
Civil War

Chapter Eight

Arundel Castle
Autumn 1139

That September, Maud's fleet of ships slowly glided up the River Arun through a morning mist. The Sussex coastline faded, to be replaced by the motte and tower of the great castle of Arundel. She watched from the deck of the *Lion*, peering through the dispersing fog. Other ships following the *Lion* had more than a hundred knights and even more Arab horses packed into their holds. Maud leaned over the rail and sniffed the salty air and earthy whiff of the marshes. She glanced up at the clearing sky to watch a heron in flight, its body long, lean like a scribe's dark line, and elegant, soaring as it was caught by an air stream. Her heart swelled. This was England; this was her homeland; this was her time. She *would* regain her stolen crown. Her landing was hardly an invasion, but she was convinced God was with her, because her cause was just. God would provide her with an army. Today, she was entering England by stealth, but she hoped and prayed that supporters would rally to her. Anticipation shivered down her spine and she gripped the ship's rail so tightly that her knuckles turned white. The castle wharf edged closer and became clearer until there was a slam and a jolt. The ship's anchor was dropped. She shaded her brow to watch sailors scurrying on the quay as they docked. They had landed below the towered castle.

By the time she stepped down a plank onto solid ground, the mist had completely cleared and the promise of a bright autumnal day lay ahead. They waited patiently on the pier until all her other ships had docked and the knights had led their horses from the boats. She leaned on Robert's right arm and Mabel took his left, as, laughing, they rediscovered their land legs. They looked about for their own mounts, which Robert soon spotted, already bridled, reins held firmly by his squires. Helped by Robert, Maud mounted Doucette, her white palfrey, who – after a few moments of instability – discovered her land legs too and shook her mane in appreciation, glad to be free of the ship's confinement. Robert lifted Mabel onto her mount, and then, in turn, their women.

Smiling, Mabel reached over and touched Maud's arm. 'Eight years, Maud, since you have been in England. Breathe in its air and smile today, for surely God will assure your success. Stephen will have displeased our heavenly Father by threatening Bishop Roger of Salisbury. Enjoy your moment of arrival, never forget it, and I'll warrant there are bishops other than Bishop Roger who will be pleased to support your cause.'

'I shall relish every hour I remain here,' Maud said, raising her head high on her long, elegant neck. 'I hope Adeliza will be as welcoming as her letter promised.' She glanced over her shoulder, because it occurred to her that, whilst those on the wharf were respectful, recognising their nobility, none had recognised her as the old King's daughter. No one here knew she was their rightful queen. Wisely, she had heeded Robert's warning and not permitted her household knights to fly pennants, ordering them not to wear their armour. Their ships could be supposed to be merchant vessels with a valuable cargo of Arab horses. She smiled back at Mabel and said, 'May God bless our enterprise, for many a man may not.'

They had decided to come to Arundel as September closed, knowing that the bishops' party, led by Stephen's brother, Henry of Winchester, had called a Church council to discuss the legality of the King's seizure of bishops' lands and castles. Stephen thought the bishops were acting in an ungodly manner by keeping armies and building castles on Church lands. They were a threat to the King's power and owned too much wealth. Their first loyalty was to the

Pope, not Stephen. If they claimed they were, in fact, protecting those dwelling on their territories, this was partly true. If they said their loyalty was to the King, these castle-building bishops were lying. Stephen, who had kept peace in England during the first years of his reign and had fought the Welsh and the Scots to safeguard his borderland, now threw up his own fastnesses, granting ruthless favourites privileges and dispossessing the old King's loyal supporters who had not sworn loyalty to him, such was his fear of the clergy's increasing power.

When Roger of Salisbury, Henry I's trusted treasurer, was accused by Stephen of illegally appropriating some of the King's monies, the King declared that, since these warrior bishops were men of God, they should not have such great possessions or their own knights, but live more humbly, as Christ had done. In winning his case in the Church council against Roger of Salisbury, whom he had cruelly imprisoned, Stephen lost the trust of Henry of Winchester, his own brother. And, when he refused Bishop Henry his support to be appointed the primate, Archbishop of Canterbury, Bishop Henry had then obtained the position of papal legate in England, an even more powerful position, and one that put him beyond the King's control. Bishop Henry built his own castle in the royal city of Winchester and called it Wolvesey Castle. His brother, the King, was not happy, even though the clever Bishop promised Stephen his unswerving loyalty, but Stephen clearly knew he needed his brother's allegiance, for he left him alone.

Stephen's minions had been patrolling the coast relentlessly, as he feared Maud would invade. He had dealt ruthlessly with rebelling nobles, as well as the indignant bishops, throughout the summer, and he suspected that Robert, who had, during the previous year, renounced allegiance to Stephen, might return to England from Caen, determined to cause trouble and reclaim his confiscated castles.

Robert had persuaded the exiled Count Baldwin to distract Stephen from the landing at Arundel by behaving like a pirate and attacking royal ports further west along the coast. Maud smiled, now, as she thought about Count Baldwin's escapades, and she remarked to Mabel, 'I wonder how successful Baldwin has been at Wareham. He will be careful to draw Stephen well away from Arundel, but can we trust Adeliza?'

'As long as Adeliza is convinced you are not about to draw her into outright rebellion, and this is a family visit, Maud, she will welcome us women and a few household knights. Never forget, her husband is for the King. Adeliza might never, in truth, gainsay him.'

'I shall guard my tongue.'

'Amen to that.'

Maud held her reins so tightly that her hands felt numb, because she *was* worried about her reception. Moving off, they slowly wound their way from the wharf, up the curling motte pathway, and trotted over the lowered drawbridge into the courtyard. The horses stamped and pawed the earth as they were reined in. Stable boys raced to take hold of their horses, while Robert and others helped the ladies dismount. They gathered around Maud as protectively as a vixen guards her cubs, which always made Maud smile, since she did not consider herself in need of protection, rather the reverse. She considered they needed her to shield *them* from danger.

Adeliza welcomed them from the bottom of the steps in front of the stout keep's entrance, leading to the first-floor hall. She was followed by a troop of maids, who offered silver bowls of scented water with which to wash their hands and faces, as was the custom. She embraced Maud warmly and certainly seemed pleased to see her, but, even so, Maud sensed a degree of reserve in her manner — wariness, even.

'Where is Earl William, Adeliza?' Robert spoke Maud's own thoughts aloud, as he rinsed his face.

'With the King.' Adeliza's eyes appeared troubled. 'William did not want me to welcome you. He mistrusts your motives, particularly as that adventurer, Count Baldwin, has been attacking the coast, around Wareham.' She narrowed her eyes as she offered him a linen towel to dry himself, speaking quietly so that they could not be overheard. 'Do you know anything of this, Robert?' Adeliza's sharp eyes momentarily glanced beyond Maud. 'Or you, Maud? Since I see the pirate's wife, Lady Ela, is amongst your women.' Her glance once again slid to where Baldwin's wife stood with the other women, talking to Mabel, as they, in turn, were offered water and towels.

Maud feigned surprise. 'Countess Ela wishes to visit Wilton. She has friends amongst the nuns,' she said smoothly, and found it easy to look Adeliza in the eye, for that bit was true.

'Oh, so the Countess intends taking the veil?' Adeliza's tone was cool.

'Not at all. She hears they have a cure for severe migraines.'

'As they do,' Adeliza said, her voice growing a little softer. 'Let us hope that she can visit the abbey whilst you are here, and that, knowing his wife is in England, her husband will leave our coasts alone.' She shrugged. 'Come into the hall. Take refreshment and rest. Your apartments are ready. And, after you have rested and given thanks to the good Lord for your safe crossing, then you must tell me all your plans.'

'In truth, I have none,' Maud replied, as they climbed the stair-case, feeling slightly panicked. 'My intent has been to visit England and, most importantly, to see you, as we agreed in our correspond-ence. I, too, might ride west to pray at Wilton and visit Reading Abbey to pray there for Papa's soul.' She paused and looked at Adeliza, who was studying her. Maud felt a sudden rush of guilt at the way she was lying to her friend. 'Robert must visit Bristol to check on his properties and sons. His daughter Mathilde is betrothed to Ranulf of Chester, and I hope I can attend the wedding in Bristol too.'

At this, Adeliza narrowed her violet eyes. She *was* suspicious. Maud cast her eyes down. She had not intended attending her niece's wedding.

Robert, behind them, played along, as if unperturbed and amused. He called, smilingly, 'Ah, yes, and never mind a wedding, my haste to Bristol is because the King will not grant me his protection. I renounced my homage to him, and so I must travel quickly, by

lesser-known ways, to avoid being ambushed by his Flemings.' Maud
turned and sped up the stairs, attempting to conceal a smile, though
her lips were twitching with a longing to laugh at Robert's veiled reference to the plot hatched to ambush him in Normandy a year
previously. The King had clearly known about it, and it had precipi-
tated Robert's reneging on his oath of homage to Stephen.

Adeliza looked uneasy again as she entered the hall, but she said
lightly, 'Ah, I see. You are wise not to lay yourself open to danger.
Please, wait until tomorrow, because I have planned a banquet for
you this afternoon.'

'Of course, my lady,' Robert said. 'Though I must depart before
the sun rises. Mabel will remain here to attend Maud until I return.'

Adeliza looked from Maud to Mabel. She shook her head in a
puzzled way, but obviously had decided not to interfere. She moved
forward, twitching her skirts, and said in a brisk manner, 'Come, I
must show you my improvements here. Your chambers have fireplaces, Maud, and we have constructed an inner staircase that wends
its way through the tower.' She waved her hand around. 'I have, as
you can see, improved the hall.' She glanced at a side trestle where
maids were pouring out ale and setting out platters with various
cakes. 'Now, please eat, all of you.'

Maud accepted a cup of ale gratefully, for she was thirsty. Her
ladies swooped on the almond cakes and Robert helped himself to a
tankard, downed it quickly, and helped himself to another.

Maud sipped her ale, declined the cakes and glanced at a wall
painting opposite depicting a hunting scene. She set her cup aside.
'The ale is freshly brewed and welcome. It is good to be here again,
Adeliza, to taste ale like this and eat English cakes.' She reached out
to her stepmother and took her hands in her own. 'I have missed
your friendship since Papa's death. We can have a few weeks of leisure, here. The weather is glorious. We must chase birds along the
river, as we did in years past. I have even brought my sparrowhawks
and falconer, hoping we shall.' Her voice grew genuinely excited at
the thought of riding and hunting in England again, after years and
years of absence – almost a decade, indeed.

'It is a lovely time of year for falconry,' Adeliza said brightly, sounding more relaxed at last. She too had drunk a cup of ale. 'The trees are golden. But we must avoid the marshes – they are treacherous.' Smiling broadly, Adeliza ushered Maud and her ladies to the new staircase spiralling up the tall tower, which she insisted was to be Maud's domain for her visit. Adeliza's apartments lay in the opposite tower. 'I am with child again, Maud. Don't you remember how I once wondered if I would ever have children?'

'As I wondered for myself. Look at us – both mothers, now. And, just to think, I have three sons. And Geoffrey adores them. I thought Geoffrey truly dreadful, and he is still selfish and vain, but he is a good father to our boys.'

Adeliza laughed. 'Men can change, softened by a woman's patient touch. Geoffrey is quite a warrior, I hear.' This was clearly a reference to Geoffrey's ruthless determination to take over as many castles in Normandy as he could.

'Yes, but let us not discuss this today. I am not Geoffrey.' Maud smiled.

'Not so violent, one would hope. I cannot see you riding anywhere in armour, Maud!'

Maud smiled; though she must never say it to Adeliza, her thoughts were warlike. I shall wear armour, if ever I must lead an army, she thought to herself.

They reached her chambers and Maud saw how sumptuous they were, painted gold and green. She pressed the bed coverlet down, declaring, 'A luxurious feather bed! Thank you, Adeliza. Last night, I laid my head on a mattress beneath a ship's awning.' Laughing, Maud gratefully sank onto the padded chest at the foot of the bed, into which her maids would lay her linen, once it was unpacked.

'There is another chamber further up the staircase,' Adeliza said, 'for your women's comfort, a solar all to yourselves, and, above that, another spacious room which Mabel and Robert have.'

Observing smiles of gratitude on Robert and Mabel's tired faces, Maud recognised Adeliza had been extremely welcoming to them all, and, for a moment, she felt another twinge of guilt. Adeliza sent

Maud's women away to find their quarters, and Robert and Mabel excused themselves to follow the ladies, leaving Maud alone with her stepmother.

As the others vanished through the doorway onto the stairs, Adeliza gently lifted Maud's filet and veil off her head and, laying both aside, touched Maud's plait. 'And here we are again, as if no time has passed at all since Henry's death. Your hair is as fine and black as ever, and your neck as long and elegant. How I enjoyed combing these locks out on your wedding night. You have kept your beauty and are still lovely, despite the strain of Geoffrey's birth.' She smiled and lowered her voice, adding, this time with a hint of mischief, 'Count Brien will be as entranced by you as ever. He always had a great love for you. Everyone knew it. We must send for him, and we can all fly our falcons together again, as we did in your father's lifetime.' She paused and drew a deep breath. 'May I ask how long we shall have your company before you leave for Wilton?'

'It depends how long Robert will linger in Bristol, on wedding plans, but perhaps for a few weeks.' She lowered her eyes. It was best she did not linger at Arundel overly long. She did not wish to place Adeliza in danger.

'You are welcome to my castle, and your knights will be comfortably accommodated in the bailey, where they'll have their own hall and kitchen.'

'Thank you. I would love to see little Alice before thanking the Virgin for blessing our voyage. I imagine she is the picture of her mother.'

'She has my eyes, they say.' Adeliza sounded pleased. 'Before dinner, we shall visit her. Rest now, Maud, for an hour of the clock.' She pointed to a candle marked out with hour spaces, which had been placed on a nearby table. 'There is time to sleep a little before dinner. I have requested it to be delayed until after Sext. I shall send for you.'

With smiles and a sweep of her gown, Adeliza turned to leave. Glancing back, she said, 'Brien's mummers came to Arundel last month. Alice sings as beautifully as ever. What a shame they are back in Wallingford. Perhaps Brien can bring them with him to play for you.'

'That would be most welcome,' Maud said, trying not to sound too interested.

Once Adeliza had departed, Maud lay down on the feather bed and drifted into sleep, dreaming of mermaids and stars, and the suit of chain mail which she knew Robert would discourage her from ever wearing.

Maud's ladies settled in within days and were delighted to gather around her fireplace in the evenings. Robert had set out the morning following their arrival with a few knights, planning to travel west on little-known roads. Maud maintained the charade of a social visit as she and Adeliza rode along the riverbank, gilded by autumnal sunshine, their sparrowhawks on their gloved wrists, beady eyes darting everywhere once their hoods were removed, ready to soar into the clear blue sky, far above the water.

They shared memories about the past and fond anecdotes about their respective children, especially Alice, who, at almost a year old, had begun to walk and say the odd word. It was all part of Maud's plan, though she did feel guilt at her deception, and all week she wondered how Robert was faring, especially if he had now reached Bristol. If he was successful recruiting others, she had no intention of returning to Anjou. Wilton was, of course, a distraction. Robert intended meeting Henry of Winchester. Sooner or later, Stephen would discover her whereabouts and, if he did, they would need someone close to him to convince him, as Maud had convinced Adeliza, that her visit to England was merely social. Visiting Wilton was as good a reason as any other.

Only Mabel was privy to Maud's constant anxiety. They would escape into the castle garden to wander alone through Adeliza's rose bushes, gathering fallen petals for her. 'Robert should send us word soon,' she quietly said to Mabel on one such fragrant morning. 'He will meet with Brien and the others – great strategists, such as Miles of Gloucester. Adeliza will not be able to locate Brien, even if she has sent for him.'

'Robert will return to escort us to Wilton.' Mabel laid a reassuring hand over Maud's.

'If Stephen does not arrive first,' Maud said in a concerned voice. She gently shook off Mabel's hand and bent down to smell a late flower. Raising her head again, she added, 'By summer, I shall regain my crown, God willing. Like this rose, I shall bloom again.'

They had sat down to a supper of cold meats, bread, pies and salads in Adeliza's bower hall following a joyous afternoon's hunting, but there was tension in the air. Adeliza had questions in her eyes and was scrutinising both Maud and Mabel closely, her violet eyes moving from one to the other. Something had clearly disturbed her equilibrium in the short time it had taken them to reassemble after the hunt. Maud grew fidgety and picked at her food.

Within moments of the servitors departing, Adeliza addressed Maud, her voice agitated: 'A messenger informed me today that the King is en route to Arundel. He will try to capture you, Maud, if you remain here. You can go back to Normandy, or you can stay here and risk subjecting us to a siege. You well know that Stephen is expert in siege warfare.' She folded her arms and stared into Maud's face, her own pale. 'My husband will be with the King and, though you have my loyalty, I must not disobey my lord and I cannot face being besieged.' Her hand instinctively cradled her belly and her eyes flew to the corner alcove where a nurse was playing with tiny Alice. She leaned forward. 'Look at me, Maud. Two babies. I want a safe future for them.'

It was as Robert had suspected. Adeliza would not endanger her family by openly lending Maud support. Mabel opened her mouth to speak, but shut it again at a warning glance from Maud.

Maud drew a deep breath and chose her words with caution. 'Adeliza, I have not come here seeking a war with Stephen. I wish only to spend time with you, and to revisit my homeland.' She looked Adeliza straight in the eyes and said, with a tremor in her voice,

'Perhaps I can make that visit to Reading Abbey, if the King permits.' She allowed a tear to flow and added, 'And, if the King comes here, surely you can simply convince him that I am your guest.'

Adeliza frowned. 'I trust you are not deceiving me, Maud, for we have always been frank with each other.'

Maud instantly shook her head. 'Adeliza, you know that I have no army, just my personal knights.' She gestured helplessly. 'A hundred household knights could not wage war against Stephen's thousands of troops, even if that was my intention.'

Adeliza's response was tart: 'I shall convey this to William. It is all I can do. But you should return to Anjou and safety before Stephen takes you prisoner.' She cut into an apple pie and began to serve it. 'Now, eat, and we shall see. Perhaps Stephen will not attack us, after all. Let us pray it shall be so.'

Maud nodded calmly and accepted her slice of pie. But her mind was in turmoil. What if all went wrong? It did not bear thinking of. Besides, where was Robert?

The Forest of Dean

Robert raised his hand to prevent his fifteen knights moving forward. Twilight had fallen on the forest and the quiet was only punctuated by the fluttering of roosting birds amongst a canopy of russet leaves. A number of horses were tethered beside a woodland chapel. Robert dismounted and approached with only two knights, signalling to the others to remain out of sight. As he came closer to the chapel, the tethered horses snorted and pawed the earth. A lean white hound arched up from beneath the tree to which it was secured, its golden collar glittering with tiny jewels, and began to bark ferociously. All attempts at a silent approach vanished in an instant. Robert waited patiently.

A tall, straight man with a noble bearing and a sandy tonsure emerged from the chapel's arched doorway, only moments later. Robert inclined his head. It was Bishop Henry of Winchester, Abbot of one of England's most powerful abbeys, at Glastonbury, younger brother of King Stephen of Blois and grandson of the Conqueror. The elegant Bishop stepped forward and greeted Robert with a sardonic smile. He thrust out his hand and Robert bowed and kissed the Bishop's ruby ring before straightening up. The Bishop's help was important for his plan to bring Maud safely to Bristol to have any chance of success. He had been informed by Abbot Anselm of Bury St Edmunds that Stephen was intending to lay siege to Arundel.

'So, you have returned, Earl Robert,' Bishop Henry said. 'And I hear the Lady is in Arundel Castle. A social visit . . . so my spies tell me.' He laughed, but his beady eyes remained no less sharp. 'They have been hawking along the river all week. I assume you wish to meet me because my brother is on his way to Arundel to, for certes, take her prisoner. Such a lovely captive my cousin Maud will make. Courageous of her to return to England.' He paused and made the sign of the cross, sighing ostentatiously. 'These have been difficult times. It is dangerous for you, Cousin Robert, to be abroad.'

'I can defend myself and my own interests,' replied Robert sharply.

There was a moment's silence. The Bishop folded his hands in front of his stomach. At last, he said, 'So how may I assist you to further those interests, my friend?'

He has ever possessed a silver tongue, thought Robert. He cleared his throat and said, 'Bishop Henry, you are papal legate, with greater powers than any other cleric in England, and power in Europe. I want you to ensure my sister's safety. She is of blood royal and, as our holy father the Pope's representative in England, only you can insist the King, your brother, respects her right to visit England, her stepmother and hopefully our father's shrine in Reading Abbey. She wishes to donate the precious relic which is that of Saint James's finger bone to the Abbey.'

Bishop Henry opened his arms in a placatory gesture. 'Of late, I do not have my brother's ear. What can I do? If he takes Maud prisoner, I cannot help her. And he *will* take her. Be assured, Adeliza will give her up. She will not want to incite the wrath of the King . . . or her husband.' He stroked his chin momentarily. 'But

Saint James of Compostella's finger bone . . . Well, now, the abbey should have this.'

Robert closed his eyes and sent up a silent prayer to Heaven that Maud had indeed thought to bring the relic with her. She rarely parted from it, he knew, and she had mentioned that she intended to give it to Reading Abbey before they left Angers.

Aloud, he said, 'Then, Bishop Henry, you must use your persuasive tongue to influence your brother, the King. Tell him he would be breaking chivalric code if he took his royal cousin, once an empress of the Holy Roman Empire, as his captive. This strategy would antagonise the Pope, and you are, *Legate* Henry, in a position to convince Stephen of God's and Christendom's displeasure if he was to lay a finger upon my sister's person or to obstruct her travel within his realm. She does not possess an army – rather, simply, a band of household knights for her personal protection. My sister is not invading his realm . . . so convince your brother to send her to me in Bristol, where I shall take responsibility for her. I am, after all, her older brother.'

'And if I do as you request?' Bishop Henry asked, with curiosity.

Robert knew that Henry was considering his own interests. Henry knew Robert was not necessarily being strictly truthful. But, equally, he realised that, if Maud were to invade, it would be best for him to think pragmatically, in case she was successful, and Robert was gambling on the wily priest's self-interest and greed.

Robert folded his arms and studied the other man, making him wait for an answer. At last, he said, 'If you are successful in convincing the King not to persecute the Empress, I shall ensure that Count Geoffrey does not touch any of your properties in Normandy, and I shall personally make you an endowment so that you may found a forest monastery.' He noted the Bishop's eyes lighting up. 'Or, if you prefer, I will give you a manor of your choosing. Not in Kent, obviously, since my possessions there have been confiscated by the King.'

Bishop Henry's expression grew thoughtful. 'Normandy, because I want a new manor there and a monastery where I might retire to the Cotentin – Caen, perhaps.' He swept a lean, jewelled hand along his rich burgundy gown. Robert waited again. The Bishop, at length, nodded. 'Agreed. It's a pact. I shall suggest escorting her to you myself. Where to? Bristol, or Bath, or some other place?'

'I shall let you know that by a fast rider. I have my spies, too.' Robert looked into Bishop Henry's grey-rimmed, misleadingly innocent-looking hazel eyes, with determination in his own. 'Do not deceive me, Bishop, or your brother, the King, will learn of our meeting.'

The Bishop didn't flinch. 'You will receive word of the outcome in your eyrie castle.' He smiled like a cat that had just lapped a bowl of cream.

Maud had hoped Stephen would not come to Arundel. His spies would know she had few knights with her, not enough for an invasion. She was wrong. On a chill morning, just after the calends of October, Maud stood huddled into her fur-lined mantle on Arundel's gatehouse battlements, anxiously watching Stephen's military host approach through the early morning haze that hung in patches over the marshes. Stephen had brought with him at least a thousand armed men, embroidered pennants fluttering, colourful against the ghostly grey mist. As the fog cleared, she caught sight of her cousin, the golden circlet on his flaxen head indicating his regal status.

Stephen was long-limbed and, though she could not see his eyes, she recalled that they were as green as sea glass. He wore a golden band on his helmet and seemed completely in control of his troops, seated upon his dark charger. There was no doubt in her mind that he was much changed since they had last met. She could sense how he possessed a kingly presence, as did a Roman emperor determined not to relinquish an ounce of power. Her anger sat like a spitting cat in her stomach as she watched him draw his troops up before the castle motte. It was apparent, too, that he had identified her, since he sat erect on his black stallion and stared straight up at her, looked away and then spoke to someone who had drawn their mount up next to his own.

Beside her, Adeliza gasped, and Maud could well understand her creeping fear. The scene below them was deeply unsettling. Her stepmother raised her arm and pointed with a shaking finger. 'There he is – that's my husband, William, beside his King.' She dropped her hand and turned to face Maud. Her violet eyes had darkened with hurt and anxiety. 'Look what you have done, Maud. You have brought Stephen's troops to my very gates.'

Maud shook her head. 'I never intended this, Adeliza. I am innocent.'

'I pray to God and all his angels you are speaking the truth.'

Moments later, William had separated from Stephen and was riding towards the drawbridge.

'Oh, no.' Adeliza drew in a long breath and released it with a sigh. 'The King is sending William in advance, Maud.' Adeliza was clearly near to tears. 'I dread to think what will happen now. I only hope you haven't destroyed us.' She gathered up her brocade cloak furiously. 'I had best go to the hall –' her voice became a hiss – 'or into Hell's jaws, it would seem. Stay here, or take refuge in your own chambers,' she snapped at Maud, as if she were disciplining one of the castle hounds. 'That might, at least, seem innocent. I'll tell William you are embroidering the Madonna onto an altar cloth, and that your women are mending clothes for the poor. In fact, I shall provide you with a basket of garments.' She turned on her heel and swept off impatiently, her cloak billowing about her.

Drogo slipped forward to Maud's side.

'Sewing, indeed!' Maud exploded. 'I refuse to be confined to my chambers. In fact, all my ladies can join me up here. Stephen will not, if he possesses a grain of chivalry, wage war on women.' She summoned a quivering page. 'Go and fetch my women,' she ordered. 'Bring them here. Go – go at once!' The boy turned, fast as a scurrying rat, and scuttled down the staircase to the courtyard. She watched him race on towards the keep, as if the furies of the Norse Valkyries sped him on.

'What shall we do?' asked her captain. 'Your knights await my orders.'

'Nothing. We cannot appear threatened, nor threatening – though, apparently, they must consider I am. We are certainly outnumbered. But it's me he wants, not Arundel, I suspect.'

'I don't think he *will* launch an assault, Empress. Look over there, the ground is too marshy. A prolonged siege would be difficult – costly, too – and, besides, he will be aware that Earl Robert could – now you, my lady, are in England for all to see – muster forces in the west, over by his castle of Bristol, maybe supported by the Welsh and knights whom Stephen foolishly deprived of their lands, instead of wooing them.'

'Perhaps. So, you think he will negotiate terms?'

Drogo grinned. 'He'll know Earl Robert is on the loose. I suspect he will not attempt to capture you. A siege would be a grave insult to Lady Adeliza – and to Earl William, who supports his claim to the throne. I hope the Earl stays with his lady now, for it would strengthen her ability to negotiate something to your benefit.'

Thinking of Adeliza's fury, Maud was not so sure. Knowing that Robert had intended to meet with Bishop Henry, she clung to the hope that the King's brother, the papal legate, would help them.

The sun was climbing in the sky and the mist had cleared. As the long morning continued, Maud's women joined her above the gate-house, surveying the vast host below them erecting shelters. She didn't see Stephen again, because he had vanished inside his own tent. She did, however, see Bishop Henry arrive in a cloud of dust, with an entourage of knights and clergy. Bells were ringing from the castle chapel. Sunlight glinted from the jewels on the Bishop's rich mantle and the gilt trappings of his black charger. Stable boys ran to remove the magnificent horse to a distance beyond the reach of an arrow. She watched anxiously, wishing Robert or Count Brien were with her, as the tall figure of Henry, gowned in samite, disappeared inside Stephen's tent.

Maud turned to her ladies. 'There is no point in remaining here, now. Go to Sext today. Pray hard to the Madonna for our safety. We shall not remain hidden and fearful, cowering away in our chambers, stitching shirts like devout maidens. We'll eat dinner in the hall.'

'They'll attack the castle,' whispered one lady to another, her voice shaking with terror. 'And they'll kill us all.'

Maud's sharp ears heard the more courageous Lenora say, 'I am sure there are secret ways in and out of here. And the castle is well provisioned. We certainly won't starve if the King sets up a siege.'

Countess Ela said to Maud, 'I've not heard from Baldwin, but I expect he's sailed down to Cornwall.'

'It is useless to speculate,' Maud said. 'I am going to chapel and then to dinner. Come with me.' She marched to the stairway, but stopped short when Drogo called to her.

'Look, my lady. Waleran and his twin brother have arrived too.'

Maud turned on her heel. 'The carrion crows are gathering.' She raised a hand above her forehead. 'Stephen has his elite followers with him. Well, they broke their oaths to me and the lot of them can go and burn in Hell for it, all three of them – Waleran, Bishop Henry and Robert of Leicester.'

'Hush, Maud,' Mabel whispered into her ear. 'You speak of a papal legate. Take care what you say.'

'They deserve all that's coming to them, Mabel. They will feel my wrath when I am Queen.'

Earl William's reception of Maud that afternoon was cool. He waved Mabel, Lenora and Ela to a bench on the other side of Adeliza, whose eyes appeared clouded and red-rimmed with weeping. He was a tall, slim man, with shoulder-length dark hair and solemn brown eyes, and he was dressed neatly in a woollen gown of green and scarlet, edged with bands of gold. Maud noticed his hand shook nervously as he gestured for her to sit by his side. She made sure that her posture was commanding. She was more than ready to justify her presence at Arundel, and equally prepared to deceive him, just as she had Adeliza. She was an empress; she was a queen.

As she accepted a napkin from a page and placed it over her shoulder, she was astonished when William, not raising his delicately accented voice, said softly, 'Maud, we can guess why you are really here, but we intend to support your visit to us. So, listen carefully.'

Without further denials, she gave him her full attention.

'I shall remain in the castle with Adeliza and send word to the King, assuring him that I am convinced your reason for being here is simply to visit your stepmother and pay your respects at your father's tomb.' He sighed. 'Hopefully, if I do this, we shall not be subject to a siege and you will be able to continue your stay with us peacefully, but –' he slightly raised his tone – 'afterwards, you must return to Anjou, taking your knights with you.' He pursed his mouth as if he were a priest about to resume a sermon. 'Adeliza is with child, as you know. You must understand that we cannot endure the strain of a siege.'

Maud remained silent, dimly aware of the muted conversations around the hall and the clinking of dishes being delivered to the table. After the servitors had moved along the board, she said, trying to conceal the smile that threatened to play about her lips, 'Thank you, William.'

William lifted his jewelled cup and nodded. 'We shall do the best we can for you. Now, tell me, how fare your sons? What news do you have of Anjou?'

Maud spoke of non-controversial subjects, such as hunting and children, as she nibbled at a tart of onions and salmon in aspic, served with salads and slices of pork in a quince sauce. If Robert had carried out his part of their plan to raise support in the west, and she could visit Wilton Abbey with Mabel, Lenora and Ela, all might yet be well. It depended on William convincing Stephen that she was harmless. Her mind strayed to Count Brien, hoping that he too would declare for her and that she would see him again soon. Brien would always hold a special place in her heart.

Following dinner, she accompanied Adeliza to Vespers. Two services in one day was an act of piety too many. After she had gazed at the painted cerulean ceiling of Adeliza's chapel and the shining green tiles, she contemplated the rotund priest in his pale linen gown. Only then did she bow her head, touching the small silver crucifix on her breast, and prayed with all her might that Stephen would not besiege Arundel Castle, following this request with a prayer for the success of Robert's mission.

'Blessed Lady Mary, intercede for me, for surely as a mother of a heavenly prince you must understand my earnest desire to safeguard my own son's rightful throne –' she drew breath, adding – 'and my own.'

Messengers rode from camp to castle and back again, over two tense days, during which Maud stalked the battlements, watching the activity in the camp beyond the moat. Occasionally, Stephen appeared; once, she spotted him staring up at the place where she stood. Was she imagining that he saw her from so far? It was strange that she had spent so long hating him, but had barely seen him in her life.

On the second afternoon, Maud's attention was caught by a sudden movement in the enemy's camp. A delegation, including Waleran and Bishop Henry, accompanied by a parcel of monks, was riding towards the lowering drawbridge. She could feel the rumble of their horses as they cantered under the gatehouse tower and into the castle's courtyard, where stable hands took charge of their mounts.

Turning to Drogo, she exclaimed, 'Stephen has apparently sent his elite to parley with us. I hope this is not an ill omen.'

'All may yet be well,' responded the calm Drogo.

Just as he said this, a page came racing up the outer stairway, taking several steps at a time. Catching his breath, he gabbled, 'My lady, the Bishop of Winchester is here and wishes to speak with you in the great hall.'

'Does he, indeed?' Maud arched her eyebrows imperiously at the news that wily Henry, Stephen's brother, had arrived. Had Robert persuaded him to her cause? 'Speed back on those mercury wings you seem to possess, boy, and inform Lady Adeliza that I shall be on my way when I'm ready.' She did not intend dancing to Bishop Henry's tune, no matter what news he had to relate to her.

She turned to Mabel and Lenora. 'He can wait. I shall select my gown first. I will not speak with him, a veritable peacock, wearing this drab wool.' Her hand strayed to the serviceable garment she was wearing that day. 'My blue silk with pearls on the sleeve borders and my burgundy ermine-trimmed mantle, I think. I intend to dazzle that gaudy priest today.'

Finely dressed, from her diaphanous flowing veil and golden filet to her dainty reindeer-skin boots, and followed by her elegant ladies, Maud swept into the hall. She paused briefly before inclining her head regally in the direction of the wily Bishop Henry and the despicable Waleran of Meulan, today without his brother Leicester, determined that the obeisance due to her rank be shown.

The pair bowed low, then rose. Maud did not curtsey. With exaggerated courtesy, she stepped forward and lowered her head to kiss the ring on Bishop Henry's outstretched hand. As she had foreseen, he was as richly clad as she was, despite the recent constraints of a smelly military tent. As papal legate, he commanded respect from all, though she would have preferred to spit at his feet. The customary greeting dispensed with, she remained distant and polite.

Ushered by William, they sat round a table on the dais, whilst her women withdrew to an alcove and sat with their hands demurely folded. Within the time it took for a spit of wax to drop from the hall candle clock, the sly Waleran had prefaced the discussion – after a studied, unpleasant glance at Countess Ela, Baldwin's wife. Baldwin had apparently attacked and fired Waleran's family property on the south coast. Maud choked back a desire to laugh and wished she had a bird that would snip off his unusually beaked nose.

Waleran came swiftly to the point, as succinct as ever, his eyes as hard as pebbles. 'The King has decided you must not compromise Earl William and Lady Adeliza further with your presence here at Arundel. Bishop Henry and I shall escort you to your brother Robert in Bristol and *he* can take responsibility for your welfare. Arrangements are being made as I speak.' He paused. 'It is generous of King Stephen to consider your niece's imminent wedding to Earl Ranulf, but –' he exhaled a dramatic pained breath – 'the King is your cousin, after all, as, indeed, is Bishop Henry. With chivalrous intent, the

King will permit you to join Earl Robert's household. I see his wife, the Lady Mabel, amongst your company, and –' he glanced at poor Ela again – 'the wife, too, of the despicable Baldwin of Revers. Any rebellion on either of your parts will be met with severe measures, including repression of the peoples of the west.' He narrowed his eyes at her. 'That is all I have to say. I take it you will agree, Countess Maud?'

'Empress Maud,' she replied coldly. On hearing a gasp from Adeliza, she moderated her tone and attitude. 'Yes, I will consent. It is generous of Cousin Stephen. I send him my greetings and thank him for guaranteeing my safety of passage from Arundel.'

'We depart tomorrow at dawn. A small group of your household knights may accompany you. The others must return to Anjou. Select a dozen.' He pointed to Ela. 'And that woman must return with them. She is banished from the kingdom.'

This was a better outcome than Maud had hoped for. At least she had not faced banishment, like poor Ela. Stephen evidently did not know of the plans she and Robert had made to muster support; and, from the south-west, Robert's stronghold, they would be in a position of power. William and Adeliza had helped her, after all, and for this she was grateful.

Bishop Henry looked at her with softened hazel eyes flecked with gold, though they gave nothing further away. 'It will be a pleasure to accompany you west. May God bless our journey.' He made the sign of the Trinity in the air.

'Amen to that,' gasped William. 'May good Saint Christopher keep you safe, Empress Maud.'

Maud knew that he would be relieved to see her gone from his own protection, but she did not miss Adeliza's gaze clouding over and the glint of tears in her eyes.

Later, Adeliza came to her chamber in the tower and, first addressing Ela, said, 'Countess, you will be escorted to Wilton as soon as Stephen's camp breaks up . . . and another lady of your choosing shall go with you. You won't be troubled there.' She looked at Ela's swelling midriff. 'It is enough that you are near your time. Wilton will be safe for you.' Turning to Maud, she said, 'God bless you, dear Maud. May we meet again in better times.'

'Thank you, Adeliza. Thank you for everything.'

'I wish I had more courage to support your cause, for I believe you have a just cause. This was no innocent visit. No, say nothing further, Maud. Best I am innocent.' The two women embraced, not knowing if they would ever meet again. Adeliza smiled as she whispered, 'You will see Count Brien yet, dear friend.'

Maud's heart beat faster, and she, too, smiled.

As Maud's party rode west, four days passed, with overnight stops at abbeys and small manors. Waleran, whom she disliked intensely, left them on the fourth evening to travel south, much to Maud's relief. Meals taken in Waleran's company had been silent. He watched her every move, making her feel more like his prisoner than a great empress with a just claim to England's throne.

Around noon on the fifth day, Maud could see a line of horsemen approaching along the Bristol road, riding steadily through a persistent drizzle. As they drew nearer, she saw Robert seated high on his charger. She turned her head and said to Bishop Henry, who rode by her side, 'My lord, it appears you need not escort me further.' She added pointedly, 'Waleran, that snake, deserted you along the route because clearly his own business is more important than my safety and yours, but I thank you, my dear Cousin Bishop, for your protection.'

Bishop Henry gravely inclined his head, but chose to ignore the slight on Waleran. Even so, she noted a smile curling about his lips, suggesting he had no love for the Beaumont twins either.

'I wish you well, Empress Maud,' he said, and raised his hand in a wave, acknowledging Robert, who was almost upon them. 'Now you have all the escort you need, we shall turn about. My duty is done, and I can leave you in your half-brother's care. I'll return to Bath Abbey this afternoon.' Eyes narrowed, he stared hard at the approaching riders, though his expression remained carefully bland.

Robert was accompanied by a group of dispossessed earls, men whose lands Stephen had confiscated, or from whom Stephen intended stealing. Beside Robert rode William Fitz Allan of Shrewsbury, a tall, pale man, with a severe Norman soldier's haircut, off-puttingly military, though his smile was pleasant. On his other side was Robert's eldest son, William, who was in his twenties still and resembled his father. He grinned from ear to ear, having just spotted his mother, Mabel, with Maud. Behind them trotted Baldwin de Revers and Miles Fitz Waller, the latter custodian of the royal castle of Gloucester. Miles had aged since Maud had last met him – there was much grey in his thick black hair. But, finally – and she laughed with pleasure to behold him – came Brien Fitz Count. She had not seen him in five years, but he was as roguish in appearance and as agile as ever he was in his youth. He deftly held his horse back from racing forward too close to her party.

The Bishop's attention to these particular earls was not lost on Maud. She understood in a heartbeat the Bishop's realisation that there would be a challenge to Stephen's throne. But it did not matter, for, with these devoted lords on her side, she felt hopeful of success, and the memory of Stephen's threatening forces, mocking her as she left Arundel, and Waleran's hatchet-like, unpleasant face, began to recede.

Bishop Henry's greeting to Robert was perfunctory, but Robert spoke with warmth as he rode up: 'I won't forget your good will, Bishop Henry, or my promise.'

'I won't permit you to,' Bishop Henry replied. He turned his stallion's head, waved his hand and cantered back down the Bath road.

'We are safe at last,' Maud murmured to Mabel, who was clucking over her husband and son. But, although Maud's words were directed to Mabel, her eyes were fixed firmly on Brien.

113

Chapter Nine

Gloucester
December 1139

On the Saturday dedicated to Saint Lucy, a last ember day of prayer, one of seven special days of fasting and prayer throughout the year, Alice, Xander and small Pipkin loaded their wagon with costumes, instruments and props to begin a three-day journey to Gloucester and Empress Maud's court. A half-dozen of Count Brien's knights were to accompany them.

Their small party followed the southern route towards the ancient city, taking the London road that led west out of Wallingford. At times, the winter roads were difficult to navigate and, on several occasions, the Count's knights had to dig their wheels out of mud when the cart veered into ditches, their rebellious horse protesting and neighing. Alice, her skirts hitched up, dragged Neddy back onto the road, her legs covered with cold, sticky sludge. As Xander pushed, she pulled, helped by little Pipkin, until, finally, the knights lifted all back onto the road, just in time, managing to save the wagon's precious load from disaster.

As their journey continued over low hills and through gentle sloping valleys, Alice shivered with cold, longing for the comforting warmth of the Yule log, delicious Christmastide fare to eat and the joys of the mumming they were to perform at the Empress's Christmas court in Gloucester Castle. She remembered from her childhood that King Henry's yearly crown-wearing had been held in Gloucester, though the fashion had died out since Stephen had become King. She did not know why, except that King Stephen rarely visited

Gloucester, particularly since Earl Robert, whose castle it had been, had quarrelled with him, and the King, keen to keep a grip on his kingdom, was too often on the move, even at Christmas. Crowns were precious and wearing them in a ceremonial manner was for peaceful times. The kingdom was not so peaceful, these days.

'I expect, soon enough, the Empress will be holding *her* crown-wearing in Gloucester,' Xander said, breaking his silence and reading her thoughts, as he occasionally did.

'I hope so,' Alice responded, with a glance over her shoulder.

Little Pipkin, now in his twenties, but still small in stature, was curled up amongst their props, covered with a mangy fur cloak that had been rejected by Countess Tilda, snoring loudly.

Alice turned back to Xander. 'Only another day and we'll see Lady Maud again,' she sighed. 'I wish this journey over. It's so cold.'

'I've known worse,' Xander said, but he huddled deeper into his thick cloak.

Alice patted her satchel and the action comforted her; she possessed a secret. For a time, she did not speak, but remained thoughtful. The only sounds were crows flying overhead to roost in the trees, the snorting of horses and the clanging of chain mail. She was dreaming of Jacques, the knight of Anjou she had known during her time there. When the Empress had reached Gloucester that autumn, Jacques had written Alice a note – a scrap of parchment delivered amongst the communications flying across the country between the Empress and Count Brien. She had been in the castle with Countess Tilda when the Count, reading his correspondence, had snatched up the folded paper with her name. Raising one of his elegant eyebrows, he had passed her the note. She squirrelled it away in her belt pocket, dying to read it privately. But he did not remark on it – Brien knew how to keep a secret.

That night, in the privacy of her loft chamber, Alice recollected mistily that Sir Jacques had danced with her at Empress Maud's court in Anjou. And that, on her departure for England, the charming knight had kissed her hand, causing a delicious shudder to travel along her arm and down her back, into her fur-booted toes. He'd said he hoped they would meet again, but she had heard nothing from him, until she received the wisp of a note saying, *I am in Gloucester with the Empress. Perhaps you will sing for her at Christmastide. It would bring me much joy to hear your sweet voice again.*

He has not forgotten me, after all, was her immediate thought, but a melancholy thought chased it. Perhaps he is too far above my own station in life for anything to come of it.

She had folded the note and placed it in a little bone-plated jewel box, which she concealed underneath a silk scarf Empress Maud had given her when she last sang a plaintive lament at Maud's court. She patted her satchel again, and the small casket reassuringly bumped against her hand.

As they journeyed further west, the weather became even more bitter, the air icy. Alice shivered and wrapped herself tightly in a blanket. After another long day of travel through frozen woodlands, the tree branches resembling stiff frosted fingers, their captain rode up, saying they would stop for the night soon. By dusk, they had reached the village of Cricklade, where a wooden three-storey inn loomed up against the darkening sky. Candles and cresset lamps glowed through the shutter slats. It seemed welcoming and busy. Xander drove the wagon under an archway into a yard with a huge stable, where there was plenty of space to shelter the horses belonging to Count Brien's men.

The captain paid for their accommodation in advance, securing a private chamber for Alice and her brothers. On inspection, she found a coarse linen sheet on which to lay her head, and a pile of woollen blankets, none too clean, but adequate. Her brothers were offered hay-filled pallets by the doorway, whilst Count Brien's knights occupied the stable loft.

Once they had stabled and fed Neddy, they crossed the frozen yard to the inn's hall and found places at one of two long trestles. As they waited to be served a supper of warm pease pottage with beef, other travellers entered the inn, including a tall Benedictine monk, with a hood pulled tightly up, almost concealing his face. The monk's hooded eyes scanned the hall until he found an empty space on the bench behind them. Alice, twisting around, saw him sit down beside a pleasant-faced, white-garbed monk of the Cistercian order – of unusual muscle for a monk, she noted – and introduce himself; she thought it of interest to see the two contrasting vestments side by side. So as not to appear too inquisitive or be drawn into conversation, she turned back.

The food arrived and she soon forgot about the odd pair, though she often liked to amuse herself by eavesdropping on the conversations of others. Tonight, she was too hungry and, since the food tasted better than it looked, she forgot her initial interest in the two clerics. As they all ate, the busy room buzzed with speculation that King Stephen's wicked rule would soon be over and good King Henry's daughter would bring peace to the land. Though she felt safe in the west, where Maud clearly had support, Alice was careful not to declare her own loyalty to the Empress, and earlier, with a finger pressed to her lip, she had said to Pipkin and Xander, 'Tell none where we are going. You never know who may be listening. The King will have planted spies in every town between the City and Gloucester, seeking out intelligence. Remember, Lord Miles is the custodian of Gloucester Castle and it is well known he is loyal to Count Brien and Earl Robert. If anyone asks, we know nothing. We are simple mummers, required to play for Lord Miles and his family over Christmastide.'

Her brothers had nodded and, lifting their cups of ale now, they began to discuss a play they would perform on Christmas Day. Alice was to be the lady rejecting an evil suitor, played by Xander, and Pipkin would be the knight rescuing her. It was to be performed in song and her brothers would play the harp and glittern. Alice was to sing laments, followed by a carol of joy when she was reunited with her lover.

They had just finished discussing it when Alice's sharp ears caught something of the conversation being conducted behind her. She glanced over her shoulder. The muscled Cistercian was saying, in a hushed tone, 'Bishop Roger of Salisbury, the old King's treasurer, died in November of disease caused by the biting insects. I heard his heart was broken by the King's evil treatment of him and his nephew, last summer – imprisoning him, stealing his castles and accusing him of theft.'

The Benedictine replied, but she could not see his face. 'The King's treatment of the bishops has done him no favours, granted. I heard the Bishop of Ely, Bishop Roger's nephew, has joined the Empress's court in Gloucester.' He sniffed, as if he had smelled an unpleasant odour. 'Seems many of the great earls are gathering in Gloucester too.' He swallowed a noisy gulp from his ale cup. 'You've come from Gloucester, you said, Brother James. Do you know who is for Empress Maud?'

Alice shifted on her bench to hear more.

'I *have* hailed from Gloucester,' said Brother James, the Cistercian, slurring his words slightly. 'My own abbey is far to the north. Tintern, they've named it. But I was present at the Lady's court for a few weeks, visiting a member of her clergy. Lord Miles, of course, is loyal to her. Robert Fitz Herbert was there, having just taken Malmesbury and Trowbridge for the Empress. Brave men, all of them.' He raised his cup.

'Oh,' the Benedictine said, with a greater degree of curiosity oozing into his voice. 'I hear Lord Miles is likened to a great bear. Looks like one, too. I saw him in Gloucester once myself.'

'Have you heard how Lord Miles captured Hereford, too, for the Empress, Brother Antonio?'

So, they are on first-name terms, thought Alice, more curious herself than ever. She had met Lord Miles often in Wallingford Castle and liked the kindly man.

Brother James seemed somewhat drunk, continuing, 'They have control of the south-west, too. Reginald, the old King's other bastard, took an oath to support Empress Maud. Others will follow.' He patted his white cloak, his voice betraying a sense of pride. 'I have been charged with a message for the King's Marshal, John Fitz Gilbert of Marlborough. He'll join the cause once he reads it, I'll warrant. And he's a savvy warrior, who will bring others over to Empress Maud.'

The Cistercian paused and Alice heard him take another slurp of his ale and set the tankard down on the trestle with a clank.

'Seems, Brother Antonio, we monks live in changing times,' he continued. 'Too many mercenaries and bandits roaming the countryside, taking advantage of unsettled places, be it town, village, woodland hermitages or remote abbeys. No abbey is safe. None will be protected from Stephen's men either, now he takes issue with the bishops owning castles and keeping private armies.'

'Nor safe from Maud's militias either,' replied the Benedictine monk. 'Not if they are hungry enough.'

'True.' Brother James banged his tankard down again. 'I am to my rest. It's a long ride down to Marlborough Castle.' He added, 'God go with you, Brother Antonio. Where are you heading, may I ask?'

'You may, because I'm visiting the monks of Gloucester Abbey and will stop there for Christmastide.'

Alice heard the further clatter of tankards pushed aside, as both monks shuffled out of their places. She bowed her head, thinking, There's something about that Benedictine monk I mistrust. I like him not. He is not as innocent as he seems.

She peered from her drawn-up hood, watching them pass by. The hawk-eyed Brother Antonio looked straight at her.

Brother James said loudly, *'A timore belli libera nos, Deus.'*

Oddly, the Benedictine monk looked blank.

Brother James translated, 'From the fear of war, deliver us.'

'Of course,' Brother Antonio replied, tapping his ear.

There was a hum of conversation, the rattle of dice and calls for ale all around.

The Benedictine tapped his ear again, as if to emphasise that he was, of a sudden, hard of hearing. 'God go with you, Brother,' he said, before disappearing out of the door.

Brother James wove his way through the benches towards the inner staircase at the end of the eating hall.

Alice was correct, she was sure, to be wary of a Benedictine monk who had little or no Latin, and whom she suspected heard perfectly

119

clearly. She wanted to hurry to the stairway to warn Brother James that his companion that evening had been false and might even be dangerous, but she hesitated. It was, after all, only a hunch, and she would appear very foolish if her suspicion was ill founded. A heartbeat later, she had another idea. She could tell Brother James that she had overheard he was travelling to Marlborough and knew the main route to be impassable because of mudslides. One of their guards could escort him to Marlborough; Count Brien's knights knew all the lesser-known paths through this part of the countryside.

She leaned towards her brothers and tapped Xander's hand. 'Just a moment, you two. I wish to speak to Captain Hubert.' She nodded towards the alcove where he was playing a game of merills with some others. She hurried over to their table. 'I beg forgiveness for disturbing you, Sir Knight,' she said, in her most polite tone.

He looked up with a broad smile. 'Why, Mistress Alice, what can I do for you?'

She nodded towards a quieter corner.

'I'll be but a moment,' he alerted his companions. 'And don't move my counter, either of you.' He followed her to an empty bench by the wall.

'I heard something interesting,' she said, a little hesitant. 'At supper.'

'You did, young Alice, did you?' the kindly old captain said.

When Alice confided her suspicions, his brow creased and he nodded. 'The monk should never have revealed his mission. That, in itself, is of grave concern. You were right to alert me, Alice. He sounds overly trusting. I shall see to it, my lady.' He patted her arm in a reassuring manner and added, frowning, 'There's no sense in risk-taking. Any message to Sir John will be of grave importance, if it comes from Lord Miles. Think no more of it. Get your rest. Sleep easy.'

She fell asleep as soon as her head hit her pillow – and this despite the grubby blankets and her brothers' snoring.

As they entered the stable on the following morning, Alice noted their captain already in conversation with Brother James, the

120

Cistercian. When their wagon rattled through the inn's archway, she was aware that two knights had left them. There was no sign of the Benedictine. Clearly, he had already departed, possibly during the night.

Snow fell in soft fat flakes and, although it was not so desperately cold anymore, it slowed their journey to Gloucester. They ate sheltered in the wagon, huddled under a canvas cover, munching chicken pasties purchased from the inn and downing their ale straight from a flagon wrapped in a blanket to stop it freezing. It wasn't much, but it sufficed to keep hunger away until they rode into the bailey of Gloucester Castle just as the sun was setting and the Vespers bells were chiming.

In the busy bailey, a blacksmith was clanging his tools, sharpening swords by the blaze of a fierce fire that had melted the snow around his forge, creating an enormous puddle. Chickens squawked in their pen. Horses were led to the stables. Falconers carried blindfolded hawks to the mews. Maids crossed to a dairy and water carriers were busily breaking surface ice and filling buckets at a well. The best sight of all was a great Yule log on rollers being dragged over the yard by a posse of laughing squires. Alice saw Empress Maud herself, seated high on a buff-coloured stallion, more appropriate for a knight than a lady. She noticed Alice and raised her hand in a greeting, shook her magnificent horse's reins and rode to the keep's staircase, where her squires helped her dismount. She then hurried up the steps to the hall in her sweeping green fur-trimmed mantle, her veil, held in place by a gold circlet, flying out behind her. In that moment, Alice thought her beautiful.

After Hubert helped Alice from the wagon, she asked him what had happened to Brother James.

'As you overheard, he had documents and a letter for Sir John. He was grateful for my offer of two of Count Brien's knights to travel with him. He agreed it was better to be safe than sorry, and even said he had wondered himself about the monk who called himself Brother Antonio. He admitted the ale had loosened his tongue and claimed he thought all in the inn were for Empress Maud. Foolish man. He won't be trusted again.' He grinned, showing a set of yellowing teeth. 'I shall speak with Count Brien. You are most observant, Lady Alice. The Benedictine had vanished by morning, as if spirited away by an ill wind.'

'Alas, I am not a lady,' Alice said humbly.

'You are more of a lady than many I have known.' His tone was that of a kindly grandfather. 'Those young men of yours will see your horse is stabled and fed, and I shall employ stable boys to guard your wagon. But first, I'll find out how you are to be accommodated. Follow me. Your brothers will join us for supper in the hall.' He called over two stable boys, took their names and charged them with watching over the horse and wagon. 'If you don't, I'll have your balls,' he threatened. They looked as if they believed him, each round-eyed and scared as a hunted hare.

They crossed the yard and climbed the long stairway up into the castle keep. When they reached the top, Alice turned around, sensing she was being watched. Staring down, she saw none other than Sir Jacques looking up at her. He lifted his arm to wave to her, and she was so thrilled to see him, with his dark eyes and curling brown hair, that her heart sang with joy. Jacques had been married once, she had heard, but his wife had died. He was a bit older than she, perhaps around thirty years. He had often flirted with the ladies in Anjou, and the Empress's junior ladies all admired him. Yet it was Alice to whom he had paid most attention when there was dancing in the hall. And he danced well, his body subtle and quick to turn, and she had loved it when he led a round dance, spinning her around so fast she grew dizzy. And she admitted to herself that his boldness excited her.

She did not see much of Jacques, however, until Christ's Day Eve. On Christmas Eve morning, the Yule log was lit with great ceremony. After Sext, Alice and her brothers were summoned by Empress Maud to an antechamber behind the dais. The Empress was attended by Count Brien. Alice noted with amusement that the Count was wearing shoes with such long points she feared he would trip if he attempted to dance. Dame Margo often made fun of his love of fashion, though Alice had no part in it – she loved Count Brien, having known him since she was a small child. His hose today was part-coloured red and gold, and his tunic was scarlet and edged with gold embroidery. His beard was neater than usual, and his hair, still black though he was easily forty summers old, was worn fashionably long and curling, touching his embroidered collar.

Alice glanced about the chamber. The Empress's ladies were gathered around an embroidery frame close to a glazed window that let in streams of sunlight. It had stopped snowing, but the days remained chill. Alice, Pipkin and Xander were ushered closer to Maud. The Empress had changed. She appeared more confident, possessing a more forceful bearing; she seemed taller, queenly, and she was regally dressed in a gown of burgundy damask lined with miniver. Two braziers glowing hotly with coals stood by the side of Maud's stately chair. Alice gratefully felt their heat reach out to warm her and wished she had the nerve to stretch her fingers towards one. She felt apprehensive, even though in past encounters Maud had always been kind to her.

They bowed low.

Maud's clear voice rang out: 'My, my, Xander, how you have grown since we last met! And you, Pipkin, too, if it's possible. I believe God has destined you to remain small of stature.' She laughed a tinkling laugh. 'Come closer, all of you, and sit on the stools.' She laughed again lightly. 'And so to the business of mumming.'

Alice felt relief. Maud had immediately appeared less aloof with that laugh and the mention of mumming. She had even remembered the boys' names. Clearly, Maud knew that a queen should not forget even her non-noble servants.

As they sat on low stools, Alice noticed that another figure, a bear of a man, had joined the Empress since they had entered the chamber. He stood beside Count Brien, just behind Maud's chair. It was Lord Miles himself, and he was smiling at her. She smiled back, not in the least afraid of him.

Maud folded her hands in her lap and said, "Tis Christmas Eve. This afternoon, you will entertain the castle children with one of your puppet performances. In the evening, before supper and the solemn Mass, you will sing suitable psalms in Latin for my lords and ladies, which I know you have mastered well. You entertained us most agreeably in Angers and you will remain for a time with us here too. We do have other entertainers . . . but you are the best of them all . . . and we have dancing for the whole twelve days of Christmastide. You will be required to perform on Christmas Day, on New Year's Day, at the Epiphany feast and for the Feast of the Holy Innocents as well. For the rest of the holiday, you may practise and, naturally, when you are free to do so, join the revels at my court.' Maud drew breath. 'I trust your accommodation with my junior ladies is to your liking, as usual, Mistress Alice?'

'Of course, Empress, you are most kind,' Alice said. She knew most of the women who had travelled to England with the Empress and she liked them all.

Maud studied the two young men for a moment. 'And you are happy to sleep in the bailey hall, Xander and Pipkin?'

'Yes, my lady,' Xander said, speaking for Pipkin as well. Alice knew Pipkin would always agree with Xander. It was an acceptable arrangement, as they preferred to sleep closer to the stable, where their valuable props were stowed away.

Count Brien stepped forward. With a toss of his dark curls, he said, in a low voice, 'I believe we have to thank you, Alice, for the safety of our messenger?'

'Brother James, the Cistercian?' Alice said. 'I was honoured to help, my lord.'

Earl Brien laughed and exchanged a roguish look with Lord Miles. 'No Cistercian,' he said. 'Safer to travel disguised as a monk than as a knight, to be sure. Even so, he was happy to have my knights as an escort. Thanks to your observant ears and eyes, our messages will arrive with Sir John, and he, too, will swear loyalty to his future queen.'

So, both monks had been disguised as members of holy orders,

Alice realised. And one – a knight, at that – had a loose tongue. He would not be used for such secret message-carrying again. She glowed with pride that they were grateful to her for her sharp observation.

Alice's joy was complete when Sir Jacques sought her out at supper, after she had sung.

He bowed to her, his curling brown hair falling over his forehead, rising with a flushed face and bright smile, and she felt the ladies seated around her fluttering, smiling and displaying curiosity at the interest shown her. Young Lady Anna was blushing. Lady Beatrice coughed and looked pointedly towards the older Lady Lenora, who was staring crossly from the dais table at Jacques, as if she would sweep him from the hall. This alarmed Alice. She did not want to risk the senior lady's disapproval and gave an almost imperceptible shake of her head. But, ignoring the Lady Lenora, Jacques smiled at them all. His eyes stopped when they reached Alice. Calling out to her, he said, with a little bow, 'May I escort you and your brothers to the Christmas Mass, Mistress Alice?'

There was a slight rustle of interest amongst the ladies. A pretty but nameless mummer girl – it was to be expected that a knight might try to attract her. But surely it could be nothing more.

'Thank you, Sir Jacques, we would be honoured,' she said, trying to sound dispassionate. Rising to her feet, she waved her brothers over to the maidens' section of the long trestle below the dais. Immediately, she caught the pair winking at each other behind the knight's back. She glared at them and told them Sir Jacques was escorting them all, that evening. The brothers smiled and politely inclined their heads.

Alice and her brothers, shepherded by Jacques, joined the candlelit procession from the castle to the abbey church. She could hardly concentrate on the precentor guiding the monks' choir as they sang *Te Deums*. By the time they were returning to the castle, the snow had stopped drifting down and the clear night sky had filled with stars. Sir Jacques pointed up to the frosty heavens. 'There is the Hunter. He is called Orion. See his belt. Follow three stars in a straight line.'

Her brothers' eyes followed his.

'It's interesting,' Pipkin said, fascinated.

'Come on –' Xander hurried him along – 'we must get back to the bailey hall to sup with Count Brien's soldiers. I promised to play and sing for them all. Sir Jacques will escort our sister to the great hall, and besides,' he added, looking around, 'there is plenty of company. Look, there's Lady Anna up ahead.'

Alice hung back, pleased to be alone, though not exclusively, with Sir Jacques. Though others returning to the hall pressed on, she dawdled and kept peering upwards at the night sky. 'I can see it!' she exclaimed.

Sir Jacques will never bore me, she thought to herself. I think he could be my twin soul. Oh, Saint Cecilia, I truly do, and I never thought to discover a soul companion.

'Come on, your brothers expect me to see you back safely. I can see the Empress's ladies already there.'

'Thank you. You have indeed sharp eyes to see all those shapes in the stars.'

'I shall hope to show you more another time,' he said gently, a smile warming his eyes.

Her breath caught in her throat.

They threaded their way through the crowds and, as they parted by the hearth where the Yule log glowed, he said, 'I thought I might never see you again, Mistress Alice.' His brown eyes were liquid in the lamplight, fixed on her as he thrust his hand into his jerkin and withdrew a gleaming silver brooch shaped like a small bear. 'I love the stars. This mantle brooch speaks of another constellation you can find during winter in the heavens. Please accept this token of my intent for our future . . . if you are agreeable . . . and should I survive the coming war.'

She felt herself blushing, yet without hesitation she said, 'I accept your gift with gratitude, my lord.'

'And . . . if you are ever in great danger, send it back to me.'

126

'If I can find you,' she said sadly, mindful of how she thought he had forgotten her before, and how wars brought about terrible displacement and loss. Should she dare love, when Jacques' family would want more for him? She should not trust him. 'I hope I never am in danger,' she said aloud.

'And I share that hope.' He took her hand and, turning it over, pressed the brooch into it.

If he was really pledging his intention to wed her with this gift, she must be honest with him. He might not realise that she came from peasant origins. 'Sir Jacques, you must know that I am of humble birth. Your family will expect you to woo an heiress with lands of her own.'

He lifted his hand away and she was left clutching the brooch. 'I have no people,' he said quietly. 'They died long ago. Once, I had a wife, and she died too. And I am without children. My wife died in childbirth, and my son too . . . It makes me happy just to be in your presence, Alice, and one day I hope I can make you happy too.' He leaned down and kissed the hand that still held his gift. With these sweet words, he was gone.

Alice wondered about him. Had he really no people? Why had his wife died in childbirth? Then she thought to herself that, sadly, it happened. She shuddered. Childbirth could be so dangerous. He was speaking the truth. Of course he was.

Those left in the hall were dispersing. Others were pulling out pallets from chests and retreating into alcoves. Alice held the brooch so tightly, it marked her hand. Despite Sir Jacques' attraction to her, he had not proposed marriage. Maybe this was just a dalliance for him.

They could only meet briefly throughout Christmastide, but she watched him from a distance, noting how he flirted with Empress Maud's ladies. They all flirted back, like butterflies flitting about the herbal in summer. He responded to the attention with smiles and flattery, and this made Alice unhappy. What could she do? If she remarked on it, she would appear to care too much, so she looked the other way. She kept her own counsel and spoke of him to no one. Yet, although Alice tried hard not to care, it was torturous when young Lady Sophia, a pretty blue-eyed blonde with a habit of batting eyes, often giggling and foolish, opened her hands one day to show the other young ladies a marzipan mouse she said Sir Jacques had procured for her from the pastry chef as a treat. *Oohs* and *Aahs* followed. Alice glanced away and pretended to busy herself stitching a rip in a puppet's tunic.

A day later, Sir Jacques offered to help Xander and Pipkin round up castle children to be part of the tableau for the Feast of the Holy Innocents. Usually, he was engaged as part of Empress Maud's retinue, escorting the Empress and her ladies to and from the feasting, or to the abbey church. And, when Maud rode out hawking through nearby marshes with Count Brien, Earl Robert and her ladies, Sir Jacques was amongst the knights who guarded the noble party. Alice's brothers accepted his assistance. She tried to look busy, polishing the wood of her harp so it gleamed. He brushed past her and whispered a compliment into her ear, his dark curls stroking her cheek. She could feel his breath and felt a delicious shiver pass through her arm.

Despite her chagrin, Alice's heart fluttered and danced when he came near and offered her little treats, such as a marzipan mouse. On one occasion, he gave her a small orange from far away. Its scent was seductive. He paid her more attention than the others and she was in love, even though she feared that anything or anyone could snatch it all away in the time it took for her eyes to blink.

As the twelve days of Christmastide passed, Alice observed how Empress Maud enjoyed presiding over her small Christmas court. Though not yet a queen, the Empress behaved as one, seeming more aloof than before. She was so busy with her nobles that she rarely took notice of Alice. Her attention and smiles were mostly reserved for Earl Robert and Lady Mabel, for Lord Miles and his wife, but, Alice noted, most of all for Count Brien.

Alice was aware that she, herself, was distantly related to Countess Tilda, and, not for the first time, she puzzled as to whom her real parents were. What if, thought Alice, my real father was someone of great significance? One day, I shall uncover that secret. One day.

For now, she hugged her other secret close. She touched her brooch from Jacques as if it were a talisman. It was a constant connection with the knight she loved, but, at other times, when he paid attention to the ladies attending Empress Maud, she really did wonder if it was wise to give away her heart. She reminded herself that she had not previously wished to marry where she did not love, and was now twenty and three; she was growing old. She felt she could love this knight, but something niggled her – what if Sir Jacques was not all he seemed? Apart from the odd chaste kiss behind an arras, he never seemed to expect more from her.

On the day following the play for the Feast of the Holy Innocents, Jacques whispered into Alice's ear, 'I am helping with the falcons today. Why don't you come to the mews and see them? They are gorgeous creatures. One day, I'll teach you how to hunt with a sparrowhawk.'

Seeing what she was sure was genuine admiration in his dark eyes, she smiled. 'Pipkin and Xander might like to see the falcons as well.'

'Well . . . yes, bring your brothers with you, Alice.' There was a little disappointment in his tone, but it mattered to her that her brothers approved of him. Besides, she had by now decided she was not going to be an easy conquest. She was ever aware that the ladies of the court smiled at the handsome widower knight from Anjou as he passed through the hall.

At the castle mews, Xander and Pipkin hurried from perch to perch, fascinated by the variety of hunting birds housed there. The little sparrowhawks were Alice's favourites.

At length, Jacques lifted up a peregrine falcon and showed it to the eager young men. 'This one belongs to Earl Robert. His name is Leander.'

When he removed the hawk's hood, the creature looked so fiercely at Alice with its yellow beady eyes that she shied away. But her brothers were thrilled, and even more delighted when Jacques permitted them to pull on a leather hawking glove and, in turn, hold the hawk on their wrists.

After they reluctantly left the mews, Xander took Alice aside and whispered, 'I think Sir Jacques has serious intentions regarding your future, my sister.'

Alice nearly jumped out of her mantle at these words. She did not want her brothers to suspect, not yet. She simply wanted them to like her knight.

'Really?' she said evenly. 'What do you mean, my brother?'

'It has been obvious over the Christmas festivities. He helped us with the Holy Innocents play and he often stares at you. Take care that his intentions are honourable.' Xander's teasing eyes had grown solemn.

She felt colour creep up her neck, knowing she had of course worried about this herself.

Pipkin said, 'I am sure Alice would never allow her head to be turned by him. Besides, I like Sir Jacques . . . and I like falcons. I want to learn more about them.'

Wanting to help Pipkin, because she could see that he loved the birds, Alice turned her thoughts away from Jacques and made a suggestion: 'We shall be returning to Wallingford soon enough. I wonder if Count Brien might let you train as a falconer. We won't be mummers forever. We all must think about the future.' She reflected sadly that, if she did not marry, her own future was likely to be spent in a convent.

Chapter Ten

Gloucester
January 1140

Maud felt miserable for days when Count Brien announced he would have to return to Wallingford in the New Year. He had remained at her court in Gloucester since she had arrived in October, only returning home briefly as that month ended. They had enjoyed a happy reunion over Christmas, the years of separation melting away as if they had never existed. Their friendship and affection for each other blossomed as they feasted, danced, hunted and planned strategy against Stephen, closeted in the royal castle's great chamber, poring over maps and lists of those disinherited knights who had promised her their support. Though Stephen had taken many old estates in the west for himself or his favoured supporters, great conquests – including Hereford – were made that autumn. Miles, Robert and Brien had become Maud's most loyal supporters and her closest male companions. She made them chief amongst her advisors, and this trio joined her at every gathering of the council.

She enjoyed Brien's company most of all. When strategic planning and campaigning grew exhausting, he would join her in her antechamber, where they would discuss old tales they both loved – the legend of Tristan and Iseult and the history of the Trojan War. She particularly relished the story of the wooden Trojan Horse, sent into the city in the guise of a gift. If only she could deceive Stephen and capture *her* City, especially the Tower of London. Her eyes widened into enormous dark pools when she read that, at night, a door had opened below the horse's belly and armed soldiers emerged from inside the horse to pour out into the streets of Troy, totally destroying it. It would take more than such a ruse to win the hearts and minds of Londoners. The most important citizens were the merchants. Stephen's marriage to Matilda of Boulogne had opened up easy trade routes for them.

'If only we might have such success against my cousin Stephen,' she sighed.

'We shall, in time,' Brien assured her, with a laugh that rang through the chamber as melodiously as the chapel bell that regularly called them to prayer. 'And you, my Empress, are fairer than Helen of Troy and more patient than Penelope.' He glanced over at Odysseus, the handsome hawk he usually kept on a perch in the great chamber, or in his own bedchamber, high in the keep of Gloucester Castle.

Maud glanced over at the other perch, holding one of her own sparrowhawks, which she had named Elysium. She stood and moved to the window embrasure, stooping gracefully and then rising to feed it a dead mouse. She kept several, caught by the castle cats, in a basket on the floor tiles. She was conscious that Brien's eyes were following her every movement.

'You *will* be Queen of England and Normandy,' he called over to her, setting aside the book and coming to stand next to her. Lowering his voice so her women could not hear, he whispered into her ear, 'You are always queen of my heart – my Helen of Troy.'

She felt a blush mantling her cheeks. Brien could say such things – to a queen, it was traditional. 'Am I really and truly?' she returned softly, glancing into his brown eyes, which were streaked with gold and soft as honey. 'That *is* a knightly thing to say.' Whilst she knew she could not be unfaithful to Geoffrey because of scandal and Church disapproval, she had often thought it would serve Geoffrey right that she was loved by another. After all, it was a total disgrace if a married woman lay with another man, yet not so if a husband was unfaithful. A child conceived with a man other than her husband would be unforgiveable, yet her husband could father as many bastards as he desired. Even so, Brien's devotion to her was returned many times over deep within her heart.

Maud, in truth, was delighted by Brien's admiration for her and his flirtatious remarks. She appreciated being free of Geoffrey, imagining that she was a young princess again, unwed, admired by all – able to make her own decisions, supported by men who had loved her father and who now were devoted to her cause. Whilst rapport with Brien was confined to the warp and weft of the fabric of chivalry, she loved him back and always would. Yet a relationship other than that of platonic love could never exist between them. It was painful to deny him her body, which she sensed that he coveted, but she could not risk a morsel of scandal about her affections and desires. Her purpose, and she believed it God's purpose for her, was to regain her crown, ruling in her own right, as the queens of Greek legends ruled, owing nothing to any man. She was indissolubly married to Geoffrey of Anjou, and the mischievous, handsome Brien was married to the aging Countess Tilda. Yet, she was glad, very glad, that Tilda never travelled with Count Brien, and that the Countess lived her own life away from the courts of both Maud and Stephen, travelling her own estates, endowing abbeys and negotiating trade with merchants in London. Their marriage was one of convenience and Count Brien never had a bad word to say about his wife, however much Maud might prod at him. He would, if ever he was asked, say, 'My Countess Tilda is a good and devout woman.' Tilda was already into her fifth decade.

Brien liked reading Maud the stories of Odysseus' adventures – sailing the seas, seeking return to his wife Penelope.

'He crossed stormy seas to return home to Ithaca, and then . . .'

'And then Penelope did not recognise him . . .' Maud shook her head.

'And she had so many suitors . . .' Brien's dark eyes twinkled with mischief.

'But his old nurse recognised him by a scar he had taken whilst hunting, years before.'

'Faithful nurse.'

'I would recognise you, always.'

★

On the morning of the Feast of the Holy Innocents, Count Brien summoned his knights and departed for Wallingford. He had heard a rumour that the King might attack his fortress. Count Brien kissed Maud's hand and reminded her again of Wallingford's important position on the Thames, halfway to London. Lord Miles and Earl Robert had agreed Wallingford must be defended. Maud understood, but still felt as if a stone had lodged in her heart.

'I shall return soon,' he promised. His forehead was creased with worry and his dark eyes were saddened. 'I need to make sure of Wallingford's defences and I must ensure Tilda's safety. She will be returning from the City.'

They agreed, but Maud felt his absence until long after the New Year had passed.

Later in January, missing him turned to concern. She had received news that Stephen was moving towards Wallingford and that he was planning to build a fort at Crowmarsh Gifford, across the river from Brien's fortress.

Maud gathered her advisors, headed by Lord Miles and Earl Robert, in her war chamber. She barred the doors so no one could overhear them as they discussed several plans, one of which concerned Count Brien's safety.

'He will know about Stephen's advance, but I can send messengers to warn him about the new fort,' suggested Earl Robert.

Miles shook his head. 'If Stephen is moving around the countryside, he'll have his own spies. Your messages, Robert, could be intercepted. By Christos, we may not be as fortunate as before, when Alice the mummer suspected our courier to the Marshal might be intercepted.' He thought for a moment. 'If I send messengers to Wallingford, or even troops, Stephen may change his tactics and cut us off.' He tapped a map spread on the table with a pointer. 'But, if we are sure he is already closing in on Wallingford, Mistress Alice could deliver a message to Brien, a warning and a promise that, if Brien is attacked, I shall counterattack –' he grinned – 'but with an element of surprise.'

Maud frowned, then smiled. 'There's our other half-brother, yet another of my father's sons by a fond mistress, young Reginald, in Devon and Cornwall, and, arrogant and impulsive though he is, he's still a soldier and a knight. Drawing the King to Wallingford leaves East Anglia and Devon vulnerable, but it gives us time to consider both. We could create such a diversion as Miles suggests.' She paused a moment for approval, as they all seemed to look her way, eyebrows raised, clearly amazed that a woman had such a grasp on strategy. She added, 'Can we trust Alice? It is true that, if she travels back to Wallingford by a route north of the London road, she may reach Brien before Stephen strikes.' Maud turned to her brother. 'What do you think, Robert?'

'I say that Alice has already proved herself worthy of trust. We have nothing to lose. Stephen appears ready to besiege Brien's castle sooner than we expected. You are right, Maud. If Brien holds firm, it gives us time to secure the west and attack the King at Wallingford at the same time. I have troops ready to march for the south-west.' Robert grew enthusiastic about her suggestion. 'It's a clever plan. You, Miles, can join me, but, south of Devizes, turn north again and rescue Wallingford.' He smiled a grim smile at Maud. 'You had best persuade the girl. Hopefully, she'll agree. I shall have a small guard escort the mummers north of the London road. The captain I'll assign as their escort will inform them of their new route once they set out. Perhaps you, Maud, ought to write the warning letter to Count Brien.'

Maud agreed, as pleased as her greyhound on receipt of a meaty bone. After all, she had known Alice for years. Brien had several times hinted that good noble blood ran in the singer's veins. The girl would never betray Brien, to whom she owed much, and, besides, she would hope to ensure her adopted family's safety. Maud would tell Alice to move them to Wallingford Castle. If Stephen struck, the surrounding villages would be vulnerable to pillaging by Stephen's wicked troops.

Maud summoned Alice to her great chamber. Today, she was wearing a plain blue woollen gown, her plaited hair caught into a knot within a dark net. Graciously, she proffered a leather purse, fat with silver pennies.

'This is payment for the entertainments, which we greatly enjoyed,' Maud said, with hopeful confidence, though in her heart she was wondering if Alice really was up to the task she intended entrusting to her.

Alice sank into a reverential curtsey and replied humbly, 'Thank you, my lady. You are always generous. It was a privilege to play for you.' She bowed her head and, rising, turned to leave.

'Wait, please, Alice. I have something else to say to you. I have known you loyal to Count Brien for many years, now. Is this not so?'

Alice spun back around, her face filled with obvious adoration for Brien. 'Yes, my lady, Count Brien is kind to my family and to me.'

Maud stood up from the desk at which she had been sitting. This was going to be easier than she had first thought. She smiled warmly and said, 'So I understand. I have need of someone loyal and reliable to undertake an important task, and you are the only one whom I can trust with it.'

Alice's eyes grew round with astonishment that she should be trusted so. She gulped, but nodded in acknowledgement of the compliment.

Maud lifted a letter from her writing table, sealed with wax and folded flat. 'See that Count Brien receives this. As you know, he left for Wallingford some days ago.' Maud's voice grew hushed as she leaned closer to Alice. 'My intelligence tells me the King is riding towards Wallingford Castle with a great army and he is likely to besiege it. I have also heard that the enemy has thrown up temporary castles to the south and east.' She touched the waiting letter. 'Since Earl Robert tells me you will return to Wallingford Castle this very week, my letter should reach Count Brien in time . . . if you agree to carry it to him.'

She added, by way of explanation, 'The castle is endangered by our enemies. You see, Alice, he must be warned, so that he may make preparations to withstand a siege, and, importantly, so he knows that, if necessary, we will counterattack the King's besieging

136

troops.' Maud seemed to be choosing her next words carefully. She spoke slowly and with deliberation, as if she was thinking aloud: 'If the King attacks Wallingford, Count Brien must be ready with protection for his people and with his food stores laid in. I am trusting you with the letter, Alice, because it is safer that it is conveyed by one whom the enemy would never suspect, rather than any military messenger. Who knows where King Stephen's spies are hidden? But do not place yourself in danger, and destroy the letter if there is a risk of it being discovered by the enemy; it contains nothing that I have not told you already.'

Maud continued, her blue eyes concerned, 'Not a word to anyone. Stay close to your brothers and your guards at all times, especially when lodging in inns or monasteries.'

Alice had heard Maud out in silence, but, nonetheless, her mind was racing. This was a huge responsibility. She briefly closed her eyes. When they reopened, they were clouded with anxiety, but she managed to say, in a firm voice, 'Our guard promises it will be only three days' travel to the north of Wallingford, and it's a safer route. I shall do my best to deliver your letter, my lady. My family and our friends are endangered too. You can trust my integrity.'

Maud seemed relieved. She swept her hand down her plain blue gown. Her dark eyes were filled with concern and her voice was gentle, if firm, as she said, 'I believe you, Alice. And your family must seek safety in the castle before it is besieged. The countryside around Wallingford may not be spared.'

Alice noted the Empress's care and consideration, and the simplicity with which she spoke, in no way condescending, and with earnest eyes. Alice felt she was the most important person the Empress knew, a sense inspiring courage and devotion to the often severe woman standing by the desk, now asking for her help. She could do this, carry the secret message and help Count Brien, who she suspected was much beloved by Maud. She nodded and accepted the letter.

Maud watched as she placed it in her scrip, below a pretty bone-plated box, which, no doubt, contained personal treasures.

'Thank you,' Maud said. 'Remember, it is for the Count's eyes only. You will be well rewarded when this war is ended.' Maud smiled. 'May the Madonna guide your journey to safety, Mistress Alice.'

With these words, Maud dismissed her, and, pleased that the interview had gone as she intended, she sat at her desk and resumed her writing of letters.

By Epiphany, the mummers were once again loading props into their wagon. But, this time, they were being tested as to their trustworthiness. The risks were great. There could be bandits on the road, lurking amongst the trees. They might be ambushed or at the very least questioned by Stephen's guards, who may have set up checkpoints. They could even be caught up in skirmishes, getting captured and searched. Alice must be ever alert and ready to destroy the precious letter that would reassure Count Brien that, if he was besieged by Stephen's troops, there was a plan to bring down the siege. She had memorised the Countess's words of warning and promise of help, though she did not know the detail. Above all, she must warn her family and bring them inside Wallingford Castle's safe strong walls. And she had to reach Wallingford with the warning as quickly as was possible. She prayed for fine weather and no delays. They would be protected by only two guards and their captain, chosen by Earl Robert. The group would travel to the small wool town of Witney, dropping down to Wallingford from there.

Watching their preparations from her chamber window, Maud, too, hoped that the roads would not become too icy; the weather had turned sharp and cold. She shivered at the thought, called a servant to close the shutters and retreated to the fireside. She murmured a prayer to Saint James, whose relic was still within her possession, to watch over the travellers.

Sir Jacques came to bid Alice farewell, helping to secure their baggage and props. Alice, feeling wistful at leaving him and wishing that he could have been her guard, did not hesitate to follow when he drew her aside into the herb garden. He took her hands in a firm clasp.

'There have not been enough private moments for us to talk lately, and I must be quick, Alice, as I am needed in the castle. My love, I promise we shall be together one day soon. Forget me not, for I shall not forget thee.' He bent his dark head, drew a tiny dagger from his belt and, reaching up his hand, cut off a lock of her hair. He put it into a tiny purse and tied it with a cord. Slipping the cord over his head, he tucked it beneath his tunic. 'I love you, Alice.'

As she heard his words, her eyes misted over. 'And I you,' she replied softly.

He pressed his lips against hers and she received his precious kiss. How long would it be before she would see Jacques' sweet face again? These were anxious times.

As Alice and her brothers rumbled over the drawbridge, a Benedictine monk riding a palfrey and accompanied by a group of knights passed by. He peered from his course black cowl straight at their cart. As he rode by, his eyes met Alice's, then dropped. She twisted round swiftly. In that brief glimpse, she was sure this was the monk she had seen on their journey to Gloucester. He had the same hooded eyes and shifty bearing. It would be difficult not to recognise their wagon, which was painted gold and green. Yet, he had no reason to be suspicious of them, except that the message for Marlborough had reached its destination safely and he must have wondered why.

If there were armies approaching Wallingford, she was relieved they were travelling by a different, more unexpected route. Little Pipkin grumbled, 'It does take longer.' He sighed. 'And how I miss my Meg.' Meg was Pipkin's sweetheart, but, as Alice reminded him, there was the consolation that they were returning to Wallingford with a generous purse of coin. She nodded to where Xander kept it tied to his belt, concealed under his cloak. 'Think of this, Pipkin: there'll be enough to set aside money for a wedding soon.'

Pipkin grinned. 'I hope she hasn't forgotten me.'

As for Xander, Alice often wondered if he was destined, one day, for the cloister. In truth, she thought sadly, if Sir Jacques does not keep faith or meets a sad end in this war, a life in a nunnery could well be my own destination. She shrugged. But, for now, I have a task and a purpose I cannot reveal to a living soul. I pray, dear Saint Cecilia, if Wallingford is besieged, the Empress's army will rescue the town.

Her family and older brother, his wife, Annie, and their brood of small children were all endangered. In that moment of understanding, she realised how much she cared about her older brother and his difficult wife. She closed her eyes and whispered a second prayer, this time to the Virgin. 'God spare us all. War is sliding closer and closer.'

Chapter Eleven

Gloucester
Spring 1140

In March, Miles had not waited to report his success to Maud in council. With his great wolfskin mantle slung about his shoulders, and fresh from the siege at Wallingford, he threw open the great chamber's door with a grand gesture, causing her women to scatter to the window benches. He did not apologise for frightening her ladies or interrupting her reading of the story of Saint Matthias, chosen by eleven remaining apostles to replace Judas Iscariot. (His image was carved in a number of Gloucestershire churches, and it was his feast day.) She rose to her feet and angrily chastised Miles for his unchivalrous manner; then, relenting, she sent a servant to fetch hippocras and cakes from the kitchens. Miles was ever like a bear crashing into a forest glade.

'Catch your breath, Sir Miles,' she said. 'Refreshments are on their way. Remove that stinking wolf thing you wear. Give it to a servant.' She clicked her fingers towards another page. Miles shrugged off his mantle. She wrinkled her nose and waved to a large, cushioned seat a distance from her own chair. 'Sit over there. Tell all.'

Miles had the grace to look abashed, but he did as she requested, handing the smelly cloak to two pages, with instructions to brush away the mud.

He leaned forward. 'Forgive me, my lady, but my news cannot wait. We have relieved the siege. Our . . . I mean *your* stratagem was a success. The mummers, Alice and her brothers, warned Count

Brien in fair time. Stephen's troops were raiding to the north of Wallingford and Alice had just avoided them. Brien's people drew enough stores inside to see them through many long months, and Alice was able to bring her family safely inside the castle. And, my lady, Brien bravely led his own garrison out in sorties against the enemy.'

'Slow down, Miles,' she said. 'So they are all safe. Thank God. But tell me everything – I want to absorb it all.'

Miles took a breath and continued, 'The King came with a large host. He tried to shut them in with a ring of besiegers. He soon realised supplies had been laid in by Brien and his people. With such abundance, the garrison at Wallingford could last out for several years. Even so, the enemy tried hard to destroy the castle. Stephen, as you know, had built forts in the area to help supply his troops and maintain the siege. It must have cost a fortune! All a waste.' He grinned, displaying broken teeth; not a pleasant sight.

'Aye,' she said. 'Using my father's treasure. Stephen will run out soon enough, I'll warrant, with his great siege weapons and with paying his Flemish mercenaries.'

'Indeed, my lady. Anyway, Stephen had departed by the time I arrived with relief troops, leaving others to maintain his siege. He headed for Trowbridge, which we had already strengthened. So, as hoped, Robert has successfully drawn him south. My troops set off through quiet routes under cover of darkness, through rains and mud, and, when we surrounded them, the King's garrison surrendered without a fight.' Miles grunted. 'I hope your dungeons can accommodate the bastards.'

Maud clapped her hands together gleefully.

He laughed. 'We'll swell our war chest with ransoms. Stephen will need Midas's gold to get his knights released.'

'Well done, Miles.' Yet, as she praised him, Maud shuddered at the thought of Stephen's knights imprisoned in her own royal castle of Gloucester. She would ask that they be removed to Bristol . . . Then she bit her lip, reminding herself that war meant many inconveniences such as unwashed knights in her childhood home.

Miles lifted his cup of ale and swallowed. He closed his eyes for a moment and Maud thought she heard him swear under his breath. There was clearly something left to tell.

'Miles?' she said. 'What is it?'

'Stephen was using a church for one of his command posts and caused much destruction there. God will punish him. Count Brien was furious. That courageous knight will not stand for such wrongdoing.'

'Nor I,' Maud said tartly. 'Where is the King now?'

'He never captured Trowbridge, despite all his siege engines. He's in London with his Queen.'

Maud grimaced once again at the thought of that supercilious woman, Matilda of Boulogne, wearing the crown she considered her own.

Miles added, 'Stephen has left troops in Devizes. As you know, it's one of the most important royal castles in the south, one which guards routes north towards Gloucester and south to Devon. He is closing in on us. But there's more. Earl Robert, your brother, made your other young brother, Reginald, Earl of Cornwall. And, my lady, I regret to tell you Reginald is unpopular there. Alas, he has damaged churches too. The Bishop of Exeter excommunicated him, and his wife has gone mad.'

Maud shook her head disapprovingly. She proffered the plate of almond cakes. Miles swallowed three as if they were mere bites. He drew another long swallow from his ale cup. Maud nibbled a cake, sipped her ale and frowned. 'Reginald is hot-headed. He never thinks before he acts.' She had never been as close to Reginald as she was to Robert.

'I fear so, my lady. No stratagem, there. Robert will regret that boon.'

'I need to give this some thought, Miles,' she said, folding her hands slowly in her lap. She leaned forward. 'And I need you and Brien in council, sooner rather than later, along with Robert and myself.'

Miles made her disquiet worse: 'The King steals from grain stores

143

to feed his armies. He is pillaging castles and villages, and attacking abbeys. Women are raped by his mercenaries. Children are speared by his soldiers. I have heard my own people say, "Christ and his saints are sleeping."'

'And today is Gloucester's favourite saint's feast day. Saint Matthias will cast curses on us, if we cannot rectify this anarchy.'

Miles reached over and touched her arm. It was a fatherly gesture. 'God is on our side,' he said quietly.

'Send for my brother Robert and for Count Brien,' she said firmly, determined to plan anew. 'Perhaps Alice might be of use again. I would like her here in Gloucester too.'

A week passed. Maud watched from the keep of Gloucester Castle as Count Brien trotted his stallion over the drawbridge, leading his knights, all helmeted and armed and with shields strapped to their backs. His head was bare and his tousled mass of dark curls, caught by a sudden breeze, blew around his face as he rode. She always felt her heart beat faster when she saw him. Her eyes followed Brien's white horse until he vanished beneath the gatehouse and into the lower bailey.

After a sodden late winter, soft spring breezes blew through the castle. Washing was laid out on bushes to dry and the April sun was shining, glinting off the chain mail worn by Brien's knights as they filed into the bailey. A little maiden had brought Maud a posy of primroses and placed them with sprigs of thyme in a pottery cup on her chamber window ledge. It was thoughtful of the child, and the flowers' delicate scent filled the chamber. However, on days in March when the wind had too often changed direction, Maud had caught the unpleasant aroma of horse dung, pigs and fowl that pecked around the courtyard below. She remained by the opened shutters, watching as the last horsemen of Brien's retinue came through the gate.

Just below her high window, she saw Dame Margo seated on a palfrey, followed by Xander and Alice, both riding palfreys as well. Maud was aware that her knight, Sir Jacques, had long admired the young woman. She sighed deeply, wondering what to do about

Alice, who was now in her mid-twenties. Perhaps she should ask Sir Jacques about his intentions. He was handsome, with warm brown eyes and a winning smile, but Maud was sure Alice was not the only one who had received his attentions. She had noticed her handsome household knight's winning ways with her ladies. Closing the shutters, she hurried down the narrow wooden staircase to her bedchamber, calling for Lenora to help her change her gown for supper.

Maud swept into the great chamber. A round oak table stood below shelves filled with rolls of maps. As it still grew chilly at night, a fire blazed and candles had been lit. She had ordered servants to clear the table and deliver platters of meats, cheeses, bread and a dish of preserved fruits with a jug of cream. Goblets, bowls, spoons and napkins completed the preparations. They each carried their own eating knives. Her own knife, with a jewelled hilt, was sheathed on her low-slung belt. If an assassin ever dared to attempt murder, she was armed and ready.

Count Brien was first to arrive for supper. He embraced her warmly and, as she momentarily laid her head on his shoulder, she felt her eyes swim with tears. She raised her hand and wiped them away. He had survived a terrible siege and now, here he was, laughing to see her and recount the tale. Brien, she was relieved to note, was unscathed. As he released her, she breathed in the familiar scent of musk that always hung about his person. His collar, embroidered with golden discs, grazed her cheek. His cuffs matched, and, as she stepped back from his embrace, she saw his boots had his favoured pointed toes. This was the fashionable, roguish, brave champion she loved with a passion, but could not ever contemplate taking to her bed.

'Maud,' he said, shaking his curls. 'You are as beautiful as ever. How do you fare?'

She felt colour rise into her cheeks. She had chosen to cover her head with her prettiest flared headband studded with pearls, from which a scalloped short veil framed her handsome, oval face. Even though she was well past five and thirty years old, she knew she still suited young women's fashions. 'I am well, Brien,' she replied. 'Happy you suffered no injury whilst defending Wallingford.'

'Ah, I have Alice to thank — and of course Miles, who came to relieve my garrison as would a Greek general of old, riding an Arab stallion, covered in mail from head to leather-booted foot and with a wolfskin covering his armour.'

'Oh, that hideous mantle!' she said with disgust, and would have made a further disparaging comment, except her brother, followed by Miles himself, entered the chamber. Brien and Maud quickly drew apart.

'Be seated,' she said to them all, gesturing to the chairs drawn up around the table. 'Brien by my right, Robert to my left, and you, Miles, across the table.' She clicked her fingers at two servitors, who entered to pour wine, first for herself and Brien. She waved them back, saying reproachfully, 'No, bring ale for my Lord of Gloucester and for the Lord Miles.' When they returned, she ordered them to leave the jugs on the table and depart until she sent for them.

For a time, they ate and spoke of their families and her letters from Geoffrey, who was taking control of more border castles in Normandy. She tapped a letter lying by her side on the supper table, one she had received that very day. 'Geoffrey writes he has taken control of Pirou Castle, and Caen too. He is making gains.'

'That is good.' Robert seemed to scrutinise her face. 'Do you miss Geoffrey?' he asked, after a few heartbeats had passed with no response from her.

She lifted the letter and wondered if she should let Robert read it. She decided not. It was her letter, after all. She set it down again and glanced up. 'I am sure Geoffrey has others to warm his bed,' she said, and laughed lightly. 'But we have found friendship.' She thought for a moment on how they had discovered an angle of repose, and, to her surprise, she felt her eyes misting over. 'I suppose, on occasion, I do miss him, but I miss my sons more.'

'Hopefully this will end soon,' Robert said, reaching over the table and touching her arm reassuringly.

There could be no going back now. They had invested too much. They were both, she and Geoffrey, fighting for the boys' inheritance. He was making gains, but hers were slow. They would come. She must not abandon hope. She blinked away her tears.

Finally, supper finished, they pushed their plates aside. As the evening edged towards the midnight Angelus, their conversation turned into a serious strategic discussion.

'So, Stephen has crossed into Devon,' she said, and looked Robert straight in the eye, meaning she knew about Reginald and was concerned about the King's advances in the south-west. 'He has summoned all the barons of Devon to his aid. And you, brother, retreated to Bristol? Was the retreat unavoidable?'

Robert frowned, laid his tankard aside and said, 'Maud, I had no choice. Our brother, that cub, Reginald, behaved foolishly and alienated the people of Exeter. Now, he's holding up in Cornwall.' Robert shook his head. 'Making him an earl was a mistake.'

'Clearly as mad as a box of frogs,' Maud remarked. 'Mad as his wife.' Her face darkened and she felt her temper flare up. 'Some brother, indeed. He'll not have any earldom from me, if he doesn't wage war rationally and act honourably.'

'I shall take him in hand, Maud,' Robert said. 'In such a mood, it would be prudent not to alienate our young brother. That could send him to Stephen's camp. But, I agree, he must mend his behaviour.'

No one spoke until Miles nodded over at Robert. 'But we have another, more serious problem now. You explain it, Robert.'

'Robert Fitz Herbert . . .'

'Who is he?' Maud's eyes widened. She could not place this person at all, but there was something familiar to this name . . . She scrabbled through her memory and it came to her. 'He's one of ours, but never much liked – a despicable creature, if I recollect correctly.'

'He's wily, and he's evil. He has taken Devizes from the King, which may appear as good news, but it is not. Maud, that man is a mercenary, one I have seriously considered dismissing, for he is a sinful man. He has boasted of murdering priests and stealing from abbeys whilst in our service. We must bring him down, because, I fear, he does not hold Devizes for you, but for himself. He is a huge threat to our cause. He will bring others over to his side, hoping to acquire land and treasure.'

Robert rested his head in his great gnarled hands for a moment. He had known that waging war against Stephen would be difficult, but he had not imagined problems mushrooming from amongst the power-hungry in his own army. He had assumed Fitz Herbert to be loyal and had miscalculated. The man was a known rogue.

Looking up, Robert added, 'He is already trying to intimidate local landowners, or bring them over to his side. He must be stopped. It brings our just invasion into doubt. Our followers will turn against us. This is a danger to our campaign's integrity and success, Maud. I even sent my own son, William, to reason with him, but he turned Will away from the gates. If foolish Reginald displayed unreasonable behaviour around Exeter, it is nothing to what Robert Fitz Herbert is capable of. We must stop him, but how? He does not proclaim for Stephen, nor does he keep faith with me, his commander – or even accept our messengers.'

The candles guttered. The air stilled. Somewhere outside an owl hooted into the chilling April night. Those around the table were silent, minds racing. Brien rose from the table and moved to the shuttered window, his long-toed boots slowing his pace. He stood there for a moment. Maud thought he was about to open the shutters and allow the night in, but he was taking time to think. After a few minutes, he spun around on his booted heel, nimble as a dancer at a feast. 'I have it! Why don't we send to the Marshal, John Fitz Gilbert of Marlborough, encourage him to pretend sympathy and offer to treat with Fitz Herbert. He could invite the mercenary to Marlborough, offer friendship, flatter him – and then take him prisoner.'

'Ah,' Maud said. 'But, if Fitz Herbert is patrolling around Devizes, he could easily intercept a messenger. It's not far from Marlborough.'

'Exactly, but I think *Alice* and her brother might get through to Marlborough,' Brien said.

There was a short pause as Robert, Miles and Maud listened, slightly stunned.

'You did say you might make more use of her loyalty and acting skills,' Brien added.

'Dangerous,' Robert said at last. 'I would not wish her to fall into that man's clutches.'

'It would require great courage.' Miles looked around, but chuckled through his enormous grey beard. 'Mistress Alice can do it. She can be disguised as a female merchant, a widow travelling south from Bristol with her steward, delivering spices. You trade in pepper, cinnamon and in saffron, Robert. Precious ingredients. Valuable. If they were intercepted, the bastards would just steal the pepper boxes.'

'I do have all three spices stored at the moment, but she'll need a guard,' Robert said thoughtfully, stroking his chin.

'I can manage that,' suggested Brien, beaming around the gathering, his eyes twinkling. 'Dame Margo can accompany her, and a maidservant.'

Maud had been thinking of Alice's face in that dark corridor in Rouen, the day of her betrothal. Alice alone with the monstrous Fitz Herbert was not something she wished to permit. But she now had an inspired thought. She could provide Alice with protection and simultaneously test Sir Jacques.

'Let me send Sir Jacques, too,' Maud said. 'He is one of my household knights. That will be an incentive for her, as he has been flirting with her and so I would hope he will guard her carefully. They are, indeed, sweethearts, I suspect – though, then again, he is admired by most of my young maidens.'

'If you think this Sir Jacques trustworthy,' Brien said.

'I believe him to be, yes. He could have returned to Anjou, but has remained here. All must be sworn to secrecy,' Maud said. 'You write the message for Sir John, Robert, and arrange a box of spice and one of pepper as a gift.'

Two short days later, and Alice was clad in a suitable travelling gown and perched side-saddle on her palfrey. Xander, Dame

Margo and young Beatrice, Empress Maud's maiden, accompanied her, and, to Alice's secret delight, Sir Jacques rode behind her, guarding the closed wooden cart carrying the pepper and spice boxes. A half-dozen soldiers clad in chain mail and helmets rode both front and behind, led by Brien's fatherly, dependable captain, whom she had known from her earlier journey to Gloucester.

Earl Robert had said to Sir Jacques, jocularly, as they departed, 'I hope you do not lose my pepper. Hard to replace – but, then again, if you do, we'll retrieve the lot once we take Devizes.'

'Do not tempt fate, Robert,' Alice had heard Brien reply, as the party set off.

Alice carried Robert's letter in her scrip, hidden within her bone casket. When Maud had spoken with her, to inform her of her mission, she had said that the journey should take two days. They would stop in Cirencester, where the Abbot, a friend of Earl Robert, would welcome them and would not ask awkward questions. Carrying merchant goods was not unusual.

It did, however, bother Alice, when they rode into the abbey precinct, that a Benedictine monk crossing the yard closely resembled the cleric she had seen at Christmastide. At least *she* looked different today, wearing a widow's wimple and sitting side-saddle on a palfrey, and she was sure he hadn't recognised her. Xander, too, looked altered, since this time he wore a brimmed hat and a blue cloak of fine scarlet. She doubted that he was recognisable. And the monk would not expect her to be travelling with a maid, a sizeable guard and a small, square, windowless carriage concealing boxes of valuable spices and pepper.

The abbey house smelled of new wood, Alice breathed in the smell of new wood as she was shown to a lofty chamber with a large feather bed, which she would share with Dame Margo and Beatrice. They dined in the refectory with the monks, and she was relieved not to see the Benedictine amongst those dining. The Abbot took his place by her side, but, because silence was observed during the meal, there was no conversation. Sir Jacques sat opposite, with Xander. He tried to catch Alice's attention with smiles, and she had to swallow back an urge to burst into laughter when he mimicked hand signals used by the monks as he requested bread and the great dish of mashed peas to be passed his way.

So far, Alice and Beatrice had both enjoyed their trip, though Alice was acutely aware she must guard Earl Robert's letter with her life, and so she kept her scrip under her cloak, even as she ate supper. Having Jacques so close lent her confidence. It was a pleasant evening and, with no sign of the monk at supper, the monastery felt like a safe haven. She longed to be alone with Jacques, wondering if they dared risk sneaking into the abbey garden after dark. One glance at Dame Margo decided her against such a bold plan. She quietly sighed. It might be easier to find a private moment on their return journey.

The next day, Xander took acting the part of Alice's steward so seriously, he was ever drawing his own palfrey close to hers, nearly causing Beatrice to unbalance when he would say, 'My lady, what clement weather we are experiencing today.' Or, 'My lady, do you need to rest awhile?' And, once, he declared, 'Such poor pottage they served us for dinner in that inn! Do you wish I complain on our return?'

Alice laughed at his quips, Beatrice giggled, but Dame Margo frowned him down, and Xander moderated his behaviour.

All was still light-hearted until, approaching mid-afternoon, their party entered an ancient stretch of woodland. Sir Jacques, who had gone ahead to scout out their route, rode back with a look of concern creasing his forehead. 'My lady, it is too quiet here,' he said to Alice. 'I'm going to alert Count Brien's men. They appear to have closed in on the wagon, which is fine, safe and good, but we are too close to Devizes, and not close enough to Marlborough.'

Before Alice could respond, as if someone hidden had been listening to Jacques, an arrow shot past her and over the heads of the soldiers to lodge itself in the wood of her spice carriage. The horse pulling the small wagon shied. Xander's horse reared up and Beatrice, clinging to his waist, screamed. Xander deftly managed to bring the palfrey under control and the whole retinue stopped. The guard surrounded her. The spice carriage came to a sudden halt, its horse neighing and straining on its leads whilst Earl Robert's driver was nearly pulled from his seat as he tried to control the whinnying animal. Bows were raised just as another arrow came whistling by. Alice's heart raced. She was sure they were all going to die right there, deep in a beech wood, on a lonely trail towards Marlborough. Count Brien's troop of six archers let loose a volley of arrows, but, as they did, as if a magician had waved a wand, the sun vanished and they were plunged into wholly unexpected darkness.

After a tense pause, a quivering Dame Margo whispered, 'God has decided to save us, my child. He has blinded our enemies.'

Of Sir Jacques, there was no sign.

'No,' Xander hissed. 'It may be God's will, but I believe what has happened is called an eclipse. One such happened seven years ago. This is similar. It occurs when the sun is prevented from shining by the passage of the moon, which moves in front of it. This will pass very soon, I believe, but we should carry on forward as stealthily and as quietly as we can. No one can fire arrows at us whilst the darkness lasts. Sir Jacques will be up ahead, waiting for us. He has great knowledge of the skies and will understand this occurrence.' Xander's shadowy finger pointed into the dark, urging them forward.

The guard appeared to agree, as they all slowly continued along the pathway, their horses unsettled and protesting, so they were not very quiet at all. Alice tried to recall when exactly in the confusion she had last seen Sir Jacques. Beatrice grew calmer when there was no pursuit, but she appeared to bury her face in Xander's cloak; Alice could just make out her bent outline.

Steadily, they walked the horses forward, along the pathway and through the unusual darkness. It all seemed to take a very long time. Alice was sure she heard rustling in the trees to her left and hoped it was not the forest outlaws shadowing them. At length, the sky began to lighten gradually, and she could see they were finally exiting the beech forest and would be able to pick up their pace. What she could not see up ahead was Sir Jaques riding his jennet. They walked the horses forward several miles, leaving the trees behind, but there was still no sign of him. Had Jacques ridden on to Marlborough to fetch help?

She was perplexed and anxious and, as the late afternoon sun began to show once again, now sinking westwards, she called to the captain, who rode just ahead of them, to stop. She expressed her fears for Sir Jacques' safety.

The kindly captain tried to comfort her, saying, 'It will soon be sunset, Lady Alice. We cannot risk returning to search that wood. The best we can hope for is that, if Sir Jacques was snatched by out-laws, they will seek a ransom. They will know from spies that he was guarding a lady travelling to Marlborough, and Jacques will confirm you are a widow, with spices in that wagon to sell to Sir John Fitz Gilbert. If he does, we can expect a messenger demanding payment for his return. My guess is we have encountered Fitz Her-bert's men. We cannot risk your being captured as well, but I suspect that rogue, Fitz Herbert, will accept our spice boxes in return for Sir Jacques' freedom, and they will, for certes, demand payment. That's how it works.'

She thought with a jolt once again of the Benedictine monk she had seen in Cirencester. With the earlier enjoyment of the ride into the woods in such convivial company, she had forgotten all about him. He could have ridden to Devizes with information, this possi-bility explaining why he had not been in the refectory for supper on the previous evening. But a small voice at the back of her mind said, *What if Sir Jacques has gone over?* She had not known him for so long. He had no family, and no ties to Maud, either. Might he have been flirting with Alice only for amusement?

She had to be content with the captain's response. She gulped and prayed to Saint Cecilia, her favourite saint, *Bring Sir Jacques safely back to us, my lady of music.*

They entered the gates of Marlborough Castle as darkness fell. Sir John, a tall young soldier who looked as if he would brook no non-sense from anyone, betrayed not an ounce of emotion when Alice delivered her message from Earl Robert. He glanced up from the letter and studied her for a moment through piercing blue eyes, as if taking her measure. 'It will be arranged as they request. As for Sir Jacques, I received word at sundown from a man whom one of my men, searching about the castle for those in terror of the darkening skies, discovered riding towards Marlborough with a message for me from Robert Fitz Herbert—'

'That was quick,' Xander interrupted. 'What does it say? Clearly, Fitz Herbert and his rogues were not frightened by the darkness in the heavens.'

Sir John frowned at Xander from under heavy dark eyebrows. 'Like me, he will have seen the strange phenomenon before, back in thirty-three, during the old King's reign . . . when I was his Marshal. A fearful occurrence, sent by God, indeed, and a warning to all who commit evil and those who are oath-breakers.' He paused for a moment, then said, 'Do not interrupt me again, young man. The messenger we caught hold of claims to work for Robert Fitz Herbert. He says, Sir Jacques will be taken to Devizes. The messenger knows the captured knight was travelling as a guide with a certain Lady Alice, a widow, who has possession of a valuable spice wagon on its way to my castle with spices for my kitchens here and for the King's pantries.' His face broke into a reluctant smile. 'No one knows I have given Maud my loyalty, as yet.'

Alice exhaled. All was well.

'Useful, as Robert knows,' Sir John continued. 'Fitz Herbert will accept the spices as payment for Sir Jacques' release. So, I propose we can achieve two objectives, here. I shall send word to Robert Fitz Herbert in the morning and invite him to my castle. You will depart at dawn and return straightway to Gloucester. Leave the wagon for all to see in my custody. Fitz Herbert is a man of great greed and he will be delighted to acquire the spices. And he will learn that I am his ally. I am my own man, here, with nothing obvious to connect me to either King or Empress, these days.' John Fitz Gilbert stroked his black beard. 'And he will not be returning to Devizes, except to dangle before its gates at the end of a rope.'

'Can it work, Sir John?' said Captain Hubert.

'Oh, yes, indeed. I have not as yet engaged in any warfare for Empress Maud, though the lady has my loyalty and she will soon enough have my oath. Our enemy is one who seeks power beyond his abilities. If his man sees you all departing without the spices, he will be convinced I have extracted them from you. I do not want Count Brien's men here, anywhere in view, when the bastard arrives.'

'Where is the messenger now?'

Sir John grinned, showing a set of white teeth. He was enjoying this, Alice realised. He likes games of cat and mouse.

'He's in my kitchens, swiving a lady of the night.'

Dame Margo gasped in shock.

Sir John looked amused. 'Naturally, I know of many such. When at Westminster we kept a stable of prostitutes, some very fine ladies indeed, fallen on hard times.' He grinned. 'Now, you will all, including your men, Captain Hubert, be escorted to the bailey hall, well out of sight. You will rest. My ostlers will see to your animals. The cooks in the lower hall will give you refreshments and my steward will see you off my property at cockcrow . . . so get what rest you can. And tell Earl Robert I shall take good care of his spices until he sends for them.'

He laughed again, and Alice saw that John Fitz Gilbert was a man who was not easily taken advantage of. He was solid as a well-constructed stone wall, and a man of cool wits, determined to outwit the Devil himself. He inspired trust, and Empress Maud was fortunate to have him edging onto her side.

In the tiny chapel attached to the lower hall, kneeling on its earthen floor, Alice fixed her eyes on a tiny pale alabaster Christ on a wooden cross and recited three Pater Nosters, praying hard that Jacques would return to her unharmed. As she murmured, Fitz Herbert loomed up in her imagination as a shapeless hairy monster, a devil incarnate, with fiery eyes.

After that vision, Alice found sleep elusive, despite a good supper and sharing a bed with the sensible Dame Margo and kindly

Beatrice. She could not stop thinking about Jacques: he could be forced into betraying them if pressed by that Devil. No, surely not Jacques. He would remain resolute and loyal to the Empress. How could she have such suspicion? Moreover, it was likely the Benedictine monk had ridden to Devizes . . . She tossed and turned and listened to the chapel bells chiming out the hours, one by one. She would never sleep soundly again until she was reunited with Jacques. How could she have doubted him?

The journey back to Gloucester was uneventful. The waiting to know if her knight was safe was agony.

Chapter Twelve

Gloucester
Summer 1140

A silent, subdued Sir Jacques rode into Gloucester three weeks later, with the spice wagon intact, accompanied by a number of Sir John's knights. Maud, with Brien in attendance, summoned her knight to the dais in the great hall of the castle. When he knelt before her, she saw he was thinner than he had been before his capture. He was no longer the dashing, chivalrous knight so admired by her ladies.

Maud stepped down from the dais, raised him up and led him to a bench by the central hearth. She sat in a cushioned chair whilst Brien sat on the bench beside Sir Jacques.

'Come, come, Jacques, you are free. The demon is no more,' Count Brien said gently. 'You are a courageous knight. I am aware you had a rough time in that devil's cells, but you are here now. That's what matters. You are intact, and not even a fingernail wrenched from your hand by the sadist.'

Jacques managed a half-smile. 'It's what he was doing to others, not to me, that's upsetting, my lord. I heard their cries for help. Hell could not be worse.'

'No more,' Brien said. 'His prisoners have all been freed and tended to.'

Maud had sent for spiced wine and cakes. The servitor filled their cups. Jacques accepted his quietly.

'What occurred, Jacques?' she said in a quiet voice. 'Can you speak of it?'

Jacques took a deep drink, cleared his throat and spoke: 'I was pounced upon during the great darkness. That was fearful enough, because I thought the Devil had taken me – which, in a way, he had. Of course, from my study of astrology, I understood the moon had temporarily blotted the sun's light, but, before I could ride back to tell my party, a net was thrown over me and I was taken prisoner. I thought of Alice as I was bound and dragged on a hurdle through the forest, through that great blackness, not knowing who had taken me. Lights moved before and behind me. I could see through the grey as the sky began to clear. They had torches and were helmeted. They carried spears and wore bows on their backs. They were fearless of the great dark, so I assumed they were devils. They never spoke.' He paused. 'They . . .'

Maud said, with firmness, 'Jacques, you know that these were no devils or spirits. They worked for a man as evil as Satan himself, and that man is now dead.'

Jacques nodded. 'I know and I suspected it. They took me to Devizes, once the sky properly cleared and the sun returned . . . I was tied and dragged over the countryside on that same hurdle, bound and gagged so I could not speak, until I was thrown into a dank dungeon, where I was chained to a wall. I received no food and tried to lick water running down the wall behind me. After a few days, though I had no real sense of time's passage, my lady, a loaf of stale bread was shoved my way and my hands were untied. This misery continued until Robert Fitz Herbert came and questioned me, threatening to put out my eyes if I lied, holding a dagger below them.'

'And did you . . . lie?' said Brien.

'Yes, I certainly did.' Jacques swallowed. 'It was hard. I clung to the story that I was travelling with the widow of a spice merchant to Marlborough to sell cinnamon and saffron and ginger. And he asked, "What else?" His thugs beat me with the flats of their swords, and then I mentioned the pepper.'

'He believed you?' Maud said.

'He must have, because he removed the knife from my eyes. He somehow knew already that we carried a valuable cargo. I was given a bowl of pottage and, later that day, taken to Marlborough. The rest you know already . . . I was looked after well by Sir John, who had invited Fitz Herbert to dine with him and talk business, and to take charge of the spices in return for my freedom. Sir John's men overpowered Fitz Herbert's guards. There was a sword fight, but Sir John easily won, and the Devil's creature was taken prisoner. He was hanged before the gates of Devizes Castle on Saturday last.'

'A just punishment and a warning to others,' said Maud. She spoke aloud an ill wish she had carried in her heart for days: 'May his soul rot in the hell he deserves. May he suffer all of Satan's tortures. An eye for an eye and a tooth for a tooth.'

Brien stared at her, clearly surprised at the viciousness with which she pronounced those words. She cared not a whit. Her father had been a ruthless king and she had learned from him that, to survive as a ruler, she must be unforgiving too – and decisive. She would not allow her sex to be perceived by men as a weakness. Again, the face of young Alice being attacked at knifepoint by Geoffrey flashed into her mind. Danger from men was everywhere. Women must be strong, fierce and clever to protect themselves. She would be.

She turned to Sir Jacques, altering her tone to speak firmly but pleasantly: 'I am keeping Alice with me. I believe you are fond of her. You may speak with her, but you will be on your best chivalrous behaviour, if you wish to remain my knight and if you intend to woo her.'

Sir Jacques bowed his head and said, 'I thank you, Empress, and I do wish Alice to be mine, if she will have me.'

Maud noticed that his eyes were full of tears. He certainly seemed subdued since he had been imprisoned. She felt a rush of righteousness. For some reason, the quiet, loyal Alice had become a person Maud – who trusted rarely – was fond of. Perhaps this escapade had given Sir Jacques pause, and he would be ready to take care of Alice. Maud hoped he recognised that she had eyes everywhere and that she would ruin him if he hurt Alice.

Unrest throughout England continued. Maud controlled the west and south-west, but, to her increasing chagrin, Stephen held the rest of England in a cruel grip. Women were raped, bandits roamed the forests terrorising ordinary people, abbeys were looted and people went hungry. Waleran, the wavy-haired, hooded-eyed, dreadful Beaumont twin, lost Worcester to Earl Robert and, in turn, he torched Robert's favourite manor of Tewkesbury. People constantly prayed for deliverance. Maud spent hours on her knees, too, in the castle chapel, on chill tiles, counting out prayers on her rose-hued beads, hoping for a victorious yet peaceful resolution.

By Whitsuntide, it was Henry, the wily Bishop of Winchester and papal legate, who sought resolution. He held a peace conference near Bath. Stephen's dreadful Queen represented her husband, and Earl Robert spoke for his sister. Whilst Maud remained behind the walls of Gloucester Castle, she wrote frequently to Bishop Henry, promising that, if she was granted England's queenship, as was her right, she would respect the Church's entitlement to lands and abbeys, ever reminding him:

My father kept peace in the kingdom. Stephen of Blois has permitted chaos to reign throughout England. My people desire and need the peace my father created to be restored. Stephen broke his oath and God is watching. It will please our Lord in Heaven that the false king is doomed.

But nothing was resolved. When Robert returned to Gloucester, Maud met with him in the castle's garden on a day of iris-blue skies, an innocent day that made the world seem so safe. Birds sang in the trees, the sun warmed the earth and the scent of June roses wafted along the gravelled pathways. Corn and barley grew tall in the fields beyond the castle walls, but Robert and Maud were both saddened.

'Queen Matilda and her advisors are intractable. She is a formidable enemy. The Bishop despairs. He has gone to Blois to consult with Count Theobald.' Robert shook his head. 'Stephen's Queen is ruthless.'

'Well, so can I be, if necessary,' Maud said resolutely. She tapped her chin impatiently with her forefinger. 'Bishop Henry must choose his side.'

'Aye, but Stephen is his brother,' Robert reminded her. 'The Bishop owes him family loyalty, distasteful as Stephen's actions towards the Church are.'

'Nonsense, Robert. Stephen broke faith with my father's wishes. Bishop Henry must choose right over wrong.' Feeling tears of frustration fill her eyes, she repeated the word 'Nonsense!' and fled, running from the garden into the small Marian chapel by the entrance. There, burying her face in her hands, she prayed again for the return of her crown.

Robert returned to Bristol, but Count Brien remained with Maud in Gloucester and, in his good company, her mood lightened. They hunted when the weather permitted and continued to read the stories of the siege of Troy and Odysseus' travels to Ithaca, their hands occasionally brushing as they turned a page. Their sparrowhawks, like twins, sat contentedly on perches by the window embrasures in the great chamber, watching them pore over unfurled maps with studious beady eyes. Meanwhile, unrest and strife continued far beyond Gloucester's walls.

June was a beautiful month and, when a fair came to Gloucester for St John's Eve, the castle's passageways rattled with excitement. Maids, pages, cooks, stable lads and others all visited the fair. Maud, too, decided she needed a change of scene. Planning to visit the carnival herself, but wishing to feel free and unrecognised, she chose to be disguised as a local lady. To complete her deception, she persuaded Brien to accompany her as her chaplain, and to have a tonsure shaved. Her idea appealed to his sense of mischief, and so he agreed, but he touched his shaven head and looked at where his dark curls lay on the floor, lamenting, 'Will my curls ever grow again? I shall need a wig, now.'

Maud solemnly shook her head. 'Never, but you still look handsome, my lord cleric.'

As servants, they took Alice and golden-haired Beatrice, with Xander trailing behind them, all carrying baskets. Xander, Maud noticed, had grown moonstruck by the sweet, quiet Beatrice, which, for now, Maud chose to ignore. Xander, she had noted, was ever watching out for Beatrice in corridors and at the bottom of stairways, waylaying her for conversation and causing her to laugh at his jokes.

It was a pleasant relief from the confinement of the castle to wander amongst the booths that offered lengths of fabric, various kinds of pottery, cheap jewellery, needles and threads, metal mirrors, felt hats, filets to secure veils, combs and even holy relics. The smell of fresh gingerbread and meat pies would make anyone's mouth water. They made purchases and soon their baskets were nearly full to the brim.

Eventually, Maud paused before the tray of relics and gently touched a vial of what was being sold as Christ's blood. Mimicking a local accent, she remarked in English, rather than in Norman French, to Brien, 'Father Tomas, I should purchase this relic for my ill husband, do you not think?' She lowered her voice and added, so the Benedictine monk selling the items could not hear, 'The monk looks like a fake. The relic is without doubt a fake too.'

Brien nodded, peered closely at the relic, glanced up and said in a clear voice, with enough gravitas to be very convincing, 'I believe you should consider it, my lady, for Sir Godwin's chapel. But let us think on it.'

Maud wanted to laugh, but choked her chuckle back.

The Benedictine appeared disappointed as Brien guided their group away from the stall. 'It's quite, quite genuine, my lady,' the monk called to her. She ignored him.

When they had walked away some distance, Alice stood on tiptoe, as she was shorter than Maud, and whispered in her ear, 'My lady, for certes, that is the man who betrayed your messenger to Sir John, and I warrant I saw him in Cirencester too. I think he rode to Devizes with information about the spice wagon. He's a spy.'

Overhearing, Brien raised his eyebrows. 'Are you sure, Alice? A spy for Stephen?'

'Yes, maybe, but most likely anywhere he can make trouble and further his own interests – and, as night becomes morning, I am sure.'

'Is he indeed?' Maud nonchalantly fingered a length of silk and moved on towards a collection of hooded goshawks tethered to wooden perches.

Brien, meanwhile, strode back to the relics and purchased the vial of blood. Maud could not hear the exchange, but she suspected Brien was speaking Latin, for the monk just smiled, took Brien's pennies and gave him the relic.

Returning to them, Brien said, 'This will be coloured water. By nightfall, that Benedictine monk will languish in the cells. And he does not understand the Latin tongue.'

It was midday. The Angelus bells sounded from all the churches within the town. No one paid attention and the fair continued. As they were leaving, Maud turned to Xander. 'Give Count Brien that basket. Go back and buy a hat for yourself. Take Alice and Beatrice and allow them to find needles and threads, and find Jacques. Tell him to question the monk.'

Xander chaperoned Beatrice and Alice back through the lanes of stalls, whilst Count Brien escorted Maud through a postern gate that led into the garden. They sat on a stone bench, a basket between them. At first, they did not speak. Maud was tired and happy just to be quiet in his presence.

After a short silence, punctuated by the buzzing of fat bumble-bees, Brien turned to her. 'It was enjoyable today, Maud, but you really should not venture out with only myself as an escort, even if I look like this.' He gestured to his robes and pointed to his head and chin, bursting into a piratical laugh. 'I shaved off my beard to please you.'

She smiled, laid her hand over his and said, 'Brien, you truly are blind today. I had a dozen of my own knights disguised about the place. As for that monk, you will have him in the cells by Vespers. Sir Jacques will take him in with pleasure. Now, let me see that vial he swindled you with.'

Brien opened the small jar, wafted it underneath his long nose, then put his little finger inside and tasted it. 'Coloured water and flour used as thickening.'

Maud laughed. 'One more of Stephen's lackeys for the noose.'

'No, he may well be a real cleric, albeit no speaker of Latin, and you cannot be responsible for his death. We should have Sir Miles try him in the quarterly court and ban him from the county.'

She considered this. Much as she disliked admitting it, Brien was right.

He said quietly, 'No more disguises. No more risk-taking. I would not lose my lady and my Queen.'

There was something in his voice that was neither courtly flirtation nor joking. Maud looked up, unguarded, and her blue eyes met his dark ones. She could not help but gasp – and then he was drawing her into an embrace such as she had never permitted before. He dropped a kiss on her head. 'Ah, my lady – if only.'

He had never before declared his love for her so openly. She pulled back, smiled up at him and, reaching up, touched his shaven pate. 'Who knows what Lady Fate and God will decide?'

He wailed and touched his head. 'Who knows when my locks will grow back? I need a new hat.'

'Granted as a gift – a hat of velvet and silk.'

They kept carefully apart for the next few weeks, but, all the same, Maud was broken-hearted when, a few weeks later, Brien left for Wallingford, his head concealed below his newly padded helmet. It would soon be harvest time and he wanted to make sure all was well. Yet again, Maud lamented that duty to others, to Tilda and Geoffrey, and the pursuit of an inheritance, kept them apart.

Brien suggested Alice and Xander remain with Maud. It was a pleasure for her to see the pure happiness these two enjoyed by singing and playing at her small court. Sir Jacques had fully recovered from his experience of capture. He now wooed Alice openly. At first, Alice appeared withdrawn, but as time passed she was smiling upon Jacques again and Jacques had become as devoted as Maud's affectionate greyhound, simply named Grey, to Alice. His flirtatious manner had grown serious and had focused upon Alice ever since his unpleasant experience in Devizes' dungeon. And Maud had decided that Xander and Beatrice, who was a minor Norman noble's daughter, were clearly meant to wed. *Who would have ever thought me a matchmaker?* she mused, a trifle wistfully. *But then, I was forced to marry someone I could never love.* Maud wanted to help them in particular because she had never been permitted her own choice of lover and her own happiness in marriage, but not yet — not before she regained her kingdom. She sighed her impatience. *When would this be?* Stephen held sway over much of England. He remained King.

Winter 1140

In November, Bishop Henry returned to England from France, without support for Maud anywhere on the continent. Maud, advised again by Robert and Miles, sent him promises that she would restore abbeys that Stephen had demoted. She swore to support England's clergy. But the situation was one of stalemate. Stephen appeared as strong as ever and had retaken Devizes.

As Christmastide approached, Geoffrey wrote her a letter, which reached her via a wine cargo entering Wareham. Their boys were growing up without her. He understood Maud's position, but Henry often spoke of missing her. She folded the letter and thought of gifts she could send her sons. Perhaps swords engraved with their names. English smiths were talented. The best gift of all was impossible, for she could not return to Anjou until her crown and their inheritance was secured. She and Geoffrey disagreed on many things, but on this they were of one mind.

Earl Robert kept Christmastide at his castle in Bristol. He had been so much away from his family and he needed to spend time with Mabel, whom he loved dearly. Maud had declined their invitation to join the revels at Bristol, preferring, she declared, to remain in Gloucester.

Robert hoped the Christmas season would give him a respite from campaigning and allow him to gather his thoughts and strength. He believed Stephen to be keeping his Christmas court either in the Tower or Westminster. Robert's children, his sons William, Hamon, Robert, Richard and Philip, were all with him, which made Christmas a happy family occasion. He spoiled their younger daughter, Anamabel, and enjoyed her light-hearted company. His older daughter, Countess Mathilde, remained with her new husband, Ranulf, in Chester, watching over Ranulf's demesnes. His other two sons were growing up in Anjou and Normandy. In the days approaching Christ's nativity, Robert passed many happy hours in prayer and meditation in his painted chapel, and enjoyed private time with Mabel.

The Christmas Day feast arrived and, by then, he felt restored to his optimistic self. The hall smelled of beeswax candles, spice, holly and mistletoe. The table was laden with Christmas food – delicate salmon in a parsley sauce, roast boar, cured deer meat, huge pastry coffins filled with various fowl, great bowls of peas and newly baked bread. There were cheeses, fruit tarts and saffron cakes, marzipan shaped into fantastical creatures, and dishes of syllabub.

Mabel reached over to him just after he had laughed at a band of colourful and talented tumblers. She took his hand in her own and squeezed it. He responded, enjoying her closeness and the fresh scent of lemon balm, glad most of all that they still enjoyed bed play, even though he was almost fifty and she had, in September, seen her fortieth year.

She whispered into his ear, 'Our sons are growing into very handsome boys, like their sire. And my namesake promises to become a great beauty.'

'Like her mother,' he whispered back, lifting her hand and dropping a kiss onto it. 'We'll be thinking of betrothal for Anamabel soon.'

'I hope he will be more pleasant than Ranulf of Chester –' she tapped his hand with the hilt of her eating knife – 'your choice of husband for our other daughter.'

Robert grimaced, but returned to her with, 'Surely Ranulf is a good match for Mathilde. He has not yet supported either side in the conflict, but he's held firm onto Chester. David of Scotland, Maud's uncle, has had his eye on that castle for years.'

Mabel snorted. 'Ranulf is, for certes, guarding his own best interests, but I don't trust him at all. Mathilde has written of her loneliness and unhappiness.'

'Yes, I know, my love, but it is early days. They've only been married a year. She'll adjust.'

Robert did feel a twinge of concern for his daughter, but he kept this to himself. He turned from Mabel, not wishing to pursue the topic of Ranulf of Chester further, and watched his younger daughter lead a round dance, laughing and enjoying the holiday mood. Had it not been for the war, he would have settled her future already. He watched his daughter's innocent joy as she spun around and raised her hand to encourage her beloved papa to join in the merriment.

'Come on, Mabel,' he said, offering his wife his hand. 'Let's become dancers too.'

'If you insist.' She rose from the table with a pleased smile.

He proudly led her into the carol, feeling the war had drawn far off that night, knowing simple joy at his own hearth.

It had rained heavily for days, but no one had minded. The Yule log ceremony, the mumming, the entertainments accompanying the twelve days of Christmastide, punctuated by solemn masses and perfectly pitched plainsong, had been a distraction from the weather as well as the war.

On the morning of the Feast of Epiphany, Robert and Mabel were passing a quiet hour in their bedchamber above the hall, when an insistent knocking against their door caused Mabel to start, a pile of silken ribbons sliding to her feet.

'Who's there?' Robert called out, slightly irritated because they had requested no interruptions.

'It is I, with a messenger, Papa,' William, their eldest, shouted through the door. His insistent tone did not bode well.

167

'Enter,' Robert said, setting aside a small silver box that he had decided would be a gift for Anamabel.

William pushed a messenger wearing a sodden mantle forward, saying, 'He's come all the way from Chester, riding hard through the night.'

The courier's cloak dripped puddles onto the floor straw. 'By Christ,' Robert said. 'Look at you – drenched as if battling Noah's Flood. Spit out your message, lad, and then get to the kitchen for a dish of broth and a warm hearth.'

Mabel clutched at her piece of glittering embroidery, a gift for a bishop.

'Sire, my lord, my lady, the King has besieged Lincoln Castle.'

Robert turned to Mabel and saw shock in her eyes. Lincoln was a great distance from Chester Castle. What, by Christ's cods, was this about?

'It is held by Lord Ranulf of Chester's brother, William of Roumare, the Earl of Lincoln.' The young man paused, drew a wheezing breath and continued, 'My Lord of Chester and his brother seized it from the King's garrison whilst the King was in London and the castle was guarded by a garrison and the castle's castellan. Earl William claims the King has no right to Lincoln's castle. With only a garrison and castellan, he saw an opportunity to capture Lincoln's great castle for himself.'

'How by the rood did they manage to capture it?' Robert asked. This was curious. Surely Stephen's garrison would not hand Lincoln to Earl William and Earl Ranulf without a fight.

'My lord, they sent their wives in under a pretext of a friendly Christmastide visit with the castellan's lady. It was Lord Ranulf who arrived with three attendants to escort the ladies home from their visit. No suspicion was aroused until he and his attendants seized what weapons they could and, as planned, William of Roumare burst in with a large company of armed knights. That is how they both took total control of the castle and of Lincoln city too. They drove out all the castle guards.'

Robert raised his fists to his head in frustration. Stephen would not let any attack on Lincoln pass. 'Go on,' he said, dropping his hands to his sides again.

'It's the King's city, so the citizens of Lincoln sent to the King for help, and King Stephen came to Lincoln with a great force. My Lord Ranulf escaped and is now in Chester. His brother, Earl William, and both their wives are besieged in the castle. Lord Ranulf sent me to say to you, he swears fealty to the Empress. In return, he begs you help him, because he is raising a host to fight the King and free his wife, who is still within Lincoln Castle.'

Mabel hastily rose to her feet, the embroidery sliding to the floor, splashes of colour bright against the green reeds. She drew a deep breath and gasped, 'You mean Stephen is besieging my daughter in Lincoln Castle and her husband has left her there, trapped, alone?' Her tone was one of disbelief.

'Yes, my lady.'

'Go,' Robert ordered the messenger, before Mabel gave vent to her anger. 'William, take the lad to the kitchens. Tell the maids to find food and warm clothing for him . . . and a bath.' Robert wrinkled his nose. He turned to Mabel and said, 'We *will* raise troops and join with Ranulf. Stephen will not dare to harm a hair on my daughter's head.' He spoke again as the lad reached the door: 'And you will return to Chester on the morrow with our promise of support. But first, tell him, he must take an oath of loyalty to the Empress.' Turning back to his stunned wife, he said, 'We'll fight Stephen. Ranulf will raise troops and come to Gloucester. I'll call up a muster, along with Sir Miles, Count Brien and the others.' He felt his shoulders tighten. 'This will be the end for Stephen. Mabel, rest assured, it will be the false king's end, because . . . because . . . God is on our side, the side of right.'

She shook her head and wept, saying, 'God abandoned us when he allowed my daughter to be a prisoner in Lincoln Castle.'

Robert embraced her and gentled her until she had wept her fill. Then he said quietly, 'I shall stay for the feast, but tomorrow I must ride to Gloucester.'

'I know,' she said, her voice fracturing. She was fearful and her heart was breaking.

The Feast of Epiphany passed in a sober manner, in sad contrast to Christmas. Robert and Mabel retired early, but Mabel passed much of the night on her knees before a Madonna shrine in their chamber. Just before dawn, Robert felt her climb into bed beside him and fall into a deep sleep.

As dawn broke, Earl Robert rose, kissed Mabel's brow and, after a whispered farewell, left Bristol to ride for Gloucester with a large troop, ready to continue the war and rescue his child.

'I promise you, I will bring our Mathilde home,' were his last words to Mabel.

Chapter Thirteen

Lincoln
February 1141

A milky dawn greeted the second day of February, Candlemas, as Earl Robert sat erect on his white charger, contemplating the tight crossing over the Witham, a tributary of the River Trent, outside Lincoln.

'We'll try further along the river. You can see this ford is far too narrow for our army,' he said to Miles, and turned his stallion about.

Miles nodded his agreement and raised an arm to indicate their troops must follow.

Maud had remained in Gloucester whilst Robert raised the troops. As her brother advised, she had pragmatically accepted Ranulf's declaration of loyalty. They gathered their forces and, by the end of January, Maud's armies were ready. As well as those serving Miles and Robert of Gloucester, a number of knights disinherited by Stephen wheeled east towards Lincoln, gathering pace like winter storms threatening the horizon. Their numbers were further augmented by fierce Welsh allies.

Maud had been active in greeting the commanders and encouraging the troops as they mustered, and she grew as steely and determined as if she were actively leading them to battle herself.

'Robert,' she asked, again and again, her face stony and her stance restless, 'cannot I ride forth as well?'

'No, Maud,' he would say, with incredible patience. 'Your hopes will stand or fall on our actions. You must remain here to keep control of the west. We need to set out with all haste. Can't you see the dangers of a mid-winter campaign? We will not risk your safety on the Fosse road, where it will be raining and muddy and bitterly cold. There will be a battle –' he banged his fist on the arms of his chair – 'and, if we lost you, your son's inheritance would be gone in the flicker of a candle.'

'So, I'm like a queen on a chessboard.'

'You are safer in position here,' Robert countered firmly. 'Let us keep it that way.'

She moodily saw the sense of his words. 'Stay safe yourselves and God go with you,' she said, with reluctance, to Miles and Robert, as they rode away from Gloucester, their banners raised proudly above their armies as a steady rain fell.

Now, Robert was aware of danger from arrow fire from within the city, if crossing the river was too slow, so he found a better fording place half a mile away. Unfortunately, the opposite bank was guarded.

He turned to Miles and Ranulf, who trotted behind him, and called over his shoulder, 'If we get across the river fast enough, Stephen will be trapped between us and the castle.'

'He'll try to break out of the town walls if we attack, or he might just withdraw,' Count Brien said, bringing his horse alongside the others.

'I think he'll stay and fight,' Miles said, shifting his weight on the saddle. 'His father was called a coward when he retreated from Antioch during the Holy Crusade. He won't risk being named likewise.'

'Like father, like son, eh?' Ranulf grunted. The Earl of Chester was a lean, wiry young man, not yet out of his twenties, courageous without doubt, but possessing an arrogance which Robert was beginning to find irksome. His gingery eyebrows seemed to meet over pale blue eyes, and he had a nasty habit of bullying his horse, unnecessarily applying the whip when he was irritated, which was often. Ranulf had persistently complained that they were not moving fast enough. He complained about the weather. When they stopped to eat, he grumbled that the food was cold. No one else protested in this annoying manner; they were hardened soldiers and used to privation. By the time they reached the Trent, Robert was beginning to think Mabel had a point. Ranulf was shifty (though charming enough to Empress Maud), and he was petulant when faced with difficulty. Even so, he wielded power in the north and was an able warrior, so Robert tried to show tolerance towards his daughter's husband. However, Count Brien appeared to dislike the young man intensely. He studied Ranulf for a moment with a look of disdain in his dark eyes, and looked away without speaking.

'Stephen will not want to be trapped inside the city's narrow streets,' Miles said, moving back to strategy. 'He will move his troops onto open land.'

'You are right,' Brien said. 'He will. If I were Stephen, I would.'

'But now,' said Robert, removing his helmet and scratching his bare head, 'we have to make the crossing, and quickly.' He spun his stallion around, glancing at the vast host waiting for guidance behind them. He swung off his mount and walked the stallion along the riverbank for a while, all the time watching the swelling water and the ford. He made a final decision and called the commanders and a group of his bravest, most agile knights forward. Once they had gathered, he laid out his plan. He told Ranulf that the men under his command should cross the ford once Robert made it safe. Miles and Brien could cross through the shallows further along the river. They must move with speed.

Robert led the way without hesitation, guiding his horse with encouraging murmurs, stepping into the freezing water. He aimed to disable the guards on the opposite bank and allow as many horsemen and infantry over the bridge as realistically possible. The rest could wade through the watery shallows further downstream.

A trusted group of his own men followed him, splashing into the river upstream from the bridge. With a low mist hovering on the water, partially concealing them from any archers, it only took moments to cross, and they were soon overpowering Stephen's guard. Once they took control of the ford, the knights and infantry under the command of Brien and Miles followed. Ranulf, his troop and the Welshmen, who were mostly on foot, crossed over the bridge.

By noon, the two armies had drawn up on open ground outside Lincoln. Followed by Robert, Ranulf rode to the front, before a low hill, and addressed his father-in-law and the host, saying, 'To you, invincible leader, and to you, my noble comrades in arms, I render thanks from the bottom of my heart, for you have generously demonstrated that you will risk your own lives for love of me. So, since I am the cause of your peril, it is right I should put myself in danger first and be the first to strike out at the line of a treacherous king who has broken his peace after a truce had been allowed. I shall now split open the royal squadron and prepare my way through the midst of the enemy with my sword . . .'

Robert, who had been listening intently, thought to himself, This is bravado, not strategy. He waited until Ranulf had finished and climbed the knoll, so he stood above him. Raising his sword, he began to speak to the army, looking down at Ranulf first:

'It is right, my lord, that you should demand the honour of striking the first blow, both on account of your noble blood and because of your exceptional valour.' He paused before continuing, 'But I am not to be surpassed, because I am the son and the grandson of two most noble kings. As on grounds of valour –' at this, Robert indicated the troops with a wave of his sword – 'there are many excellent men here whose prowess cannot be outstripped. Yet, I am driven by a different motive. King Stephen has cruelly usurped the realm, contrary to the oaths given to my sister. By throwing everything into disorder, he is the direct cause of the deaths of many thousands . . . He has plundered those who are in rightful possession by law of lands in England.'

At that, a great cheer rose up.

Robert realised he must also deliver a warning. There could be no easy retreat through the marshlands they had just crossed. They would have to fight their way into the city. Momentarily, the sun shone into his eyes and he closed them against the blinding light.

After a cloud passed over the sun and the moment had passed, he looked heavenwards and raised his sword again. 'God will aid our victory,' he declared loudly, convinced that the Lord was on the side of right and theirs *was* the side of right. He finished by saying, 'Waleran of Meulan is a trickster; Hugh Bigot is an oath-breaker, liar and perjurer; the Count of Aumale, William le Gros, is so lecherous that his wife has left him; Simon of Northampton is a braggart; William of Ypres is treacherous, filthy, obscene, evil. And, as for King Stephen, he has grown fat on murder.' He drew breath. 'All of them are tainted with perjury!' Robert folded his arms and waited. Even his son-in-law looked at him with admiration in his pale blue eyes.

There was a blood-curdling cry. Hands were raised to Heaven, to a sky cleared of mist, where fast-moving scudding clouds were crossing over the pale winter sun. The knights buckled themselves into their chain mail and Robert reorganised their lines. Totally in overall command, he placed himself centrally with his knights, beckoning to Count Brien.

'Brien, soldiering is not your best talent, but you are courageous and a fine tactician. Stay close to me and you will survive to charge another day. That is to be your tactic today. No heroics. Let survival be your motto.' Robert did not allow Brien time to respond. On this battlefield, his word would be law. Following Robert's speech, Ranulf did not argue either, and, as instructed, he moved to the right, whilst Miles drew up the disinherited knights under his leadership. Robert moved the Welsh infantry in front. As he gazed up the slope, he realised Stephen had arrived in Lincoln expecting a siege, not a battle. The enemy were apparently short of cavalry.

He saw the fair-haired Stephen on his stallion, in a central position, with a mounted force of earls, and to the right he was sure he recognised the detestable Waleran by the manner in which he leaned over his favoured white stallion. He spotted William de Warenne too, but there were others whom, from a distance, he could not easily identify. What he did notice was that the knights around Waleran appeared to be arguing. As the enemy began to charge down the hill, it became apparent that no single commander on either wing had taken control. They will not make quick decisions, he realised. His eyes scrutinised their right flank, where Flemish and Breton soldiers, William of Ypres and Count Alain of Richmond were moving swiftly towards his Welshmen. William of Ypres attacked their Welsh infantry, mowing them down within heartbeats. Others of the Welsh survived and dispersed, but, as they fled, Count Alain and William of Ypres chased them towards the marshes.

'Stay in place!' Robert yelled out, glancing towards Ranulf, hoping he did as he was ordered.

Robert signalled to his own cavalry to charge forward. Moments later, they were engaged with Stephen's. For a time, he and Brien cut their way through Stephen's ranks. When they gained a brief respite, it was to watch Alain of Richmond and William of Ypres fleeing the field amongst their troops. Robert sent up a brief prayer: 'Thank you, Lord. We may yet win the day.'

Stephen himself was still fighting bravely, but Robert could not reach the King because he and Brien were again surrounded by the enemy cavalry. They fought like devils, back-to-back, their mounts snorting whilst, all around, sparks were leaping from the clash of helmets and the crash of swords. He heard the fearful hissing of arrows coming from the direction of the city walls, and, briefly glancing up, he saw they were being fired by ordinary citizens from the parapets. Shouts echoed around the field, and the battle grew fiercer.

Stephen stood on the field with a small number of knights, even as the ground emptied around him and his knights were being unhorsed and captured by Robert's men. Lone horses were wildly racing around the field chaotically. Stephen was brandishing an axe, having lost his sword as well as his mount.

'Charge!' Robert yelled to his cavalry. He could not help admiring the King's courage. He was like a lion, wielding that axe. Robert's knights fought their way closer to him. Robert heard a great thump and a clang resound through the air as a stone whizzed past, as if from nowhere. It felled the King. Robert urged his horse further into the melee, but, before he reached Stephen, there was a shout.

'Here, everyone! Here! I have the King!'

Stephen was being helped to his feet by a tall knight, whom Robert recognised as William de Chaigues, one of his own household knights. Immediately, Robert shouted to him, 'Do not harm the King!' He rode up to the stunned Stephen, gently removed his helmet and said, 'My lord, the fight is over. Cousin, you are my prisoner.'

Stephen raised his head, glared at him and said, 'For now, it appears that I am, Earl Robert. But time will tell.' He looked defeated, thin and tired, but at the same time he retained a dismissive, somewhat arrogant bearing that cried *I am your King*. His pale blue eyes spoke the words he did not say: *You betrayed me once and you will regret this day.*

Robert escorted his prisoner up the hill to the castle, accompanied by a heavy guard and followed by his troops, who prodded their prisoners forward at the tips of bloodied swords. Stephen was helped onto a gentle mount, a brown palfrey. Robert himself led the King into the castle precinct, saying, 'You will be well accommodated until you are recovered, my lord, and then we shall escort you to Gloucester.'

'You'll send word to the Queen in Windsor that I am alive?' was Stephen's surly response.

Robert mumbled agreement and ensured that Stephen was given a fine apartment, where he was to be permitted a few days of rest. He also sent a surgeon to tend Stephen's aching head, and a maid with a brew of poppies to help him sleep. Only then did he seek out his daughter.

Mathilde was being cossetted by her husband. Long may Ranulf's contrition last, thought Robert to himself. Yet Mathilde did not appear to be reassured by her husband's concern. And why should she be? Robert mused. Ranulf had used her to get inside the castle, and, once Stephen arrived, he had abandoned her to a siege.

Her expression became aghast as cries and screams penetrated the castle walls. Ranulf had let loose his wolves as soon as victory had been declared, in punishment for Lincoln's appeal to Stephen. Its citizens were now paying a bloody price.

Mathilde wept, on seeing her father. 'I begged mercy for them. Papa, stop this revenge. It is too cruel.'

Robert held her within his arms and wiped away her tears with his fist. 'This is war, my sweet lass. The people brought Stephen here to Lincoln and fired on us from the city walls. Now, they are paying the price.'

When Mathilde grew calmer, she withdrew to the bower hall with her maids.

Robert spoke firmly to Ranulf: 'The bloodshed around the town must cease. Mathilde is distressed, and no wonder.' He folded his arms across his surcoat, still bloodied from the battle. For a moment, he waited. When Ranulf did not answer him, he continued: 'With your good will, I think my daughter should pass a month or so with her mother. I'll send Mathilde back to Chester after Eastertide.'

Ranulf scowled, but said, 'If you insist, Earl Robert . . . I suppose, now, the Empress will be crowned Queen?'

'We'll see. God willing.' Robert took the great chair on the dais. Ranulf took another, and Robert elaborated: 'There must be further discussion with the Bishop of Winchester. I shall escort our royal prisoner to Gloucester personally. No harm must befall him, Ranulf. Stephen is an anointed king. I shall suggest he is incarcerated in Bristol Castle.' He grinned. 'Ironic, since that was Duke Robert of Normandy's prison.'

'But it was an honourable imprisonment,' Robert added, in a quieter voice. 'Stephen will also be kept honourably.'

Ranulf raked a hand through his reddish hair. 'I shall travel with you to Gloucester and on to Chester. Mathilde may remain with her mother throughout Lent. My brother will keep the peace here, in Lincoln . . . and restore order. The prisoners' ransoms will swell the Empress's coffers . . . and my brother's too. He can rebuild Lincoln.'

'Agreed, but you will order a stop to the mayhem and murder out there forthwith.'

Ranulf inclined his head. 'I can but try . . . We did well this day, Earl Robert,' the young man said, and left the room.

Scratching his head, Robert wondered if Ranulf would remain loyal to the Empress. No matter what passed, his son-in-law would never use his daughter as a part of his scheming again. He rose wearily to seek a private chamber and bathe, for his limbs ached, and his cuts and bruises stung. It had been a brutal day.

Chapter Fourteen

Gloucester
Late February 1141

The February day was chill and bright. Empress Maud glided around the scriptorium, pausing to warm her hands at one of the many braziers set about Gloucester Abbey's long upper room. As she looked over the shoulders of the diligent monks, she marvelled that the scribes could work in such bitterly cold conditions. Huddled in their robes, shivering over their work, they wore fingerless mittens. It was so frosty outside and so chilly in the room, she wondered why the inks they used did not freeze.

Warming her hands over the glowing coals, her sharp eyes noticed ink pots placed on a stand close to the hot charcoal braziers, and she realised that was why the colours the monks needed for their illustrations remained fluid on such bitter mornings. Soothed by the brazier's heat, she stood behind a monk who was adding a little mouse pursued by a black cat up a letter *M*. His work was so delicate and engrossing that he was unaware of her scrutiny.

Maud had come to the scriptorium to collect a book of verse detailing the fight between Achilles and Hector during the Trojan War, a small codex which the monks had worked on for months. She intended it as a name-day gift for Count Brien – a necessary distraction from the never-ending wait for news from Lincoln. Why had she received no intelligence of the campaign's success, or even its failure, which she scarcely dared to contemplate? The rains had stopped. Days were crisp, if cold, and nights were frosty, but a messenger might still take a week to ride between Lincoln and Gloucester. She bit her lip. Patience was not her virtue, alas.

She stood still, listening to the sweep of her ladies' cloaks on the scriptorium's tiled floors, a blackbird singing outside and the constant scratching of pens on parchment. Lost in thought, Maud did not at first feel a gentle touch on her arm.

'Madame.'

She started and turned around. The Abbot of Gloucester Abbey was hovering by her side. Gilbert Foley was a serious young man, tall, with a sandy tonsure and brown eyes as soft as the treacle sweets she liked to eat.

He leaned down and whispered to her, 'My lady, you have visitors.'

Maud glanced around, expecting to see them here, within the long workroom.

'No, my lady,' the gentle young Abbot said, a smile curling about his lips. 'They are not here, but they are waiting for you in the Abbot's house . . . I think you must come at once.'

Since conversation was not permitted in the scriptorium, she summoned her ladies with a wave of her hand. They were gathered around a handsome young monk, who was enjoying their attention. He smiled when the women left his desk and hurried to the Empress's side.

Her household knights were waiting outside the scriptorium, and, once Abbot Gilbert, Maud and her ladies had left the workroom and were standing under the gable protecting the outer staircase, they came to take up position behind her. She gathered her fur-lined mantle closer against the chill and said to the Abbot, 'Now speak, Abbot Gilbert. Tell me who awaits me in your hall.'

'It is Count Brien and Earl Robert, who have returned from Lincoln – with another.'

Though her heart leapt at this news, she was quick to hear diffidence in Abbot Gilbert's voice and an irksome reluctance to say more. Surely they had not faced defeat?

'They are safely returned to us?' she asked eagerly. 'And another, you say? Who is this other?'

The Abbot spoke in a hushed voice: 'I was told to escort you to the hall. I dare not say more, Empress.'

'Count Brien and Earl Robert are well?' She tried another tack to loosen the reluctant Abbot's tongue.

'Most well, my lady. Please, come with me. All will be revealed.'

Glancing down, Maud gathered up the hem of her green wool cloak. Bordered with golden braid and lined with ermine, it complemented the purple gown, edged with embroidered lions. Her head was adorned with a favourite gold filet, her silk veil falling in pleats from her intricately plaited hair. She preened a little, considering that she looked every inch the Empress, a true Queen of the Romans, more than ready to receive her returning warriors.

Maud raised her head as she entered the Abbot's small private hall. Her guard posted themselves around the walls, though Sir Jacques, now a captain, followed with her three attendant ladies to stand to attention behind her. A sunbeam struck through the glazed window, momentarily blinding her. Two men were dropping to their knees. Hazily, her eyes made myopic by the sunbeam, she saw a third man being pulled onto his knees by one of the others. This figure appeared stiff and awkward.

A gasp from Sir Jacques was followed by a collective intake of breath from her ladies. As the sun vanished and her sight cleared, Maud saw what she was meant to see. A cry caught in her throat, but she stifled it and immediately drew herself even more upright, her head higher than ever on her elegant neck.

'Rise,' she said, in an imperious tone, to Brien and Robert. She then turned her attention to the third man crouched before her, and, raising a long slim hand, she pointed down at him. 'Stephen, you will await your fate at my leisure.'

The cousin whom she had glimpsed from the walls of Arundel Castle, and whom she remembered as handsome, now had grey shooting through his hair. He was tired, unshaven, and clad in homespun garments – hardly the rich garb of a king. Despite the surprise, she grasped the situation within a heartbeat. This was a downcast and defeated man.

As Robert and Brien rose to their feet and he remained kneeling, Stephen lifted his head and spoke in a hoarse voice: 'As you wish, Cousin Maud.' He cleared his throat. 'Not quite the greeting an anointed king expects.'

'A king!' She snorted with disdain. Her heart was thumping with excitement, a rush filling her veins. She would not refrain from treating him as he deserved. She glanced at Robert and Brien. 'This self-styled prince is my prisoner, and it is in my gift to decide whether he lives or dies.'

'Maud,' Robert said, cautiously, 'I believe your council will decide. But, for now, Stephen of Blois is indeed a prisoner.'

She addressed Abbot Gilbert, who was hovering by her side: 'Have the prisoner confined in your antechamber, behind a stout and locked door, whilst I speak with my brother and the Count.' She turned her back on the kneeling man and snapped her fingers at the knights standing around the walls. 'You, you and you – take him. He is to be watched every moment, even when he drinks, when he eats, sleeps and pisses. To converse further today would insult my father's memory, which my cousin has so unlawfully defiled.' She turned on the Abbot, who seemed stunned into immobility by her vehemence. 'Go, now!' she ordered. 'Do as I request. And send servants with refreshments for us.'

'Maud,' Robert said softly, 'you will be Queen as our father decreed, but please exercise a little kindness towards our cousin. He must eat too.'

She inclined her head in reluctant acknowledgement of his intervention, but did not speak. Stephen had purloined her crown and he could starve, for all she cared.

The Abbot stretched out a hand to Stephen and helped him to his feet. It seemed to Maud that the warlike, bold and brash Stephen was already much humbled, for he shuffled after the Abbot like an old man. Her knights dutifully followed.

Robert called after them, 'Abbot Gilbert – ale, bread and cheese for the prisoner, if you please. We shall be some time with my lady.'

The Abbot nodded, unlocked the door with a large key hanging from his belt and, opening it, stood aside for Stephen to enter his own private chamber.

Stephen glanced at her and, in that moment, Maud noted a terrible sadness in his watery sea-green eyes. She steeled herself not to feel pity for him and, turning her back again, walked to the window, its glass near enough the shade of her cousin's eyes. She stared down into the abbey courtyard, which was heaving with soldiers, heavily armed and clad in chain mail. All about them, horses were snorting and stamping, the steam of their breath rising up into the frosty air in white puffs. Her sense of elation mounted. These brave men had won her a crown, thanks to Robert's unswerving loyalty, his strategies and military prowess. With God's blessing, her father's will could be done at last. Yet, she well knew, if she was to be a queen in a world accustomed to kings, she must harden her heart.

She spun around on her heels, drew a deep breath and addressed Robert in a voice as sharp and clear as a monastery bell: 'Did you not think to send forward a messenger to tell me of Stephen's capture? I cannot help but wonder at your oversight.' It was an unfair remark, but she needed to show her position.

Robert approached with his hands outstretched, his tone verging on the impatient: 'Peace, Maud. We did not want word of our royal prisoner spread about the countryside, nor to run the risk of any rescue attempt.'

Maud's eyes flashed at the word 'royal' and Robert paused, adjusting to her mood.

'We travelled with haste; now we are on your own lands with Stephen in Gloucester, secrecy matters less. The world can know who our prisoners are. But – please may we all be seated, Maud? There is much to say.'

She nodded, realising belatedly that she must seem ungrateful. They sat in chairs by the long hearth, without speaking. Within moments, refreshments arrived, ale was poured, the atmosphere lightened and Brien, who had been silent since Maud had entered the chamber, caught her eye and smiled.

'Tell me all,' she said to Robert, her tone considerably less imperious. 'You have accomplished much and I am truly grateful. You have won me my throne, and here you are to recount the tale. I dearly wish to hear it.' She looked from Robert to Brien and back again, and asked, her forehead creased with concern, 'But I do not see Miles. Is he safe?'

'Our bear is well and hearty . . . if tired,' replied Robert. He began to describe the battle, and how Stephen was taken, adding that Stephen had shown great courage.

Brien grinned and added his own description of the battle. 'We lost many brave Welshmen from our front lines,' he said. 'Our cavalry was stronger than Stephen's and we were better disciplined.'

'I hope you do not now expect me to feel sorry for the usurper or that she-wolf of a woman whom my father married him to,' Maud said, unable to restrain her sense of injustice any longer.

'No, Maud,' Robert said, and took a gulp from his tankard. 'We must protect him, particularly from those dispossessed earls whose lands he redistributed to his own supporters. It would not be seemly for you to allow harm to come to an anointed king. The Church could object. Your father kept his brother in honourable confinement for twenty years, and safe. The important thing is to ensure your right to the throne, as your father determined.'

Maud sipped her own ale. 'I am listening. How? Stephen will still have supporters and I enemies.'

'It can be done with the Church's help. First, we must consult with Bishop Henry of Winchester and the clergy, and we must convince those barons who supported Stephen of the legality and justice of your claim to rule.'

Maud drummed her fingers restlessly on the arm of her chair. It was irksome that, following a great victory, the old arguments were being repeated and dissenting barons must be persuaded that she was their rightful Queen. She *was* able to rule, and had already done so, as an Empress of the Holy Roman Empire. Assuring them of her capability would be a challenge, but one she would steel herself to meet without hesitation.

Brien added, 'There will also be the problem of Normandy.

Geoffrey will have more conquering to do . . . and that of English hearts and minds also.'

'He is an experienced warrior,' Maud said, though her tone was chilly. She still found Geoffrey's infidelities difficult to countenance, all the more so because she was obliged to remain a loyal wife to him — outwardly, at least. If she was unfaithful to Geoffrey, she would be condemned by the very Church she needed to win to her side. 'Geoffrey is more than able and he will be thinking of our sons' inheritance.'

'But,' Brien added, 'the barons and clergy must all understand the oaths they took to support you were binding oaths. Everything that belonged to King Henry is, by right, owed to you, his daughter, as you were born in lawful matrimony.'

At these words, Maud noticed that Robert lowered his head. He was the son of a king's mistress, though he had always been treated as a prince by her father.

Looking up again, Robert said, 'It is, as we all know well, written in the Book of Numbers, in the very last chapter, that daughters have a right to succeed to their fathers' estates if there be no sons. But it may seem to some that the weakness of a woman's sex prevents a daughter from entering into the inheritance bequeathed by her father.'

'That is nonsense!' replied Maud, scornfully. 'Weakness, indeed! I have already been both a queen and an empress.'

'Nonsense to your mind, yes,' Robert continued, 'but many think it. The Lord, when asked, promulgated a law that everything the father possessed should pass to the daughters of Zelophehad, and they might go where they wished.'

'Indeed,' Brien added.

They did not mention another verse stating that daughters should not marry outside their tribe, which she had done. Geoffrey was a kinsman, though they had sought papal dispensation for their marriage to be valid.

Robert said, 'In natural law, in man no less than animals, there is closer love for a daughter than a nephew.' He glanced over at the door behind which Stephen was confined.

The Abbot, who had returned to them in time to overhear their debate, ventured to say, 'All is written in scripture as recounted by Count Brien, and, my lady, you never disobeyed your father. You carried out the duties of imperial rule virtuously and piously until your husband's death, and you responded to your father's summons. You returned to him from German lands. You obeyed King Henry also when you took a second husband, whom we all believe to be brave and resolute.'

Geoffrey might be courageous, but he was also arrogant and controlling, Maud frowningly reflected. When she was Queen, she would obey no man, nor display any weakness.

The Abbot was coming to a conclusion: 'Indeed, my lady, there is no just reason for you to have been disinherited by Stephen, your cousin, that sorry creature,' he said, pointing a long finger at the door.

'I shall hold Stephen prisoner in Bristol. He will recognise Maud's right to the throne, and he will vacate it,' said Robert. 'And I shall request a meeting with Bishop Henry. He may be Stephen's brother, but he's too canny to stay on Stephen's side.'

Abbot Gilbert added, 'In turn, I shall speak with the clergy I know and we'll write to Archbishop Theobald of Canterbury.'

'Archbishop Theobald is from my favourite abbey, that of Bec,' Maud remarked brightly. Expelling a breath, her shoulders drooped slightly. 'Yet I suspect Theobald's loyalty to an anointed king will prevent him from declaring for me. Stephen must agree to ensure that Archbishop Theobald acknowledges my claim.'

Robert reached out and placed his hand over Maud's. 'Stephen will, I assure you. I shall ask Bishop Henry to put pressure on him, on Archbishop Theobald and on all the magnates who have championed Stephen of Blois.'

'And, if Bishop Henry gives me his support,' Maud replied, 'I shall be grateful for it.'

A new era was about to open in her life. The queen had taken the king from the chessboard.

Chapter Fifteen

Winchester and Oxford

Maud, accompanied by Brien, Miles and Robert, the Abbot of Gloucester and her numerous supporters, rode out of Gloucester towards Wherwell, where she was to meet with Bishop Henry, the papal legate.

Robert reminded her, 'Bishop Henry is the one key supporter you need for the Pope, who has previously recognised Stephen as King, to accept you as rightful Queen. His influence on the Vatican is crucial. He will influence England's bishops too. Our meeting with Bishop Henry will be a prelude to your reception in Winchester by the most important of England's bishops and abbots. Please, Maud, be forgiving that he is Stephen's brother. Remember how he brought you from Arundel to Bath.'

'Only because he thought I was better kept there than in London, where Stephen could box us in.'

'Perhaps, but he did think Stephen treated the bishops without respect.'

She shook her reins impatiently. Bishop Henry, necessary as he was to her success, was a two-faced snake.

The priory where the meeting was to be held was surrounded by woods. Maud's cavalcade rode under trees that were dripping rain; it was a day which felt worryingly ominous, though her spirits refused to be dampened. Followed by Bella, a recently acquired sleek greyhound, Maud entered the priory hall to be greeted by Bishop Henry himself. The Prioress led the noble party into the refectory, where a fine dinner was set out. The mild aroma of fishes in various sauces was overwhelmed by the scent of wet wool. A hint of incense clung to Bishop Henry's fine gown, which was richly embroidered with Madonnas and angels. It was, moreover, edged with golden threads, causing his expensive garments to shine in the candlelight. Maud wished she had worn an embellished gown herself. Still, her green wool riding dress was more comfortable for a ride through sodden lanes.

If ice was to be cracked over the Bishop's support for his imprisoned brother, it was more likely to be done over Lenten fish with a sauce of almonds, a fine pease pudding spiced with pepper, followed by saffron cakes and apple tarts. The Bishop appreciated a good board. He was distant but deferential towards Maud and her brother, though keenly aware of his exalted position as papal legate, referring frequently to the eminent bishops he knew in the Pope's curia. Even so, Bishop Henry and Robert seemed to be on friendly terms. After dinner, they strolled along the covered walkways, side by side.

Though outwardly civil, Maud did not warm towards Bishop Henry during the dinner. Instead, she directed her attention to the Prioress, an elegant woman, with whom she had mutual acquaintances. When she accompanied Maud to the antechamber door after dinner, the Prioress said, 'My lady, I must attend prayers now. You will have your flock, just as I have mine, and you will, by God's grace, manage them well.' She inclined her head and departed with a serene smile.

Once they were seated around the priory conference table, the Bishop initiated a discussion about how a future, with Maud ruling instead of his brother Stephen, could be envisioned.

'Firstly, I am relieved to know that my brother is not harshly imprisoned, but rather is kept in comfortable circumstances, watched over by Lady Mabel, whose ancient noble family I have great respect for. I trust my brother will remain in good health.'

Robert inclined his head, acknowledging the compliment to his wife. 'Indeed, he has enough freedom to move around his apartment and visit the gardens for fresh air and exercise,' Robert said.

Bishop Henry steepled his fingers beneath his chin and wasted no more time on pleasantries. He came straight to the point, addressing Maud: 'I acknowledge that your father wished you to inherit, but you were not quick to claim the throne. Many powerful men supported my brother, Stephen of Blois. The great nobles were becoming restless and there was a danger that England would fall into a state of strife. Your father had ruled with an iron fist.' He sighed. 'But, alas, Stephen promised much and delivered little. He favoured his own supporters, alienating those whom he dispossessed.' His smooth tone hardened. 'Worse still, my brother attacked the clergy, especially Bishop Roger of Salisbury, in a most unacceptable and wicked manner. Stephen attempted to undermine the very authority of our Church. This much you know.' Henry sat back in his great armed chair, and Maud was aware that his limpid gaze was deceptive; he was observing her closely. There was a pause. 'And now you have imprisoned my brother,' he said, repeating the obvious.

'He is kept honourably in Bristol Castle and, as you mentioned yourself, my lord Bishop, the noble Lady Mabel has charge of his custody.'

At that, the Bishop raised a sandy eyebrow. 'Well, it does appear that women these days are much raised up into positions of authority.'

Maud forced herself not to bristle, but her fingers tightened on her armrests. She replied calmly, 'We are competent rulers too, as you must know from the example of Melisande of Jerusalem, married to my husband's father. She rules; he is her consort.'

'Of course, but she takes the advice of men, especially her prelates, so I hear tell.'

'As I hope you would advise me,' said Maud, demurely.

Bishop Henry glanced heavenward and opened up his hands, as if giving a blessing. 'I believe God has approved your rule, else my brother would not be your prisoner.' He folded his hands again and leaned forward. 'I suggest you are known as "Lady of the English" or "Lady of England" until you are crowned. It would not bode well to have two Queen Matildas in the land. As you know, Matilda of

Boulogne resides in Kent, which she holds firm. I doubt she will acknowledge you as Queen, Empress Maud. As time passes and you win London over, we shall see what ensues.'

With Matilda of Boulogne loose in the kingdom, creating mischief in Kent, there could be further difficulty. Stephen might be generous, but Matilda of Boulogne was a she-wolf. The sooner that woman was exiled from the kingdom along with their children, the safer Maud's grip on England's crown would be. There was not enough room on one throne for two queens.

Maud had never liked Bishop Henry. He possessed a silken tongue, but it was that of a serpent. Also, she could not forget that, in supporting his brother as King, he had broken his oath to her father.

'Well, my Lady of England,' he continued, 'and my lord Robert, I will strike an agreement. I shall keep faith with Empress Maud as long as she consults with me on policy concerning Church business, such as the distribution of abbeys and bishoprics, and, naturally, appointments.'

Before Maud responded, she listened to the rain beat against the shutters and was glad of the fire in this chamber, its blaze illuminating the golden threads of Wherwell's rich hangings. She studied the image of Gabriel on an embroidery, opposite. The blue-eyed angel seemed to smile down on her.

'Do you need time to consider your response?' Henry interlaced his long fingers under his chin, a hint of steel in his voice.

'Maud?' said Robert, his eyes fixed persuasively on hers.

Brien and Miles were clearly anxious too, but she was reluctant to allow the wily, smooth-talking legate to control what she believed to be her right: the appointment of new bishops. Even so, she needed his support, and Theobald, the Archbishop of Canterbury's support too. And, if she agreed to Bishop Henry's conditions, she might more easily manage Theobald than Henry himself.

'Cousin,' she said clearly, 'my lord Bishop, I agree that the Church will have the final say on the appointments and other Church business.'

Bishop Henry sat back, looking satisfied. 'Now, all that remains is to arrange a procession through Winchester to the cathedral, so all can see that the Church approves the Lady of the English.' He glanced towards the closed shutters at which rain lashed, and above which fat wax candle flames quivered in their sconces. 'Let us set it up for a week hence, to allow time for the clergy to travel here and for the weather to improve.'

Maud and her women were given chambers in the priory. The men lodged in nearby manors. It seemed as if the whole of Hampshire was providing shelter for her supporters and their knights. The English supported her. In bed that night, Maud stretched her toes and imagined her coronation. The Bishop had suggested a procession to Winchester Cathedral, so all the bishops attending could see this as a prelude to her coronation: *Winchester is a royal city, that of your mother's royal Saxon ancestors. You have to be seen to be believed*. She was in total agreement with him, as was Robert.

On the day of her entry into Winchester, the first time she had presented herself as Queen outside the south-west castles and villages, Maud announced, 'Purple and gold, my warmest reindeer fur boots and my ermine cloak. Knot my plait at the back of my neck and secure it with the band studded with rubies. I am an empress, Queen of the Romans – and now, apparently, Lady of the English.' Turning to Lenora, she said, 'You will carry the casket containing Saint James's finger bone in the procession. You must walk before the other ladies.'

'Such an honour,' Lenora said, then hesitated. 'Should not the Prioress have that right?'

'She will have Wherwell's own favoured reliquary to carry as she leads her nuns in the procession.'

Maud shooed Bella the greyhound, who had been nosing around her gown, into a corner. 'You will not jump on the Lady of the English today,' she called to the creature, as she swept about the woven floor mats, twisting about to peer at her elegant gown. Maud, feeling elated, mimicked the Bishop's silvered voice: '*My Lady of the English, we cannot have two Queens in the land at the same time. It would be confusing.'*

At first, her ladies gasped at her daring to mock a bishop, but then they all laughed heartily. Maud enjoyed surprising them.

'Oh no, Bishop Henry,' she said, making her tone icy. 'You must remember I am the only Queen of England.'

Bishop Henry, the Tree of Jesse studded with winking jewels adorning his vestments, received Maud in the Bishop's castle, once Wolvesey Palace. Its courtyard was filled with those bishops and abbots who had made their way to Winchester. A huge number of squires and stable lads tended to stamping, snorting palfreys and jennets. A few abbots rattled through the gates in small box-like carriages painted with godly images of angels, crosses and biblical scenes.

Before noon, a stately procession led by Maud and Henry walked to the cathedral. It was a gentle spring day, the sun shining softly in a hazy blue sky. The mood was jubilant and the populace of Winchester welcomed her, tossing flowers as she passed – primroses and other spring blooms. On arrival at the cathedral doors, Maud was welcomed by Nigel, the Bishop of Ely, a middle-aged cleric whom she knew well, his thick black tonsure gleaming in the sunlight, and there also was Robert of Bath, Abbot Gilbert, and Alexander, the lined and grey-eyed Bishop of Lincoln, who had aged decades since she had last seen him. She supposed the Battle of Lincoln and subsequent massacre of his townspeople had distressed the Bishop deeply. For that, she was sorry. A gathering of local nuns and monks swelled numbers in the cathedral's nave. But the most important prelate of all remained absent. Theobald of Bec, Archbishop of Canterbury, should have been there to lead the ceremonies and recognise her imminent queenship.

Theobald's absence was concerning.

'I wonder what the Archbishop Theobald could be so busy with that he cannot be here,' she said at dinner, to Bishop Henry.

He patted her hand as a kindly grandfather would, though he was not much older than she. 'I shall call a Church council and settle this matter. He *will* attend, once summoned by the papal legate, my Lady of the English.' He seemed to preen as he referred to his title. 'Many of England's clergy have given you their promise of fealty today. You have the Treasury keys in your possession. We progress you towards your throne, but there is still much to be done before you can finally claim it.'

Seated on her other side, Robert set his wine glass on the table covering and murmured softly, 'Be patient. If they request Stephen's renouncement of the throne and his agreement to their fealty oaths to you, he will not stand in your way. He might well believe his life depends on it, and that God wishes you to be Queen, or else he would not have lost the battle at Lincoln. It is your right and also your father's will that you be crowned. I shall remind him, if he has forgotten this.'

She nodded, because Robert's advice was wise and she knew that he would manage Stephen's recognition of her rights. Much as Maud hated Stephen, she recollected that he had not taken her prisoner at Arundel Castle. She must, in turn, treat him with respect.

Turning her attention to Bishop Henry again, Maud thanked him for the delicious feast he had provided. Lifting a mouthful of salmon with her spoon, she complimented his cooks on the lemon sauce.

He said, 'I have lemons brought from Spain. And, on occasion, oranges as well.'

When she was Queen, she thought, she would order all the most exotic fruits for her table, including lemons, oranges and even pomegranates.

Maud took up residence in the royal castle in Oxford – a large, comfortable stone castle, with an ancient tower. Archbishop Theobald and any hesitant magnates remaining loyal to Stephen had been ordered to travel to Bristol to confer with him. If Stephen agreed to free them from oaths to him, they promised they would willingly offer the Empress their loyalty.

She received word, a week later: Stephen, as Robert had predicted, concurred and freed all from their oath of homage to him. He renounced his kingship, seemingly afraid that, if he did not, he might mysteriously vanish one night. Even so, if everything went wrong now, Maud was aware that Stephen might yet decide he had acted under duress, and, just as bishops and nobles had acknowledged Stephen after her father's death, they might switch their loyalties again. She reminded herself that, if she was to survive, she must be a firm and even a ruthless queen.

Her uncle, David of Scotland, wrote to say that he was making the journey south to support her and intended attending her coronation in London. However, Robert advised her that the burghers of that city would not easily recognise her right to the throne. London, he pointed out, had enjoyed easy trade with the continent under Stephen's rule thanks to his marriage to Matilda, the heiress to Boulogne.

Maud paced around Oxford Castle, up and down stairways, restlessly crossing and recrossing the hall and banging the lids of coffers in her chamber because the burghers of London, despite repeated requests, remained silent concerning where their loyalties lay.

A week after Robert had warned her of these difficulties, a letter was intercepted. It was written by an unnamed cleric of the abbey of Westminster to another in Winchester. When it was brought by Count Brien to her antechamber, Maud sat on a cushioned bench by the window and read aloud: '*God willed that King Stephen should be cast down for a moment that his elevation might be loftier and more surprising. England is shaken with amazement by the King's capture . . .*'

She sprang to her feet, tore up the letter and flung it into the charcoal brazier.

'These are treasonable words!' she raged. 'Find the author of them at once and throw him into prison. He should lose the hand that wrote this.'

Furiously, she crossed to the table, lifted a small pot containing scented herbs and threw it at a wall, where it broke into many pieces.

Brien folded his arms, watching her gravely, but saying nothing.

A page ran from the chamber, shouting for a broom. Maud continued to spit fire: 'I believe Matilda to be responsible. She will have spies everywhere in the City.'

'It came from the abbey at Westminster, unsigned, as you well know,' Count Brien said gently, and, coming closer to her, he laid a hand on her arm, trying to soothe her as he would a restless colt. 'Now you have cast the letter into the fire, Maud, we cannot compare the hand that wrote it, should other such notes be sent to abbeys around the country.'

She sank into a chair, leaned back against cushions, closed her eyes and muttered a torrent of curses.

When she had calmed down, Brien fetched her a cup of wine and assured her, 'My own spies will seek out the monk – or, indeed, nun – responsible.'

'Please do,' she said, quietly sipping her honeyed wine.

But Brien could not discover the culprit and Maud became increasingly anxious to be crowned in Westminster. It was her intention to make a great procession into the City, demonstrating to them all who now held power. She said to Brien, as they walked in the garden where roses had burst into bloom, 'I may be a woman, but I am determined that my reign will be likened to that of a king rather than a queen.'

She began to assert her position by creating new barons. She raised Miles to Earl of Hereford, which Robert and Brien felt to be well deserved. Miles the bear knelt before her in Oxford Castle's great hall to receive his charter, his sons and his capable wife, who had managed Maud's household in Gloucester as well as her own, at his side. Miles studied the parchment, which had Maud's seal affixed to dangling ribbons in the bottom right corner. It showed her as a seated crowned figure and was similar to her previous one. She was pleased with this revised one, because it also named her as Lady of the English. When she raised Miles to his feet, she saw tears swim in the tough old warrior's eyes.

'Oh, Earl Miles,' she said softly. 'You are irreplaceable and the honour to create you an earl of England is all mine.' It was odd how, though she had a smaller court than ever in her life and was away from her royal cousins, husband and children, she felt as though she had a closer family than ever before. Robert, Brien, Miles; Alice, Lenora, Beatrice, Xander, and even little Pipkin – even, she mused, the trustworthy tough warrior, John the Marshal. These people had become her family.

That evening, as she partook of supper in the castle garden with Robert, Miles and Count Brien, she announced it was time to plan a procession towards London on Saint John's Day. 'I don't wish to delay any longer. David, my uncle, will arrive from Scotland very soon. Once he joins us, we should plan my crown-wearing.'

Robert looked up with concern in his eyes. 'You are right, Maud. However, we must ride the long way around to the City, because Windsor Castle is still holding out for Stephen, and the burghers of London remain slow to recognise your queenship. There could be an attack.'

'And,' Brien added, 'you will need the loyalty of Geoffrey de Mandeville, Custodian of the Tower. De Mandeville has not declared for you yet.' He thought for a moment. 'We can go a long way around to Westminster and negotiate terms as we travel. You can offer him more than the Earldom of Essex, which he was granted by Stephen. He is, I believe, anxious to recover his family's fortunes in Normandy.'

'Worth it,' Robert agreed. 'Matilda of Boulogne has been using her Flemings to harass Londoners on the southern banks of the Thames. It would weaken her if we have Earl Geoffrey on our side. He will help us persuade the Londoners.'

'Agreed,' Maud said. She turned to Brien. 'Can I not honour you, too, my loyal friend, with an earldom?'

Brien said solemnly, 'No, I am content as I am, particularly since I have no children to inherit my lands. However, may I make one request?'

'Anything,' she said, as Bella nosed about her gown, hoping for titbits from the supper table.

'I see Bella is hungry,' he remarked, before answering: 'It is lands that I seek, but not for myself, rather for the monks of Reading, an abbey close to both our hearts.' He gave Bella a piece of meat from his plate and, when he looked at Maud again, his eyes filled with love and sincerity.

She smiled. 'Brien, the abbey will have more lands. You will always be my sincere knight, who puts abbeys, God and his lady before his own needs.' She reached over and took his hand. 'Thank you for your loyalty,' she said. She dropped his hand and clasped her own together in anticipation. 'And here are Xander and Alice, come into the garden to play and sing for us!'

Alice began to sing a haunting ballad in her pure clear voice, as her brother accompanied her on the harp. Everyone was entranced. A full moon shone down, the sky was a myriad of glittering stars and Maud was truly happy, enjoying the moment, yet hopeful she would soon be crowned England's Queen. Bella rested her silky head on her paws as she settled by her mistress's feet. Maud glanced at Brien and he smiled back at her. The moon continued to cast its saffron light over the garden as Xander played a flute with skipping notes, dragonflies flitted about the roses and, for now, all was at peace and Maud was with those whom she loved best.

Out in the gardens, away from others, Alice and Jacques walked hand in hand along a pathway lined with Madonna lilies. The heavy scent of the flowers was seductive. Glancing over his shoulder, Jacques said, 'Alice, we are forgotten, I believe. I need to speak with you privately. It cannot wait.'

Bemused, she nodded and permitted him to lead her through the gate into the orchard. Ever since his return from his imprisonment in Devizes, he had seemed more subdued and serious in his nature. The ladies had been deprived of his gifts procured from the kitchens, and even his stories, songs and jokes. They sat on a small hillock below an apple tree that was bursting into blossom. For a time, they remained in comfortable silence. She turned to face him. 'Jacques . . . what is it?'

'I realise I haven't always treated you fairly.' He glanced down at his feet. She waited. He looked up into her eyes, his own eyes clouded over. 'I shall be straightforward. The future is another time, if you are willing to share it with me . . . share it with me, wherever it takes us. If you refuse, I shall understand, but I hope you—'

'Stop, Jacques! Just do not disappoint me . . .'

'You will . . .?'

'Wed you. Now, let me see . . .' She paused and drew breath. 'You have suffered. Maybe not enough . . . but . . .' She glanced up at the night sky. 'Nothing is permanent in life, but, for me, love must be as sure as the stars that dwell in the sky up there. It is for all time.' She found herself smiling. 'Look, that is Venus up there, and she must have cast a spell upon me, and I shall . . .'

'Marry me?' He gasped as if he could not believe her words.

'Yes, because I do love you.'

'Oh, my love, when? When can we wed?'

'Before midsummer, in my own village church, with my family around me. If we can get leave to go there.'

'Alice, I love you with all my heart, for now and until eternity.' He pulled her into his arms and kissed her hard.

She had never thought they truly had a future together, but God had answered her prayers. From the garden, they could hear a harp playing. Slowly, they pulled apart and, arms entwined, wandered back towards the orchard gate.

Chapter Sixteen

Wallingford
May 1141

Announced by a page, Alice entered Maud's antechamber. Curtseying, she requested permission to speak. Maud glanced up from her charters with a half-smile. She knew what this was about. Sir Jacques had already spoken to her of his desire to make Alice his wife. It was a pleasant diversion during a very busy month. King David was on his way south and plans were being made to set out for the City and her crowning. Her mood was especially benign and, after all, May was a perfect month for courtship.

'What is your request?' she said, laying aside her pen. 'Speak, Alice.'

'My lady, now the countryside is at peace, I wish to visit my home. Xander does too. Our family has returned to their farm and would welcome Xander's help for the summer harvest.'

Maud twirled her pen in her fingers. 'And . . . is there more to this request, Alice?'

'Well, yes. We have been with you for a year, my lady, and I would see my people, and I wish to . . .'

'Ah, you would like to introduce Sir Jacques to them.' Maud finished Alice's sentence for her, before the young woman began stuttering and fumbling her words. Mind, she thought, Alice is no longer so young – not the fifteen-year-old girl who sang at my wedding to Geoffrey. And, she was pleased to see, Sir Jacques – the thinner, wearier knight who had returned from captivity – seemed to have eyes only for Alice.

'I grant your request, Alice, and, since I have no immediate need of my household knight, I would like you to wed in your village. Sir Jacques has already asked me for your hand, Alice. It is also a matter for your father and Count Brien, but they will grant it, without doubt, knowing of my wish for your happiness and of the loyal service you both have given me.'

'Then, if Count Brien permits, we shall depart as soon as it is convenient, my lady.'

'And, when all is decided and you are married, you will return to me as husband and wife, to Westminster, in time for my crowning. I wish you to sing at my coronation feast, Alice, and, as usual, appropriate accommodation will be granted to you both within my castles.'

Alice knelt to receive Maud's blessing. She felt tears at the edges of her eyes. She was to marry for love, and to be asked to sing at a coronation was an honour indeed.

'Three weeks only, though. You must be in London by midsummer.'

'Yes, my lady,' Alice said. She skipped along the passageway as she left Maud's presence and hurried to confide her news to Jacques. She was dreaming of her wedding day already. Jacques was not the perfect knight she had dreamed of when she was a child, but, somehow, this was even better. He was now her friend as well as her betrothed, and she loved him with all her being.

Maud watched from the doorway in the stone keep of Oxford Castle, with Count Brien by her side, as Alice, Jacques and Xander rode out through the castle gateway.

'Xander will return soon, I believe,' Brien said, smiling. 'He has eyes for your maid, Beatrice.'

'Will her father agree to her marriage to a jongleur? He is her inferior in rank.' She folded her hands. 'As Alice is inferior to Sir Jacques – by birth, at least.'

Brien turned to face her. 'Ah, now, there you are mistaken. Alice is not of lowly birth. Her father was a knight and cousin to Tilda. He is deceased and without heirs. When you retrieve his lands from Robert of Leicester, she will inherit an estate.'

'So *that* is the mystery attached to Alice. She is of the nobility, but illegitimate, just like my brothers and sisters. And that Beaumont twin withholds her inheritance?'

'She is, but I chose not to place her in danger from Robert of Leicester — an evil man, if ever there was such.'

'I wonder, will I ever get a promise of fealty from those brothers?' Maud said, with caution in her voice.

'If Earl Robert and Bishop Henry have their way, yes, they will all come grovelling to you, my Lady of the English. You have the Archbishop's blessing. Stephen agreed it.'

'Now my coronation can follow.'

'Yes, but let us worry at this no longer today. Come inside to the fireside and read that book you gave me for my name-day gift.'

Maud laughed like a girl half her age, delighted at the thought of passing a pleasant hour in Brien's company.

Alice sat on a white palfrey called Augustine, a gift from Sir Brien, as they rode out of Oxford on a gentle, sunny May morning that smelled of new shoots, celandines and primrose. It was only a morning's ride south to Shillingford, and, with such wonderful news to tell, she anticipated the reunion with her adopted parents with joy. Her excitement was enhanced by her pride in the handsome mail-clad knight who rode by her left side, mounted higher than she on his stallion. Xander looked very fine too, she thought, as he rode on her other side, wearing a new woollen cloak pinned with a silver owl fastening, a gift from Beatrice.

Their wagon and props remained in Gloucester because the decision to travel to Winchester and then Oxford had been taken so quickly following the King's defeat at Lincoln. Earl Miles assured Alice he would send it forward to them once he returned to the castle, but Xander was impatient and grew determined to fetch it himself.

'My instruments and the puppets!' he wailed like a petulant child.

'I only have my harp and flute with me. What if they should be damaged?'

'Unlikely,' Jacques reassured him, as they rode along the river path close to Abingdon Abbey. 'However, if you must cross counties again, I shall accompany you with my two men-at-arms.' He glanced over his shoulder at the guards who were accompanying them south from Oxford. 'The Empress can spare you two, eh?' he called back, awkwardly twisting around in his saddle. 'A month in the country, Alan and Johnny? How does that suit you?'

Tow-headed Alan grinned, showing a mouthful of broken teeth. 'It suits well, my lord. We are yours to command.'

Johnny, a slighter younger man than his fellow guard, said, 'It makes a change. Give me a barn to sleep in and a bit of honest farm work and I am as content as a dozy hound.' He nodded, his copper head of hair shaking as he emphasised his pleasure at being away from soldiering around Oxford for a month.

'I may perform at your wedding, after all,' Xander said, turning to Alice.

'Your flute and harp will suffice.'

Xander piped up again with a refrain she had of late heard too often: 'I wish it were me thinking of my wedding day.'

'That will come right, in time. I have a good feeling,' she said confidently.

'Your good feelings are not always right.'

'This one is. I am sure of it. Once the Empress is England's Queen, she will command Beatrice's father to permit her marriage to you, Xander.'

'But she is an heiress.'

'A minor heiress, who deserves a good husband,' Jacques said quietly. 'A husband who has shown great courage. What say I teach you to sword fight whilst we are in the country? The lads back there will help. They know many moves.'

Xander brightened at once. 'That would please me. I am accurate with a bow and arrow already, and swordplay appeals.'

★

Alice had not seen her adoptive parents for more than a year. The family had spent the terrible months of the Wallingford siege trapped inside the castle. After Stephen's troops had departed, they had returned to the farmstead. It was situated a few miles further north of the villages that had been fired.

As Alice rode along field tracks, she could see how seeds sown during the previous month were sending up green shoots of barley. August would see a bountiful harvest. She hoped for a Whitsun wedding and, although she and Jacques had already been handfasted in front of witnesses, she longed for a celebration and a priest's blessing, as well as her family's approval. Even if Xander did not retrieve his rebec in time, there would be replacements at the farmhouse.

'My horse's shoe has taken a stone,' called Johnny.

'We are near the village,' Xander said. 'The blacksmith's daughter is my brother's wife. He'll be at the forge.'

As they rode into the village, the first thing Alice observed was that cottages had been rebuilt, repaired and freshly thatched. They dismounted at the smithy and the burly blacksmith set aside his tools and exclaimed, 'So my lady Alice returns! And my, my, Xander.'

'Indeed,' Alice said, leading the docile Augustine by her reins. 'It's good to see you too. How are the others?'

'Your brother's farm and that of your parents were the only farmsteads untouched by the King's men. Folk here would be suspicious of loyalties, except your ma and pa were at Wallingford Castle and Count Brien's men were guarding the property.'

'What damage did the King's men do?' she asked.

'What did they do? They did as soldiers are wont to do in a war. Rape, pillage and thievery.' He indicated the church which stood by the crossroads. 'Eight men lie in graves there, and a few women too. It has been a time of hunger.'

'I am sorry to hear it. But my parents' farm stands. And you survived, with Dame Gertrude?'

'Aye. Everyone needs blacksmiths. Even the enemy.' He drew a hoarse breath. 'And I hear the King is the Lady's prisoner, held tight in Bristol Castle. Is it true the Lady will be our Queen and bring peace to the land?'

'God willing,' she said.

'And those be her men?' He pointed at Alice's escort.

'They are, and one horse needs shoeing. Took a stone on the road from Oxford.'

The blacksmith peered at the horse Alice indicated. 'Looks in great discomfort. I'll see to it whilst Gertie gives you all a cup of ale. She's been brewing today, God bless her.' He whispered into the jennet's ear and received a whinny in return. 'She'll be right as can be within the time it takes you to swallow a tankard of ale.'

Alice supposed all of Count Brien's fiefs would be pleased the King was a prisoner. Villagers and townspeople who had suffered armies trampling their fields and through their streets could hope the Empress would bring peace. It was, she realised, a good time to raise the villagers' spirits with a wedding. Everyone here had suffered. It was fortunate that the blacksmith and his wife survived. She even felt charitable towards the sharp-tongued Annie, her sister-in-law.

'May Wallingford never suffer another siege,' she murmured, as they entered the garden behind the smithy. She touched the silver cross hanging under her cloak, a parting gift from Empress Maud.

'Mistress Alice, well I never,' gasped plump Gertrude, and she poured them all ale as they sat under the sycamore and Alice made introductions.

Ingrid was standing by the farmhouse door as they trotted into the yard. Hens clucked around, then scattered, a pig grunted from his pen, and Alice was pleased to catch sight of their dovecote, over in the orchard, peering through trees full of ripening apples. Here, time stood still, despite the war. Walter and Pipkin hurried from the barn, their sweaty faces smothered with smiles. At once, Jacques jumped from his stallion and helped Alice down from Augustine. Alan and Johnny dismounted. Xander sprang from his jennet, looking from his mother to his father and to Pipkin, clearly unsure who to greet first.

'Such fine horses!' Walt said, as he reached them all. 'Come and see your ma, Alice. She has been watching for you since Sext.'

'Oh, it's a relief to see you so well and safe.'

'We did have a spell in the castle, and we were concerned as to what we would find on our return, but nought here was fired. Now, the village was a different story.'

'We heard it from the blacksmith,' Xander said.

Walter shepherded Alice and Jacques over to Ingrid, raising a hand to Xander and the guards. 'We'll just stable them horses and be back with you as soon as you can flick a stick at a fly.' He nodded to the two guards and said, 'You lads come with me, and you too, Xander. Horses before human needs. You can tell me your names as we get them brushed down, fed and settled for the night.' He seized hold of Argos and Augustine by their reins and led them into the barn, followed by the guards and Xander leading his jennet.

Pipkin trailed behind, calling, 'Take care they don't disturb my sparrowhawk. She's resting.'

'We knew you were coming,' said Ingrid to Alice.

'How did you know?'

'Count Brien sent Dame Margo, yesterday, with gifts from the castle — luxuries for a wedding, she said, and a wedding gown for you, Alice.' She studied Jacques, shading her broad brow from the setting sun with one hand. 'Welcome to our farmstead, sir. Any friend of Alice — nay, a betrothed, no less — and respected by our benefactor, the Count — is a favoured guest here, without a shade of doubt. So, come inside, rest and eat . . . You must be famished, riding all the way from Oxford.'

'Thank you kindly.' Jacques bowed low.

As they stood in the porch, Ingrid said, 'Jacques can take Xander's chamber and Xander can sleep in the workshop with the musical instruments.' She looked at Alice. 'You know we took them down to the castle for safety during the siege. And you, Alice — well, you know where your bedstead is. When you go up the staircase, you'll find it all ready and Dame Margo's gift on the bed, all wrapped up in linen. If the gown doesn't fit, I can adjust it.'

They paused in the broad porch and Ingrid indicated bowls of water, soap and linen on a shelf, so they could wash their hands and faces. After that was done, she led them into the hall, where a fire glowed low in the central hearth, with a pot of rabbit stew hanging from a bracket. It smelled of herbs and mutton, and Alice felt her mouth watering. Glancing sideways, she saw the trestle was laden with meat pies, tarts and cheeses.

Ingrid ladled the meaty stew into a row of wooden bowls placed on the hearth ledge. As savoury steam rose from it, she said, 'Don't let it cool too much. Sit there on the bench by the trestle.' She laughed and then studied Alice and Jacques for a moment. 'When the others arrive, we have a wedding to discuss. Our message from the castle is that it's to take place in the village church on the Sunday following Whitsun. That gives us just over a week for preparations. And, when you are sent for, Dame Margo said you are to ride to Westminster for Queen Maud's crown-wearing.'

Alice was surprised that Ingrid knew so much, and that all this had happened without her knowing. She was momentarily silenced, but had just gathered her wits to remark on it when Xander entered the hall drying his hands on a linen towel, wringing it out and carelessly tossing it aside onto the hearth ledge.

'And you, Xander,' Ingrid said, giving him a bowl of steaming stew, 'eat. The cart with your puppetry and viol and glittern is on its way from Gloucester Castle . . . in time for the wedding.'

Xander's eyes shone like a full moon. 'Well, by the rood, that is a miracle, because all I have had since Gloucester is my small harp and flute.'

The others gathered around the table, tightly fitting onto the benches.

'Now, who are these men?' Ingrid said, placing the rest of the bowls on the trestle.

'Oh,' Pipkin piped up. 'They are the Empress's men.' He introduced them.

'In a way,' Jacques said. 'They are mercenaries from Anjou. I have borrowed their service.'

Ingrid said, smiling at the two of them, 'In that case, you are welcome too. You can either lay your heads in the barn or in the hall.'

Alan spoke up: 'We'll be happy with the barn tonight. We'll not need to stay, now the cart is on its way, so we'll be off to Wallingford come morning.'

Clearly, Alan made decisions for both soldiers, thought Alice, setting her spoon down and wiping around her emptied bowl with a crust of bread.

Alan glanced at Sir Jacques. 'If Sir Jacques grants his permission.'

'We'll have no escort to the City, if you go,' Jacques said softly, his face clouding with concern.

For an intake of her breath, Alice wondered if Jacques feared the roads.

Alan reassured him somewhat by saying, 'You won't need us. It's a main route straight there. But, if you do, Sir Jacques, send to Wallingford and we'll come.'

After supper, once they had gathered around the hearth, Pipkin told them he hoped to wed Meg after harvest time. His future was assured, since he would inherit the farm of his betrothed's father. She was an only child. 'Her pa is pleased and so am I,' said Pipkin, grinning like a farm cat that had just snatched a mouse. 'I cannot be a player forever.'

'So, Papa won't have your help here?' Alice ventured, as she stretched her hands towards the fire.

'He'll have Godwin.'

'We have employed more serfs to work the land here, a half-dozen granted us by Count Brien,' her father said, lifting his tankard. 'Not all the time. They have other duties.' He smiled at Alice and Jacques. 'And now, we had best get on with planning your wedding, Alice.' He slapped Jacques' back in a friendly manner. 'And a fine one it will be too. You have chosen a good man, here, Alice – so Dame Margo tells us. Noble, as you deserve.'

Jacques glanced up from his tankard. 'I am but a poor knight, though I have title to land in Anjou and a reeve minding it all. I can offer Alice a fine manor house, but I am not of the great nobility.' He looked a little downcast. 'I look forward to showing my demesne to Alice, though that can only be when the Lady of England does not have need of my service here.'

'We are glad to house her here for longer, and you, too, Jacques, when you are not needed. We have plenty of room for you both.'

'My thanks to you, Walter. We shall be with the Lady as often as not, but . . . it is restful here.' Jacques glanced around. 'And I feel your kindness everywhere in this hall.'

Her family had made Jacques welcome. Within one evening, it was as if he had always been part of their family.

Chapter Seventeen

June 1141

Alice's wedding day dawned with clear blue skies and birdsong. Doves were flying in and out of the dovecote, a blackbird was chirruping, thrushes sang, and Alice, after drowsily stretching, remembered what lay ahead and leapt out of her bed. She could hear a broom sweeping across the yard.

Clucking hens were banished to their coop. Extra cooks had been employed for the feast that afternoon and the yard was emptied so that trestles and benches could be set up. She could, if she listened hard, hear Ingrid overseeing the preparation of salads and other dishes, toing and froing to oversee the baking of fresh bread in the lean-to bakehouse attached to the farmhouse. The delicious smell of a whole sheep cooking on a spit in the meadow behind the farmhouse wafted up to Alice's chamber, which stretched over half of the upper floor and was reached by an outer stairway.

Annie came rattling into the yard on a cart, to help Alice bathe in a tub lined with linen. There was the added luxury of soft scented soap from Spain, contributed by Dame Margo.

'Hurry down, Alice!' she yelled up the staircase. 'The water is warm. The tub is set up in Ingrid's chamber, behind the hall. Your gown, stockings and garters are already laid out.'

Alice flew down the stairway and into the hall, dressed in her shift and with her hair in two thick plaits. Annie helped her bathe and she washed Alice's luxuriant fair hair with the soap, which smelled of bergamot. She dried the tresses with a towel, combed it out and called for buttermilk and bread with butter and honey. Alice declared she was too excited to eat. 'You'll not go hungry to your wedding,' Annie scolded, hands on hips.

By the time Alice was laced into her new gown, she was in an intense state of nervous anticipation. For a moment, she again wondered if she was wise marrying anyone, and wise to trust Jacques . . . but she drew a deep breath and decided, yes, because she loved Jacques with all her heart and knew he loved her. In their world, love matches were rare, but Lady Fortune had smiled on her.

Alice glanced into a large disc of polished metal owned by Annie and drew another deep breath. She resembled a lady from a troubadour's ballad. Her silk wedding gown was as blue as the Virgin's mantle. The day had begun perfectly. She was grateful that Annie had grown kinder now she was the mother of four children and pregnant with a fifth. The eldest, a girl, was already nearly nine years old, and would be Alice's attendant today. The boys were aged seven, six and four. Annie had lost two babies, but her current pregnancy looked set to come full term. She was glowing with health and oozing kindness, and, though still pious, not at all condescending anymore.

When Alice pushed aside the leather hanging and entered the hall, Ingrid was waiting for her. 'One more thing,' she said, seizing a wreath of summer flowers from the work table – marigolds entwined with cornflowers – and placing it on Alice's hair. 'To enhance your beauty.'

Glancing around, Alice realised the comfortable, plain hall that usually smelled of woodsmoke was filled with the flowery scent of weddings and summer. It was festive, hung with rue, roses, vervain and greenery from the hedgerows.

Xander arrived as she was admiring it all. 'Godwin and Jacques will meet us at the church. Godwin is to stand as groomsman.' Jacques had stayed at Godwin's farmhouse over the past nights. It meant her husband-to-be would not see her until they gathered in the church porch. 'Can we depart soon?' Xander said. 'Pipkin, are you ready to play that glittern?'

Pipkin stood to attention, looking taller than he usually did. He was wearing a new tunic the colour of mustard flowers. His fair hair

211

and beard had been neatly trimmed and his blue eyes glinted with happiness.

Alice stepped out of the farmhouse just as the church bells were ringing for Sext. Ingrid and Annie, with her children, gathered behind. The musicians, Xander and Pipkin, moved to the front of the procession, ready to walk the mile to the village.

Then, Xander remembered: 'Ah, Alice, you must not walk. Just a moment.' He handed his pipes to Annie and dashed to the barn. He returned leading Augustine, decked out with hollyhocks and daisies. Turning to the eldest of Annie's sons, George, he handed him the reins and helped Alice onto her horse's back. Alice hooked her left foot over the pommel, ready to ride to her wedding. 'You have the honour of leading her,' Xander said to George, who puffed out his chest with pride as he accepted his important role.

They left maids behind, as well as Annie's talented cook. When they returned from the church, a bridal feast would be laid out on bleached linen cloths thrown over trestles placed in the shade against the farmhouse walls. Men, women and children joined the procession as the wedding party approached the village, including a band of drum and cymbal players. It was not long before the church came into view. As Alice dismounted to walk the final steps towards the churchyard, she was surprised to see a great number of Count Brien's knights lined up by the church gate. They all stood to attention as she approached, their chain mail glinting in the sun. A banner Count Brien loved to show, with a griffin embroidered on it, fluttered in the breeze. A heartbeat later, she saw Count Brien himself, standing near Godwin and Jacques in the church porch. He had dispensed with the hat he often wore and she noted how his hair had grown in the year that had passed since his dark locks were shorn. Black curls nestled again below his chin and no evidence of the hideous tonsure remained. Her heart glowed with pride. Count Brien had come to her wedding!

Her mouth widened into a delighted smile when the tall, serene village priest said, 'Count Brien wishes to speak before you exchange rings.'

Count Brien cleared his throat and began to elaborate: 'It is customary a bride brings a dowry to her marriage and she in turn receives a morning gift. Lady Alice, for this is how she is to be known henceforth –' he turned to Alice – 'I can announce, and I have Countess Tilda's permission to do so, my Lady Alice, you are . . . in truth . . . an heiress, and I swear this before Christ, you are due to inherit lands currently in the possession of Robert de Beaumont, lands that were part of your natural father's estate. Now that the Empress is to be England's Queen, these will return to their rightful owner. I shall, in addition, grant you some acres of my own as a morning gift.'

The villagers looked astounded. Their puzzled, weather-worn faces turned from Alice to Count Brien. They probably think it really is the Count who is my father, Alice thought – even if he's too young. Still, it mattered not. She was to be mistress of an estate in Anjou and would eventually have land in England as well. Her lack of dowry had not troubled Jacques, but it pleased her that she now had something to offer him. How she longed to know who her father really was – though she supposed, like any promised charter, this must wait too.

Count Brien nodded to the priest, saying, 'The wedding can commence.'

Jacques was elegant in his new surcoat of pea-green, and his cloak was pinned with a traditional brooch she had given him as a wedding gift. It was silver and engraved with intertwining little roses. Annie's father had paid a silversmith, with whom he was acquainted, to fashion it for her. She studied it, delighted to see it glint on his short cloak. They bowed their heads and faced the priest, who blessed their rings, then, when they had made their wedding vows, they exchanged them. After the ceremony, they gazed into each other's eyes and their lips met. This was a kiss she would remember all her life. The wedding party filed into the church for the nuptial Mass.

Later, Count Brien quietly excused himself as they stood greeting people in the porch, saying he was on his way to Oxford to join the Empress. 'We shall meet in Westminster, Sir Jacques. Countess Tilda sends her apologies. She is unwell and Dame Margo is tending to her.' Brien's eyes looked sad as his gaze lingered on the couple.

'Ah,' Alice ventured, 'it is, without doubt, stiffness of the ankles again. I shall send her a cream of arnica and camomile.'

'And, for that, Alice, she would be grateful.' He smiled a benevolent smile at them. Brien never would say a bad word of Tilda. He turned away to leap onto his waiting black charger.

That night, after a joyful afternoon of feasting, surrounded by merrymaking villagers and family, Alice and Jacques climbed the stairway to her chamber and, when she tossed her garter down from the top, Xander caught it. She whispered to Jacques, 'I hope he keeps it for Beatrice. Surely God will grant him as much good fortune as we possess.'

The chamber had been tidied by maids who had made the bed with fresh crisp linen and scattered fresh floor straw with camomile. Alice and Jacques undressed each other with no shyness, because over the past months they had come to know each other. In fact, she wondered if she could be with child already. A full moon shone through the window past their pale bodies, casting a silvery light around her chamber that was now theirs.

After they left off their lovemaking, Alice pushed aside the bed sheets and, climbing down from the bed, crossed to the window ledge to peer out onto the yard below. Xander and Pipkin were still playing country songs of love. Villagers were twirling around in circle dances and Ingrid was weaving around a ring, leading the others.

Jacques softly called her back to bed. She returned to him. He put his arms around her and said, 'A year and more ago, I was lost, shocked by my experience in the dungeons of Devizes Castle. My return safely to you, my sweeting, helped me recover my courage, and I thank you for your love with all my heart.'

As an answer, she snuggled close and whispered, 'Embrace me again, for I love you with all my heart too.'

'I pray,' he said, 'that, when this war is ended, we can travel to Anjou.'

'That would be exciting,' she whispered back. 'And we must visit my lands, when we discover where they are.'

★

All was not well in Westminster. Maud and her retinue had travelled in early June to the City, hoping she would be welcomed, but disputes had blighted the days leading up to her coronation. She was tired and the weather was hot. Robert was wrong, she told herself. He advised her not to tax the City merchants heavily to put money in her coffers, saying that she should appease these men who had supported Stephen because he had links with Boulogne through his wife's possessions there.

'And, Maud,' he said, when she, he and others had gathered in council – a meeting he chaired, to approve plans for her coronation, including a procession through the City to the Tower – 'Bishop Henry wishes to make a request.'

She snapped, 'What now? Speak up!'

'If you appease the merchants and protect trade routes to this end, you must allow Eustace, Stephen's son, to inherit Boulogne. It would be a gesture that will pay off and show your astuteness, wisdom and generosity of spirit, my Lady of the English.'

Maud felt herself become intractable. If she gave way on these issues, she would show weakness, not strength.

'No, Bishop Henry. No, no, no. The merchants will pay me an increased tax and Eustace will not have Boulogne. It remains a crown possession.'

'One that only became such when Stephen was married to Matilda of Boulogne, a match forged by your own father.' Bishop Henry's face was reddening with anger. 'It is natural that Stephen's son inherits Boulogne.'

Maud shuffled scrolls around before her, tapping one of the documents from which her seal hung by a red ribbon. Glancing around the table, she said, deliberately deepening her voice, 'And I have selected a new bishop for Durham, one that will please my uncle, who has supported my cause.'

'I see,' said Bishop Henry, his bushy brows raised. 'Yet I do not see, because that does not please those who feel your uncle still has designs on northern power for his own family and Scotland. I suggest you think on this appointment again, my lady.'

'Empress,' hissed Maud back at him. 'And soon to be Queen.'

These men would not gainsay her decisions. She raised her head high and glared at the Bishop of Winchester.

'And now I have jewels to select for my crowning and a fitting for my gown, so please excuse me, my lords.'

She rose, and they all rose too. As she swept away, she noted Bishop Henry's blackened countenance and his downturned mouth.

Alice and Jacques reached Southwark, on the outskirts of London, on the eighteenth day of June, travelling from Wallingford to attend Maud's crowning in Westminster Abbey. But what they did not know yet was that London would be a harder city to take than any battle in the campaign leading up to Maud's coronation. The next few days were to change everything. The approaching coronation was the event that would start the true Anarchy, as the chroniclers would later call it: the bloody civil war that would set all England in flames.

They were unaware of any unrest, or that, to avoid attacks around Windsor, the Empress had approached Westminster from St Albans. Their own journey, following summer-scented routes edged by verges filled with flowers, by fields where hay was made alongside green hedgerows, had been pleasant and ambling. Their horses carried packs with only necessary clothing, though Alice had included her blue silk bridal gown because she intended wearing it on Maud's coronation day.

As they rode into Southwark, south of London's bridge, Jacques spotted a large, whitewashed inn, with a handsome wooden board hanging over the street entrance, depicting a swan. It had three storeys and an archway leading through to stabling behind the building. He reached over, took hold of Alice's reins and slowed their trotting horses to a walk, saying, 'This inn will be used by merchant wagons travelling south towards the Kentish ports, or north into the City. I say we stop here for the night, rest the horses, refresh ourselves, demand a tub –' he grinned and she saw the twinkle in his eye she could never object to – 'have our cloaks brushed down and enjoy a good supper.'

That would please her too, she said, and so they turned the horses under the archway into the yard, dismounted and gave their mounts to an ostler. It was, the man assured them, only a matter of greasing the innkeeper's fist with enough silver pennies, and a private chamber with the promise of a bath and supper would be theirs.

He knew his master well. Within a short time, Alice was pleased to enter a spacious room under the eaves. It was clean and the linen fresh. Maids trundled up the stairs with a tub, later sloshing up once again with buckets of warm water.

'Come,' Jacques said to her, after they had dressed in fresh garments. 'If we hurry down, we can dine in the common hall and we might pick up the atmosphere in the City. Surely they will be preparing to celebrate the forthcoming coronation. Count Brien's messenger said it would be on Midsummer's Day. We can celebrate too, Alice, because tomorrow is St John's Eve.'

As they stepped onto the staircase, Alice tapped her husband's arm to get his attention. The hairs on the back of her neck had risen, for some reason. Was it only the natural surliness of city-dwellers, or perhaps the fact that the businessmen and burghers looked concerned themselves, with knotted brows? Something was surely going on. 'Don't reveal we are close to the Empress, Jacques. It is best to remain anonymous.'

He turned to her. 'Really, Alice, I want to shout her praises to the heavens,' he replied. He shrugged. 'But, if you wish not, I won't.'

'I think it wiser to be cautious.'

They found themselves sharing a table with an assortment of people, some departing the City and others heading into it. Alice did not like the belligerent looks on the faces of many of the men seated with them. Most wore fine garments, and there were even two long-faced nuns who said they were from Bermondsey Abbey, visiting St Helena's Abbey in the City. When Alice smiled, they did not respond in kind. The table was soon full of talk concerning the arrival of Empress Maud at Westminster.

One narrow-eyed merchant, who was travelling from London

towards Dover, said, moving his tankard from his mouth, 'She has negotiated her entry to the City. Following the coronation, she wishes to process to the Great White Tower.' He shook the tankard angrily, spraying his neighbours with ale. 'But none of us burghers want her.'

'Geoffrey de Mandeville,' added a fat-faced man, raising his brow. 'The Keeper of the Tower, Geoffrey de Mandeville – heard his name, have you?'

Alice looked at Jacques, squeezed his knee below the trestle, glanced up and shook her head. She hoped her husband would not be angered at this talk and betray them.

The fat burgher continued, 'He betrayed us all and offered Maud his support. She has accepted his fealty and, as for him, he never complained when she demanded taxes from us burghers.' He glared around the company. 'That's what it'll be – taxes to keep her in cloth of gold.'

The merchant said, 'He'll rue the day. She'll bring evil to the City. There's an unwomanly ruthlessness there. She's capable of gouging out your eyes if you cross her, like her father could and did. There'll be rioting, if she's crowned. London will be her mulch cow, milked dry. She'll bring us hardship.' He shrugged. 'I'm travelling to Kent to meet our rightful Queen Matilda, if I can. She promised to hand over castles to Maud, but a delegation has already talked sense to her, and I've heard say she's changed her mind. Well, my friends, I've a fine manor house in Kent. It'll be safer there, after Queen Matilda's army reaches London.'

Jacques' face had reddened to the colour of the merchant's cloak, and Alice felt colour creeping up her own neck. So, Queen Matilda was moving towards the City with troops.

'Will Londoners make trouble at Maud's crowning?' Alice asked, trying hard to sound innocent. No one spoke immediately. They were staring at her as if *she* were the she-wolf. She said, glancing from furious face to furious face, pausing and focusing her eyes on the two nuns, 'She will be crowned, surely?'

'Not for certes. The Bishop of Winchester proclaimed her Lady of the English, but she's not yet crowned, nor will she be crowned if us Londoners have the courage to act,' said a young, angry-looking man with yellow hair, whose face was covered with wens. 'Stephen's our rightful King and God's anointed.'

Mutterings ran all along the board, because this youth had gone too far. Although these were treasonable words, they seemed to give others courage.

Another well-clothed man, probably a crafts master, rose and banged his fist on the table, making Alice near jump from her skin. 'She won't be crowned if the City rises up against her. No one wants that woman as our queen. We already have a queen. She's good Queen Matilda. That other is a difficult woman, an apparition of greed. Her father was a cruel man and she will be likewise, cold as ice and nasty as the Devil. We do not want her destroying our city.'

'She could retreat from the City, mind,' said the lad with the wens, folding his skinny arms.

The fat merchant said, 'The she-wolf could return and lay siege to London. She'll have our King's siege engines in her possession. Look what happened in Lincoln. Massacre and rape followed that battle. Not as if the King can break out of Bristol Castle and save us. No one wants her.'

Alice felt a hot retort rise to her lips, but she clamped them shut and quickly swallowed.

The merchant stroked his chin, as if deep in thought. 'If London rebels, other places will follow. Cities and castles will refuse her. Abbeys won't acknowledge her,' he pronounced.

'Arrogant witch. She could burn us to the ground.'

The innkeeper shouted over. 'There's news!' He pushed a Benedictine monk forward.

Alice recognised him and lowered her head immediately, staring down at her cooling bowl of pottage. How was *he* free? Miles must have sent him on his way after a few nights in the cells. She curled around on the bench, looked away and pulled her wimple closer, adjusting it so not a hair showed. If the monk did not remember her, she was sure it would be because she was wearing a matron's wimple and neither Pipkin nor Xander were with her. But would he place Jacques? She kept her eyes lowered.

The room hushed when the monk announced, in a booming voice that sounded as pleased as a huntsman announcing a kill, 'Queen Matilda and William of Ypres have led an army through Kent. They'll reach Southwark by tomorrow's eve. The City will rise up to support her.'

There was a great cheer.

The thinner of the merchants shuffled in his seat and eyeballed the now white-faced, shocked Jacques. He said to him in a low voice, 'Get away from here.'

Alice leaned closer to hear him better.

'We'll be trapped between two armies, if we stay. My house in Thame Street could be ash by sunset. I warn you, my friend, protect that wife of yours. As I see it, there'll be fighting and burning and no coronation. Turn back to from whence you came, or you are welcome to accompany me to my manor in Kent. You look like decent folk.'

Jacques shook his head and said, 'My widowed aunt dwells in the City, by Aldgate. I must fetch her over the bridge before they close it . . . if trouble truly is brewing.'

'As you will.' The merchant turned to his neighbour and began grumbling about armies gathering, death and destruction.

Alice and Jacques were forgotten as the diners set to their supper, talking amongst themselves, some asking the Benedictine monk questions. Alice and Jacques sat quietly listening, until they judged it safe to slip away without arousing suspicion.

They left by a low door to the side of the eating hall and climbed up the stairway to their chamber.

'We dare not stay longer here than we must. Get a little rest, Alice, because we'll hurry away as soon as it is light. We cannot enter the City in case we are trapped. We can ride along the river and find a ferryman to get us over to the Palace of Westminster.'

'Will we be in time to warn Count Brien?' Alice said.

'I pray we will. All our lives may depend on it.' He chewed his lower lip as he fell into thought.

'What is it?'

'They'll have spies, and may know already. I suspect our Lady of England may have to wait longer for her coronation.'

Alice found her mouth twitching into a smile, despite their peril. 'Your aunt was an inspired comment. They'll think we have rushed into the City to her rescue.'

'Pray Christ it is so. 'Tis midsummer and, with few hours of darkness, we shall be off, my love. Unfortunately, early light may be to Queen Matilda's advantage as well.'

They gathered news as they rode through villages south of the river. There was a great army approaching. Villagers were trying to get ferry rides over the river, thinking they would be safer in the City. Others were travelling in the direction of Southwark, hoping to cross into the City over the great bridge.

Alice could see smoke rising far in the distance, curling above fields and rooftops. 'I could not tell if the smoke is William of Ypres's army or maybe midsummer bonfires,' she said.

'Too early in the day for those,' Jacques said gloomily, after watching dust rising back along the river. 'It'll be an army. We must get across.'

It was frustrating, but no wherry was to be found. All were occupied. They could see the spires of Westminster's abbey on the other side and Alice prayed hard: 'Please find us a boat to take us and our horses over, dear Saint Cecilia.'

As they turned a bend in the river, Westminster vanished from sight. They reached the village of Putney before they discovered a suitable craft willing to ferry them across the Thames. A cacophony of church bells began ringing, and they would still have to ride back to the palace of Westminster.

'May God save us all,' prayed Alice, glancing back over her shoulder, because, in the east, smoke was edging closer. 'I never in my days heard so many bells ring Vespers.'

Chapter Eighteen

Westminster
Midsummer 1141

Midsummer's Eve arrived at last. Maud watched the throng of nobles drifting into the hall from Westminster Abbey, a triumphant smile tugging at the corners of her mouth. She had not attended Sext, having observed the earlier service of Prime. Vespers would be the prelude to her coronation. She stepped to the edge of the dais and peered into the great gathering of her supporters. Robert and Count Brien stood with her, looking for the missing Bishop Henry, concern growing on their countenances. Miles was moving through the crowd, weaving his way around garlands of flowers and herbs that hung from pillars to celebrate Midsummer's Eve; he too was seeking the Bishop.

The air was redolent with the scent of freshly baked bread. Maud murmured to Earl Robert, 'It's midday and he is not yet here. He did not attend Sext, you say. So where is he?' Her short-sighted eyes scanned the hall again, for a moment watching busy servitors bearing in platters of venison, roast swan and dishes piled high with golden-crusted pastry coffins containing small birds. These aromas were all delicious, but Maud had no appetite. She hardly glanced at the tables covered with pristine linen and set with silver, or the great pots of roses placed upon them.

Miles rushed to the dais. 'Bishop Henry has not been seen about the palace, in the abbey church, nor is he on the river. No one knows where his attendants are either. He has left Westminster.'

By then, Maud was clenching her hands so hard, her nails were marking her skin.

Miles added, 'The stewards are seating guests. We must continue without him. Archbishop Theobald is with the other bishops. I can ask him to speak grace.'

Maud nodded, and he rushed off to consult with the Archbishop of Canterbury, who, by choice, was heading his own table of bishops and abbots.

She felt Robert's touch on her arm. 'Maud, please take your seat. As Miles says, the feast must begin. Food will cool quickly. Look, they are carrying in bowls of your favourite mushroom soup.'

He was trying to distract her, but it did no good. A sixth sense nagged at her. Something terrible was amiss. She shrugged her shoulders and shook her head, but allowed Robert to guide her to her place.

The Bishop had still not arrived by the time the servitors came to clear away the soup bowls. Maud, now even more concerned, turned again to Robert. 'Is it true Ypres has been pillaging, south of the river? Perhaps Bishop Henry is trapped.'

Robert shook his head. 'I doubt it, though I have heard villagers are crowding the river with whatever crafts they can get hold of, fearing the worst is about to happen. I've asked De Mandeville to send into the City to find out if it is still safe for you to process to the Tower.' In return for his coming over to her cause, Maud had recognised Mandeville as Earl of Essex and Custodian of the Tower.

From his place beside King David, De Mandeville, hearing his name mentioned, called along the high table: 'The Bishop is doubtless in his new palace of Southwark, being warmed by a whore.' Others laughed at the ribald jest, but Maud frowned disapprovingly.

King David tried to diffuse the tension with a loud guffaw, and dragged long fingers through his white hair. Then, magician-like, the Scots King twitched his moustaches in a grandiose manner. 'Ah, to be sure, the Bishop is held up looking for his cope, clad in his braies, searching through his wardrobe for damasks and silks like those worn by a noble, rather than a modest bishop's garb.'

Even Maud began to smile at this absurd image. 'Few bishops' copes are modest, Uncle,' she said. 'Certainly not Bishop Henry's.' She leaned along the trestle towards Geoffrey de Mandeville. 'Well? Any news from the City, Earl Essex?'

'None as yet, my lady. I had expected word this afternoon.' He did not seem too bothered by the Bishop's vanishing, nor by the rumour that the City might rise against her crowning.

It was when the servitors began distributing platters of venison, salmon and swan, and were refilling goblets, that a messenger wove his way through the trestles and approached Count Brien, whispering into his ear.

Maud raised her brows. 'Is he from the Bishop?'

Brien shook his head and bent to speak to her quietly. 'My lady, no, but Lady Alice and Sir Jacques have arrived. They request speech with me.' Lifting his napkin from his shoulder, folding it neatly on the table, he stepped down from the dais and walked along the length of the great hall to the studded doors. Maud could not see him once he passed out of the hall, but she noted how the Countess Tilda's face, beneath its severely starched wimple, looked as curious as Maud felt.

As a distraction from concerns about both Bishop Henry and the Londoners, the conversation turned more positively to whether Maud should take up residence in the Tower or remain in Westminster once she was crowned. A quarter-hour or so passed and Brien had not yet reappeared, when another young man rushed into the hall from a side entrance. He pushed through the benches and trestles, heading for the steps, his eyes searching for someone in particular. Climbing up to the dais, he leaned over the table and spoke to Earl Geoffrey over a platter of beef. Earl Geoffrey of Essex grew as white as the ghost of old King Harold, a joke Maud used to share with Brien when they were children, imagining that the Saxon Harold's ghost walked the corridors of Westminster Palace by night.

'By Christ!' Earl Geoffrey exclaimed, rising from his seat. 'Christ's cods, my man here has just passed through Ludgate and the Londoners are calling men to arms. The church bells are pealing.' He stopped speaking and placed a hand to his ear. 'Listen, I hear them myself. It's the truth. The City is rising. They're coming here.'

'It cannot be true!' Maud exclaimed. 'What about my procession? What about my crowning?'

At that instance, Count Brien returned. He leapt up the steps onto the dais and stood before her. 'It's true enough, my lady. Listen – can't you hear those bells?' The air stilled as they stopped and listened. It sounded as if all the church bells of London were ringing at once.

Brien said, 'Jacques warns us of an approaching mob. He and Alice rode from Wallingford and heard of trouble brewing in London when they stopped for a night in the Swan, at Southwark. The Benedictine monk we saw at the fair in Gloucester was at the same inn, stirring up trouble. Queen Matilda is riding with William of Ypres and their troops are ranged along the river from the City's western gates as far as the bridge.'

Maud's hand flew to her heart, which was beating too quickly. 'Can't we hold them off?' she asked.

'Not a mob,' said Geoffrey de Mandeville. 'Not a London mob, madam.'

'He is right,' Robert said, tossing his napkin down and rising to his feet. 'We must retreat. It's a trap and Bishop Henry—'

'I know. The Bishop of Winchester may be behind this,' Maud interrupted, with bitterness in her voice. Her hope of a crowning was fading by the minute.

'He must have been making a pact with Matilda all the time. I knew that fox was wavering,' King David gruffly remarked, as he, too, stood up.

'Where are Alice and Jacques now?' Maud said to Brien.

He pointed to the far end of the hall. 'I sat them at the board. It's the last food they might get this day. There is no time to waste. We must make haste.'

The bishops were looking her way. The Archbishop of Canterbury, who was to crown her Queen tomorrow, looked puzzled and as if he was waiting for her direction.

'Everyone must leave,' Robert said. 'Shall I tell them all we are departing?'

'No, I shall announce it.' Maud scrambled to her feet. What could she say? How could she explain it? She would say as little as she need say and not display her disappointment. Importantly, there must not be panic.

She stepped to the front of the dais and raised her arms, her sumptuous, embroidered gold silk sleeves falling back to reveal her jewels. Her guests fell silent. She spoke with a confidence she did not truly feel. 'There is an army waiting along the river, one greater than ours, and a mob approaching from the City. We must abandon the palace at once, leave everything and save our own souls. May the Lord bless and protect us all.' There was no need to say more; they could hear the bells.

'An orderly exit!' Robert called out.

'Which route?' someone yelled.

'North and west.'

There was a hurried scuffle of benches scraping across the flagstones and chairs tumbling backwards as their occupants scrambled for the doors. Corn marigolds, hedge roses, St John's Wort, fennel and yarrow were scattered as pots crashed to the ground and smashed into smithereens. Amongst the chaos, Miles and Robert took charge. Whilst Miles sent for horses to be brought into the courtyards by squires, Robert stepped into the mass of people who were rushing to the doors and hurried through them to speak with the Archbishop. The Archbishop never replied to Robert, but made the sign of the cross, organised his abbots and bishops into an orderly exit and sent for their carriages, horses and guards. Count Brien calmed his wife, Tilda, reaching for her stick and calling for Dame Margo to come and attend her. He ensured they were both safely mounted on their palfreys, and warned them to stay close to Maud's ladies and her knights.

Robert, calm as ever, with Mabel by his side, marshalled the guests from the hall. Druid-bearded David of Scotland helped. Maud watched for a moment as her mother's brother shepherded others through a side door to the courtyard. She spoke firmly to her own ladies, who were shaking with terror, convinced at any moment that a rabble would break into the palace and ravage them. Robert's daughter Mathilde and her deplorable husband Ranulf helped to calm her terrified women. Once Maud raised her voice, all of them obeyed. If she had to abandon her crowning and save their lives, by the rood and all that was holy, she would do so with honour and courage. They left by the side door to a second courtyard, where their horses waited with squires and ostlers.

As the abbey bells rang for Vespers, her court was already mounted and riding in an orderly fashion from the palace, all of them, including the clergy and Archbishop Theobald, following the royal retreat. It was hardly the procession originally intended as a spectacular entry into the City, rather a retreat from its angry citizens, no doubt stirred up by Winchester, the papal legate, himself. As they rode through the villages, Maud was sure she could hear City bells ringing in the distance, conscious of a mob pouring through Aldgate, already looting the Palace of Westminster. They had escaped with their lives and only the clothes on their backs.

Once they had passed through Edgware, terrified villagers scattering, the long column rode as fast as the Devil's horsemen. The orderly retreat began gradually to fall apart. Maud found herself with only her own knights and her uncle, as well as Robert, Miles and Brien, her ladies and her knights' families. The rest had veered off, riding towards the safety of their abbeys, their own lands, castles and manors. Maud's pathetically reduced convoy turned towards the quiet river known as Edgware Brook, hoping they had outpaced any of Queen Matilda's men who might have followed in pursuit.

When Robert considered it safe to stop, they set up camp. Not far away, drifting from a nearby village untroubled by the great events of Westminster, they could hear drums playing, music and singing, and they could smell smoke from midsummer bonfires. King David, helped by several squires, was able to erect a campaign tent, which miraculously he had brought on a packhorse as they escaped. He offered it to Maud and her women, and she gratefully accepted.

'So, you had the presence of mind to retrieve this,' Maud said, striving to appear normal.

'The packhorse was the only one we took. You'll have to make do with a thin mattress and a rough blanket, niece.'

'It will suffice,' she replied, trying to keep her anger out of her voice.

'I've posted guards.' He passed her a water skin. 'And ye'll be sharing this. 'Tis all we have till daybreak.'

Exhausted, Maud drifted into a deep sleep without dreams. She was awake by dawn. When she exited the tent, Robert was seated on the ground outside, as if he had been there all night, guarding her. He lifted a basket roughly woven from green reeds, filled with newly baked bread and little rounds of cheese, and, to her amazement, he produced a wine skin. He presented her with a silver vessel so she could drink. 'Such a luxury,' she remarked.

After sharing bread and cheese with her brother, she said, 'Have any scouts caught us up, and what is the news?'

'The mob broke into the palace, raided the royal apartments and stole what they could.'

She cleared her throat and spat out a mouthful of wine. 'No fire?'

'They were more interested in theft than fire. They grew drunk on the wine, took all they could carry and passed out. There'll be terrible heads by the time they get their plunder back through Aldgate.'

'And the false queen. Where is she?'

'The scouts say she crossed the bridge, entered the City and took the Tower.'

'Where is the Tower's Custodian this morning?' She glanced about their makeshift camp, hoping to see De Mandeville.

'Certainly not with us,' Robert replied. 'He'll be in the City, making peace with Matilda. Winchester will too, for Bishop Henry is another one for turning his coat. We could lose the clergy. Archbishop Theobald and the bishops sought refuge in Ealing Abbey last night, and he is returning to Canterbury, my lads say. Queen Matilda may even get hold of the Treasury at Winchester.'

At this, she spat again and swore. 'And *he's* not to be trusted.'

'No, but he's Stephen's brother and the Pope's legate, and Matilda will promise him great power. Bishop Henry was furious that you refused Eustace his inheritance of Boulogne.'

'But that was our trade route. He could not be permitted to control it.'

'A tricky issue. Also, the Bishop wanted a part of government and you refused him this too. You also supported a candidate for the bishopric of Durham favoured by David of Scotland — one clearly not favoured by Bishop Henry. I heard him complain that you were difficult and, if you remember, I warned you against the appointment.'

She shook her head. 'I am careful of those I dare not trust, like my father once was. Bishop Henry is wily, a snake.' She folded her arms, determined not to fall out with Robert. Dropping the subject of Bishop Henry, she said, 'Where is Brien, this morning? Why is he not here with us?'

'Brien has ridden west towards Oxford with his own troop, his wife and mine. Mabel must return to Bristol at once and ensure that Stephen is more securely guarded.'

'Put him in chains,' she snapped.

This time, Robert changed tack. 'Jacques and Alice showed exceptional courage, having ridden hard to warn us of the mob's advance. I thought it right they, too, continue ahead with Count Brien.'

Maud nodded her approval with a thin smile. They must all get to the west as quickly and best they could. She fully realised this, but how heartbreaking it all was. She glanced away, determined the tears filling her eyes would not spill over. This was to have been the day she became a queen.

Robert drew a long breath. 'We'll break camp now, ride as far as Reading Abbey today, and tomorrow Oxford. Then we'll decide how to deal with the Bishop of Winchester.'

'What about Ranulf of Chester, and Miles?'

'Miles has departed for Gloucester, and Ranulf will be riding for Chester with my daughter, Mathilde, and her ladies.' Robert grinned. 'He'll remain neutral, I believe, but he'll worry that your uncle might attempt to wrest Chester from him.' He chuckled, glanced towards the river and pointed to the hedging. 'Look, David himself!'

At that very moment, the white-bearded King of Scotland appeared through the hedgerow. He was shaking water droplets from his white mane and was only wearing his shirt and braies. A servant trailed behind with his clothing. In his thick Scots accent, he said cheerily, 'A dip in the river sets me up for the day. I feel as perky as a twenty-year-old again. Ready to move on, Maud?'

Her tears were at once banished. She felt a hysterical laugh rise from her belly and settling in her throat. To David, it was as if they were on an overnight hunting expedition, not escaping from an army or lamenting her abandoned coronation. She would not lose heart. She had mislaid her crown for now, but she had not yet lost all hope – not at all.

'I shall be glad to return to the comforts of Oxford Castle –' she crossed her arms and squared her shoulders – 'to plan our attack on Winchester. I want my Treasury there secured.' She turned her head and glanced at the tent. 'My ladies appear to be awakening. We'll be ready to depart once they have refreshed themselves with this.' She held aloft the wineskin, then, lifting the tent flap, called for Lenora and Beatrice to hurry up. Glancing down at her gown, she added, 'What a waste of good silk.' Her elaborate clothing was crumpled and sweat-stained.

Oxford

It only took another day's hard ride to reach Oxford. Once there, Maud steeled herself and began preparations to fight. She received a letter from Count Geoffrey telling her that Henry had grown into a precocious eight-year-old, and of his sorrow that her crowning had been delayed, as he put it. The good news was that Robert de Beaumont had made peace with him and supported him in Normandy. She lifted the letter to the hanging cresset lamp to see the next lines with more clarity, then dropped it onto the table and said, 'Read it, Robert. It looks as if Stephen still has support from that hatchet-faced, duplicitous Beaumont twin. No mention of the other.'

'Waleran will travel to Geoffrey as well. He'll be intent on protecting his best interests — Meulan, for a start. It's their family seat.'

Maud sank into a chair and cradled her head in her hands as Robert read Geoffrey's letter. Looking up at him, she said, 'What do we do now?'

He paced the great chamber, stopping by a window that overlooked the stream. Further along stood the castle's mill. 'God help us if we were to be besieged here in Oxford and the mill was ever taken. We'd lose our source of bread. In fact, just in case, we must store grain.' He visibly shuddered. 'Oxford is too close to London. You would be safer in Gloucester, Maud.'

'Oxford is closer to London. I hope to recapture the City. Besides, whilst we have Stephen in Bristol, we are safe.'

He looked thoughtful. 'We need to know Bishop Henry's intentions. He'll have flown like a homing pigeon to Winchester. Perhaps I'll pay Wolvesey Castle a visit and enquire as to where his loyalty lies. He commanded everyone to serve you, even Archbishop Theobald. If he has shifted his position, we'll attack his castle and take the Treasury in Winchester. You, Maud, should go to Miles, in Gloucester. You can gather our forces together again . . . and send to Chester for Ranulf's help. He's in no danger from the Scots whilst David is in Oxford. We'll need all the help we can muster.'

Having a plan always restored Maud's spirits. She felt happier. 'I'll do it, Robert. We'll gather our support in the west again. Brien will ride to Gloucester with me. He'll come from Wallingford soon.'

Before Maud set out for Gloucester, she reinstated Jacques as one of her commanding captains within Oxford Castle, and she welcomed Alice back into her service, saying she would be glad if she would sing for her again and that, perhaps in September, Xander might join them. The younger woman was glowing with good health and happiness. The marriage was apparently a great success and that gladdened Maud's heart.

'I think Xander would be pleased to return to your service as a court musician,' Alice said, as they sat together on a stone bench in the herb garden of Oxford Castle, trampling the camomile that grew between the paving stones, releasing its soothing scent.

Maud had sent ladies Lenora and Beatrice to cut the lilies and hollyhocks that grew by the walls, to place in the chapel. Small clouds scudded across an azure sky. It was a peaceful day and Maud was glad of it. It was good to be back in Oxford.

'And, if I may,' Alice continued in her musical voice, 'I would like to make simples, now that you have granted Jacques and myself our own house in the bailey.' She touched her belly. 'I think, my lady, I may be with child.'

Maud reached out and touched Alice's hand with her long fingers. 'That, Alice, is the best news I have heard in some time. I am pleased you are happy with the bailey cottage. It's your new home, for as long as you want it – let us say until Jacques can take you to Anjou and, indeed –' she sighed – 'until I can wrest your rightful lands from Robert de Beaumont and your estate is safe for you to visit. Sadly, a humble home is little to offer you, but I hope it suffices for a time.'

'It suffices well, my lady,' Alice said. 'It has its own garden and, from the back of the second storey, we can see the river. The sun setting becomes haloed with brightness and we see liquid gold and reddish copper reflections on the water.' She lowered her voice. 'We even have a privy that overhangs it.'

'An important amenity. When is your child due?'

'January, my lady.'

'Midwinter, so . . .' Maud was counting. 'An eight-month child.' She laughed. 'Conceived in May.'

'May, I believe,' Alice said quietly, looking down at her folded hands.

'I hope this child will bring you and Jacques much joy. And we could do with your talent with simples.'

Beatrice and Lenora were strolling along the pathway with a basket of flowers. Maud rose, intending this as a signal to Alice that the interview was over.

'One puzzling thing occurred at the inn in Southwark, Empress,' Alice said.

'Puzzling? Queen Matilda took London, and that's the puzzle — how she managed to raise an army and do so.'

'Yes, but the Benedictine monk we thought to see the end of was hovering about the inn and he announced her movements.'

'Well, well — he certainly manages to survive. Let us hope he comes to a bad end.'

'Like the castle cat, he seems to have many lives,' Alice said, as she departed.

Gloucester

Maud established herself in Gloucester Castle, where she wrote to all her supporters saying she would continue to fight for her crown. A day later, Count Brien rode in from Wallingford. She received him in the great chamber, holding out her hands, longing to touch him. His countenance was full of concern. He did not smile, but whipped a letter from his satchel.

'I received this letter from the Bishop of Winchester,' Brien said, with a frown as dark as his grown-out tonsure, his black curls touching his embroidered collar.

She raised her brow. 'Really, Brien? So, our tarrying Bishop has decided to communicate with you but not with me. What has he said?' She felt her anger surfacing and wanted to speak words a lady should never utter. She swallowed them, indicated a chair, and steepled her fingers, ready to listen.

He sat opposite her at the council table and began, 'I suspect I am not alone in receiving such a communication. And I've written my response.' He drew a long breath and exhaled it with a sigh. 'Bishop

Henry has declared for Stephen again . . . Robert will know this, by now . . . and Winchester has encouraged everyone else to return to Stephen as well.'

This was a terrible blow. When she opened her mouth to call Winchester one of the names she had not as yet uttered, Brien added, 'No one will, of course. He wrote to me saying I was in danger of being numbered amongst the unfaithful men of England. Has *he* not changed sides, and is *he* not unfaithful?'

Maud closed her mouth again, but gave him a look as sharp as a razor's blade. 'He's a snake in the grass,' was all she said.

At once, with a flourish, Brien produced another folded parchment from his tunic pouch and opened the letter he intended as his response to Winchester's outrageous note. 'Let me read you a part of my response, Maud. I have said, *I should be numbered amongst the faithful men of England, for I have obeyed the lawful command you gave me. King Henry gave me land, but it has been taken away from me and my men because I am doing what you ordered me to do. As a result, I am in extreme straits and not harvesting one acre of corn from the land he gave me. You should know that neither I nor my men are doing this for money or fief of any kind, either promised or given, but for loyalty.*' He smiled at Maud, his peaty eyes flashing.

'Well said, my dearest Brien.' She felt her own eyes fill with tears at the sincerity of Brien's enduring loyalty, and in that moment her love for him flooded her whole being.

Brien reached over the table and took her fingers, interlacing them into his own. 'I listed all who supported you. And I ended with a challenge.' He grinned. 'Listen. *I, Brien Fitz Count, whom good King Henry brought up, to whom he gave honour, am ready to prove what I assert in this letter against Henry, nephew of King Henry, Bishop of Winchester –*' he paused – 'or by judicial process.' He released Maud's hand and folded his letter, replacing it in the satchel along with the Bishop's correspondence.

'He won't like being threatened with trial by combat. Who are you sending with that response to him?'

'Oh, Maud, I think Lady Alice and, if you permit it, your knight with her. They can return to Oxford with Robert.'

She managed to smile. 'You have my permission to return to Oxford and send them with the letter. They might enjoy the adventure, though I doubt there will be any reply from Bishop Henry.'

After Brien left her presence, she swore, calling Bishop Henry all the words she had suppressed in Brien's presence. Knave, bastard, c—t. . .

A few days later, Waleran de Beaumont came riding into the castle courtyard with a small retinue and, with his usual arrogance, demanded to speak with the Lady of the English. She watched him dismount from an upper window. What was that betrayer doing entering her castle yard? She told the page who announced him to make Waleran comfortable in the great hall and she would come down shortly.

'Oh, and first find Count Brien in the mews,' she thought to add. 'He intends riding to Wallingford today. See if he has already departed and, if not, tell him to meet me in the great chamber.'

'Yes, my lady.' The page scuttled off to do her bidding.

Waleran could wait on her convenience, so she deliberately took her time to receive him. She composed herself, picked up a mirror of polished steel, peered into it, adjusted her head veil and, followed by Beatrice, who was demurely carrying her spindle and wool, glided down the stairway to meet with Brien.

'Waleran has arrived?' Count Brien said as she entered the great chamber. 'I was just about to depart.'

Maud sank into a large, cushioned chair, and Brien took the chair opposite, nonchalantly crossing his long legs. She noted he was wearing a new pair of leather riding boots – though, for comfort's sake, she was pleased to see the toes were of a modest length.

She placed her elbows on the table. 'I shall hear what he has to say, but he won't be lodging here. He can shift for himself in an inn or ride back to Worcester, or wherever he came from. Before I meet him, let us decide not to trust a word he says.'

Brien responded with, 'Worse than our Bishop of Winchester.

235

Waleran must want to secure his lands in Normandy, just like that despicable twin of his.'

'If he changes sides, we can stop him helping Matilda.'

Brien shook his head. 'Accept his loyalty and send him on his way. Do not trust that hatchet-faced, slippery eel, not for all the coin in the Winchester Treasury. He must have no intelligence of any of our plans. With luck, he'll sail for his estates in Normandy and Geoffrey will deal with him.'

'Geoffrey will give him short shrift if he tries to double deal with us.' She stood and smoothed down her summery, pink linen gown. 'Now, let us go into the hall and see what this traitor has to say for himself.' She called to Beatrice, who had been spinning discreetly in an alcove by a long window. 'Come into the hall with me, Beatrice. *You* can attend me today.' She called for her page, who hovered by the arched doorway, ready to open it, and ordered the youth to advance before them and announce her.

'Straighten that rumpled tunic first,' she snapped at the page, sharp as needles.

His face reddened as he hurried to do as she asked.

Her carriage as upright as her steward's rod, she put on her most haughty expression as she walked before Brien and Beatrice into the hall to greet Waleran, intending to leave him on his knees as long as she felt she dare.

236

Chapter Nineteen

Winchester Castle
August 1141

When she sat down with Robert and her chief counsellors in the great chamber of Winchester Castle, Maud said quietly, 'I know I have made mistakes, Robert, and I wish I had paid heed to your counsel in London. I never should have alienated the burghers by threatening to tax them heavily. Not only is the Bishop of Winchester being slippery, but Mandeville will turn to Matilda too.' She paused. She had not wanted to be contrite, but she did not wish to lose Robert's total trust in her either. She did not want the earls' support just because they had made their oaths all those years since, but because they believed in her. She said, 'I suggest we make a pact with De Mandeville, offer him sheriffdoms and justiciarships in London, and even the Bishop of London's castle at Stortford. He hates the Londoners, of course, but we can make no peace with them without his agreement as to terms. We must regain control of the City, and he can help us.'

Robert replied warily, 'I am not at all sure of him. He is in Guildford with Matilda and William of Ypres. Of more immediate concern —' Robert leaned forward and looked at every face seated around the conference table — 'Mabel has written to me that Stephen has twice been caught outside the walls of Bristol Castle, in the bailey.'

Maud was horrified. The thought of Stephen wandering around at night, engaging the soldiers who guarded him, using his genial manner to win them over, was a concern she had always had over his honourable confinement. 'I told you, Robert, he must be put into chains. There can be no opportunity for his wandering.'

There were murmurs of agreement from her commanders, particularly from John Fitz Gilbert, a man who was undoubtedly astute, and who could be as ruthless as any enemy brandishing a scimitar.

David of Scotland leaned back in his chair. 'Here we are, in Winchester Castle, besieging the Bishop at Wolvesey Castle, Maud. What do we do now?'

'The Bishop told Robert he was not supporting Queen Matilda, saying his only concern is the Church. This, naturally, is not to be believed, since he wrote to Count Brien and numerous others telling them to renounce me.' She noted Brien's nodding head. His reply had been delivered and no response had been given by the Bishop. Alice had returned to Oxford empty-handed, and she and Jacques were with her now. 'We have no option—'

'But to keep Winchester penned inside his castle,' Miles said, crossing his arms over his great chest.

'Indeed, he who is not with me is against me,' Maud said. 'I sent Bishop Henry another message yesterday.' She shook her head. 'He will be in his stronghold, in the south-east of the town. Winchester is prosperous and it was the capital of my mother's ancestors. Their tombs lie in the cathedral.' She narrowed her eyes and smiled her feline smile. 'It is mine by right. Bishop Henry has until the morning to respond.'

Maud's messenger returned, saying that the Bishop had already left Winchester. She sat once again in the great chamber with Brien, Sir John and David of Scotland.

'So, he slipped out once he heard we were here with an army,' Brien said, on hearing of the Bishop's departure.

'Apparently, our wily friend left by the east gate with his guard,' Maud said. 'Robert has gone to Wolvesey Castle. If the gates are barred to him, he'll send a warning spear in to them.'

John Fitz Gilbert banged his fist down on the table, making their parchment map of Winchester shake. 'The castle garrison will have engines, and Bishop Henry will have left instructions for them to resist. By Christ's arse, he is a coward. He'll be off to whimper his complaints to Matilda.' John Fitz Gilbert raged, 'I would not trust his commands to the Wolvesey garrison to possess a modicum of any knightly chivalry. Where's Miles, Maud?' He scanned the anxious faces around the great chamber.

'He has taken a troop out along the high street to guard Robert's back.'

Sir John grunted. 'The castle garrison will soon enough give up if they're under a siege, and, without the Bishop to command them, they'll lack advice. What does the Bishop think he can do if we have Stephen in chains? What does Matilda think she can do?'

David grinned and stroked his beard. 'She'll risk her husband's life.'

'She'll know we won't harm a hair on his head,' Maud replied soberly.

Brien, who was standing by the window, shouted, 'Come and see this.'

They all hurried to the long window embrasure and peered out. Smoke was rising from most of the roofs to the south-east of the high street and flames were spreading, snaking along the upper storeys of shops and merchant houses.

Maud gasped in horror. 'The source must be in the Bishop's fortress.' There could be no other explanation. 'Robert is out there, and Miles too.' She looked at her commanders' shocked countenances. All were horrified by how quickly the fire was spreading. 'Some of my ladies asked me if they could visit the stalls on the high street today. I granted it.'

'Maud, it is time to bring out our troops,' Sir John said firmly. 'There could be rioting and there'll be need for firm law and order . . . and help to put out those fires. I wonder, could the Bishop's bastardly garrison be shooting firebrands from his castle?' He turned to the Scottish King. 'David, could you, for now, stay with our Lady? I own houses in the town. By Christ, they'll be fired too. It'll be dangerous. We must go out and Maud must stay here.'

Maud gasped at John's controlling audacity. She opened her mouth to make a sharp retort, but closed it again. He was her Marshal, who understood horses and hawks, and whom she did not want to lose, now that he had come over to her side rather than sitting on the fence.

He bowed his dark head to her and said, 'We'll find your ladies. Which are they?'

'Alice, Beatrice, Anne and Joan, Sir John. They went to purchase herbs and embroidery silks.'

John nodded. 'Brien, come with me. If they are shooting fire from the castle, up there, it'll be because they're intent on destroying the town.'

Within moments, they had gone to don mail and helmets and ride out.

Maud hurried to her small Madonna chapel, with Lenora following, and sank to her knees before the little wooden statue of the Virgin. She prayed, clicking her amber prayer beads anxiously. 'Bring them all back to me safely.'

She felt Lenora touch her arm and whisper, 'Sir John will bring them back, my lady. He is reputed for always doing what he says he will do.'

Alice could not understand what had happened. One moment, she was selecting herbs from a stall to make into salves and infusions; the next, the street was filling up with smoke. She opened her purse and pressed coins into the herbalist's hand, anxious to get away, but he was abstracted, his shocked eyes gazing along the street. He accepted her coins in his large sweating hand without even checking her payment was correct. Following his gaze, she could see that buildings nearer the east gate, close to Wolvesey Castle, were catching fire.

Her basket thrown over her arm, she raced across the street to where Anne and Joan were selecting threads from a silk merchant's shop. 'Where's Beatrice?' she shouted at them. 'The street is on fire. We must get back to the castle. Hurry! Where is she?'

Joan began to cough. Pungent smoke was drifting towards them and into their noses and mouths. 'She went to find ribbons,' Joan gasped. 'The shop is just along there.' She pointed, coughed again and drew her veil across her mouth.

Alice didn't hesitate. She thrust her basket into Anne's hand. 'Take this, Anne, and put your threads in it. Both of you go back. Go now. I'll find Beatrice.' For a moment, Anne waited, but another drift of smoke – thicker, this time – came their way in a fat grey plume and she grabbed hold of the shaking Joan's arm and dragged her out into the street. They raced towards the royal castle, bent almost double from coughing.

The high street was ablaze – stalls, buildings and goods. People were fleeing. Flames licked roofs and spread from building to building, dropping enormous, scorching cinders on the ground, where they flared up, igniting other houses. As Alice searched from side to side, peering through the gathering smoke for Beatrice, she was caught up in a surge of scattering crowds. She tried to recollect the colour of Beatrice's mantle. People were running with hoods pulled up, despite the day's heat, and linen veils dragged across their mouths, many clutching children by the hand. She paused at stalls selling ribbons, either trampled into the dirt or damaged. The further she ran, the more thatched roofs were on fire, yellow flames licking up and out through darkening smoke. No Beatrice. There was shoving and cursing as she pushed her way along the high street, racing in the opposite direction to the fleeing citizens, to the source of the fires. Finally, she reached the south-east end of the street, where the nuns' abbey had caught fire. The Nunnaminster's roof was alight. Nuns were pouring out onto the streets, crying and screaming and panicking. She felt a tug on her cloak. Spinning around, she recognised Beatrice, her face blackened with soot.

'I tried to warn the stallholders,' she cried. 'They are shooting firebrands from the walls of the Bishop's castle. Look!' She pointed up towards the walls of Wolvesey Castle.

'Thank Heaven and all the holy angels, you are safe,' was all Alice could say, as she stared through the sparks and cinders towards the

241

Bishop's gatehouse, seeing the terrifying sizzling sparks that were raining all around them.

Yet another burning brand flew straight onto the thatched roof of the nunnery, setting it alight. Close to them, a small man's surcoat was on fire, yellow flames licking viciously around him. Alice tugged off her cloak. Risking her own hands, with Beatrice's help, she pulled it around him in a desperate attempt to smother the blaze. She could smell his singeing hair, and sooty tears streamed from a pair of desperate yellow eyes.

All at once, he began yelling in agony. She had managed to stop the burning, but his face was a mess of growing, reddening sores. If only she had her salves with her! With cinders descending in an ominous dark rain, the little man pulled away, her ruined mantle dropping from him. He shed the ragged bits of burned clothing and began to run with the flow of fleeing nuns, shopkeepers and citizens, who all, a very short time earlier, had been enjoying a summer's day ambling along Winchester high street, shopping in the markets or tending their gardens. They poured out from merchants' houses and from the nunnery, and raced away from the torched stalls. Glancing back at where the firebrands hailed from, Alice realised the Bishop's men had, indeed, set fire to their own city. She bent down and tugged her precious silver bear brooch from the ruined cloak. It was hot, but she clasped it and pushed it into her belt purse.

'Run, Beatrice!'

They ran.

Robert's face was blackened with soot. Firebrands were flying from mangonels placed on the other side of the castle walls. How could the Bishop have allowed this? It went against all Christian teaching. He would never forgive Bishop Henry for leaving a garrison with instruction to do all that was necessary to destroy Winchester, so that the Empress had nothing left here to occupy.

As heavy stones were fired on them from the walls, Robert turned to see Miles with his guard on foot, carrying crossbows and sheaves of arrows. He called along the wall to Miles, 'We'll head for the New Minster and organise there.'

Robert then turned his prancing horse about. It was snarling and attempting to rear up, but Robert ignored it, quickly gained control of his mount and encouraged the charger along, his back bent low, twisting through the scattering, swarming crowds, until he was galloping into the grassy close of Saint Swithun's Minster. Miraculously, the building was untouched. He fell on his knees before its great door, surrounded by monks and priests who, on seeing him, knelt around him and sent up a prayer for mercy.

Moments later, Sir John and Count Brien rode in from the high street.

Count Brien shouted over to John, 'If you help Robert and Miles organise relief here, I'll ride back into the side streets and send the injured and lost either here or up into the royal castle. The minster seems to possess clearer air, and there are nuns and monks who can tend to the wounded.' He turned his stallion around and headed off.

Sir John swung off his mount and began to help Miles and Robert organise chains of buckets, brought to them by monks. 'We have opened the city gates. Best encourage people to take flight into the countryside. Only the east gate now remains closed. That one is too close to the Bishop's castle. Saint Lawrence's Church is burning, Earl Robert, and the Nunnaminster and houses in Swithun's Street are alight, as well as all the buildings along the high street.'

Robert said, 'We must try to put the fires out. It's all we can do, now.'

Tirelessly, as the bells tolling from the city's many churches sounded out the town's panic, they filled buckets from the wells. Directed by Sir John, Miles and Robert, the soldiers formed long lines stretching all along the high street, passing the water from man to man. Those injured and too old to flee were carried into the minster, where nuns, monks and priests tended to them as best they could. Once all was organised, Miles mounted his horse to leave the safety of the minster, taking archers with him, intending to pick off the Bishop's men up on the walls around the castle.

Sir John, working alongside Robert, said gruffly, 'Count Brien has proved himself courageous this day, out there in the thick of it, trying to save whomever he can.'

'Count Brien is one of the best men you'll ever meet, John. Pity you've not seen his courage before. He would give his life for our Lady.'

'I'm glad he cares for more than his hawks and charming the ladies. We'll all be fortunate to survive this day. Two of my houses in the town are gone and my tenants burned within. Brien found two of Maud's women stumbling towards the castle, one of them bruised and bleeding, up near the castle gates. They'd been knocked off their feet in the stampede to the west gate. He sent them back inside the castle under escort, but there's two more ladies still missing.'

Robert grunted a response. 'Take over here, John, for a bit. I'm going further up the high street to see what can be done. Perhaps I'll find them. Who am I seeking?'

'Lady Alice and Lady Beatrice. I searched hard as we rode down here, and Lady Alice's husband is out on the high street looking for her too.' He glanced up. 'At least the Bishop's devils have stopped sending out firebrands. It may be a temporary lull. Or perhaps they fear more might destroy their castle too.'

'Miles's archers meeting their mark, with luck.'

The breeze changed direction. Flames began to blow backwards towards the south-east, over the city walls towards Hyde Abbey. Robert saw people staggering out of houses on the other side of the close with whatever belongings they could rescue; others were scooping water running down the central channels on the high street, those meant to take away rubbish, and were trying desperately to fill buckets to douse flames licking up the walls of their houses. Horses were spooked and running wild about the street, neighing and stamping. Chickens and pigs were racing around in a mad frenzy. It was all Robert could do to manage his own stallion, even though Hercules was well trained and had known the chaos of battle. The stink of smoke, the burning and the acrid smell of dampened thatch permeated the streets. It was hopeless. The city burned on. The smoke had become so dense that, in places, it was difficult to see. Robert leapt off his rebellious horse and began to lead it. He leaned down, picked up some cloth from a trampled booth, tore it, dampened it and tied it over his charger's nose and mouth. He directed as many as he could to soak down roofs, whilst dodging collapsing timbers.

Someone shouted out, 'Saint Martin's Church in Fleshmonger Street is burning.' On seeing one of Brien's men orchestrating a chain of water buckets from a well by Brook Street, which ran parallel, Robert redirected a number of them there. The flames that had engulfed the church had died down into a glow, but the roof had begun to collapse inwards.

Alice and Beatrice were sheltering near the church and, on seeing them safe, Robert breathed a deep sigh of relief. Sir Jacques came up to greet him, saying he had searched for his wife and her companion everywhere and found them helping people get away to the gates. Brien and Jacques were organising others into an orderly band, drawing up water from a well further down, on the bottom corner of Fleshmonger Street, to douse the thatched roof of the ancient church.

Alice was helping the priest, bandaging his arm with strips of linen, and now she glanced up. 'Count Brien saved the relic. Father Ignatius, here, was trying to protect it and a golden cross. He was overcome with smoke. His arm is burned.'

She pointed to Beatrice's soiled cloak and Robert opened its folds; it contained a crystal reliquary. Beatrice was sitting on the ground beside it, guarding the bundle, gazing at the church as if mesmerised by the dying flames.

It was not far from here to the castle. Robert called to one of his men and said quietly, 'Escort Lady Beatrice and Lady Alice to the castle, then return here.'

Count Brien laughed. 'Lady Alice has already been up to the

castle and back. She returned with a basket of salves and bandages. She won't leave, and Beatrice won't go without her.'

Jacques paused before he lifted up another bucket, speaking to Alice in a gentle voice: 'I think, for the sake of our child you are carrying, you must return to the castle. You have done all you can here, my love. I insist you accompany Beatrice and that relic back to the castle . . . to Lady Maud. Leave the salves and bandages. We'll do what we can with them.'

Alice nodded a hesitant agreement. Taking Beatrice's hand in one of her own and lifting the bundle containing the reliquary in the other, she began to slowly follow the guard back towards the high street and the castle. The traumatised Beatrice never spoke.

Robert called after the guard: 'Take Hercules with you too and see he is rubbed down and stabled. I am better off without him.'

As night fell, flames lit up the darkness for miles about them with an awful beauty. The Bishop had destroyed the ancient city just so that Maud's army could not have it; as a result, the people of Winchester were to lose almost everything. Whilst Maud's commanders tried to save lives, many more died in the fires. The burning of flesh made the whole city smell like a tannery. Maud had passed much of the day watching the unfolding disaster from various high windows, or pacing the solar, feeling completely helpless as she awaited reports from her sheriff.

When Alice returned with Beatrice, Maud took them to the ladies' dormitory, where she told them to bathe and rest. Placing the crystal reliquary that contained Saint Lawrence's tooth in Alice's care, she asked her to take it into her chapel once Beatrice had fallen asleep.

'People are wandering around like sleepwalkers,' Winchester Castle's castellan, William Pont d'Arch, the Sheriff of Hampshire, told Maud. 'Do I have your permission to gather up alms for those suffering?'

She said, 'I am coming with you – with my guard. They will help.'

'It is not wise for you to be on the streets. People are either angry or wandering around out of their senses.'

'They need to see me. They welcomed and cheered me in April, and they must see me again now. They must know that I care.'

'As you wish. Perhaps you could offer succour? People need bread. Many have lost everything.'

Maud hastened to the kitchen to organise food for the needy gathered in her bailey and for those wandering the ruined city.

Once outside the castle, she saw the somnambulant citizens of Winchester for herself. Many wretched folk were walking about dazed, with candlesticks and crosses held high, praying for deliverance. As she and her guards worked their way along the high street towards the minster, she moved amongst them, offering bread and ale.

Sir John appeared from the minster close, having heard that she was on her way, and, with his mail-covered legs akimbo, he barred her passage. His face looked thunderous.

'My lady, it is unsafe. The wind may get up again and change. An assassin could leap out in the darkness and—'

'What darkness?' she said, pointing up at the northern sky, which was lit up by flames that had already risen beyond the northern wall.

'Hyde Abbey is burning over there,' he said, following her raised arm. 'There are fires all about us. Get on that horse your groom is leading and please return to safety.' His harsh voice grew gentler. 'Don't you see? If we lose you, my lady, we lose our cause.'

She saw his point and requested that her guards leave the rest of the baskets of bread with Sir John.

The red-faced Marshal managed a sooty grin. His dark hair was streaked white with ash. His cheeks were puffed out and his skin was reddened where there was no grime. 'Like the miracle of loaves and fishes, without the fish,' he quipped.

'Indeed, Sir John, but of course the Nunnaminster will possess a fish pond and, once it cools down and we can access it, I'll warrant the fish will have survived.'

*

The wind rose up again. Embers relit. The fires raged all night. By morning, the city of Winchester was in ruins. They heard that Hyde Abbey had burned right to the ground. Hundreds of homeless people took refuge where they could – in the bailey, in the minster close, in churchyards – and others fled the city with only the clothes on their backs. Twenty churches were destroyed. The lords had worked all night, desperately trying to save people, stop fires spreading and ensure Wolvesey Castle was guarded so closely that none could leave it. But worse was to come. At first light, Maud's spies came rushing to the castle with terrible news. They had been posted on the Guildford road. A great army led by William de Ypres was riding towards Winchester on behalf of Queen Matilda, in King Stephen's name. This could be the end of Maud's hope to retrieve her stolen crown.

Maud hurried into her chapel, fell on her knees and prayed for deliverance.

Chapter Twenty

Maud discussed their desperate situation with Robert in an alcove of the solar. In the two years since Robert had first come to her and Geoffrey in Anjou to put forward his plan for retrieving her crown, she had never felt so hopeless. She had always felt that there was better ahead – from her subdued and unqueenly landing at Arundel, to the triumph at Lincoln, and even during their embarrassing retreat from London in June. The great conflagration in Winchester had appalled her, but now there was even worse to solidify their rout. Matilda the false queen's armies had surrounded Winchester and – Maud and Robert had just heard – they had burst into the ruined town. They attacked Robert's men and created a double siege, trapping Maud and her court inside the royal castle. And, although this was her castle, the royal seat of her father's government and his father's, and Maud did not wish to relinquish it, she did not wish to die here either.

'We are holding one road into our end of the city, which leads to Wherwell Priory,' Robert said. 'So far, the priory has been sending supplies to us from where it stands, some ten miles away. But if the priory is taken, we shall all suffer hunger.'

Maud rested her head in her hands. Should she give up? Should she return to Geoffrey?

Robert continued, 'Sir John is holding the Wherwell road for us to allow goods to come in that way, but, for certes, Ypres will try to take John's base of the priory. Given the forces Ypres commands, there'll be no quarter for Sir John's battalion if they get control of Wherwell. They do not respect churches, ungodly as they are, and they'll not care about the nuns either.' He rubbed his chin worriedly. 'The truth is, I have not heard from the priory in two days, Maud.'

Maud drummed her fingers on the windowsill. 'We're caught like fish in a net . . . there must be a way, though. We sent to the south-east for relief. Where are they?' She looked up at Robert. 'I'll warrant the false queen has Bishop Henry in tow.'

He shrugged. 'She has capable commanders, and all are ruthless. She'll have William de Warenne of Surrey and Gilbert Fitz Richard de Clare. There's the Londoners, too – a huge militia.'

'What shall we do?'

'We need grain for bread and whatever other foods we can get through the Wherwell road.' Robert scratched his head. 'I need to know what is happening there. Why has Sir John stopped sending supplies? If the enemy is there, well –' Robert held up his palms – 'we need to know.'

Maud thought for a moment. 'We could send Alice – she's clever and reliable – with Beatrice. And we should also send Jacques to protect them and help gather intelligence. We could disguise them as nuns with a monk on a visit to Wherwell.' Maud could think of no other solution and she was, in the end, reluctant to leave Winchester.

Robert sighed. 'It's a possibility. I suppose, as long as they do not approach from the Winchester road, but across fields and tracks, they could ride the few miles to Wherwell. If anything happened to them . . .'

'They must take all care to stay undetected,' Maud said. A small flicker of hope began to warm her again. 'Even if disguised as clergy.'

Alice and Beatrice were calmly spinning in the solar, listening to the usual rumours humming around the large airy chamber above the hall. A month had passed, but the smell of fire damage still seeped in through opened shutters. Wolvesey Castle remained under siege and they were almost encircled by Queen Matilda's army. Rumour had it that Maud had promised to rebuild the city. Most who remained camping in gardens or in their ruined properties accepted alms from the castle. Many supported her and loathed the bastards residing in the Bishop's castle. After all, the Bishop's men had burned their city, destroyed properties and ruined lives.

Food was fast running out, so the castle cooks had been saying over the past week. They lamented there were too many mouths to feed. If Alice went out to the kitchens to fetch anything for the bower, a plate of cakes or a flagon of ale, heads were shaken. One said, 'We have so little of everything. We need flour, peas and grain to feed the hens . . . and soon they'll all be eaten as well as the castle pigs –' the cook placed her hands on her broad withers – 'and even those grand horses you all ride.'

Alice looked up from her work as Maud approached their window seat. She set aside her spindle, rose to her feet and curtsied. Beatrice did likewise.

'Ladies, pray please sit.' Maud's voice was hushed. 'I must request a favour of you both.'

Alice's mind ticked over fast as a beetle crossing the window ledge scurried into a crevice in the wall. Those familiar words, *I have a request*, suggested a new mission, and since each of the tasks she had undertaken for Maud had been more difficult than the last, whatever the Empress was about to ask of her now was most likely to be very dangerous and frightening. A memory of Jacques, his trials at Devizes and how he was traumatised flashed through her consciousness, and she found a smile playing about her lips. Jacques was changed after that time, more serious in his demeanour, and, after all, that task had brought them together in marriage. She had been so relieved to see her love safely returned from the bleakest of dungeons, she could not refuse the more sombre Jacques.

Alice took a deep breath, looked searchingly at Maud and calmly folded her hands. Beatrice's mouth tightened with anxiety.

When Maud explained the precise nature of the favour she was asking, Alice immediately replied, 'I am happy to undertake this.'

She looked questioningly at the younger woman. 'But are you, Beatrice?'

'Yes –' she nodded – 'it's not nearly as dangerous as helping during the fire. I was terrified by it and thought we were to be toasted alive – but, my lady, it has strengthened me too. I came through it unscathed in the end. I discovered courage, I believe, and, yes, I can do this.'

Maud swallowed. 'You will have to be very brave and certainly very cautious. If you see danger as you approach Wherwell, you must return to the castle straight away. If all seems well, you just need to obtain a report for us from Sir John. It is crucial we know he is safe and can help us here. We shall starve if he cannot get food through to us.' She drew a long, anxious breath. 'This is a dangerous mission, so do not underestimate it. It is one that will herald success for us, or failure.'

Alice nodded and clutched her hands together, her countenance fierce. Beatrice was listening closely, her eyes as bright as a lantern's glow. They were focused and paying careful attention, which was good, for they would be facing possible capture.

Maud smiled her reassurance and said quietly, 'Jacques will escort you disguised as a monk bringing you into the priory. Beatrice, you can feign illness and a need for advice from the infirmary. You inhaled too much smoke in the city. You have heard of the renown of Wherwell's treatments.'

'My lady,' Alice said, trying to smile, despite her fear, 'I really do need herbs from Wherwell Priory.'

'And may you find what you need, Alice, and return unharmed. You will depart as darkness falls, assuming Jacques agrees. There is a waning moon tonight. It's enough to give you some cover, yet a sliver of light to see your way. Avoid the main route. The road to Wherwell is free of Matilda's troops, but you never know where they may lurk in order to attack our supply wagons. Stick to the field tracks. Stay out of plain view.'

'Do we ride?'

'Yes, on your own palfrey, Augustine, and Beatrice can ride one

of mine – Diana is gentle enough. At least both animals remain
well fed, for now. If you can bring any small grain sacks back as
well as intelligence from Sir John, that would be very welcome . . .
assuming it is safe. The nuns would provide a cart and horse.'
Maud gave them an encouraging smile, and more reassurance than
she truly felt.

They were fortunate, thought Alice, not to encounter Queen Matilda's forces after they set out at dusk to ride the ten miles to
Wherwell. Slipping out of the west gate, they took field routes where
they had some concealment from overhanging oaks and tall hedgerows, rather than the road – though, on the few occasions they
crossed near the main route, there was no evidence of the enemy.

'Where are they?' whispered Jacques, scanning the Wherwell
road from the shelter of his monk's cowl. He pulled back on Argos's
reins. Beatrice brought her beautiful white palfrey up behind him.
No one spoke as they sat listening. Something was wrong. Alice felt
it in her bones. A fleet of sparrows flew above her, straight as an
arrow shot, yet there was no birdsong, even though dawn was not
far off.

'We must be near enough halfway there,' Alice said. ''Tis odd,
because I expected to see sentries and to have been stopped by them
by now.' She touched the wooden crucifix hanging over her
breast. Her hair was tightly bound up beneath her nun's wimple, and
felt unfamiliar. Despite her unease, she was relieved to be away from
the sieges within and without Winchester, from the monotony of
days passed confined to the castle, and away from the constant danger presented by enemy soldiers who were making sorties into
Winchester's ruined streets. The only gate Maud's forces now controlled was the west gate. Daily, there were skirmishes within the
town itself. She reached over and stroked Augustine's neck. 'We'll
be there soon,' she whispered. 'And I promise you the biggest bag of
oats you've eaten in weeks.'

Some miles further on, they were riding up a grassy hill which,
once descended, should have brought them parallel to the priory. As

they approached the summit, Alice saw a thin plume of smoke curling up from the direction in which they were headed. She felt her heart thumping within her ribcage. A familiar acrid smell was drifting on the breeze. Jacques reached the hill's brow first. He raised his hand in warning and slid down off Argos's back. Alice saw the anguish on his face as he turned back and said, 'Wherwell has been fired.'

Alice came off the familiar Augustine's back with ease, whilst Beatrice, inhibited by her nun's habit and an unfamiliar horse, dismounted more awkwardly, helped by Jacques. Alice's legs were wobbly and shaking. They stood in a row on the hill ridge, shading their eyes with their hands. A mile from the priory, the smell was that of burning straw.

Beatrice clutched Alice's arm in terror. 'It's happening all over again,' she gasped. 'If we go any closer, we'll be caught up in it.' She pointed. 'Look into the distance, towards the church tower. It's burning. I think some of the priory is, too.'

'How large is the garrison there?' asked Alice. 'How many men, Jacques?'

'Sir John leads three hundred knights. By the saints, I wonder – could they have they got away?'

'If they have, they are certainly not running in our direction,' Alice answered. 'And not if they've been captured or killed, either. I fear for the nuns. Was Sir John not protecting them?'

'I want to move nearer to find out,' Jacques said. 'You and Beatrice stay with the horses.'

'No,' Alice said firmly. 'There's nowhere to hide, except to go back a few miles into woodland, and I do not wish to be trapped there. We'll go forward together, keeping to the field track under the trees. Perhaps we'll stop and wait for you in those trees, just a little further on.' She pointed to a copse to the left and below the hill.

'Then we had best move slowly. Stay close together and pray we are not attacked.'

'No,' said Beatrice, who was displaying great courage, Alice noticed, though her teeth were chattering with fear. 'I think they are all still trapped in the abbey. The enemy would go east from there, to Guildford, bringing booty and prisoners with them. Oh, it looks as if they are putting the fires out now.'

It was true. This was not like Winchester. The church tower was smoking and some adjacent buildings were alight, but much of the abbey itself looked unharmed. As they drew closer, stopping at around a half-mile's distance from Wherwell, they could hear shouts and cries drifting towards them, as well as the clang of weapons and feminine screams. They dismounted within the copse of trees.

'Stay here, and I'll move forward on foot,' Jacques said. 'I'll see if I can find out anything more, though what we can see from here speaks for itself. We should turn about and get back to Winchester before that force does, with their demands for ransoms and surrender. You'll not be collecting herbs today, Alice.' He gave her a grim smile.

'Last thing on my mind, with that in view.' She pointed to the smoking church tower. 'Godspeed, Jacques,' she said. 'Stay close to the hedgerows. You may be wearing a monk's habit and have tonsured your head, but you are still a knight.' She managed a half-smile. 'And at least you understand Latin.'

They drew their horses into an adjacent copse, under a stand of beech trees, and, holding hands, they waited and waited. To Alice, it seemed as if Jacques was never returning. Her heart felt as if a stone was lodged in it. If he had been taken, how could she live without him? Of a sudden, there was a wild ringing of the abbey bells, discordant rather than musical. She clutched hold of Beatrice's arm. It sounded as if some kind of battle was being fought up in the church tower. The bells were not ringing in any normal manner. Occasionally, it even seemed as if they were being struck by the backs of swords.

After a while, the women heard the sounds of several people crashing through the beeches. This time, Beatrice seemed the calmer one. Alice tensed until she saw Jacques' familiar silhouette pausing to look about him.

Shaking with both terror and relief, Alice hissed, 'Pray holy Saint

Cecilia! It is you, Jacques.' She squinted again through the foliage. 'And who is this?'

Hiding behind Jacques' habit, she made out a boy and a girl, their faces smeared with dirt and smoke. She guessed them to be from around ten to thirteen summers. The little maid was clutching Jacques' hand. The boy was older, she realised, than thirteen, just small. He hung back.

'I found them crawling along the field furrows, through corn stubble. They were in the abbey. Eva and Thomas are their names.'

'Are you nuns?' Eva asked, still clutching Jacques' hand.

'For today,' Alice said.

The children looked well fed, if simply clothed. Both were tow-headed and wide-eyed. Eva spoke clearly: 'Soldiers came and attacked the other soldiers.'

Thomas said, 'You should not go near the abbey. The nuns have locked themselves in the refectory. The church was fired with burning brands. Sir John and a few others were up in the tower, but they fought their way out. A fire brand caused the lead to melt. It got into Sir John's eye.'

'How do you know all this?' she asked.

'When the soldiers let the horses out of the stable, I captured him his own horse, and lucky he was for it. I sent it into the orchard. Another couple of horses were already tethered in the orchard to graze. Oh, Sir John, he was in a bad way – wasn't he, Eva? Injured terrible. I tore the bottom of my shirt, gave him a cloth to tie over his eye and head. I caught another horse for the knight was with him. They got away. Sir John's knight said to me, "Get out now, whilst you can, lad." I ran back to the stables, and Eva, here, was trying to hide under a horse trough. I found her in a dark corner, under some hay. Horses were all gone. There's a small door behind the straw bales where Eva hid, so we squeezed through, ran back to the orchard and into yonder fields.' He jabbed a finger at Eva. 'She's to be a nun, one day. She's my friend and I am her protector.'

Eva let go of Jacques' hand. She folded her arms in a determined manner. 'I love God, but I don't want to be a novice. My parents are dead. I won't go back there. Thomas will look after me and I can work.'

'I see, Eva. What do you do at the abbey, Thomas?' Alice asked.

'I look after the horses, of course. It's how I got to know Sir John. I groomed his horse. How else could I know about the good grazing in the orchard? Lucky, that was. God blessed Sir John this day,' he said simply. 'And I look after the Abbess's two sparrowhawks.'

'My brother loves the hawks too,' Alice said. She looked at Jacques. 'What do we do? Why has none other come our way?'

Jacques said, 'Dead or prisoners. There's nothing we can do at the abbey.' His eyes were weary as he focused on Alice. 'Yes, the King's army have taken prisoners. You are right, Alice. None as yet were coming our way, but, if they feel it safe to escape, I'll warrant, once darkness falls again, they'll be making for Winchester . . . survivors such as young Thomas, here, at any rate. The bastards are forming a column of injured and prisoners. Saw it for myself. I slipped into the orchard too and climbed up a tree by the field-edge wall.'

'The wall?' said Alice idiotically, and Jacques' tired face broke into a smile.

'The monk's habit was a nuisance, I can tell you. But 'tis how I spotted this pair in the field. Ypres's men are not coming this way – not yet. Once they go, they'll take what food they can raid as well. We cannot go in there for fear of discovery. It's all but over. They were taken by surprise before dawn.'

'That's right,' said Thomas. 'Not going back either.' He folded his arms over his thin chest.

'I wonder where Sir John was headed. You say he rode off?'

Thomas shrugged. 'By a back lane, but who knows where to. The nuns will go to Andover if the nunnery has no food. They talked about moving there when Sir John came to Wherwell. This was their plan, but then the enemy descended upon them like demons from Hell. There be fine ladies there too, in the priory, and orphan children.' He glanced at Eva, as if to say she was one such. 'The soldiers took the lutes and treasures and hangings and silver . . . and they loaded sackfuls of food onto their horses, and those fine horses they stole too,' he said, shaking his head.

Alice drew her eyes down to his torn shirt, hoping it was clean, or else Sir John's wound might become infected. 'Well, I pray Sir John gets a doctor, wherever that brave man has gone.'

Beatrice said, 'Jacques, what about the nuns? Should we not help them?'

'We must pray they are coming to no harm. You heard the lad – they'll try to get to Andover. The best we can do is get back to Winchester before Ypres does. We must warn the castle. So . . . no more talking, for now . . . Thomas, are you coming with us?'

The lad nodded.

'You take Sister Beatrice's palfrey, in that case, and, seeing as you know horses, you'll stay close to me and handle that palfrey well. Eva will ride behind you. If we are stopped, you are servants to Sister Beatrice and Sister Alice, mind. You came from the Nunnaminster in Winchester, seeking provisions from Wherwell – herbs and flour – but turned back when you saw smoke. Oh, and by the way, the nuns of Nunnaminster are taking refuge in Saint Swithun's Minster. Mind that, if asked.' He turned to Beatrice. 'You can ride behind me, on Argos, Sister Beatrice.'

'Yes, Brother Jacques, we are wise to return to Winchester.'

Helping Beatrice up onto the jennet and taking the reins, he looked around him. 'I'll walk to the edge of the wood, here. Watch for my signal and follow when I wave you out. Single file. You first, Sister Alice, and, Thomas, you'll follow. Are we in agreement?'

They all nodded, but Thomas looked baffled for a moment and asked, 'Where are we really going, if this is the Lady Maud's palfrey? The castle? Another nunnery?'

Alice laughed. The lad was sharp. 'You'll find out soon enough, but you'll be safe, I promise, and so will Eva, and that's all that matters for now. But we have to get back first.'

When she heard about Wherwell, Maud – who had not eaten, so worried was she at the lack of food for her household – felt faint.

Brien helped her to her chair. Thank heavens, always, for Brien, thought Maud, letting her hand brush the back of his neck. Now more than ever, she wished to be held by him. But Brien was loyal to Tilda.

Brien had brought Alice, Beatrice, Jacques and the two young people into the great chamber behind the hall to meet with King David, Earl Robert and Miles. The girl and boy hung back, but Jacques pushed them forward. They were clearly in awe of her and the noble persons with her.

'You say Sir John got away?' she asked again. Her voice betrayed her fear, she knew. This had not gone well. Though – thanks be to the Virgin – Alice, Jacques and Beatrice had returned to tell the tragic story. Then she grasped what this would mean. They were lost. Winchester would be sacked by the false queen's forces. She might well be taken prisoner – and, whilst Stephen was still held by Mabel in Bristol Castle, that would count for nothing if she was taken by Queen Matilda. Her cause would be lost. She blinked back her tears of frustration. 'Sir John?' she repeated, trying desperately to chase away the fear haunting her and to sound in control of her emotions.

'With another knight,' Jacques repeated.

'I wonder where he is,' Robert said, anxiously scratching his head. 'He has not ridden here, though I suppose he would consider it too dangerous and assume the road was guarded by royalist troops.'

'It'll be to his own castle of Lugershall, for certes. It lies twenty miles to the north-west of Winchester,' Miles said calmly.

'I pray the nuns and all the other women of Wherwell are safe. I hope there were some horses, carts and food left.' Maud shook her head. 'If they took plunder, or despoiled virgins, God will never forgive them – or her, that evil woman who calls herself a queen,' she said sadly. She looked at Robert, feeling sorrow gather in her eyes. She was sleeping badly. She was exhausted, and so, so desperately in need of rest.

'They'll seek ransoms and we'll have to abandon Winchester if we are to get any of our captured knights given back alive,' Robert said quietly. 'We have hardly enough food left here to feed ourselves, let alone the people out there in the bailey. Wherwell as an outpost was our only hope. We need to consider what next, Maud, before it is too late. Ypres is ruthless. I don't think we can wait for Ranulf to bring us help from Chester and, in any case, I suspect he is capable of deceit. We can't send to Anjou either. Geoffrey is holding firm in Normandy.'

David said, 'The earls fear us Scots taking their northern lands. My noblemen will want compensation if they ride south. That would cost you dear.'

Maud said, 'Yes, indeed, not from Scotland.'

Brien touched her hand and, with his eyes, drew her attention to the little group returned from Wherwell. At once, grasping his signal, she remembered Alice, Jacques, Beatrice and their young charges.

Managing a thin smile, she said, 'Alice, Beatrice, Jacques, go to the kitchens. Find what food you can. Say I sent you. Take that pair with you, and can I ask you to take them into your charge?'

Without hesitation, Alice said, 'Yes, my lady. I shall see they are cared for, and have food. I am sure Jacques can use a boy good with horses, and I could use the little maid here, to help me, for now. We'll find them fresh clothing and bedding. Can Eva sleep in our bower chamber until we return to Oxford?'

'Yes, she may. It's the least I can do.' Maud sighed, wondering how many more lost children she would have to find homes for, or abbeys to care for them. 'But when we get word to Wherwell or Andover, they may want her returned to them,' she said with firmness, noting how the child scowled.

After they had departed, Maud faced her council's long faces. They had now used up the good fortune of a lifetime. She knew they would have no option but to retreat.

Stragglers from the attack at Wherwell Priory struggled into Winchester through the west gate over the next few days and nights. Wretched, silent little groups of men-at-arms and surviving crossbowmen tried to avoid Ypres's patrols on the old Ickniell Way, just as they had done a week earlier on the way to Wherwell, and – as Alice and her companions had been – some were disguised as the religious. Considering it carefully, Robert warned Maud once again that they must retreat before there was no possibility of escape or relief. They had no food, he said. The queues in the bailey were too long. People were quarrelling over crusts. Soon, it would be rat soup and cat meat, he told her . . . after the horses were slaughtered.

To his relief, persuaded by David, Miles and Brien, she agreed. Maud could be stubborn, but she, looking thin and so, so, tired, clearly knew it was their best option, and their only one.

Robert conferred with Miles and Brien, David and Maud, all seated in a hushed group around the council table.

'William of Ypres holds the Andover road for Queen Matilda, so we must take the route west and avoid his barriers. The Salisbury road will be safe, once we are through Stockbridge and over the River Test. Maud, you will leave first, before dawn, with Count Brien and his squadron of fast-riding and able knights.'

Maud's eyes briefly met Brien's over the table. He raised an eyebrow at her.

'Your ladies, including Alice, together with Jacques, a guard, and the little lassie and lad, will ride with the Archbishop of Canterbury shortly after, carrying a flag of truce; they'll also be accompanied by archers, as well as the Archbishop's own knights. The enemy, even William of Ypres, will not dare attack him. Your women should don nuns' habits. Their instruction will be to part from the Archbishop after crossing the river and ride west for Sir John's fortress of Lugershall with Jacques and his men. After *their* departure, another squadron rides from the west gate, led by Miles and David.' The look he gave them all was firm. He would brook no disagreement. 'They will catch you up at Lugershall. We ride to Devizes and Gloucester from there, using abbeys to break the journey when we are safely away from Ypres and his armies.'

There was a moment's silence as they absorbed the plan, after which he said, 'And I shall take up the rearguard. Any attack will most likely come from the rear. We will all have to cross the River Test. That, too, will be challenging. Like Andover, it's another potential site for an ambush.' He leaned over the map spread out on the council table. 'Do you all understand?'

They nodded. Maud departed to tell her women to pack.

'We'll regroup at Sir John's fortress,' Robert told the others. 'Our final destination will be Gloucester, where we should be safe. It's far from London, and I hold power there. Our departure will be staggered, but we should all be on the road before daybreak.'

Well before dawn, Robert drew the departing troops up in an orderly fashion in the castle bailey. Torchlight glowed around the bailey walls. He glanced up. Stars glittered in the night sky and a crescent moon hung like an eerie suspended boat amongst them. He watched his sister mount a charger and, riding astride, her cloak's hood drawn close about her face, trot forwards out of the city gate onto the ancient Salisbury road. He walked up and down the remaining group, instructing them when to depart. Before he took up the rear of the column with his own knights, archers, crossbowmen and infantry, he first knelt in the bailey, in a pool of torchlight, and prayed they would all reach Lugershall safely.

'Bring our dear Lady from the jaws of Hell into safety, and God preserve those souls left behind.' He knew well what happened in cities when besieging troops rode in. He hoped all men would have the sense to hide their daughters, and that Bishop Henry and Queen Matilda, a mother herself, would see that the survivors of the fires in August were not punished for their support of Empress Maud.

He climbed onto his black charger and prepared to follow Miles and David and their troops out of Winchester's west gate.

Chapter Twenty-One

Lugershall, Gloucester and Rochester Castle

As Brien and Maud approached the River Test, she sensed danger. They had ridden fast, but the Test was still near Winchester, and the enemy was on the move. Dawn was breaking. 'We don't have far now,' Brien called over to her. 'The Archbishop should not be too far behind. We'll reach Sir John by nightfall.'

Maud was more used to riding a palfrey than a charger. Whilst she did not wish to show her discomfort, the saddle was chafing the inside of her thighs and her soft skin smarted with sores. She dared not pause to look. They were galloping harder than she ever had before. 'Are you sure we are not being watched?' she said anxiously. 'I feel enemies all around us.'

'No, there would have been barriers across the road and we have not encountered any so far,' Brien said. 'We just need to get over the Test, all of us, so the others can have a clear crossing. When I give the signal, you must push your steed through the water. The Archbishop most likely will cross over the ford, up there.' He pointed, and through the trees Maud could see the Test flowing fast into the village of Stockbridge. 'We'll cross down there, before the village.' He pointed. 'We *can* ride through the water, there. Can you do this, Maud?'

She agreed to the crossing point and turned her mount further downstream, as Brien indicated. They began to slowly encourage the horses through the water. Their small band of advance horsemen, around twenty, had no problem. They paused on the opposite bank, watching whilst Maud crossed, her horse splashing through the fast-flowing river, with Brien leading her over the slippery stones on the river's bed. The stallion was sure-footed and they reached the opposite bank without misadventure. It was as they waited for the rest of Brien's horsemen to cross, screened by oaks and keeping close to the willows that dipped to the water, that they heard the distant sound of hoofs and voices from the direction of the village.

Brien wasted not a moment. He raised his arm and shouted at those already over the river to ride on. He screamed at Maud, 'Ride for your life! We can still get away! My soldiers will hold them back.'

Maud raised her riding whip and used it on the stallion's rump. The horse shot forward, with her clutching the reins, fearful of falling, almost forgetting the welts on her thighs and her sodden skirts as she concentrated on remaining in control of the stallion.

'Do not glance back!' came Brien's voice, crying from behind her. 'Keep up your gallop, Maud. There are not so many of them.'

She rode faster than ever, even though she could hear shouts and swords clashing back by the river.

'We cannot stop until we reach Lugershall.' Brien, catching her up, was breathless, and much of what he was saying was lost in the wind they created as they raced forward, leaping hedges, parallel to the Salisbury road.

She grasped the point. They could not stop until they reached Sir John's fortress, and she had no idea how far they had to ride to reach its safety. Her thighs felt sorer than before. Blood was trickling along her legs and she knew she had rubbed lacerations on them, but still she urged the horse forward, encouraged by Brien, who kept pace with her all the way. The dozen troops he had selected to ride with them, she knew, were unrivalled in their ability, while those who had fended off the enemy around the river soon caught them up. She had no idea if any of Brien's horsemen were lost in the skirmish, but as she galloped on towards Sir John's castle it occurred to her that only a small band had accosted them, not a great army. She wondered if the actual army was elsewhere. Miles and Robert must surely be safe, she thought to herself. As for the Archbishop, had he already turned east for Canterbury? If so, were her ladies and Jacques on their way to Lugershall? What direction would they take? There was no sight of them on the downs. Most likely they *were* following. However, once word of the skirmish reached Ypres, as no doubt it would, Robert and Miles could be caught in a trap around Stockbridge.

They reached Lugershall's bailey by dusk, having outrun any pursuit. She had drunk very little water as they rode. Now, she was thirsty and hardly able to dismount from her horse. She felt arms reach up and help her from the saddle, and heard Brien say, 'My lady, you must rest.' As she reached the ground, she felt her legs trembling. Brien took her arm. He looked exhausted. All of them were drenched in sweat and the horses looked on the verge of collapse.

She accepted Brien's support, glanced sideways and managed a wincing smile, then shook off his gauntleted hand. She straightened her back and, with difficulty, but with determination, walked forward to meet the man emerging from the keep. She stifled her shock when she saw the extent of Sir John's injuries, forcing herself not to look away. He had taken these wounds in *her* service, protecting the road into Winchester. His eye socket was covered by a puss-stained binding. His facial skin was coated with crusts and was inflamed and angry; it was coated with goose grease. She refrained from commenting. Sir John was not one to relish sympathy.

'We need shelter, Sir John,' she said simply.

'And that, Empress Maud, I give you willingly. My wife, Aline, will look after you, for I see you are without female attendants.' She saw him scrutinise her company, and he added, 'You have ridden hard this day, I see. You and Count Brien both. Your account must wait, but I gauge that you have broken out of Winchester. And Earl Robert, King David and Miles are riding on your heels, is my guess. Still, explanations must wait. Go with my lady, Empress, and she will see you can rest until supper.'

Aline appeared very shy and she wore an enormous silver cross on her breast, suggesting she was of a deeply devout nature. She hesitantly came forward, curtseyed and, without a word, led Maud into the keep and to her private chamber. Maud was grateful when Sir John's wife and her maid brought her a jug of scented water and a bowl in which to wash. Aline provided Maud with a cup of wine, in which Maud tasted herbs, and she helped Maud undress and persuaded her to stretch out on the bed and rest.

'Rest before supper. You can talk later, my lady. Meanwhile, I must see to my husband's dressings, for the wounds he has need cleansing and the dressings need changing regularly.'

'It is a terrible injury,' Maud said.

'It is, and I regret I can hardly bear to look at it, but Sir John will put up with anything without complaint. Give him enough wine and he'll just drink himself through the pain.'

Aline's gentle talk was soothing and Maud must have fallen asleep. She woke with a jolt. It felt but a moment had passed, yet it was deep night, and the moon, visible through the unshuttered window, was riding high in the September sky.

Aline was saying, 'You must leave at once, my lady. Count Brien wishes to ride for the fortress at Devizes. There is too much danger for you to remain with us, though I wish you could.'

Maud cried out when she swung her legs from the bed. There was blood on her linen. Aline asked her shyly if her flux was upon her.

'No,' Maud said. 'It was the necessity of riding astride and my legs have been chafed by the saddle.'

Aline turned to a coffer and, searching through it, produced a salve, which she gently rubbed onto Maud's torn and blistered skin. She made bandages with strips of linen ripped from a bedsheet and wrapped them securely about Maud's thighs.

'We brushed the dirt from your gown whilst you were sleeping,' Aline said, as Maud slipped it over her head. 'Here, allow me to lace it for you.'

Brien was waiting in the hall.

'Why are we leaving?' she said.

266

Brien replied quietly, 'John sent scouts back towards Winchester. One returned with terrible news. Ypres fell upon our army shortly after they rode towards the ford. They had only reached Strete. Every man was for himself. He did report, however, that the Archbishop had got away with a group of nuns, so I assume Alice and your women remain safely in the Archbishop's party.'

'Praise God for that,' she said. 'The rest?'

'Those following us were surrounded and overwhelmed. Most bolted, but Robert fought them until Ypres and his Flemings overcame them.'

There was a moment's pause.

Maud took an intake of breath and exhaled. 'Has Robert been captured or butchered to death?'

'I know not, but they will want to take Robert alive.'

'Miles?'

'We know not either,' Brien said. 'But this I *do* know, Maud. You remain in danger here. It is the first place Ypres will seek you. Fresh horses are being made ready. We must try to reach Devizes by daylight. After that, everything will be clearer and we can decide on a new course of action.' His voice was gentle. Maud knew he was making a supreme effort to safeguard her. She must remain strong and without emotion; the time for weeping would come later. She closed her eyes, squeezing back tears of despair, before swallowing hard and thanking Aline and Sir John for their kindness. Robert, her brother, whom she argued with, but always, always listened to . . .

Moments later, she was mounting a fresh horse provided by the Marshal and riding out into the night to Devizes.

Maud did not feel herself collapse. She was riding one minute, concentrating hard to ignore her painful back and smarting thighs; the next she knew, she was lying stretched out on a mantle on the hard earth. Another had been made into a pillow and placed beneath her head. Brien was looking over her. His face was filled with concern.

'What happened?' she asked.

'You fell off your horse,' he said. 'Do you not remember? We could not stay at Devizes. It was too dangerous there as well. We rested a few hours, drank a little, ate a little and set out again. Too soon, I fear. You collapsed only a few miles from the castle. I have sent back to Devizes for a litter. It is not so far to Gloucester.'

'You mean I have to travel by a horse litter, as if I were infirm or ancient?' Tears welled up in her eyes. 'I have let you down, Brien. How could I?'

Brien smiled down at her and touched her forehead. His touch was loving and reassuring. 'Dearest Maud, you must travel by litter because you are ill and exhausted, and that is understandable. Your courage is to be admired. You are fearless and oh so very, very beautiful.' He laughed. 'And you are braver than most men, and you, above all, deserve our loyalty. We can't forsake you and so we must make sure you reach safety and recover.'

'What about Robert, Miles and the others, Brien? Do you think they survive?'

'I do, Maud. I cannot be sure of it, but I feel in my heart God will save them all.' As if to empathise the truth in his short speech, he struck his heart with his fist.

After she reached Gloucester, she learned how Robert, Miles and David had been attacked as they tried to ford the Test around Stockbridge, not long after she and Brien had ridden at full speed over waterlogged marshes and into the folds of Danebury Downs, on to Lugershall.

She was resting in her solar by the glazed window, staring out through opaque glass at a late September wind scattering falling leaves through the courtyard below, when Brien came to see how she was. She looked his way and at once concealed her sorrow with a vague smile. Brien joined her on the window seat.

'Where are they, Brien? Where are Miles, David and Robert? What happened to their retreat?'

Brien appeared to swallow. His dark eyes were filled with concern and she sensed disaster. He reached for her hands and enclosed them within his own. 'Robert fought with the rearguard as they were descended upon by William of Ypres and his murdering bastards. Fortunately, his life was spared; as we well know, he is too valuable a hostage. He was captured by William of Salisbury and Humphrey de Bohun.'

She did not move a muscle. In as firm a voice as she could manage, she asked, 'And the others?'

'The retreat became a rout. I came to tell you Miles has managed to return, near enough in rags. He threw off his armour. His wife is tending to him. King David got away with a number of Scots, but he'll be heading north now. Everyone threw off their armour and scattered. Maud, we have no army now. There'll be requests for exchange of prisoners and ransoms. Robert has been taken to Rochester Castle and honourable imprisonment.'

'I see,' she said, removing her hands and looking away to conceal her tears. All they had hoped for, since London . . . She glanced back after swallowing. 'What about the Archbishop? My ladies?'

'He got away to an abbey and is on his way to Canterbury. The ladies are safely in Abingdon Abbey. They will continue to Oxford Castle, protected by Sir Jacques and his troop.'

She crossed herself. 'Thank the Madonna for their safety, at least.' She thought for a little while. Silence was only broken by the clatter of spinning wheels across the chamber, and the soft hum of conversation. Maud glanced over at the castle ladies to whose presence she owed much these last weeks, since she had reached Gloucester. She turned to Brien. 'We must get Robert back, rest, build our army again and, if necessary, send to Geoffrey for help. We are fighting not just for my queenship, but for my son Henry's future. We have Stephen still captive in Bristol. England does not have a king.'

Brien seemed to study her intently. 'Maud, you must be prepared. It may be Stephen's safety in exchange for Robert,' he said. 'This is the most likely way forward. We need Robert to guide our strategy. He must be set free. I shall request that Stephen remains closely guarded, but has his chains removed. I do not like to think of Robert losing his honourable confinement.'

'Nor I, Brien,' she whispered.

'And you, Maud, are you recovered?'

'My sores have healed well, but my heart has not.' She looked away so he could not see tears welling in her eyes.

Robert was incarcerated in a pleasant chamber in Rochester Castle. His bedchamber overlooked the garden and his small antechamber contained a brazier, a table, a bench and several cushioned chairs. Unlike Stephen, he was neither chained nor in uncomfortable captivity. But the shock of his capture and his journey to Kent had aged him. He was exhausted and he was sure there were more white hairs on his already greying head. There was much time for solitary thought. The days following his imprisonment, punctuated by the cathedral bells ringing the Benedictine hours, weighed heavily on him and were lonely for a man usually as active as he was, one used to giving orders to men whose fate he could only imagine had been far worse than his own.

Robert could hardly grasp how the retreat from Winchester had been such a disaster. He had planned it so carefully. At least the Archbishop and Maud's party had escaped the attack. Trapped within Rochester's thick walls and heavily guarded keep, he had no idea of how Miles and David had fared. Their troops were dispersed, he assumed, or captured, and many would have been killed – too many. Winning the crown for Maud was now well-nigh impossible. But he must not lose hope, and his solitary sleepless nights made him come to a new conclusion. Winchester had been a turning point. They would concentrate on winning Maud's crown for Prince Henry, rather than for the Lady. After all, he was sure that was what his father – Henry's grandfather – had had in mind when, a quarter of a century ago, the earls had taken oaths to recognise Maud's succession, and he had later insisted she return to Geoffrey to get with child.

Soon enough, Robert was summoned to a meeting with Queen Matilda, as Stephen's wife insisted on being addressed, the faithless earls advising her, with the wily betrayer, Bishop Henry, in attendance. He was escorted by two guards into a council chamber and ushered to a chair by a round table placed opposite the Queen. She was petite, around five feet tall, with soft brown eyes set in a round face that, under her white wimple, looked motherly rather than queenly. Robert reminded himself that Matilda's gentle womanly appearance was deceptive. He must not forget she was determined to preserve the throne for her husband and her Boulogne lands for their son, Eustace – without doubt, the throne of England for Eustace in due course too.

As he sat at their conference table, wearing robes of fine wool provided for him and which he hoped had never belonged to Stephen, Robert stared hard at his foes and considered any advantages he still held. He determined they would take anything from him with great difficulty. His wife still had Stephen held prisoner in Bristol Castle. Count Geoffrey held much of Normandy for himself and his son. Maud, he believed, must have by now safely returned to either Oxford or Gloucester. She could fight back if enough of their supporters had survived the retreat from Winchester. He looked up surreptitiously and, glancing around the table, his eyes moved from Matilda to William of Ypres, whose black hair was tied back with a length of rough cord, to red-bearded Richard de Clare and a number of insignificant nobles. Finally, to his utter disgust, his eyes lit on the turncoat, Bishop Henry of Winchester. Robert folded his arms and composed his face so that it showed no unease, then he waited to see which of his foes would speak first.

It fell to Queen Matilda to begin negotiations. 'So, Earl Robert – may I refer to you as Cousin Robert? – are you treated fairly?' She was softly spoken, with a high-pitched voice. A greater contrast with sharp, self-consciously regal Maud could not be imagined.

'As you can see, Cousin Matilda, my lady. As you can see.' He touched the robe of blue wool, its sleeves trimmed with squirrel fur. He was tempted to ask her what she wanted from him, but that would be inadvisable. She clearly wanted Stephen's release and Maud exiled.

Matilda narrowed her mouse-brown eyes and nodded at Bishop Henry, who immediately launched into an attack on Empress Maud's

271

character, claiming Maud was unworthy of a throne, saying he had been mistaken about Maud's qualities. She had attempted to besiege him in Wolvesey Castle and it was she who was, he considered, responsible for the destruction of the city of Winchester. He snorted down his aristocratic nose and added, 'She has broken any promises she ever made to respect England's Church. She has corrupted the Archbishop of Canterbury with her lies and she has even attacked me, the Pope's legate.'

Robert did not speak, although Bishop Henry looked at him with accusatory, hardened eyes that appeared darker today than usual, like small river pebbles.

The Bishop added, with venom in his tone, 'If the Queen had not sent an army, Winchester would never have been liberated. The Empress is, I can see now, a woman of gross arrogance, who thinks of nothing other than what she considers to her own advantage. She tried to deprive the King's son of his inheritance and me of my seat at Winchester. She has shown no consideration towards the good merchants of London, making enemies of them with punishing attempts to fine these same burghers.'

Robert considered the Bishop's words. 'But, Bishop Henry, it was you who titled her the Lady of the English and who insisted that all, including the Archbishop of Canterbury, recognised her right to England's throne.'

Henry shook his head. 'That was a mistake I deeply regret.' He looked slightly crestfallen and mumbled again. 'An error I regret.'

Matilda threw the Bishop a steely look. Robert noted how Henry seemed to shrink into his expensive furred cloak. Satisfying indeed, even though everything else felt disastrous.

'So, what is to be done, Earl Robert?' Matilda's head swivelled his way once more as she spoke up, louder than before. 'Don't you see, Robert, how giving your loyalty to the Empress and breaking your oath to the King, my husband, has been misplaced? The King may remain a prisoner in your castle of Bristol, but the greater part of England still supports him.'

Bishop Henry, having quickly recovered from Robert's accusation, positively purred like a self-satisfied cat, 'So, Robert, we will make you an offer. Come over to the Queen and her earls, release the King from imprisonment, and you will be assured that all your lands will be returned to you, including those in this county of Kent.'

They wanted him to betray his sister! Robert smiled lazily, as if their offer was nothing to him. He kept his voice quiet and replied, 'That is not going to be any kind of satisfactory end to our impasse, my lord Bishop and my lady cousin.' He creased his brow. 'Because I do not shift my loyalties as others seem to, like snakes shedding their skins.' He looked pointedly at the Bishop, who gasped at the insult. Robert continued as evenly as he had begun, 'I recollect all those who, on many occasions, made a promise to my father to recognise the Empress, my sister, as England's queen after his death. As far as I am concerned, the crown belongs to her, and if not her, to Henry her son, my father's first-born grandson. So let this be an end to your requests suggesting I have behaved without honour, and, indeed, I remind you both that others of worth will do likewise and remain loyal to my sister.'

Queen Matilda impatiently rapped her knuckles on the oaken table. She said, with her lips pursed, 'This interview has ended, but I advise you, Robert, to consider your position. Perhaps we should send you into imprisonment in Boulogne, out of mischief's way . . . out of our way . . .'

Robert interlaced his fingers and looked straight into her hazel eyes. 'And, if you do, madame, I cannot guarantee that Stephen will not end his days a captive in Ireland.' He swallowed a breath. 'I request your permission to write to my wife, so that she knows I shall remain in Rochester . . . for a time.'

'Granted,' Queen Matilda said, with a snap in her voice, her serenity dissipating and her frustration evident. A heartbeat later, she composed herself again. 'Write your letter, Earl Robert. Tell your lady we suggest an exchange – an earl for a king. Have Mabel release my husband and we shall return you to her.'

Robert stood and bowed. 'I shall write to Mabel this very day, my lady, and speak of your proposal.' He chuckled, thinking this might yet go his way, although releasing Stephen could be a disaster for their cause – or what remained of it. They had lost too much at Winchester to recover quickly, including many fine commanders. He thought for a few moments before making a point: 'Exchanging a mere earl for a king is not seemly.' He shrugged with apparent nonchalance. 'The exchange, if agreed at all, should include more. I request other prisoners of rank should also be exchanged for the King.'

Richard de Clare, who had taken William of Salisbury as prisoner and hoped to get a huge sum for his captive's release, glared at this suggestion, his face growing as pale as sour milk. Robert was amused at the thought of Earl Richard, an utter toad, reluctantly giving up William of Salisbury, his noble prisoner.

'No,' said William of Ypres, who was burly, dark and red-faced, and had not spoken until now, but had exerted a silent, frowning, malevolent presence throughout the discussion. Robert realised the bastard was also determined to get his own ransoms assured. 'That is not acceptable,' Ypres barked at Robert.

Queen Matilda sighed, as if weary of it all. 'Ypres, you will not be deprived of your prisoners. Nor you, Earl Richard. There will be no haggling over souls.' She spoke quietly again. 'Go and write your letters, Robert. We shall speak again.'

The exchange was organised by the end of October. It was Mabel who arranged the Empress's side of it. Robert was relieved that he had to swear to nothing significant and was happy to ride to Winchester, despite bitter recent memories, remaining there within Bishop Henry's castle until Stephen reached safety. But then, neither did Stephen make promises. Each man would be free to defend his party to the utmost of his abilities.

Stephen was set free from Bristol Castle on All Saints' Day. As a surety that he would be safe, Queen Matilda had ridden to Bristol, along with their younger son and the fiery-headed Earl Richard de Clare. Once she was reunited with Stephen, she would remain in Bristol Castle until her husband reached Winchester safely, and

Robert, in turn, arrived in Bristol. On the third day of November Robert was freed, and Stephen departed for Winchester. Robert, too, had given a surety, leaving his heir, William, in Winchester until Queen Matilda returned from Bristol and was again safely re-united with Stephen. The exchange of hostages took the best part of a week in November.

Robert sighed when he was welcomed into Mabel's arms. 'King Stephen will be restoring his authority in the City this Christmas-tide, and, along with Bishop Henry, he'll overturn the Bishop's Winchester agreements of last year.' He held her tightly, then pulled away and reached for a cup of wine. 'The one comfort is he'll make that silver-tongued adder, his brother, explain himself, and Bishop Henry will squirm.'

Mabel said lightly, 'Queen Matilda is admirable and loyal to her husband. She and I spoke amicably whilst she was my guest. Stephen is fortunate to have such a determined wife by his side. I would that Geoffrey was an equally generous-hearted helpmate to Maud.'

Robert let go her hands and groaned at his wife. 'Don't you go approving the enemy! She has a hard heart. We'll need to devise a new strategy now that Stephen is free and we have suffered enormous losses. We can hold the lands and castles we have already taken, by the agreement with the Queen, but I am sure Stephen will fight on to recover them from us. They may have won a significant battle at Stockbridge, but they have not won this war. But our strategy must change.' He paused to swallow more wine. 'We'll seek more troops from over the sea, from Normandy and Anjou. We'll persuade Geoffrey we are determined to win a throne for his son. Maud will have to accept she can only hope to be a regent, ruling with a council's guidance, until Henry is of age.'

'And you will propose this to her, Robert?'

He nodded. 'I think I must. She will grit her teeth, rage at me and others, and we'll carry on the campaign, but she will realise that she needs a new approach. She will not be crowned Queen in her own right. England's earls will not accept Geoffrey – and, besides, he is only interested in Normandy. They clearly simply won't accept a woman as their sovereign. We came close to having Maud crowned, but it did not work. That is the new reality, Mabel. 'Tis unfair, but we can still fight on for young Henry's future.' He sighed deeply. Winchester and Rochester had taken a heavy toll on him.

'Come to bed, husband,' said Mabel quietly. Setting aside her cup and standing on the tip of her toes, she placed her lips on his. She tasted of red wine and smelled of summer roses. It was good to be home. He had never loved Bristol Castle as much as he did that night, and, more than his own castle, he loved his clever, faithful wife.

Part Three
New Approaches

Chapter Twenty-Two

Oxford
1142

Alice was the happiest she had ever been, excepting the day of her marriage to Jacques. She had given birth to a healthy daughter in the middle of February, on a sharp, crisp evening, after the hour of Vespers, in the upstairs chamber of the comfortable house in Oxford. Despite the flight and horrors of Winchester, mother and baby were well.

Ever since they had escaped from Winchester in the autumn, Alice and Jacques had made this house, granted to them by Maud, into a sanctuary and a home – somewhere comfortable for Alice to stay during the latter stages of her pregnancy. The stone two-storey cottage, built against the bailey wall, had an undercroft for stores, reached by outside steps, and a large hall above, with a simple kitchen space at one end and a still room at the other. The fireplace and chimney flue were a luxury rarely found in ordinary houses. Another addition was an internal staircase built against the hall wall, leading to a small garderobe and two upper chambers, both with arrow-slit windows and deep sills that overlooked a garden and the busy bailey.

'We are fortunate indeed,' Jacques had said on the evening of their return from Winchester, after the red-cheeked cook, granted to them from the castle kitchens, had provided them with a hearty supper, which they had enjoyed seated before a crackling fire. 'We must find a maid to help you, Alice, since our orphans have continued with the Archbishop to Canterbury.' The girl, who, it turned out, was of minor noble blood, was promised to the Church. The boy was set to looking after Archbishop Theobald's horses.

Alice had said, with a smile, 'I would very much like a servant.'

A week later, Gudrun joined their household, the cheerful, efficient fifteen-year-old daughter of one of the castle servants. She was unremarkable in appearance, except for her warm, honey-coloured eyes and straw-coloured hair, which was thick and worn in one long plait covered with a simple linen veil. Alice liked her at once. She was relieved that Gudrun loved babies and claimed to be experienced with them, having come from a large family of younger brothers and sisters. A widowed male servant called Ned, who slept below, in the undercroft, also joined their household. Gudrun and Bess, the cook, both slept in an alcove in the kitchen and seemed satisfied with the arrangement. Alice felt she had acquired a fine household. Looking back on her childhood as a mummer, she could not believe, sometimes, that she had the steadfast Jacques, such a grand home as this seemed to her, and the benevolence of Empress Maud, who she had admired so long.

As the weeks passed, the terrifying memories of Winchester gradually faded. Alice heard tales of what had occurred after they had escaped with the Archbishop: the ambush of Earl Robert's troops and stories of knights taken captive, their armour and weapons cast aside, and tales of others who, for weeks following the Queen's surprise attack, wandered the countryside in disguise. After Earl Robert had been taken prisoner in the autumn and was then exchanged for King Stephen, life settled into a period of relative calm, the two monarchs of England living in an uneasy peace. Jacques resumed his duties as one of Empress Maud's sergeants, and Alice worked in her still room, creating tonics from hyssop and juniper in wine to cure winter coughs, as well as mixtures of rose oil and vinegar to rub on her swelling feet. This was as her pregnancy advanced into its final months.

Christmas had passed pleasantly. There was enough to eat during the season, so, as expected, they frequently joined the feasting in the castle hall, where a semblance of jollity prevailed. Alice often thought about her family. Little Pipkin had married his sweetheart,

Meg. Xander did not come to the castle at Christmastide to play his lute. Alice was too advanced with her pregnancy to perform that year, so Empress Maud invited other musicians from Oxford's churches to play for them.

As they walked up to the castle from the bailey on the feast day of Christ's Nativity, Alice remarked, 'Has Xander given up all hope of wooing Beatrice, do you think? She looks so lovely, though a little sad, this Christmastide. She asks after him, but I have had no news.'

Jacques shook his head. 'These are difficult times. I believe that, with your other brothers married, Xander feels he must pass the winter season with Ingrid and Walter. When travel is safer, he will return, you'll see. There are many vagabonds about the roads, along with robbers and homeless soldiers.'

'Maybe in time.' Then she changed the subject, saying brightly, 'Cook says we'll be dining on roast swan at the castle. As for the ladies, they'll be enjoying the carolling and dancing.' She sighed and, glancing down at her belly, added, 'I am so cumbersome now. No carolling or dancing for me. I wish the child to be born soon. I can't even balance a harp on my knees.'

'You'll be singing again soon enough, Alice.' He glanced up at the sky. 'Clear night.' He pointed to the Great Bear. 'There it appears, ever constant.' He bent down and kissed her nose.

Once Christmastide had passed, Alice organised two midwives to come to her. The older ladies from Empress Maud's company visited the happy household, where a fire always blazed in the hearth, and they were welcomed with seed cakes as well as warming cordials. Alice sent them back to the castle with clay pots of skimmed honey, red and white bryony, cucumber and a little rose water to keep their lips soft throughout the chill of winter, or with tiny linen bags containing fennel, lovage and parsley to rub on their gums and teeth. The women stitched baby garments and helped her sew panels into two of her own gowns to widen them.

Her time came and Jacques was banished to the castle hall, whilst

Lady Lenora stayed with Alice and helped the two midwives manage her birthing in the second chamber above the hall. Her lying-in lasted a week, for which Alice was thankful, and she was also grateful for the blessing given her by the kindly castle priest, Father Thomas.

Ami easily slipped from Alice, after only a short travail, on a February night with a full moon and winking stars. Jacques, Alice knew, was pacing the castle yard, staring up at the night sky, whispering prayers to Heaven, clutching a medallion engraving with the Madonna's image, praying that her life and that of their child would be preserved by God.

When the chamber had been cleaned of the evidence of childbirth and the afterbirth removed in a covered basin, Alice was washed with sweet lavender water and dressed in a fresh shift. Her bed was remade with clean linen and, at last, Jacques was permitted to see his daughter. Alice had decided to suckle her own child. Immediately, she had felt a huge maternal love for Ami, as expansive as the night sky Jacques liked to study.

The two bustling midwives hurried down the stairway and Gudrun discreetly followed. Lady Lenora patted Alice's arm and said she was returning to the castle to tell the Empress of the arrival of Alice's beautiful daughter.

'A joyous event amongst us, after so much misfortune and tragedy,' she said quietly, her Spanish accent still seeping through her words. 'She is strong and she will be beautiful, like her mother. Why, she has a crown of gold already.' She smiled at Jacques. 'Ah, Jacques,' she added, 'you are most fortunate.'

'I know it,' he said, and Alice saw his adoration for the infant as she parted the swaddling so he could see his daughter's gentle face.

Maud sent Alice a silver spoon, engraved with the child's name and with that of Empress Matilda, Lady of the English. She also sent her a purse of silver coins bearing the Empress's name, which had been cast in the Oxford mint. To these gifts, Lenora added a fine silver bowl, saying, 'As you know, it is the custom, especially as you have asked me to act as Ami's godmother.'

Alice examined it, turning it over and over, then round and round, admiring it. 'Why, it has a silver cross and a fish engraved upon it. It's truly beautiful.' She looked over at the cradle. 'Ami will treasure these gifts always.'

Lenora gave a tinkling laugh. 'I wonder, will Ami grow up to sing like an angel —' she lowered her voice, for Alice was now a noblewoman, not the girl who had accepted coins for her singing so many years ago — 'like her mother?'

'I think she will at least enjoy the puppets, when she is older,' said Alice, smiling wistfully. Singing brought her so much joy. 'Ah, it is so long since we have had puppetry.'

'It is quiet around Oxford,' Lenora said. 'Perhaps Lady Maud can ask Count Brien to send your brothers to us. I know one young lady who would be most joyful to be reacquainted with them — and with the puppet master.'

'You refer to Beatrice,' said Alice, worried that, if she prayed too hard to be reunited with her mummer brothers, she might be disappointed. There were more important prayers for God to attend than those of Lady Alice.

Alice's prayers were realised, or possibly Count Brien had so to do with it. At Pentecost, Xander and little Pipkin through the castle gateway on the familiar mummer came with gifts from the farm — baby garments lo dered by Ingrid, and a child's walking frame, tho be needed for a while. Xander had not until no spring, he explained, because he was needed season and because the roads remained da time, they came with Count Brien and hi ing the Empress in Oxford for Whitsu

Immediately, the mummers' cart knights and ladies, and amongst the and Beatrice had eyes only for e

Ami for the brothers to fuss over and sleeping arrangements to be made.

'You can both share the second bedchamber. Gudrun will prepare it for you,' Alice said, with a huge smile on her face.

''Tis a fine house, Alice,' Xander said at supper. The weather was warm, so they ate under a mulberry tree in her small garden. 'How fortunate you are to have a place to call your own, a fine cook and a bonny maid.'

'It was the castle steward's house originally, but a new one was granted him, up above, in the inner bailey. I like it down here because we are closer to the town, where I can purchase the herbs I don't grow – like coriander. Besides, we are snug and safe positioned against the wall.' She smiled, proud of her home.

Jacques raised his head from his ale cup. 'One day, we must cross the Narrow Sea to my estate in Anjou. It's been three long years, near enough, since I have seen it.' There was longing in his voice. He lifted Alice's hand to his mouth and, turning over her palm, kissed it, sending a quiver through her body. Alice was as deeply in love with her husband as ever she had been. He added, looking into her eyes with adoration, 'And perhaps, soon enough, we can take possession of your estates held by Robert of Leicester. He may have run off to his Norman lands, but, when he returns, our Empress will claim them off him for you, Alice – as is your birth right.'

'I hope it will be so, but for now I am content,' Alice murmured, she turned to lift Ami, who had begun to demand attention.

Soothed and petted, Ami soon grew quiet again. The conversa-
turned to their escape from Winchester, and Alice related
terrifying crossing the Test had been and how the Archbishop
onstantly feared ambush. 'We were fortunate to escape,' she
ropping a kiss on Ami's head, 'for we were sure there were
hidden in the trees. But, after crossing the Test, we rode
speed to Andwell Priory, all the time disguised as nuns.
bishop parted from us at Abingdon Abbey, two days after

'You had protection?' asked little Pipkin.

'We had Jacques and his troop to guard us as we rode along the river road from Abingdon to Oxford. Besides, the Archbishop travelled with many monks, an abbess and her maids, and with fifty heavily armed knights.' She shuddered. 'I never want to relive what we experienced in Winchester again. I pray daily to Saint Cecilia that we may have peace in the land.'

'As do most of us ordinary folk,' Xander said. 'We want peace so we can grow our crops, trade, play music and see the seasons pass without fear of attack.'

'Amen to that,' added Pipkin.

They decided to perform the romance of Penelope, Odysseus and Telemachus on the feast day of Pentecost. Alice knew the story well and she liked working the puppet Penelope, with her black curling hair and slippery green satin robe. During twenty years of Odysseus' long absence from her side, Penelope was aggressively courted by two suitors who, while they waited for her favour, made free with Odysseus' possessions and stole his wealth. The suitors, voiced by Xander and Pipkin, grew impatient as Penelope sent them away. Telemachus, a handsome puppet with golden curly hair and a Greek tunic, played by little Pipkin, opened the tale, setting up his father's departure from Troy. The scene switched. Alice emerged from behind the curtain, took her harp onto her knee and began to strum and sing the soulful poem of Odysseus' return to Ithaca, moving the lengthy tale forward at a pace. Odysseus had been detained by the nymph Calypso on her island, but he longed for home. The goddess Athena arranged his release. Xander, concealed beneath the small theatre's lower curtain, raised Odysseus on his stick and Pipkin introduced a gorgeous, gilded ship with waves painted below it, using a rocking motion. When Pipkin removed the ship, up rose an island. Pipkin acted in turn Calypso, Athena, Poseidon and, finally, the Princess Nausicaä, who received Odysseus kindly and directed him home, at last, to Ithaca. There, he discovered Telemachus grown up and Penelope, who, in this version, had banished her suitors and welcomed Odysseus back to Ithaca, into her loving arms.

They, of course, had shortened the familiar story, which gives Odysseus many more shipwrecks and adventures and, likewise, parts of the poem, which Alice, who knew it well, sang in a clear voice, as she strummed.

'No soldier took on so much as Odysseus.
That seems to have been his destiny, and this mine –
To feel each day the emptiness of his absence.
Ignorant even whether he lived or died.'

As she sang the final verse, she was sure she saw Maud dip her head to wipe her eyes with a linen kerchief fetched from her belt. Count Brien took Maud's hand and squeezed it. Was that something he had always dared to do? Alice wondered. She did not begrudge Maud and Brien any love; it was long since Maud had seen her sons or Geoffrey; and Brien was obviously not in love with Tilda, though he was ever respectful of her. As for Beatrice, she was staring at the puppet of Odysseus, spellbound, most likely because Xander's voice was that of the hero.

I wish all endings could be happy, as it eventually was for Odysseus, Alice thought, watching those in love, and I hope we all find home. But where is home? Surely, home is with those whom we love.

She set aside the harp. Xander and Pipkin came from behind the puppet-theatre curtain and they all took a bow to great applause.

After the performance had ended, sweetmeats were passed around. Two messengers, wearing Gloucester's favoured yellow and red colours, rode into the courtyard. Leaping from their mounts, they shouted loudly for ostlers and thrust their horses' reins towards the stable lads who had been loitering around the courtyard wall, watching the performance. Maud appeared to receive the messengers graciously, accepting a letter they passed to her. Alice watched intently as Maud immediately broke the letter's seal, unfolded it and read its contents. Without refolding it, and with a raised brow, she passed the parchment to Count Brien. He studied it with a frown gathering on his brow and murmured into Maud's ear. Servants paused their passage about the courtiers. Raised tankards were lowered.

Everyone was watching the Empress. No one spoke. She nodded to Brien, and, her face serious, stood up from her chair, tall and elegant. 'I see you are all most curious. It is nothing to cause us any great concern.' She pointed to the letter, now refolded. 'Earl Robert will be returning to Normandy and Anjou to recruit troops for our cause. On his return, we shall continue to fight for our throne.'

There was a silence. Robert was leaving? It was as if a bolt of lightning had passed through the happy gathering. Earl Robert had a way of making everyone feel safe and that, despite setbacks, they could recover that which they had lost. He made it seem possible that, with patience and planning, at which both he and Count Brien were expert, Maud would regain her lost throne. But anything could happen during his absence. Even so, they needed reinforcements, and this was Robert's intended strategy now. They needed help from Anjou.

Their initial surprise at the Earl's decision did not, however, shock Alice, because, for a few months over winter, hidden from the outside world, they had been able to forget the destruction war had brought to them. Although Stephen was, at present, reported laid up ill in St Albans with some mysterious affliction, Jacques had predicted that, once he recovered, he would open a summer campaign against them. My poor Ami, she thought, after Maud's announcement. She is a child born into the sorrow war brings to the land.

Maud and Brien departed together, sweeping up the steps into the castle, and the musicians struck up again. Dancing was organised within the courtyard. Xander and Alice packed their puppets away. As they carefully wrapped each character in linen, Xander confided in Alice: 'If Earl Robert is sailing to Normandy, I shall ask Count Brien to request that he takes me with him as an entertainer.' He lowered his voice into a softer tone. 'Alice, in truth, I intend visiting Beatrice's father. He is one of Earl Robert's Norman vassals.'

'I know, but will Count Brien support this?' Alice asked him.

'You sailing away to Caen, I mean.' They had left Pipkin to move the cart into a stable and had wandered into the castle garden to stand under a hazel tree close to the gate. A nut knocked by a crow dropped between them. 'Oh,' she said, rubbing her head. Glancing up, she shook her fist at the bird, which was already flying off into another tree. She turned back to Xander. 'Well, what are your chances?'

He folded his arms and raised his head. With determination in his voice and with a stubborn set to his shoulders, he said, 'I intend to test my fortune, Alice. I am good with a bow and arrow, and am coming along with swordplay.' His tone grew gentler. 'There'll be more than music on this adventure for me. I hope to prove myself to win Beatrice – and her father, of course.'

'Well, I wish you luck, Xander. You deserve Beatrice, and she you.'

Xander reached out and took her arm. In a warning voice, he said, 'Alice, take Ami and return to Wallingford this summer. If the King recovers, he will try to attack Oxford. It won't be safe here for you. I am sure Jacques would agree. Besides, I think Ma would love to see you and her new grandchild.' He grinned.

Attack Oxford? She did not think so. At least, she did not *like* to think so. Sounding a little pert, she replied, with her chin tilted up towards him, 'I am quite sure we are perfectly safe, Xander, but, nonetheless, I shall speak with Jacques . . . and, anyway, I should visit the family, now summer is here at last.' Hearing crying, she glanced through the gate. 'Here comes Gudrun with the hungry Ami. If the crows leave me be, I'll feed her right here, in the shelter of the tree. Xander, ask Count Brien soon, because I am sure Earl Robert will sail for Caen before the calends of July.'

'Yes,' came his answer. He, too, peered through the gate. After another second passed, he said, 'I am going to join Beatrice in that dance, out there. See, our Pipkin is leading them all.'

For a few moments, she listened to the strains of the rebec and bagpipes and watched the revellers winding their way around the courtyard in a snaking line, hands on waists, led by Pipkin playing his pipe. 'I wish you all good fortune, Xander!' Alice called after his back, as he departed.

Gudrun arrived with the wailing Ami. 'She won't stop, my lady.'

Alice sank onto the turf seat beside the tree and opened her bodice. Her baby's teeth were beginning to come through and she could hurt. Yes, all right, she would go to the farm soon. Ingrid was good with difficult babies. Four months old only, but time Ami was beginning to get weaned, she decided.

Xander set out for Normandy with Earl Robert. And, just as he had warned, no sooner had the ship sailed from Wareham than King Stephen made a miraculous recovery, moving west only a month later. He laid siege to a fortified castle Maud had set up in Cirencester. It was in the west: Maud's lands. The garrison, alerted to his advance, stole away, and the news made its way into Oxford, with those fleeing recounting that the King had burned it down to its foundations. A week passed. There was speculation that Stephen was moving his armies closer to Oxford itself.

Jacques told Alice, as they broke their fast one morning, 'You are moving out of the castle tomorrow, down river to Wallingford and to the farm. I have arranged a boat with a ferryman and a small escort. No argument, Alice. Go and pack. Ami and Gudrun will accompany you.'

His eyes were full of concern for her. He sounded as determined as Xander had been about setting out on Earl Robert's mission. She knew he was right to care so deeply about her and, though she was loath to leave him, she knew he could not bear it if anything happened to her or Ami. This was the great measure of his love. She nevertheless found herself opening her mouth in protest.

He forestalled any argument. He folded his arms and stared straight into her eyes. 'I shall worry less about you and Ami if you go to the family.'

'I might be with child again,' she said, hopelessly wishing this might change Jacques' mind. But he was right. And he knew he was too.

He seemed to soften, and he leaned over and, lifting her hand to his mouth, kissed it. He drew her into his arms. 'Oh, my love. All the more reason for you to be safe with Ingrid and Walter.'

She felt as if she was abandoning not only Jacques, but also the Empress.

As if reading her mind, Jacques said, 'And I have spoken to the Empress already. She is in agreement with me.'

At this, Alice hurried from their chamber to the still room to make various simples, just in case these were needed during her absence. It took her all morning, but the work soothed her rumpled feelings. From there, she walked to the chapel and fell on her knees before the plaster, blue-gowned Madonna, who held a very large plaster baby Jesus. She prayed that the King would not attack Oxford, and for Jacques' safety.

Alice did not want to abandon Jacques. She could not bear for them to be separated again, as they had been once before, on the journey to Marlborough. He would be placed in grave danger if Stephen attacked, but her concern for Ami overcame her hesitation, and so, that afternoon, she packed up what she could, including her casket containing letters from Jacques written before they married. As an uneasy dawn broke over the river on the following morning, Alice left Oxford with Gudrun and Ami. Glancing back, she twisted her rosary and prayed to the Virgin Mary that she would keep her love safe. Gudrun hummed a soothing tune to Ami, who waved her arms wildly, as if she too did not want to part from her father.

Chapter Twenty-Three

Avranches, Normandy
November 1142

Robert swept into the hall of Avranches Castle, in Geoffrey's Norman lands, accompanied by young Prince Henry and a few of the Prince's companions. The boys had been practising swordplay until the snow grew too heavy to comfortably continue their sport. Robert had been observing them for a short while, and had noted that his nine-year-old nephew was already displaying ability in thrusting at and evading an opponent.

He mused on Henry and his friends playing with the greyhound puppies cavorting close to the central hearth, and how Henry was always the focus of a group of boys his own age, generally the centre of attention. With his reddish-gold hair and study frame, he displayed leadership qualities and a self-confidence Robert wished his own sons possessed. Henry had inherited his mother's determined nature and his father's skill with the sword. One day, Robert thought, he would make a formidable king. Robert's task now was to make sure Maud's supporters secured England's crown for her son. To this end, he wished his nephew could train for a time at Bristol Castle and, even more importantly, begin to understand the ways of his future kingdom. By Christ's bones, Robert prayed daily that, despite the setbacks of London, Winchester and Stephen's release from Bristol, Geoffrey would keep faith with his wife and grant them the troops he requested.

Since Winchester, the usual fickle supporters had returned to Stephen. Yet, Robert was more determined than ever to fight back. His own freedom had been exchanged for Stephen's freedom, and he owed it to Maud and to his conscience that they would try again to wrestle the crown from him. When Robert had left England in late June, he considered Maud safe in Oxford Castle, watched over by Miles, Earl of Hereford, though from the distance of Gloucester. Brien was not far off in Wallingford, only a mere ten miles to the south. These two loyal knights would guard her safety during his absence.

Robert had been frustratingly delayed in Normandy because Geoffrey had insisted he help secure Avranches before any military support was given to Maud in return. It was a successful campaign. Avranches was now firmly in Geoffrey's hands, and it looked as if Normandy was soon to be entirely in Angevin control, and Geoffrey, naturally, aspired to be Normandy's new Duke.

Robert, itching to move, drummed his fingers on his thigh as he watched men strut about the beautifully decorated pillars, gathering into sociable groups, all glad to lay down arms as the Christmas season drew closer. Farmers, who were ever weather sages, said they were facing a bitterly cold winter. Their predictions were correct, Robert mused. Snow had arrived early and it was lying thickly on the ground. The earth was hibernating and the successful campaign battles were already distant in the knights' minds. As his watchful eyes moved about the hall, he noted a group of ladies gathered around the hatchet-faced Count Waleran. The unpleasant Count, to Robert's chagrin, had joined Geoffrey's court, doubtless determined to protect his own Norman lands, despite Geoffrey being married to, and supporting, Waleran's enemy in England. Waleran had only that week returned from Paris with the latest French courtly gossip. The ladies were leaning into Waleran's conversation, listening closely. Robert's ever-alert eyes swept further on.

It was time to leave Normandy. As he stretched his freezing hands out to the fire and a game of dice rattled to its conclusion, Robert was shaken into the present by a chill wind gusting through the hall door. It opened to reveal a heavily cloaked stranger – a dispatch rider, by the anxious look on his face and the small scroll he held aloft in one hand, shaking a shower of snow from his mantle and stamping it off his boots into the rushes. The ladies stopped listening to Waleran. Count Geoffrey, clearly thinking the message was for him, held on to his chess piece, but began to rise from his chair. He stared towards the Earl as the messenger headed straight for Robert, knelt and lifted the letter towards him. Robert, taking it, said, 'Who from?'

The messenger came to his feet and replied to Robert's question: 'I come from Count Brien, from Wallingford, and I would have been here earlier, my lord, but I have been riding all over Normandy for this past month seeking you.' He breathed deeply and, shocking Robert, added, 'Wareham is held by Stephen. I had to cross from Corfe.'

Robert closed his eyes. This was not just bad news, but the worst news. Wareham was his port of entrance into the kingdom, once he had ensured his promised reinforcements from Count Geoffrey. That Stephen had acquired Wareham was a blow to the help promised his sister. He should have been back in England months earlier – and would have been, had Geoffrey not used him to fight in Normandy. Opening his eyes again, he drew an intake of breath, exhaled and moaned. 'By Christ's holy bones, Stephen has recovered? And is campaigning again?'

'The letter from my lord tells all . . .' The messenger looked stricken and he drew back, as if he expected Robert to strike him once he had read Brien's words.

Slowly, Robert broke the seal, flakes of hardened wax falling to the floor tiles. He read Brien's letter. He froze. He gasped. At first, he could not take it in. A few words jumped out at him: *Oxford . . . besieged . . . trapped . . . Maud*. He reread it, the words escaping involuntarily from his lips: 'My sister has been besieged in Oxford Castle. God has abandoned us.' He raised his voice. 'I should have been in England to protect her! I have let her down.'

He lifted up the letter and stared straight at Geoffrey, who was clutching his stone bishop as if it had frozen to his hand. Robert rose. Approaching Geoffrey, he said, his voice furious, 'Do you hear this? Your wife is besieged in Oxford Castle.'

'What?' said Geoffrey. He was startled.

'Read the letter from Count Brien. Whilst we have been campaigning, my sister has been placed in grave danger.'

Geoffrey dropped the chess piece. 'I see,' he said, with a distinctive chill in his voice.

'*Do* you see, Geoffrey? She is near enough Stephen's prisoner. Count Brien says the King's force is too great for him to take on alone, and he must protect Wallingford.'

Geoffrey's brows pulled together. 'Count Brien? Well, I am sure Count Brien can rescue Maud without my help.' He was tight-lipped and there was sarcasm in his tone.

Robert cared not for what scurrilous gossip Geoffrey had heard about Brien and Maud from across the Narrow Sea. He tapped Brien's letter with his left hand. 'This says Stephen arrived in Oxford three days before Michaelmas – that's two whole months since, Geoffrey.'

Geoffrey's blue eyes now looked as if they would pop out of his face.

Robert continued, 'Miles and Baldwin, thinking Maud safe with Stephen still ill, were distracted by an attack on Cirencester and left her unprotected . . . by Christ,' he said, glancing at the letter again. 'Geoffrey, thousands of Stephen's men are in and around Oxford.' He gazed earnestly at Geoffrey. 'You must see, I have to return to England at once to rescue my sister, and to do so I need fresh troops – those you promised me.' He thrust the letter at Stephen. 'Read it for yourself.'

A childish, but very loud voice shouted out from the direction of the hearth, 'Is my mother in danger?' Young Henry was on his feet, the puppies and his companions abandoned. He pushed through the crowd already gathering around his father and uncle.

Robert turned to Geoffrey again, who was skimming Brien's words. He did not wait for Geoffrey to finish, but said, 'You promised me men.' He was trying to remain calm, but his anger with Geoffrey, who had constantly delayed his return, bubbled up and spilled over. 'I have helped you on your way to a dukedom. You must help me and your wife secure a throne. Count Brien cannot release men from Wallingford. There are not enough of them. Stephen has surrounded Oxford Castle with an enormous army. Now, you must help us.'

Geoffrey snorted down his long Angevin nose. 'I can't go to England; I must consolidate my gains here. I do hope to be made Normandy's Duke, and Henry will follow me. *This* is his inheritance, which by Christos I'll protect.'

'Ah, Geoffrey, in this you are only in part correct. England is also Henry's inheritance.'

Just then, Robert felt a small, thunderous presence by his side. Legs firmly on the floor, chin thrust out, Henry showed his own strength of character. 'I shall go to England with my uncle and rescue my mother.' His face was resolute. 'I shall be King in England, and I want to see my kingdom.'

What a single-minded force of nature young Henry was! What a king he one day could be, God willing, thought Robert, and, despite his fear, he felt a smile curving up the corners of his mouth.

Geoffrey, however, was unsmiling. He looked stubborn, shoulders set and green eyes darkening resolutely. Robert was sure he would not allow this precious princeling to visit war-torn England. The men looked aghast at Henry's determined countenance. No one spoke until Geoffrey finally addressed his son: 'You may go with Earl Robert to England, for I cannot.' He flared his elegant nostrils. 'Too many might take advantage of my absence.' He turned to Robert, and Robert felt Geoffrey's eyes holding his own with a look as menacing as the weather beyond the castle walls. 'But your uncle must keep you safe, for, if he does not, he will answer to me with his life.'

Without hesitation, Robert said, 'I shall guard Henry with my life. He will be educated this winter in my castle of Bristol, where he will study the law codes and ways of the kingdom, which is his grandfather's legacy to him.'

'See you do, Robert.' Geoffrey stroked his little pointed beard. 'I'll spare six hundred of my army, and ships to transport them to Corfe. No more.' Geoffrey folded his arms, and Robert knew there would be no further negotiation.

It was inadequate, but it must suffice. They would depart before the end days of the month. First of all, Robert meant to take Wareham back from Stephen. He would advance on Oxford once he had recruited a big enough army to break Stephen's siege. Simply, he did not have enough men. His mind was ticking over and over, strategically. If he could distract Stephen to Wareham, he might divide Stephen's army. For certes, he could not ride to his sister's rescue yet – and, before he did, he would honour his promise to Geoffrey and ensure Henry safely reached Bristol first.

Corfe, the first young Henry had seen of his promised kingdom, was bitterly cold that November, the castle as grim as a witch's cave. Having seen to Henry's safekeeping within the fortress, despite snowstorms and a difficult sailing, Robert continued to Wareham. He captured the garrison by surprise, but, to his chagrin, Stephen was not distracted south from besieging Oxford Castle, so Robert fetched Henry from Corfe, left his own strong garrison controlling Wareham, and escorted Henry as far as Devizes, where he set up his headquarters. If only Maud could hold out for another month, he would – perhaps – have time to recruit an army to free her. He knew Oxford Castle was well provisioned – though, after three months, food stocks must be running low. Stephen clearly intended to starve her out during the worst winter they had experienced in decades.

'Will Stephen harm my mother if he captures her?' Henry asked solemnly, as they rode towards Devizes through a seemingly peaceful, silent, snow-covered landscape.

'No harm will come to her,' Robert said, hoping this assumption was correct. 'But let us hope, nephew, we can raise a large enough army to rescue your mother.' Then he added, more optimistically than he felt, 'You will see your mother soon, Henry, God willing. This will be the beginning of the end. But there will be anarchy as we have not yet known it.'

Chapter Twenty-Four

Oxford Castle
December 1142

Maud's garrison had manned Oxford Castle's walls steadily and resolutely since Michaelmas, when, as Robert had heard in Anjou, the miraculously recovered Stephen had crossed the river with his army, burst into the town and sacked it, burned houses and killed any who resisted. They heard rumours of rape. During September, the population of the castle swelled, as fleeing citizens sought protection within its walls, many just in time, before the Empress pulled up the drawbridge, sealing them all inside. Throughout autumn, the castle garrison responded to attacks. Furiously, they threw burning oil and boulders down at the enemy, until there were no more stones left to fire upon them.

As Maud sat by a tiny fire in the bower hall of the wooden castle, day after day, her thoughts raced desperately, always arriving back where they had begun. By the second month of Stephen's occupation of the ruined city, stores were running low in the castle. Their paltry heard of cows were slaughtered, as were the pigs, and finally – painfully – the horses. By December, the castle inhabitants were surviving on salty fish stews and a diminishing supply of barley. She was sick of it, though she had insisted she should not be treated differently and must eat the same and as little as those who dwelt in the bailey. There were simply too many mouths to feed. The possibility of rescue was growing increasingly remote. Despair was setting in. Maud wished she could become a bird and fly over the castle walls to freedom. It was she whom

Stephen wanted. If she were not here, he would save his army's strength and leave the city.

Maud carried the weight of guilt. Over the past weeks, she had been given a long, lonely time in which to contemplate her situation, and she knew it was her fault. She had not taken the advice of Robert, Brien and Miles in London and treated fairly with London's merchants; she had driven loyalty away from her and back to Stephen. Others had left her cause after Winchester. Her army was diminished. Her arrogance had cost them any advantage they had nearly two years earlier, when she had first set foot on English land at Arundel, and she found it hard to forgive herself.

Even so. Yes, she was alone – Brien in Wallingford and Robert in Anjou, as far as she knew – and felt abandoned, but she still could not concede victory to Stephen. Why had Geoffrey not sent men and arms when she had requested these during the previous spring? If only Robert had not become delayed in Normandy, winning castles for her husband. And yet, these *whys* and *if onlys* were precious little to comfort herself with.

Maud often climbed to the top of Saint George's Tower and walked along the battlements, from where she surveyed the occupying army's camp outside the walls, the enemy strutting about the city, yelling insults up at her people, and sending arrows over the moat into the castle bailey. They usually failed to reach their mark. Stephen had drawn up siege weapons and ladders, ready for a final assault, but the arrows and mangonels became a silent threat as December deepened and it became clear that Stephen's real attack was to starve them into surrender. Heavy December snowstorms were delaying the final storming of Oxford Castle, but there was no need for it anyway. By mid-December, they had only enough food to last a few more weeks, and Maud knew that, by Christ's Day, her surrender would be unavoidable. She walked the battlements, day after day, thinking she needed a new plan – a method of escape. In despair, her thoughts grew more and more reckless and ever wilder. And this was how her plan came to be.

Maud was greeted by a spy. He had exited the unguarded postern gate in November, under cover of darkness, and, using a small coracle, had managed to get to Wallingford, down river, and back again before the millstream had frozen over. He informed her that Earl Robert had returned to England and had taken Wareham from the enemy. Now, the Earl was raising an army to rescue her. The spy also reported that her son, Henry, was in Bristol, guarded by the indomitable Lady Mabel.

Maud's heart leapt weakly at the news and tears filled her eyes. So, Robert had managed to bring Henry to England – to the kingdom that would one day be his. How she longed to see her boy. A tear slid down her cheek when she thought how long it had been since she had seen her sons. She might die here.

No. If no one came to her rescue before Christmas, she determined to find a way to rescue herself. Once she had gone from Oxford, the castle could seek fair terms and surrender. Her daily walks had helped her think with clarity.

Maud dismissed the spy, and went to climb to the top of Saint George's Tower. Already, an idea was forming. Could she escape the same way as the spy? That postern gate set into the tower had been used for provisions to be brought up into the castle in the days when the city was free; now, there was no longer any traffic up and down the wall. Maud peered down from an arrow-slit window, tilting her head. The postern was half concealed by foliage. Stephen had most likely forgotten its existence or thought it would be impossible to escape his watch from across the millstream. If the messenger had used it, could she, too? With an unusual burst of energy, she hurried back to the bower hall and sat again by the feeble fire.

After some further thought, Maud called to a page and asked him to bring Sir Jacques to her. 'You should find him on the north wall,' she said.

The page, who had a decidedly hungry look about him, scurried off to do her biding. By the time the chapel bell rang the hour of Sext, she and Sir Jacques were climbing the staircase to examine the postern gate that was set into an alcove deep within the tower's walls.

Jacques produced a key, unlocked the gate and pulled the door open a crack, pushing the overhanging snow-laden foliage aside. He peered out.

'What can you see? Is the millstream frozen over?' she asked, barely able to contain her excitement.

He quickly drew back inside and locked the door once again. Turning to her, he replied, 'They are not guarding the millstream or the postern exit. However, their camp circles all around us, so doubtless they do not consider it important to do so. They are concentrating their guard on the north and south exits. I think you are right – they may have forgotten it, or never known about it. It is set quite high up, my lady.'

'That's a mistake he'll regret,' she muttered under her breath. 'And the millstream—?'

'Is frozen.'

She was thrilled and cupped her hands over her mouth to stop herself shouting for joy. Taking care to speak in a measured manner, she said, 'Jacques, this is our way to escape.' She drew a deep breath. She must get him to agree to her plan. It was a foolhardy idea, but it might work.

Jacques was studying her quizzically.

She continued, 'This is what we shall do. Tonight, we send our messenger out to Abingdon Abbey through this gate. His cousin keeps the stables there and he can warn him to make ready horses to carry myself, you and another knight whom I can trust with my life. But we do need a tracker, if there is such a one to be found, to lead us south to Wallingford.'

But Jacques was already shaking his head. 'My lady, you cannot be in earnest. You might be able to cross the millstream, since it appears to be frozen solid, but how can we get through the camp out there without being captured? Then there is the river, the Isis. It has currents and we must cross it. The Isis might not be frozen solid.'

'Courage, Jacques. We *can* do it. You will see. The messenger knows his way and he can appear like a beggar, and he must continue to Wallingford, for that will be our destination. There are so many mendicants wandering about the countryside, soldiers will not suspect him. He'll easily slip through their lines, though not back again.'

'But we might not.'

'We must try!' Maud felt desperate again. She suddenly remembered how it had felt when she was trying to persuade her father and Adeliza not to marry her to Geoffrey. But, this time, it was a matter of life and death.

'I can make us white coverings from bedsheets, Jacques. We'll melt into the snow out there, silent as wraiths. We *can* do it and walk to Abingdon. It's not far.'

'Far enough, in this weather.' Jacques, however, was beginning to smile, catching her enthusiasm. 'I do know a tracker amongst us. He's a Wallingford man and knows every hidden route between here and there. He will get us safely downriver to Abingdon. He is an able archer and has picked off a number of the enemy from the walls up above us.' Jacques then looked around at disused winches set against the wall, studying these until his eyes finally lit on something. He turned back to Maud, who was wondering what he was thinking. 'We can try to escape this way. The drop from the postern door to the millstream would be too much for you, and the winches are noisy, so we could not use them to lower you. You'd have to climb down that ladder, there.' He pointed to the wooden ladder usually used by the castle storemen to bring up sacks from boats in better times.

'I believe I am capable of using a ladder,' she said, with a laugh. 'I escaped London and Winchester, and, by Christ's holy shroud, I intend to escape from Oxford too.' She drew herself up to her full height and exhaled deeply. 'It's a half moon tonight, and cloudy. I think, Jacques, we can escape detection. Besides, you will see Alice and your child, once we have reached our destination.'

'Well, yes – that is, if we survive and Alice is not made a widow. And your ladies? Obviously they stay behind.'

'Stephen will not harm them. Once the castle surrenders, he will send them elsewhere. It will be a part of the terms of surrender. And if, as I believe, Robert is in Devizes recruiting an army, Beatrice's

301

much-loved Xander will be with him too. He had hoped to ask Beatrice's father for her hand. I sent a letter with my approval and my promise to see he is well rewarded by me. He's a fine archer and I believe he will have had success in currying favour.'

Jacques nodded. 'That was kind of you, my lady.' He hesitated, but only a few moments passed before he said the words she needed to hear: 'So, what time do we leave?'

'As soon as night has fallen. We'll give the messenger an hour's start and then follow. The snowstorm out there will swiftly cover our tracks.'

It was indeed snowing more heavily than earlier, and Maud was sure that this and her planned camouflage would be to their advantage, for it would keep them safe and render them invisible. She hoped they would be able to follow the frozen Isis River down to Abingdon with ease, moving through the treeline, guided by the tracker, and she was determined they would not become lost.

Feeling optimistic, she sent Jacques for the tracker and sped through the barely swept snow from Saint George's Tower to her bower. Her cheeks were burning from the cold, but her anticipation mounted with every heartbeat. In the bower, she discovered her women sitting in a cold, miserable huddle by an embroidery frame, trying to embroider a Noah's Ark, but making negligible progress.

'Set aside your needles and pay attention,' she said, with more than usual firmness. 'I have a task for you.' They glanced up with puzzled eyes, and she folded her arms, pinning her frozen hands underneath them. 'But first, allow me to explain my intent.' She told her women quietly what she was planning. 'We gather up white sheets and fashion cloaks, so that we may blend into the landscape.' She finished with, 'I am leaving Robert D'Oily and Hugh de Plucknet to see that just terms are agreed on our surrender tomorrow. By these terms, you will travel to Wallingford with a guard. You will not be harmed.'

'It is too dangerous, Empress,' Lenora protested. 'If you are caught . . . or eaten by wolves . . . or attacked . . .'

'And if I am taken prisoner by Stephen it will be a life sentence for me, as you well know. I value my freedom too much to be anyone's prisoner and certainly not Stephen's. This is my only chance. My brother will need to raise an army before he can rescue us, and he will be too late, because within a week we shall have nothing to eat. Nothing but rats. Well, I refuse to dine on rats, and I know the number of cats has already diminished in the bailey. All our livestock has been slaughtered a month since, so what else can I do?' She spread open her hands in a desperate gesture.

'I see,' said Lenora. 'And so we begin to stitch white mantles. All of us?'

'Yes, all of you. Collect enough sheets to make four concealing mantles . . . with hoods.' Seeing tears roll down Beatrice's cheeks, she added gently, 'You will all soon be able to eat other than scraps again. Think about that, Beatrice, and you will soon be reunited with Xander. I am sure of it. Now, whilst you stitch, I must speak with my knights.' She was brisker than she intended to be, but there was no time for sentiment. It felt good to make plans, to take action, to organise like a general. She felt as if she were flying like a bird, or about to. An eagle, she thought momentarily. An eagle flies high.

She hurried to the hall, which, apart from the kitchen and bower, was the only chamber in possession of a fire. They had been so desperate for heat, they had burned much of the castle furniture already, and she only possessed a cushioned bench and the embroidery frame in the bower, along with their beds and cushions.

The few knights she had asked Jacques to summon to her, and the original messenger, were waiting for her in the hall, gathered by the failing fire, their gaunt faces filled with curiosity.

'You, you, you and you,' she said. 'Come with me. We must parley.' She led Alexander de Bohun, Adam, who was her clerk, and Hugh de Plucknet to her own chamber, as well as Robert d'Oily, who had taken over from his very recently deceased father as the commanding castle custodian.

She recounted her plan without one qualification or hint of possible failure. At first, of course, there were protests from the four knights: the plan was impossible, foolish, risky. She countered these

303

with the argument that, if she was to be captured by Stephen, it would be the end of everything for her, her son and their supporters, and it would mean a life sentence for her in some dark gloomy fortress as his eternal prisoner.

'If we agree, who will accompany you?' asked her clerk.

'Sir Jacques, a guide and you, Hugh,' she told him, studying Hugh intently.

Hugh nodded.

She turned to Alexander de Bohun. 'Alexander, you, as my chief of guard, and Robert, as Oxford Castle's castellan, will negotiate terms of surrender tomorrow.' She laid out her preferred terms. No one was to be harmed. It would be an honourable surrender. 'You tell him you have concern for the safety of the garrison, but please do not mention me. Make it seem your decision to overrule me. Stephen is so arrogant, he will assume you would dare.'

Alexander smiled wryly.

'Ask for nothing except the garrison's safety and that of the women. He must not accuse you of deceit, once I have gone. You know nothing of my escape.'

'It is the only plan we have,' Sir Hugh said reluctantly to D'Oily and Alexander.

Adam, the scribe, still appeared doubtful, but he was outnumbered.

D'Oily shrugged. 'We must try.'

Maud breathed her relief. 'Make ready and meet me in the tower during the hour of Compline.'

That night, after the chapel bell rang for Compline, Maud, followed by Beatrice and Lenora, who were carrying a great basket with the hastily made cloaks folded inside, met with Jacques, Hugh and their guide, Wilnuf, a thin, pale-faced youth, by the postern door inside the tower. The messenger, clad in a beggar's rags, had been sent down the ladder by Jacques earlier. Everyone else attended Compline. The castle bailey was empty because, after Compline, everyone was fed a small ration of fish stew within the hall. Lenora, who had, at first, protested about the plan, now realised it was her mistress's best chance of survival.

Maud reassured the women quietly as they climbed the inside of the tower to the concealed door: 'Worry not. We will reach Wallingford tomorrow. By the terms of surrender, which order I have left with Constable D'Oily, no one will be harmed. It is the only hope we have of breaking the siege before we all become skeletons from lack of sustenance.' She gave them a cryptic smile and faced the waiting two knights, D'Oily and the guide. Her scribe had attended Compline. 'Your mantles,' she said, and they took the white cloaks with bemused smiles. 'I am not giving up,' she said to D'Oily. Her voice was soft, but determined.

'No,' D'Oily said. 'You are not. May God and his angels protect you, my lady.'

Maud's furs made her appear bulky and she had pulled a gambeson over her gown, as well as thick hose and linen wrappings about her private parts and legs so she could ride more comfortably. She glanced at her thick, soft, fur-lined gloves and down at her stout boots. She was not the usual willowy Maud.

Hugh, Wilnuf and Jacques carried flasks of a strong honey spirit concealed under their cloaks, hooked to their belts, as well as their sharp short swords. Jacques also carried a small sack of dried bacon, the last of that provided by a slaughtered castle pig in November. Hugh had, at the last minute, thought to bring flint and tinder as well.

Maud tied a purse with coins wrapped in soft linen to her belt. Thrilled by her own daring, she threw her white mantle over her clothing. 'No more time-wasting,' she announced quietly.

She extinguished her lantern. Hugh opened the postern door and lowered the ladder, which reached the snow-covered ground and neatly rested against the wall. The scout hurriedly climbed down the ladder first. He was fast and smooth as a starving cat. He held the ladder firmly for the others to descend. Maud followed, not hesitating. Quickly, Jacques and Hugh shinned down the ladder. Once they were leaning against the wall, perfectly concealed by their white mantles, Alexander and D'Oily drew up the ladder, closed the postern door and bolted it. Then, it was just Maud and her three men, alone in the dark fields of snow.

With Wilnuf leading, they stepped from the bank onto the frozen stream. The sharpness of the cold and vastness of the sky above caused Maud to gasp; after the confines of castle and bailey, it was breathtaking. The feeling of freedom so delighted her that, stooping to touch the ground, she nearly scooped a handful of snow together to throw towards Stephen's camp.

They were standing, on a millstream, their white cloaks blending into the landscape. Stephen's encircling camp stretched out before them: a terrifying maze of snow-laden tents. The silent stone tower and the wooden keep loomed up behind. A cloud slowly moved across the moon concealing its light. It's as well, she thought. Even a glimmer of that moon could reveal them to their foes.

They stepped gingerly over the ice and crossed the hardened millstream, with hesitant movements, taking care not to slip. It was bitterly cold and a sharp wind had risen, almost blowing them over; their progress was frustratingly slow. Wilnuf raised a hand to still their movement and crept forward first. He seemed confident of the way, which was reassuring. Maud was holding her breath until she thought her chest would burst open. Smoke was rising from the camp, which indicated anyone could appear at any moment to take a piss or seek conversation with another. Choosing a route carefully, Wilnuf guided them safely in the shadows between the campfires. Another tense moment passed and he waved them forward. They kept close to the fires rather than risk any sentries that could be patrolling the camp. But, miraculously, they slipped through the tents undetected and were soon crossing a narrow ice-covered stream just beyond. They still had to cross a stretch of open ground before reaching the River Isis, which would lead them to Abingdon, and safety.

Progress was still slow in the drifting snow and huge flakes were swirling about them, whipped into a mad dance by the wind. Maud kept murmuring thanks to God that the guide knew where the river lay, for she did not. The fields were a plain of white that seemed to have no ending, melting into a dark horizon. The four of them struggled on.

When they were some way over the meadows, a cart pulled by a gaunt horse suddenly appeared from the direction of the river, as if it was sliding over the snowy land on bone skates. For a moment, Maud hoped wildly that it might become ensnared by a snow drift or capsized by the buffeting wind. They all stopped moving, desperately hoping they were not visible, but the driver of the cart looked straight in their direction, swore an oath she could not make out and lifted his whip to his unfortunate horse. As she held her breath, she heard ice crack, but he moved on over the frozen earth to be swallowed into the snowstorm blowing across the meadow. No doubt, he was certain he had seen ghosts.

She let go a sigh of relief. The guide, raising a hand, moved again, and the small party of three followed until they pressed on into the trees. She was yet again thankful to God for Wilnuf, who trudged ahead. She glanced back over her shoulder. Oxford Castle had vanished. The camp tents were disappearing, though thin wraiths of smoke struggled upwards through the falling snowflakes. Ahead, she saw the frozen river gleaming through the trees.

They had already succeeded in crossing two streams, but her spirits fell as she took in the vastness of the River Isis. This was a wide river, and if it had not frozen solid they would be undone. The Isis possessed deadly currents that might suggest it had not frozen deeply enough for them to cross it safely. They halted. Crossing over it was a gamble, but it was one they must take.

They looked at each other and Jacques nodded. She saw his dark eyes glittering above the scarf wrapped around his head, as he reached out for her hand and Hugh took her other one in his. Maud had never thought she would cling to two knights in this way. Jacques had been her knight for so long, he was part of her family. Had she ever held Brien's hand so tightly, she wondered? When they reached

Wallingford, she would grip him as if she would never let him go. Clasping hands, they stepped out onto the ice. As they slowly walked over it, they watched for cracks. Maud was sure she could hear ice settling with a crackling sound every step they took. Every time they stepped forward, she felt her breath burn in her chest. Silent prayers caught in her throat, hoping against hope that, just as God had guided the Israelites through the Red Sea, He would keep them safe as they crossed the ice. She skidded once, but was jerked up to her feet by Hugh and Jacques. If she had fallen, she suspected her body weight might have broken the surface and she could have pulled them all into the river . . . had the ice given way . . . but it did not. It held true and, at length, they were over the Isis. They had achieved the impossible, but there was a long way still to go.

Further on, safely concealed by trees and the river to their left, the guide felt it secure enough for them to pause and drink from the wine skins. The spirit slid down her throat and warmed her bitterly cold bones. She was exhausted, but, managing to smile and refusing to surrender to her tiredness, she said, 'Let us continue. I think we have only four miles to cover.'

They took the strips of dried bacon from the satchel Jacques had under his cloak and chewed as they struggled through deep snow that, by now, was filling their boots and making movement difficult. But they battled on, glad that the drifting snow was covering their tracks, blotting them out as if they had never been there.

'I thought it impossible,' whispered Hugh. 'But I think we'll make it.'

At that moment, a horn sounded in the distance.

'Don't speak too soon,' Maud said. 'We had best press on. That horn must have sounded in Stephen's camp. It's only a couple of miles back. Maybe the carter has spoken of strange beings in the meadows.'

'If so, thank God and his angels for the drifts covering our tracks. They may look for us, but all they will find are ghosts haunting their imaginations,' Hugh said. 'Your plan, so far, is working, my lady.'

She felt Hugh's admiration for her daring and courage, and it made her more determined to reach safety. The snow eased into floating flakes until they could see the sky, and, as a rosy dawn began to appear, they reached Saint Mary's Abbey, Abingdon.

'The messenger will, by now, have arranged horses,' Jacques said. 'Hopefully he has not been questioned too closely. He looks like a beggar, but, of course, the stable master at the abbey is his cousin.' He turned to Maud. 'My lady, wait here in the woods with Sir Hugh, so you are not seen.'

They all agreed on this, and the two stayed, sheltered by a stand of beeches with icy branches, while Wilnuf and Jacques tramped forward to gain admittance to the abbey from the gate keeper. Hugh and Maud knew the Abbot well because he had often visited Oxford prior to the siege. She said she was reluctant to involve the kindly man in her escape.

'Stephen is notorious for making temporary castles out of abbeys. It is better if Abbot Ingulph can say he never saw Empress Maud tonight,' Hugh agreed.

Maud and Hugh waited, huddled in their mantles, trying hard not to fall asleep. They talked to keep themselves awake, desperately clinging to the notion that Stephen did not have patrols out, but she remained uneasy about the horn they had heard. At last, just as Hugh was trying to make her laugh at a joke, they heard the snorts of approaching horses. Two steaming mounts, led by Jacques, trotted into the clearing. Jacques said, 'The messenger safely reached the abbey and alerted his cousin, who keeps the stables, but I decided it would arouse suspicion to take four horses. We must manage, my lady.' He grinned. 'After all, we are much lighter than several months ago. These two geldings can carry us all.'

'Right, we move forward,' Hugh said, as if he were leading his troops into battle. He leapt onto the first horse and, reaching down, took Maud's arm and pulled her up. Jacques gave her a push from behind to settle her, and she was grateful, because her legs felt weak, shaky and numb with cold. Jacques then took the mantles and buried them in the snow amongst the beeches.

'What happened to our messenger?' she said, as Jacques mounted the second gelding and Wilnuf jumped up behind him.

'He has gone ahead to alert Count Brien.'

They had a nine-mile ride to Wallingford Castle, but steered away from the Abingdon–Wallingford road. Instead, Wilnuf led them over a cross-country track so buried under a snowy white mantle that Maud wondered aloud how he could find it.

'I know every tree and hedge and cottage along this route,' he called back. 'I could find it even if blinded.'

She doubted this, but did not challenge his boast. His sense of direction proved sound. Wallingford Castle, a strongly defended fortress built of stone, gradually came into view. When they reached Wallingford's walls, Hugh called up to the guards to open for the Empress Maud. There was a long pause until Brien himself came onto the gatehouse battlements; Maud was so relieved to see him, a distant silhouette with his distinctive shaggy dark mane.

'Well, look whom the snowstorm has brought us!' he shouted down. 'So you have succeeded!'

His voice warmed her heart. He had not forgotten her. 'Did you doubt me?' Maud called back, her voice wavering. 'Let us in, for Christ's sake! We are as frozen as those petrified trees in the forest, back there.'

'Forthwith, Empress.'

Slowly, the drawbridge was lowered and they rode over it into the bailey, which was filled with people. Many hands reached up to help Maud dismount. She was so cold and stiff, she faltered, but Brien was there to catch her. He wrapped her in his mantle and straightway carried her into his hall, followed by a procession of retainers. Inside the hall, men and women fell to their knees as they passed. Brien deposited her in his own great chair by a blazing hearth, still wrapped in his cloak. She could not have been happier than she was at that moment, first encircled by Brien's arms and now seated by his hearth. Hugh and Jacques pushed forward through the kneeling crowd. From the corner of her eye, she noted Wilnuf, slipping away, his arm linked with a girl whom she supposed to be a relative or sweetheart. He had served them well and she vowed to reward the man generously.

Having Brien exclusively to herself lasted only moments. Countess Tilda came hurrying forward with a cup of warm spiced wine and thrust it into her hands. 'Drink, my lady, and, when you have rested, tomorrow you can answer all our questions. I have prepared a chamber for you and there is a maid. As well, there is one here who belongs to your knight and is an old friend to us both. She will bring soup, bread and meat to your chamber.'

There had been times in the past when Maud had considered Countess Tilda a dour nuisance because she was married to the man she herself loved. Though comforting and competent, Tilda was humourless. Strands of escaping hair from below her wimple were as grey as iron, and her face was lined like a spider's web. It was unkind to wish ill of Brien's wife, for she was generous-hearted. That day, Maud felt nothing but good will towards Tilda.

'I thank you, Countess,' she said, before looking at the kneeling men and women. 'Rise, and thank you all for your warm welcome. My knights and I must get warm, be fed and rested, and then we can answer your questions and tell you of our escape. This I shall say: Oxford Castle will make an honourable surrender this day.'

The mass of men and women cheered.

Brien beamed at her and the Countess helped her to rise from her chair. Taking Maud's arm, Tilda led her to the stairway that rose up from the hall through the castle. In her chamber, Maud sank onto the bed and gratefully allowed the maid to help her undress and pull a clean soft linen shift over her head. And, just then, an excited and smiling Alice appeared with bread, a bowl of stew and an apple coffin.

'Thank the good Lord and all his shining angels you have escaped that hell, my lady,' Alice cried out. 'Praise the Lady of Heaven my lord has escaped with you. Thank you for bringing him here with you.' She sat the wooden tray on the embroidered bedcover.

At first, Maud was too tired to speak, but she stood and opened her arms, enclosing Alice within them, tears coursing down her cheeks. 'Praise the Virgin, we are all safe. Tell me all. How did you come to be here in the castle?'

As Maud ate hungrily, Alice said that she had been dwelling in Wallingford Castle since September, making salves and medicines in case there was a siege at that castle too.

'Alice, you must go to Jacques,' Maud said solemnly. 'And I can see you are *enceinte*.' Alice was bonny and round. 'He will be relieved to see you and without doubt you need to see him. Shoo. Go at once. I am in need of rest. Go.'

'My lady, I believe I still have three months left yet,' Alice said in a quiet voice. She lifted the wooden tray from Maud's knees and slipped from the chamber, leaving her a honey drink laced with camomile. Maud took a sip, but, realising she had no need of it, set it down on the table by her bed. She slid under heavy quilts and almost at once fell asleep, exhausted, happy to be warm again, and even happier to have gained her freedom – and respect for her strategy and daring.

Chapter Twenty-Five

Wallingford
Christmas 1142

A week before Christ's Day, as soon as Earl Robert knew that Maud had reached safety at Wallingford, he burst into the mews at Devizes Castle with astounding news. Young Henry was feeding a mouse to a pretty hawk whilst the castle falconer watched on from where he lay, slumped on a pallet. On seeing the Earl enter, the falconer scrambled to his feet.

Nodding a greeting to the man, Robert turned to his nephew. 'Henry, if Mirabelle is your choice, it's a fine one, but return her to her perch. You won't be flying her after all, today.'

Henry looked stricken with disappointment.

Robert placed an affectionate arm about his nephew's shoulder, knowing what he had to tell would cause elation. 'I have news for you, Henry. Come with me to where we can talk privately.'

The falconer dutifully relieved the boy of Mirabelle, taking her from him gently and returning her to her perch. Robert led Henry across the courtyard and set him down on a bench in his private chamber. He could not hold back a moment longer.

Feeling his mouth widening into a smile, he took the chair. 'Your mother is free, Henry. She has escaped from Oxford Castle. The castle has capitulated and her servants have travelled to Wallingford by the terms of an agreement made with Stephen by the castle constable.'

Henry's young face was suffused with wonder. He could not speak, so startled was he.

Robert continued, 'The bad news is that Stephen has taken control of Oxford Castle, but we are travelling to Wallingford for Christmas with your mother. Later, we'll escort her back here.'

Henry could not contain his excitement, Mirabelle clearly forgotten. 'But how did my mother escape capture?'

'Your mother has the courage of a she-wolf, the intelligence of an eagle and the determination of a strong emperor. She escaped from a postern gate set deep into a tower, and crossed the ice with a few loyal knights and a guide, all of them concealed under white mantles. They walked like ghosts through Stephen's camp, followed the Isis to Abingdon and acquired mounts. They rode on as far as Count Brien's castle. Is this not amazing, Henry?'

Henry's blue eyes widened. 'It certainly is, Uncle Robert. We don't need to rescue her anymore and I shall see her again.' He leapt to his feet. 'Hurrah! When do we leave?' He was, as usual, displaying the impatience and exuberance that went with the colour of his hair.

'At first light, Henry. And you will see she is no worse for her adventure. She is, according to the monk who carried Count Brien's message, strong and healthy.'

Henry jumped up and punched the dust motes floating through the chamber. 'We'll fight back, won't we, Uncle Robert? Take England. And I am to see her again — at last!'

'Henry, you must learn to wait. We shall consolidate what we have won first. I am rebuilding an army. We hold the west and my sister must make grants to abbeys to strengthen her power base here. After Christmas, Henry, you will return to Bristol and continue your lessons. One day, you will be King, and a good king understands statecraft. A noble king is educated in strategy, becomes a patron of the arts and supports the Church. There is much for you to learn.'

'But I want to spend time with my mother.' His face darkened.

Over the time they had spent together, Robert had noticed some signs of flaws in his nephew's character that would need management. Henry had been indulged by his father, and his nurses were clearly used to granting all his childhood whims. Under firm tutel-age, the boy would learn to curb his impetuous ways and grow discerning, as well as learning to fight like a fearless warrior. For a moment, Robert thought wistfully that he would not be spending any part of Christmas with Mabel this year, but he chased the thought from his mind. There would be other years.

'Will we hunt at Wallingford? I want Mama to see Rory, my wolfhound,' Henry was saying, his voice insistent.

'I cannot promise the first. It depends on how safe the forest and river are. Stephen will not have taken Maud's escape well, so his armies could be prowling south, looking for her – though I expect he knows very well where she is. Wallingford Castle, Henry, is one of the strongest in the land. It is an enormous stone fastness, and safe. We'll travel with a large escort, so I hope Count Brien is very well provisioned this winter, since he'll have many extra mouths to feed. And, yes, Rory will travel with us, of course.' Rory was a handsome, reddish Irish wolfhound with a rough coat, and was much loved by Henry, who had taken possession of him in Bristol. Robert smiled to think that Henry adored both dogs and sword fighting. He was a noble princeling, just one in need of rough edges smoothing.

'Mirabelle?'

'I think, Henry, you are to be entertained royally. We may not hunt, but, if we do, it's likely to be deer . . . or wolves.'

Henry grinned. 'I hope we do, Uncle.'

At first, Robert did not want Maud to know he had travelled to Wallingford with Henry. He wanted it to be a surprise. When, just before Christmas Eve, they arrived in the castle yard and he alone entered the chambers occupied by Maud and her ladies, she jumped to her feet like a started hind, dropping her book. He stooped down and retrieved it from the rush matting before looking up. Maud was thinner than he had seen her, and her dark hair was streaked with silver, but she was still beautiful and her eyes bright as ever. Setting her book on the side table, he smiled his approval. 'You are reading strategy of war, I see. Publius Flavius Vegetius, no less. We can all learn from the Romans, especially Vegetius.'

'Indeed I am reading Vegetius. I may not ride out in battle, but I can inform myself about strategy. And I am not giving up . . . But you never sent me word you were coming to Wallingford,' she scolded, but, as he bent down towards her, she dropped her sisterly kiss on both his cheeks. 'Welcome, dear brother. I am glad to see you. I thought I might have a much longer wait.'

'I did send a message forward. I asked Brien to keep my journey secret from you.'

'But why?'

'Because I have someone with me who should study that book.' He pointed to the Vegetius. 'A surprise for *you*.' He turned to the doorway and called, 'You can come in, now.'

Henry entered and Maud started and put a hand to her heart, round-eyed with shock. Her voice breaking with emotion, she cried, 'Henry, my son, come closer. By Christos, how you have changed!'

She had tears in her eyes. Henry, Robert noticed, though grinning, was at first – unusually, for him – a little diffident, not sure of whether to embrace his mother or not. However, Maud opened her arms wide and Henry, who was nearly as tall as she, stepped into her embrace.

Robert quietly said, 'We shall remain for Christmas, though we must discuss our way forward after that, Maud. Today, however, you have something other than war to occupy you.' He laughed heartily and slung his arm over Henry's shoulders. 'Why, sister, I had thought *we* would rescue you, but you rescued yourself.'

'Mama, you have not changed at all,' Henry said, before Maud could reply, raising a hand and touching his mother's dark plait. 'But I think you are smaller.'

'Not so, Henry, because it is you who has grown taller.'

It was time to leave them. Robert dropped his arm and slipped away, leaving his sister and nephew together, her maids, including Beatrice, tripping softly behind him. As he closed the door on mother and son, he turned to Beatrice. He winked and she stepped back. 'Go down into the hall at once, because Xander is waiting patiently to see you.'

Her eyes smiled as he spoke and she touched Lady Lenora's arm with a polite, 'Excuse me, Lady Lenora.' Before the older lady could signify her permission, Beatrice had flown down the stairway, as fast as a bird flying from a fowler's net.

The following morning, Robert met with Brien on the battlements for a quiet parley, away from the hurly-burly of Christmas Eve. Within the hall, Christ's Eve preparations were underway. Ivy carried indoors was bursting out of panniers. Mistletoe had been hung above doorways, releasing a pleasant if astringent scent. Glancing at it that morning, Robert thought with nostalgia of Bristol and hoped Mabel would forgive him for not returning to her that season.

He absorbed his high view of the houses, small gardens and distant fields. A coating of silver snow glittered on rooftops.

Brien remarked, 'We may have a Saint Stephen's Day hunt, after all. With snow covering the ground masking sound, deer can be more easily surprised and captured.'

'Henry will be pleased,' Robert said. 'I told him we might not be taking the falcons out.'

'No, because we'll have the hunting dogs instead.'

This was a vantage point over the courtyard directly beneath and, for a while, in companionable silence, they watched the Yule log's procession across the yard towards the steps leading up to the hall. Maud, too, Henry by her side, stood below in the snow, watching the log's progression. A page circulated amongst them with steaming cups of mead. Robert smiled as Henry accepted this heady, warming drink, clearly with Maud's approval.

'Strong drink for a young lad,' he remarked to Brien, with a belly laugh.

'He can stomach it. Look, there it goes, up the steps,' Brien said. Countess Tilda was waiting at the top, ready to welcome the log. Xander's playing of his bagpipes grew louder the closer it came.

Robert's watchful eyes returned to Maud again. 'She looks none the worse for her confinement in Oxford,' he said, turning to Brien. 'And so happy to be reunited with Henry.'

'A fine lad, too. His hair is as bright as burnished gold in the sunshine. No mistaking *his* parentage,' Brien remarked. 'He'll be both lion and fox.'

'Hot tempered, too, and impatient, but eager to learn. All good things come to those who wait.' Robert paused and turned to face Brien. 'We are fighting for him, now – for the lion cub. My sister said as much to me yesterday. So . . . my friend, we need to decide on our strategy.'

'Ah,' Brien said, thoughtfully. 'I *thought* this was the real reason you wanted to speak with me up here, rather than watching the young cub down there in the courtyard.' Brien stroked his neat dark beard. 'By the way, how did you persuade Geoffrey to let him out of his sight?'

'With some difficulty. Geoffrey used me and the fighting men I raised around Caen. We spent the summer on campaign, but he will take Rouen soon enough. When he gets control of Normandy, we are, of course, in a stronger position. That helps Maud's cause. He has released ships and fighters to me, but not nearly enough, nor as many as I asked for. So, I have been recruiting from our base in Devizes. We'll return there in January and make sure we are well equipped to protect the territory west of here and south through the Kennet Valley.' He laughed heartily, now thinking about Maud's daring escape. 'Stephen must have been furious to find his bird had flown.'

'The knights and women released by Stephen all said he was incandescent with rage.' Brien chuckled, and then grew more serious as he continued, 'By all accounts, the women were terrified. Stephen's men, led by that dog Ypres, pulled the castle apart and might have allowed his curs to rape the women, except that Stephen himself put a stop to any such wickedness. He pulled Beatrice from a Fleming's grasp and apparently spoke gently to her, promising to release them all, with Maud's knights to protect them. Stephen decided to send the lot of them away before worse could happen out of his sight. He fed them and sent them on carts to Wallingford.'

'Chivalrous of him,' Robert said, 'considering he had lost his quarry.'

'He buzzed about Oxford Castle like an angry wasp, but he stung with shouts and words of threat rather than physical cruelty.' Brien placed his hands on his slim waist, pulling tight his mantle about his neck, and Robert noted Brien was as handsome as ever, with hardly a strand of grey on his dark head. Nor had Brien lost his love of fine clothing. His green wool mantle was pinned with an ornate silver clasp. It was lined with soft rabbit fur.

Robert spoke again. 'The Marshal came to see me at Devizes. He is willing to resume the fighting, but my own thought is that we should consolidate what we have achieved first and not dwell on that which is lost to us. Maud should make as generous grants as she can. The majority of England's barons and bishops will never accept a woman as their ruler and she will need to do all in her power to hold the loyalty of those earls who would fight for Henry's inheritance. And she must give land generously to western abbeys. I believe the Marshal, not a fiercely religious man, agrees.'

'How did Sir John look, considering the eye he lost?'

'The loss of an eye has angered him against Stephen, but his right eye is as piercing and sharp enough for both. He wears an eye patch and it suits him well. Women still throw him admiring looks. Lends John an air of mystery. He is a hero, if often taciturn. Besides, he is tough, lean as a hare, strong as an ox, and I'll warrant his sword is as fast as ever it was and his thrust just as accurate.'

Brien grew thoughtful. He shook his mane of curling dark hair, drew it back with slim fingers and let it drop forward again. He said, 'Your strategy seems sound, Rob. If further attacks occur in the west, or even in the south, we'll be ready and armed.'

'To the hilt.' It was Robert's turn to look thoughtful. 'You'll guard Wallingford closely. Prepare for another siege. It's our remaining most easterly fastness, so Stephen will have his eye on it.'

'He failed last time.' Brien sighed. 'I am well provisioned for months, but, much as I am loath to break company with her, escort Maud to Devizes after Christmastide. She couldn't abide a new siege, should Stephen attack this fortress. I have my armed scouts and spies out, posted along the river route towards Abingdon. My troops are patrolling the estates surrounding my castle. Given half a chance, the King's army will devour the land like a swarm of locusts. My people will suffer great hardship if he returns.'

'There'll be skirmishes, especially around Oxford. Another good reason to make sure our lands are protected. A number of land grants to the dispossessed will ensure their loyalty and provisions from well-managed harvests. We are looking at a long war, now. Take ordinary folk, such as Xander and Beatrice. Her father has agreed to their betrothal, but she is a minor heiress with land in Normandy, so granting Xander a manor of his own here would be in Maud's interests, as well as Xander's. Same with Alice and Jacques. If she grants them property close to Devizes, Alice will not be dependent on a manor too close to danger around Wallingford. A steward can manage the Wallingford land you granted her on her marriage.'

'Yes, of course, Maud must reward her knights. Stephen has made many of *his* English knights resentful by awarding castles and manors to his Fleming butchers. This will do him no favours in the long term.' Brien stroked his beard and frowned. 'The safety of my lands is, without doubt, a concern. Stephen is so close. Fortunately, Alice's family holding is well off the main route between Oxford and Wallingford. I have given them serfs to help farm it. The younger brother and his wife remain on the family manor. Pipkin works for me as a falconer. He is good with birds.' Brien's eyes darkened from brown to a shade more like ebony. 'I shall increase my guards everywhere.'

'Stephen remains indecisive,' Robert continued, thinking of the amiable young man who had become a skilful but too greedy monarch. 'He trusts the wrong people. By rewarding Flemings before Englishmen, he creates feuds between them and his barons. The barons quarrel amongst themselves too. I heard they are jealous of

De Mandeville, and I also heard the Bigods of Norfolk sit on the fence. This could be to our advantage.'

'I think we are in agreement, Rob,' Brien said. 'Miles and the Marshal would see the sense of it. By the way, Miles sent a Christmas greeting from Gloucester. He was thrilled by Maud's daring escape. He wrote she had donned wings like an angel and God had watched over her flight.'

Robert gave a guffaw as he removed his elbows from the wall. 'An interesting sentiment, coming from Miles. The bear is not in favour with the clergy, not since he took over that church in Hereford as his headquarters a few years back, something we must avoid.' He peered beyond the battlements again. 'Ah, well, I see the courtyard has emptied. Shall we join in the revels in the hall? Your Countess, I hear, has promised a standing feast today, as well as the singing of Christmas songs. There'll be little left, if we don't hurry.'

On Saint Stephen's Day, the sun shone in a blue sky, making the snow glitter, and the air remained frosty. It was a fine day to hunt. Those of Maud's court who enjoyed the chase were gathered inside the outer courtyard, already mounted. Brien sent out his huntsmen to gather information about where the deer had been sheltering. The huntsmen had marked out a stag that favoured a particular stand of beeches deep inside the deer park. On their return, there followed a brief discussion as to how they should conduct the hunt. It was agreed young Henry would ride with Robert. He was not to get too close to the business of slaughter.

Henry appeared petulant at this decision. Robert gave in a little, saying, by way of compromise, 'When it is safe, Henry, I'll allow you to move forward as stealthily as a wild cat. I'll be right with you and it might be possible for you to throw a javelin, but you must stay by me and my man-at-arms, Oswin. Do you understand?'

Oswin, a great, muscled, shaggy-bearded man, grinned and winked at Henry, who had brightened again at the promise of a bit of the action.

321

'It is easier to catch the quarry after snow has fallen. He won't run as well through the snow. Even so, Henry, it is very dangerous and I am responsible for you. Or would you want me to send you with the women?' He winked.

'My mother is riding with the men.' Henry glanced around at Maud, who had joined the assembly, taking her place alongside Count Brien. She was smothered in furs, hood to boots. They all were.

'Your mother is an experienced huntswoman. And that is why she will ride with Count Brien. But, if anything happened to you, Count Geoffrey would send an assassin after me.'

Henry closed his mouth at this and nodded.

The breakfast of pies was taken in the outer bailey and washed down with small beer. Yet again, Tilda has done us well, Robert mused. The route they had decided to follow, on the basis of information gathered by the huntsmen, was agreed and the hunters set out at a trot, riding through the walled town and out of the town's gates into the hunting park. Relays of dogs were positioned on leashes all along the route. Brien sent a lymer ahead to track down the stag. The head huntsman raised his hunting horn and blew the call. The deer were marked, several of them spotted sheltering amongst the stand of trees where the stag was noticed earlier. The hunters would ride quietly and keep track of their quarry.

Robert kept a close watch on Henry, which in part took away his own enjoyment of the hunt, but the boy rode confidently through the trees, never faltering; with his fur hood close about his head, he looked like a small bear. Up ahead, Robert spotted Brien and Maud riding close to each other. Countess Tilda never hunted. Her calling was more domestic. Maud's legs were almost brushing Brien's.

At length, the baying began. The marked stag could run no longer, and Robert became firm with Henry again.

'Now watch, Henry. It's Count Brien's hunt. He is senior of us all today and the hounds will be held back so he can make the kill with his spear.'

'But you promised I could spear the stag,' Henry protested.

'Hush. Once Brien and your mother have speared the deer, we'll ride forward and you can toss one too. How about that?'

'I suppose.'

They reached Brien, who nodded towards Henry. Robert whispered in the boy's ear and Henry threw the first spear with amazing accuracy, catching the stag in the neck. The creature buckled onto its knees and fell.

'I've done it!' he yelled. 'I brought it down!'

Robert knew that the boy would love hunting for life. They watched as the deer was dissected. Brien walked forward to them and marked Henry's cheeks with blood. He then presented him with the stag's heart.

'This is yours, Henry,' he said. 'Your first kill, I believe. Don't tell Count Geoffrey we placed you in danger, just recount that you helped fall a stag.' He winked, but he took back the dripping heart and placed it in a satchel. 'That's your supper, lad,' he added.

Robert smiled to see the delight on Henry's face. But, glancing down at the crimson blood streaking the snow with vivid red where the stag's heart had dripped, he wondered if it was truly right to kill such beautiful creatures.

Henry rode back to the castle with Brien, so Maud moved her palfrey round in a circle to trot alongside her brother. They fell back a little, so they could converse privately.

'Maud, as you know, there is to be a formal betrothal between Beatrice and Xander. He has proved a fine soldier, as well as a talented musician.'

'I am happy to provide them with a manor, if that is what you wish to ask, Robert.'

'I assured Beatrice's father that she would be well provided for. I promised him either you or I would grant them an English estate. And do you know, Maud, what he said?'

She looked straight at him with her dark intelligent eyes.

He tugged his horse back a little, closer to his sister's mount. 'Her

Papa said it was a relief to see his only child settled. He said Xander had his approval. They'll inherit his manor in Normandy. Her father said, "I look forward to a grandson soon, my lord, for he will be my true heir."'

'You men are all the same. You think only men can run estates, yet many widows do, and women must when their men are at war. And all you want from us is male heirs. Too many men with power. Too many of us women without.'

'Now, Maud, not all. After all, Mabel runs my castle in Bristol better than I do. You had best not let those who have sworn loyalty to you hear such careless unguarded words. And, besides, Henry will make a great king. He will be astute, decisive and much loved, and I wish to guide his education.'

'That wish is granted, for none are as able to tutor Henry as you and those whom you select to manage his education.' She tugged on her reins and added, 'I am happy to grant a manor for Sir Jacques, too. I shall make sure both manors are closely bordered to each other. Frankly, I could not have escaped Oxford without Jacques.'

'I wonder what Stephen's next move will be. My spy has told me he has left Oxford for London, to spend Christmas with his Queen.'

'That Cistercian you were speaking with in the hall some days since is a spy?' she said.

'For some years, he has been in my employ, a knight posing as a monk' replied Robert. 'Brother James can move between abbeys and monasteries, which makes him useful. He has learned to guard his tongue.'

'I recollect him now – and the Benedictine monk whom Alice told us of, who tried to prevent him delivering a message to the Marshal.' She shook her reins again and bells jangled. 'When I settle in Devizes, I'll take stock of all I possess. The coinage mints will issue my pennies again and I'll establish an office dedicated to land administration. We *will* protect my son's inheritance.'

Robert threw her an approving smile. 'The future is in God's care, but this is a careful way forward.'

★

Beatrice was dressed in a blue gown with golden circles embroidered about the hem for her betrothal to Xander of Wallingford. Her golden hair flowed loose, held by a circlet of pearls. Xander's green mantle was pinned at his shoulder with a brooch – an owl cast in silver, with garnet eyes.

Beatrice received a sapphire ring from Robert's own jewel chest to mark her union. Xander slipped it onto her middle finger and the couple were as good as wed, though the church wedding would take place in Caen. If they set up home together first, Sir Hugh, Beatrice's father, had said that would be acceptable. Once they had said the words declaring their troth before witnesses, they were traditionally handfasted by the whetstone in Brien's hall.

A betrothal feast followed. Brien clapped his hands, musicians struck up a carol and the handfasted couple led the company into dancing. Since Brien led Maud out into the circle dance, Robert felt obliged to escort Tilda into the carol as well, but Tilda shook her head. 'Earl Robert, my dancing days are over. My leg would not stand it. Please, ask another.'

Robert politely took Brien's empty chair beside Tilda. He spoke of small, domestic matters – of Mabel and of Bristol Castle. In return, Tilda told him how she feared her London houses were lost to her. She might never visit them again. She would ship wool out of Wareham and had decided to rent a merchant's house in the small port.

As they conversed, he caught her glancing at Brien and Maud, and noted a hint of sadness in her face. Tilda's gaze flicked back to him and, reading his thoughts, she said, 'As you know, Robert, we noble people are rarely allowed to wed those to whom we are best suited. You and Mabel are an exception.' She lowered her voice. 'Brien has never loved anyone other than Empress Maud.'

There was silence. They both looked at Maud and Brien, whose faces were alight with joy as they moved together.

'I believe it a chaste love,' Tilda said softly. 'He has never, to my knowledge, taken mistresses. The two young people betrothed today are most fortunate.' She turned to face him. 'I often think we should all be permitted to marry those we love, just as they have.'

Robert placed a hand over hers. 'Countess Tilda, you are a woman of sound sense. Brien is fortunate to have you to wife, because you have a firm friendship. Love can run its course, but true friendship endures until death itself and, God willing, journeys with us beyond the grave.'

Tilda smiled at his words. But her eyes rested on Maud and Brien, dancing together. It was clear to Robert she remained so very sad.

Chapter Twenty-Six

Devizes
1143

It was a still, peaceful September morning. The sound of blackbirds and thrushes singing drifted in through opened shutters and was soothing to Maud's ears. Placing her office where an outer staircase climbed the castle walls meant, if she desired solitude in the garden below, she could simply slip out through a small arched doorway onto the staircase. Maud wiped her pen and laid it on its cradle. Her office was a chamber lined with deep shelves, and here she took pleasure in the smell of parchment and ink. She read through a document that needed witnessing.

Devizes had belonged to Bishop Robert of Salisbury, was stolen from him by Stephen, but recovered by Maud when Stephen was her prisoner. The beautiful castle had become her seat of governance in this new time of real peace. She enjoyed the Bishop's tasteful selection of opulent hangings, with their embroidered scenes of hunting, flowers and swirling acanthus leaves, and the Biblical scenes painted on various walls. She was entranced by the beautiful chapel at Devizes, with its painted glass windows, where she prayed daily, presided over by the Madonna in her blue gown edged with gold. Maud's comfortable bed in the Bishop's great bedchamber was hung with heavy crimson damask curtains to guard her privacy and banish draughts. Her chamber had a view of the gardens. It was, in all, a more pleasant and comfortable seat than either Wallingford or Oxford.

Most days, her scribe worked alongside her, checking her land grants, sharpening her quills, and copying and carefully storing the completed scrolls in the shelves, knowing exactly where to find everything again. In this part of the west, Maud was accepted as ruler – and Stephen resented this. Her recent strategy of distributing grants of land and manors to her knights helped ensure their future loyalty to her son, and so she made sure Henry, as well as she and Robert, witnessed the most important of these.

'Master Egbert,' she called to her scribe, who was a completely bald monk, with warm hazel eyes, 'I have finished for today.' She sighed. 'Not much land left to grant, but this particular appointment is important.' She indicated the document she had checked. 'It's the one you scribed for me creating the Sheriff of Wiltshire an earl.' She rolled the document and added, 'Please see it is kept safe until it is witnessed.'

Above all other appointments, this one was most important. It was her intention to keep the Salisbury family loyal to her cause. Old Sir William had suffered a stroke and was residing in an abbey, but the earldom would continue through the family after his death, most likely through Patrick, his second son, since William, the elder son, had never recovered after being taken prisoner after Winchester, and was on the point of dying from a wasting disease. The family's support since the Winchester retreat and Stephen's recovery of his kingship had been questionable.

It had not been completely quiet, that summer. In August, Stephen had attempted a siege at Wareham, but, when Robert arrived with his newly formed army, he abandoned it. With his brother, the vile betrayer, Bishop Henry, he retreated to Wilton Abbey, intending to fortify it and, from Wilton, launch further attacks on Maud's territories. It was typical of Stephen that he would commandeer an abbey and put the Wilton nuns out of their cloisters. Only twice had this happened on her watch, when Miles had taken Hereford and when Sir John had tried to protect the road to Winchester at Wherwell. Robert had pursued Stephen to Wilton, where they engaged in a battle. Rumours reached Maud assuring her Robert had won Wilton, and, since Stephen did not intend to repeat his mistake of Lincoln, he and Bishop Henry fled the field to safety.

Maud slowly descended the outer staircase into the garden and wandered about flower and herb beds, lost in thought. It was a colourful garden, with flower beds full of gillyflowers, pansies and periwinkles, and purple daisies that heralded the arrival of Michaelmas. Shortly after her arrival, her head gardener plodded through the garden gate, carrying a basket of pears from the orchard. She graciously acknowledged him, lifting a pear from his pannier. 'Ripe enough, Master Alfred, but we won't risk belly ache eating them uncooked. When you take them to the kitchen, ask the cook to stew a dish of pears for the void at dinner today.'

Master Alfred nodded. 'My lady, it will be done at once.' He shuffled off with his laden basket into the inner bailey.

She sank down onto a turf bank to enjoy a few more moments of solitude before attending Sext. Her thoughts, this time, turned to Patrick of Salisbury, an arrogant young man, tall, chestnut-headed, and who, anytime he had appeared at her court, wore a discontented air about him. The cause, she knew, was his determination to bring Lugershall Castle back into his own family's estates. John Fitz Gilbert, her Marshal, had initially ruled both Lugershall and Marlborough Castles for Stephen. She determined not to take Lugershall from Sir John, who guarded the Kennet Valley. Nor would she countenance disputes amongst her earls. Private wars and skirmishes would, for certes, weaken her grasp of the west. She hoped granting Patrick's father an earldom might sweeten the young man's rancour.

'My lady.'

Maud glanced up to see Beatrice on the stairway.

'Madame, horsemen have entered the outer bailey, flying Earl Robert's banner. The Earl is dismounting.'

She jumped to her feet, her hands fluttering, smoothing her tunic. 'I am coming.'

Beatrice ducked through a low doorway into the bower. If Robert was here, Maud would learn just how Stephen had escaped the battle around Wilton.

★

She hastened to the hall, where servants were already laying cloths on trestles for dinner. She asked a page to bring refreshments into her office and turned to greet Robert, who was seated by the hearth. Her first words were, 'Praise God, you have safely returned to us.'

He rose and kissed her hands. 'I have good news.'

Maud ushered Robert into her office behind the dais, where Robert sank onto the bench by the window overlooking the garden she had left only minutes earlier. She arranged herself neatly in her chair.

'Well,' she said, once the page had returned with goblets of wine and a plate of small meat pasties. 'Success?'

Robert swallowed a mouthful of wine. 'Yes, that is the good news, but it came at a price. When Stephen decided Wareham was too well protected to besiege, he rode thirty-seven miles to Wilton with Bishop Henry and occupied the abbey. This you know. We pursued him with the greater army and did battle with him. Indeed, we won the day. However, there was much carnage in Wilton. Alas, a terrible price was paid for that victory.'

He paused. She knew the sorrow of war and she instinctively touched the cross that hung on her bodice.

Robert continued, 'Stephen and Henry fled the field as fast as hares pursued by huntsmen, and their lieutenants protected their retreat. Now, many important knights are imprisoned in Gloucester and Bristol.' Robert drank deeply again from his glass, and chuckled. 'We'll get Sherborne from him too, because he'll pay dearly for those we captured and who shielded his retreat.'

She smiled at the thought of taking over the pleasant castle at Sherborne. 'Another castle put up by Bishop Roger, so it will be furnished in the best taste. Stephen won't be pleased to see that go to us.'

Robert grinned. 'I'd rather we had captured Stephen, and taken our devious Bishop Henry too.'

'Is it not like a chess game?' mused Maud, as she tilted her silver goblet to her mouth. She took a small sip and said, 'I'm granting an earldom to the Salisbury family, Robert. I've distributed all I can, including two manors near Marlborough to Jacques and Xander. There's nothing left to give.'

'There will be,' said Robert. 'If we can keep Patrick of Salisbury and the Marshal from hammering each other, Lugershall safe in John's care, an earldom for Salisbury is worth it. The father is confined to an abbey and William, the elder son, is ailing. He is not long for this world. I believe a canker is eating him. He is skeletal. The Salisbury family's future will lie with young Patrick.'

Maud laced her jewelled fingers in her lap. 'Stephen's barons create private wars. His barons terrorise their people and the abbeys.'

Robert said, ''Tis true enough. I have further news of interest.'

She raised her brows and leaned forward. 'Tell it all.'

'Stephen has held court at St Albans and, on a suspicion of treason likely fermented by his barons, he has arrested Geoffrey de Mandeville, the grasping traitor who abandoned your cause in London and returned his loyalty to Stephen and Matilda so he could remain Earl of Essex and acquire further favours.'

Maud frowned and leaned back. 'Another serpent. He controlled the Tower and he held back from declaring for me in London, then placed himself at my service before the coronation he doubtless had a hand in preventing. Well, well. He has received his due. He had far too many castles, and possession of the Tower in the City. Stephen will confiscate them all. He might release De Mandeville, but, if he does, he makes another enemy. Mind, if that happens and he declares for me, we'd never trust him again. De Mandeville is as slippery as a Fenland eel.' She shook her head. 'Stephen listens to the wrong people, permits quarrels and makes enemies.'

'And, Maud, if Stephen, of a sudden, dies, we must make sure it is Henry who will sit on the throne, not Stephen's son Eustace.'

Maud's black eyes glittered anger as Robert spoke Eustace's name. 'That inept boy will never sit on my throne.'

'I am going to build a fortress near Faringdon,' Robert said, as he reached for a pasty and swallowed it in two bites. 'A fastness at Faringdon will be further protection for the south and the west, in case

331

Stephen strikes out from Oxford. I'll put my son Philip in charge of it. He is shaping up well. Twenty years old and enthusiastic.'

'Oh, do so, Robert. The responsibility will be good for him.'

Ten more years and Henry, too, would be approaching twenty years.

Christmas approached. Maud's cooks were gathering in provisions. Devizes Castle smelled of spices, greenery and scented wax candles. On Christ's Day Eve, Robert and Mabel joined Maud with their sons, as well as Prince Henry, who had made a companion of Robert's younger son, Roger. That Christmastide, they were celebrating the acquisition of Sherborne as ransom for Stephen's valued knight, William Martel.

'It will help us secure a corridor from the south coast to Bristol and your lands, Maud,' Robert said at a Christmas Eve parley with Brien, the Marshal and Henry, who was permitted to attend the meeting in the hall antechamber, but only to listen.

'A firm message to Stephen that our fight is back on.' Brien leaned back in his chair and swept his hand through his hair. 'And we are administering the west firmly with our own laws and ordinances. He'll be envious of our good rule.'

Maud glanced fondly at Brien, who had come to Devizes alone. Countess Tilda had decided Wallingford was perfectly safe and she preferred to remain there. Maud was pleased to have Brien's undivided attention once again during a season of dancing, music and celebration. She could hear strains of recorders, lutes and glitterns already sounding in the hall, and Alice's voice, still clear as a bell, rising up in a carol.

John Marshal cocked his ear to listen. He, like Brien, had come to Devizes without his wife. Aline was very retiring, he had explained, and did not enjoy great numbers of people. His wife was not a courtier. In fact, Maud was aware that Lady Aline, who had been so kind to her after her Winchester escape, was more interested in prayer than her marriage, and, although she had given John two little boys, Aline found the day-to-day running of John's manors impossible. Robert had mentioned recently after visiting them that, perhaps, she would be happier if the marriage with Sir John was annulled and another alliance forged. He knew just the lady for John.

John himself broke into her thoughts: 'Has anyone heard any more of De Mandeville? I believe Stephen released him in return for his relinquishing custody of the Tower and the castles at Saffron Walden and Pleshey. De Mandeville sped to the Isle of Ely and took over Ramsey Abbey – drove the monks out, fortified the church and occupied a number of properties around about. Word has it that the bastard sacked Cambridge.'

Robert made one of his guffaws. 'And he has not declared for Maud, nor has his associate in Norfolk, Hugh Bigod. Still, they'll keep Stephen distracted, and that is no bad thing.' He paused for a moment. 'He and Bigod are laying gelds on villages, robbing and burning. The land remains untilled. They steal from churches, abbots and bishops. They are no better than outlaws and certainly more dangerous. People will starve this winter in those sad shires if Stephen does not bring that devil to heel. It is a sorrowful state of affairs.'

Henry's eyes had grown huge as Robert described De Mandeville's wrongdoing. Maud smiled reassuringly at her son and said, 'He is not coming anywhere near our lands, Henry. Not everywhere is filled with such vicious bandits.'

Henry said, in his boyish voice, 'When I am King, I shall not permit such wicked men to live.'

'Indeed, you will not,' Maud said. She glanced around the company. 'Are Miles and his family not joining us, this Christmas?'

'I think Earl Miles has decided to join us for the New Year. He has not seen much of his wife and sons these months. He mentioned something about spending a few days hunting, but he assured me that, before New Year, they would come to court. I have set aside lodgings for the family,' the Marshal said.

'You think of everything, Sir John,' Maud said, raising her glass to her Marshal, thinking that Robert had spoken truly when he said

John Fitz Gilbert remained a handsome man, mannered, eloquent and always alert, attractive, despite his eye patch and the scarred left side of his face.

Christmas Day dawned bright and cold. There would be falconry and feasting. Time passed pleasantly around the hearth, listening to Alice's haunting voice floating through the hall. She had two small children now, Ami and Ralph, and, when she was not ten miles away on her new manor of Middleton, she was present with Jacques and Xander at court, where she entertained and, on rarer occasions, gave a puppet show for the castle children with Xander, as they had done in years past.

It was Christmas night, and Maud was listening to Alice sing verses about shepherds, mysterious Eastern kings and the birth of Jesus, when she was jolted from her enjoyment of the performance by a loud banging on the hall door. She gripped the arms of her chair. Insistent calls to open up made her fear an attack when they least expected one. At once, Alice stopped singing; Xander lowered his lute; Jacques and Alexander de Bohun rushed to the door, both shouting, 'Who is without?'

Robert, John and Brien leapt to their feet, unsheathing their swords. The Bishop of Bath grasped his silver cross in front of his chest and a group of his monks knelt praying in the rush matting. Prince Henry and young Roger of Gloucester stood side by side, legs spread, in front of Maud, thrusting their eating knives forward as if they intended defending her. Maud rose up to her full height, firmly clasping her hands in front of her green damask gown, waiting for what came next. Her maidens, including Beatrice and Lenora, gathered behind her.

'I've come with news from Gloucester Castle,' a voice called.

'Open up. That voice belongs to Miles's man, Guillaume,' Robert called to the guards at the door.

Guillaume walked straight along the length of the hall to Maud, knelt and said, in a voice that was breaking, 'Madame, I come from the Countess of Hereford with terrible news. My Lord Miles was killed yesterday afternoon whilst hunting. He took a fall and broke his neck. I rode all day to tell you. May God give rest to my lord's soul.'

Maud had known Miles since she was a child. Her legs weakened and her heart seemed to stop. Brien was by her side at once, placing a gentle hand under her elbow to steady her. Henry was at her other side, looking up at her with concern in his blue eyes.

Robert calmly leaned down, raised Guillaume and bade him sit by the hearth. As usual, he found solace in practicalities. He gestured to the castle priest, Father Adolphus, nodded to him and quietly asked everyone to attend castle chapel to pray for Miles's soul. As they began to file out of the hall, Robert sent for food for Guillaume. The distraught young messenger declined, though he asked for a cup of wine.

Maud's tears began to stream down her cheeks. They had lost their great bear. The loyal band of knights, loyal to her father, to herself and Prince Henry, had lost a well-respected companion who could never be replaced. His family would be heartbroken.

'May his soul rest in peace,' she whispered, and her hands moved as if of their own accord to the amber prayer beads that hung on a silver clasp from her belt.

Chapter Twenty-Seven

Bristol
July 1145

The feast day of Saint James fell on the twenty-fifth day of July. A fair was held in the churchyard of Saint James's Priory, a Bristol church founded by Earl Robert when he had renovated the castle, ten years before. By having a yearly fair, Robert hoped to raise enough funds to pay for a new rood screen, more elegant than that of its rival, Saint Mary's. Robert was free to attend. The war had gone quiet. Stephen had been caught up in the Fens this past year, encircling De Mandeville until the latter finally fell prey to an arrow, at Burwell Castle. When his wound ran septic, De Mandeville died.

The Empress's cause had taken a boost when Geoffrey, Count of Anjou, had finally got his wish and was created Duke of Normandy. Geoffrey had successfully besieged Cherbourg and taken Rouen Castle in April. He made peace with Louis of France after he granted King Louis the Vexin in return for recognition of his new dukedom.

'Good for Geoffrey,' Maud had said, folding up a letter from him requesting Henry's immediate return to Normandy to be trained as Geoffrey's heir. 'Well, I suppose I can officially claim to be Duchess of Normandy, now.' She'd smiled a cynical half-smile, 'Stephen is eliminated from the dukedom and we'll see how his earls who possess Norman lands behave.'

Robert had remarked, 'Mabel will miss Henry. He's lively, quick to learn – and very aware that he is learning to be a king, not a mere duke. And I hope he never forgets the lessons his English tutors and I have taught him.' Robert had sounded put out, though Normandy was significant in itself and his own lands around Caen were currently safer because Geoffrey had been created Duke of the Normans.

'Henry swears like a seasoned soldier. He sees himself as a warrior already,' Maud had said, somewhat bemused by how the years had flown. 'I hope he learns to respect the Church.' She had grown more devout as the years passed by, and had often said to Robert, *If I should die here in England, Robert, make sure my body is buried at Bec Abbey.*

Robert, too, was no longer young, and Miles's untimely death had made him realise his time on earth was running out. The Lord's grim reaper comes for us all, he mused. No one lives forever. He was seated on a bench outside the church porch, his legs astride and a tankard of fresh ale in his hand. Leaning back, he enjoyed the warmth of the stone behind him through his old linen tunic – one that, after many years' wear, had faded from indigo blue to the softer shade of the summer's sky above. The only indication he was ready to fight, if necessary, was the sharp sword sheathed by his side.

For a while, as the sun rose high in the sky, he mused over other events of the past year. He had brought about John Fitz Gilbert's second marriage to Sybil of Salisbury, a union that brokered peace at last between Patrick of Salisbury and John the Marshal. Patrick had become Earl of Salisbury following the demise of both his father and his older brother. If he was not overly friendly to his new brother-in-law, Patrick was firmly loyal to the Empress. Sir John was delighted with his intelligent new bride, Patrick's beautiful sister. As for Aline, it had been easy to get the marriage annulled, because John and Aline had been related within the prohibition of the rules of consanguinity – cousins in the third degree – though, apparently, they had not been forbidden their marriage in the first place. Still, it worked out well, because Robert encouraged his widowed uncle, Stephen de Gay, to marry Aline, and she was happier with this indulgent, adoring widower than she had ever been with the tough courtier and soldier, John Marshal.

Robert was disappointed when Ranulf of Chester, his daughter's husband, declared for Stephen. However, as with De Mandeville, there was always suspicion lingering over him as to his true loyalty — if Ranulf was loyal to anything other than his own interests. This would not end well, and it saddened Robert because not only was Ranulf of Chester his son-in-law, but he held vast lands in the north. Ranulf's unhappy wife, Mathilde, wrote to Mabel. She was dismayed by her husband's new allegiance and wrote with concern:

> . . . Ranulf's loyalty to Stephen does not feel right or safe. The King's barons are jealous of him because of his power in the north. The King listened to these ill-advised men, who called Ranulf a traitor who was determined to lure King Stephen with armies to support my husband against Welsh incursion. Stephen tried to besiege my husband in Lincoln, but abandoned the siege. Stephen wants Lincoln. My husband hopes Stephen will grant him troops to fight the Welsh along the Marches. So far, Stephen has declined . . . Forgive me, Mama, but I have to support Ranulf, as he is my husband, though it sits ill with me to do so . . . I fear for our future.

Turning the problem of Ranulf over in his mind troubled him, but he pushed the thoughts away. Today was a holiday, not a time for worry.

Robert idly watched his wife and her maids slowly weave a pathway through the stalls towards him. He smiled, for they were enjoying the fair and would return to the castle laden down with silk threads, ribbons, scented soap from Castile, perfumes and other trifles. They had paused to watch acrobats perform on the priory garth. Minstrels wandered about the town's streets and a holiday atmosphere invaded the town's inn courtyards, where there was bear baiting and wrestling. Robert had no appetite for the cruelty of bear baiting, but he did enjoy seeing men wrestle. A man close to his bench had begun to play a pleasant country ditty on a pipe, but of a sudden stopped. Robert looked around, following the piper's eyes. A rider on a brown jennet was moving with slow deliberation through the stalls, peering from side to side, until he dismounted his horse and led it towards Robert.

The rider wiped sweat from his forehead with the back of his hand. He made a curt bow. 'My lord, they told me at the castle you were here.'

'What is so urgent? Christ's toes, could whatever it is not wait until dinner time—?' Robert broke off, recognising the young man. 'You're Martin, my son's man. Has Philip . . .? Is he well?'

'Philip is well and resting in your hall.' He waved his hand towards the castle. 'He is having a twisted ankle bound by your physician and sent me down to find you.' He drew breath before adding, 'My lord, I must warn you, Philip has given Faringdon to the King.'

It took Robert a moment to grasp the significance of this news. He rose slowly to his feet, feeling his bones stiffer than they had been for years. As if to balance himself better, his hand immediately rested on his sword hilt. 'How come? Are you telling me Stephen has taken Faringdon? My son never resisted? And, if so, why? What by Christ's blood are you all thinking of? If Stephen has taken my fastness of Faringdon, this will open the way to his possible attack on Wallingford, Cricklade and – worse –' he clapped a hand against his head – 'Cirencester. What were you all thinking of? You could have sent for help.'

'We did not have enough engines, crossbowmen or soldiers to hold out against the King's siege. We had no option but to surrender the castle. It was an honourable defeat, sir. We could not have done otherwise.'

'I doubt that. Go back to the castle and I shall be there shortly. My son will give me a full account of this debacle.' Robert glanced around. Mabel was approaching at last with her maids, their panniers filled to overflowing with purchases, as he'd expected.

She took one look at his face and, smoothing down her wimple, said, 'Robert, was that Martin, Philip's friend?'

'Yes – unfortunately, yes.'

'What is he doing here? Is Philip well?'

'Apparently,' he grunted at her. 'Apart from a sprained ankle. We have raised a milksop. Philip was given responsibility for Faringdon,

339

Mabel, and he's gone and released the castle to Stephen without a fight.' He slammed a fist into the other palm. The day had lost all pleasure for him now. 'He will give me an account of his actions and they had best make sense. It's a complete disaster.'

'Come, it may not be as terrible as you think,' Mabel said, placing a hand on his arm, attempting to soothe his anger, and failing. 'We'll return to the castle and discuss this civilly.'

Philip was a young man who did not take well to criticism, especially from his father, and particularly if accused of cowardice in front of Robert's sergeants. Over dinner, Philip protested voraciously that he'd had no option but to cede Faringdon to Stephen.

'You could have held out longer!' Robert roared at his son, feeling his face burn with fury, banging his fist on the table. From the corner of his eye, he caught Mabel's frown.

They had just eaten a tasty dinner of salmon in a cream sauce, cold chicken, salads and a spiced rice dish. Robert had kept his temper throughout the meal and held back his questioning. He ignored Philip until they had finished eating. Once the raspberry syllabub was finished, he let his anger spill out like a cauldron that had boiled over. 'You could have sent a message to me. I gave you trained pigeons. If a messenger could not have slipped by Stephen's trebuchets, a pigeon could have flown over them. I expect courage to be displayed by my sons. You are a disgrace, Philip. Leave my presence.'

Philip knocked over his wine as he rose to his feet, staining the cloth crimson, like blood. Awkwardly limping, he descended the dais steps and hobbled through the hall, followed by Martin. He grabbed the sword he had left by the hall's entrance and departed, never speaking or looking back. He never bade his shocked mother farewell.

'That was harsh,' Mabel said in a quiet voice, placing a hand on Robert's arm. 'You'll have alienated him.'

Robert said, still infuriated, 'I shall have to double the garrisons of all my castles between Faringdon and Devizes, and send a warning to

Brien in Wallingford. Speaking of Brien, look how he has held Wallingford, the jewel in our Empress's crown, all these years. My own son has not even the wit to try to combat a siege, and not the sense to send a message to me if he felt he was losing.'

Mabel placed her hand over Robert's. 'He will return to us, my dear – never fear. You have been hard on him.'

'Unless he joins Stephen,' Robert said morosely.

Alice had ridden to the Bristol fair with Xander. They had put on a popular puppet show on the previous day, the story of Saint James and his journey by sea to Compostela, a favoured destination for pilgrims. Robert granted them lodgings in the castle for the duration. Alice planned to visit her family's Wallingford farm with her children, and she would take Robert's warning to Count Brien. It would take several days to travel between Bristol and Wallingford, stopping overnight in abbeys and priories. They must avoid Faringdon, veering south.

The two children rode in the puppetry wagon with Gudrun and a nurse. Gudrun drove the wagon. A guard of six protected their journey. Two days later, Alice and Xander were trotting into the familiar bailey of Wallingford Castle, having slipped by Stephen's mercenaries.

'By Christos,' Brien said, neatly refolding Robert's warning. 'I knew something of this, since Philip has lost no time declaring loyalty to the King. News spreads fast as a kestrel's flight.' He sighed. 'This will break Robert's heart, but Stephen has left a garrison in Faringdon and is now chasing Earl Ranulf of Chester through the north.'

Alice shook her head. 'Why so?'

'Stephen imprisoned Ranulf, but gave him his freedom in return for castles, including Lincoln. Ranulf is incandescent.'

'Will Earl Ranulf seek the Empress's favour, my lord?'

'Once Chester is secured, he'll declare for Prince Henry. Unlike that despicable rogue, De Mandeville, Ranulf will be welcomed. Maud has gathered support from good men such as William Fitz

Allen, Fulk Fitz Warrin and Sir Hugh de Plucknet – and, of course, Patrick of Salisbury. It won't be long before a new generation rises – younger, fitter than we aging warriors. Rob may have lost Philip to Stephen's side, but we'll have William of Gloucester and Miles's heir, Roger, and Earl Patrick leading the lion cubs for us in no time.'

The children were tugging at Alice's skirts and Xander stood quietly behind her.

Brien changed tack. 'Ah . . . you have a beautiful son, there, Alice, and Ami is grown from babyhood into a little girl. You are blessed.' Brien's eyes twinkled as he leaned down to give each child a sugared plum within a small napkin, from a dish on his table.

Alice smiled down at her golden-headed daughter, because Ami held her treat tightly, saving it for later, ever holding out. Her son soon had his mouth smeared with juice and sugar. Laughing, she wiped his face with the napkin.

Brien laughed too. 'It is almost Vespers, so stay for supper and a maid will make up a chamber for you. Dame Margo intends visiting Ingrid with embroidery silks. You can all travel upriver tomorrow.'

'Thank you, my lord, we are pleased to accept.'

'And how is your new manor, my Lady Alice?'

She never tired of talking about the manor. She had already planned to stay only a week and visit her other property, close by Wallingford. 'The manor is paradise's own fields. It is productive and my tenants are content. I spend much of my free time in the still room and dairy. My steward keeps close accounting and manages all when I am at court.' She paused. 'But Jacques is restless. He has been too many years away from Anjou.'

'If he has a trustworthy, efficient bailiff, his estate will thrive.' He looked at Xander. 'And you, Xander, are you happy with your demesne?'

Xander's face opened into a huge smile. 'It's a fine manor house, my lord, and the farm is productive. It's peaceful in Wiltshire and I pass as much time on the manor as I can. Beatrice is at court, but she visits –' Xander grew bashful – 'with an escort.' He coughed to hide

342

his embarrassment, since he and Beatrice were not as yet married in the eyes of the Church.

Alice wanted to laugh. Beatrice's escort comprised a toothless elderly dame, an adolescent servant girl and three guards. The guards preferred to spend time in the brothel, permitted by Sir John in Marlborough, rather than on the farm. The arrangement suited Xander and Beatrice well.

'We hope to wed soon,' Xander added. 'We have promised Beatrice's father a wedding in Normandy. I fear we'll be waiting a while yet.'

'Not too long, I hope,' Brien said. 'Ah, here is Countess Tilda, come from the orchard with Dame Margo. They'll be pleased to see the children, Alice.'

The two women bustled into the antechamber and both cooed affectionately over Alice's little son and three-year-old daughter.

'I wish God had given Brien and me children,' Countess Tilda said, her usually pursed mouth breaking into a smile as she lifted Alice's son onto her lap. The little boy, a happy child, tugged at her veil and smiled up at her. A puppy had followed the two women into the chamber. Spotting it, the boy cried out at once, 'Dog, dog,' and slid down onto the floor matting from his perch on Countess Tilda's knees. Moments later, both children were playing with the puppy.

'The puppy is one of five. Would you like to keep her?' Tilda said gently.

Alice politely replied, 'Thank you. We return within a week's space, so, if you have a basket for the pup, she can travel in the cart back to Marlborough.'

'What will you call her?' Countess Tilda looked down at Ami.

The little girl glanced up. 'Honey, my lady. She's the colour of the bees' honey my nurse spreads on my bread each morning.'

''Tis a perfect name.' Tilda laughed lightly and laid her hand on Ami's golden head.

A week later, Alice started back to Marlborough with her children, servants and guard, whilst Xander remained with Ingrid and his

343

father until the harvest was over. She was to deliver a letter from Count Brien to Earl Patrick, alerting him to keep his militia primed in case Stephen returned to harass the south. They stopped at an inn in Salisbury and, after enquiries, discovered Earl Patrick in the great Salisbury Cathedral, where a priest was giving out a stirring sermon on the merits of crusading.

Recognising her as she approached him, Earl Patrick edged away, whispering, 'Lady Alice, not now . . . After the sermon. It's persuasive. I might be persuaded to crusade, you know.' He turned his attention ostentatiously back to the priest, above whom hung a white banner with a blood-red cross.

There was no sense in them all waiting, so she said to the children's nurse, 'Take the children back to the inn and watch over them. In fact, Gudrun, you go too, and take two of our guard with you. This may take some time. See they have naps, both of them.' Turning to the third guard, she said, 'Wait with me.'

Gudrun hurried the nurse and children away from the crowd gathered in the cathedral, followed by the two other guards.

As the long sermon droned on, Alice amused herself watching sunlight pour in through painted glass, creating coloured patterns on the floor tiles. She tried not to study the doom painting too closely, with its figures struggling on ladders where devils prodded these cursed souls with vicious pronged forks into a massive cauldron. Her eyes moved upwards to the more comforting sight of angels and clouds, above which God surveyed the mesmerised populace listening to the recruitment drive.

The crusading priest was in full flow. Even her guard seemed gripped by a hypnotic state, his eyes intent on the priest.

'Be as shrewd as snakes and innocent as doves. Sacrifice the body to save the head.' The priest was suggesting the Pope wanted them to sacrifice their bodies in a war to save the Church in the East. There were words about faith triumphing over evil.

'I wish that were true,' she murmured aloud.

The tall, handsome Earl Patrick, standing to her side, coughed primly and uttered a loud, 'Hush,' in her direction.

344

The priest continued, 'Christian knights should follow the example of the Israelites and fight against the pagan enemy, rather than kill each other in internal wars.'

Now it was Alice's turn to clear her throat. This was too close for comfort; was this priest criticising both monarchs?

He added, in a resounding voice, 'Bishops should renounce their dioceses and wealth, preach the way to Jerusalem and pray for Christian victory over the heathens.'

Alice shook her head and quickly stopped her urge to shout out her disapproval of his whole diatribe, fearing retribution if Earl Patrick noticed. She wondered if any bishop would travel to the East. She certainly could not see Henry of Winchester sailing off to fight in the Holy Land . . . Anyway, she had listened to enough. She whipped the letter from her belt and thrust it at Earl Patrick. 'From Count Brien,' she said, and turned on her heel to flee the cathedral, hearing her guard lumbering and puffing behind her, hardly able to keep up.

This new Crusade had been called by King Louis of France. Alice had been wrong when she thought bishops would not leave the comforts of their palaces to crusade, because many did take the cross. Over the Christmas season and throughout January, news seeped into Devizes of the preaching going on throughout the land, all in a similar vein to that which she had heard in Salisbury.

She was seated on a bench in the castle bailey with Jacques, who was polishing his sword while discussing the Crusade with her. The children were playing with a ball made out of a pig's bladder. Her son stumbled in pursuit of it. He had just passed his second name day. 'Not so fast, my boy,' she called. He paid little attention, but, having caught it, stood still, holding it fast, determined not to let Ami have it back.

For a moment, Jacques stopped polishing the sword and resumed the conversation they'd been having. 'Knights who have divided loyalties because they own lands in Normandy and England, which are divided between Duke Geoffrey and Stephen, are using the

345

Crusade as a way out of declaring for either. They are sick of this long war.' He lifted his cloth again. 'If they leave on Crusade, we'll be lighting candles for many more souls next year. Apart from skirmishes, we've enjoyed peace in this corner of England, these last years.' He gave her a loving smile and she was glad he had more sense than to be caught up in the madness that would take many away, chasing after King Louis and his beautiful wife, Eleanor, the Lady of Aquitaine.

'As long as you never catch the crusading fever,' she said firmly.

'I have no intention of leaving my family for God's Kingdom, though many do make fortunes there.'

'Have you heard of any of our knights wishing to join?'

'I heard talk that Count Waleran and Earl Warenne of Surrey have taken the cross.' He lowered his voice. 'Keep this to yourself: there was a rumour circulating the guard room that Philip of Gloucester has joined the new Crusade too.'

'Earl Robert's son!' She felt her eyes widen at this bit of gossip.

'Aye, Alice, he turned away from his father to support Stephen. And the falling out between them has hurt Earl Robert gravely.'

That afternoon, as she held her candle for Candlemas, Alice prayed that Philip Of Gloucester would survive the Crusade. She hoped Earl Robert could find it in his heart to forgive his son. Alice had always liked Philip, remembering him as a laughing youth, who in past times always wanted to please his father. If he died on the Crusade, it would break his father's heart.

Chapter Twenty-Eight

Devizes
May 1147

'No.' Maud felt the blood drain from her face as she listened to John Fitz Gilbert describe her son's latest foolhardy escapade. 'It cannot be true, John. Ludicrous! Geoffrey would never have allowed Henry to sail to England . . . and with a band of mercenaries.'

Outside, the birds she'd enjoyed listening to moments earlier were still singing in the trees, and a lark called from the orchard. She *should* be happy. Spring was her favourite season and today was the first day of May. Her ladies were making bouquets of flowers and there would be a maypole erected and dancing in the village. She was free, and they had an army which was building up its strength. And Henry had all but ruined the day's simple pleasures because he had idiotically decided to invade England.

Maud paced the ante chamber, turning around to face her visitor once she reached the narrow window.

'Geoffrey, no doubt, did not know,' John Fitz Gilbert said, crossing his long legs. 'Henry set off from Normandy in secret, with a band of friends and mercenaries – which he cannot afford to pay – thinking he could attack Stephen.' He released a sigh. 'His excuse, if this can be excused, is that he desired to take an active role in events here and claim his inheritance.' He shifted his position on the bench again. 'Henry gave out the impression, to observers watching from the shoreline, that he had crossed the sea with a company of knights and was heading up an army of thousands . . .' John chuckled at this. 'Another rumour went out that he carried a great treasure from

Normandy. People saw ships on the horizon and made ridiculous assumptions.'

'I never heard any such rumours,' Maud said. 'What success has he enjoyed? None, I'll warrant, or I would know of it.' She drew herself up indignantly. 'Geoffrey is responsible. He took his eyes off Henry. Likely he was dallying with a new mistress. Such idiocy would not have occurred on my watch.'

'Henry attacked Cricklade and Purton, twelve miles from Malmesbury. He attempted this feat without proper siege engines. He only had a few climbing ladders and one trebuchet – mine, which I fetched back to Lugershall. Others lent it to him; I was at Marlborough. He borrowed my horses. I have those back as well, but not all. Henry's meagre army was beaten back. Many of his mercenaries have drifted away . . . with a number of my handsome stallions. Your son is back at Lugershall. He refused to come here with me, fearing your wrath, so I made him write you a letter, but I thought to brief you first as to the occasion. My lady, I am loath to tell you that he needs money to pay the mercenaries still with him. They are camped in my pastures and, frankly, I want rid of the pack of them. They endanger the peace of my lands. Henry's presence will attract Stephen to Lugershall like a wasp to a juicy plum.' John pulled a letter from his jerkin and placed it in her hands.

Frowning, Maud read her son's begging words aloud: '*Dearest mother and Queen, I beg you for aid. I need five hundred marks to pay my army. I need funds to return to Normandy . . .*' She groaned, lowering the note. 'Foolhardy youth. Taking no advice and making no apology. He has put Devizes at risk, never mind Lugershall. I am trying to build a base here for Henry, and, believe me, I have learned hard lessons.' She slammed the letter down on the table, making the Marshal raise his one good eyebrow. 'Stephen won't hurt him. Henry will return to Normandy immediately.' She shrugged her shoulders. 'But I have no money available for my son. Nor has Robert money to give him either.' She folded her arms and jutted out her chin. 'Had I money to give, I would not. Henry is untrained.' She scowled. 'Tell him to ask Stephen for funds to go away, and I'll warrant

Stephen will be so glad to see him off these shores, he'll cough up those marks, quick as a hen can lay an egg.'

'But Stephen could take him hostage, my lady, if he learns Henry is in England. Is this wise?'

'Stephen will be most happy to appear magnanimous. He'll not want Henry here all summer, making trouble for him. Money for Henry's mercenaries' pay, in return for a speedy departure.' She drew an intake of breath. 'Keep Henry at Lugershall until it's settled. If it isn't, dose him with poppy juice in his wine and bundle him off to me in a cart.'

John Fitz Gilbert looked thoughtful. 'It might work.' His frown turned into a grin, exposing a mouthful of fine teeth. 'I would very much like to dose young Henry with poppy and have him off my hands forthwith.' He laughed. 'The lad shows spirit, Maud. When he is ready, he'll make a great warrior and king, but the time is not yet.'

'Obviously not. I shall write to Geoffrey. If Stephen does not pay up, Geoffrey must. By the Virgin's mantle, I swear Henry has to be on his way back to his father by the feast of Saint John.'

Maud wrote to Robert and to Count Brien, alerting them to her son's folly, emphasising Henry was not to be encouraged. She expected, of course, that neither would. Above all, she determined her errant son would not wreck his chances of winning back England's crown. She had, with difficulty, learned the value of selflessness, endurance and consolidation. Her peasants were happy. Her lands thrived. Harvests were plentiful. There was less hunger reported in her domains than in the whole of Stephen's large kingdom. With many of Stephen's supporters concerned about their Norman lands, and others taking an oath to crusade, his position was likely to weaken. She wondered, as she lifted her pen again to write to Geoffrey, if she should return to Normandy herself, leaving Robert, Brien and the Marshal to hold the west. She started, and erased with her eraser knife; then, having destroyed one leaf of parchment, she began again:

My husband, Geoffrey, the Duke of Normandy,

I wish you good health . . . I believe it is time to return to you in Normandy. I am Normandy's Duchess. Henry has made a foolish mistake in coming here without our permission. The lords of Normandy must see me. They will care for Norman lands as well as their estates in England, which will mean more Norman support for our cause here. We can work together within Norman territories, Geoffrey, for our son's inheritance in England, and raise troops for a more forceful return when Henry is older and is ready to head his knights, once he has matured and is granted his spurs . . . I have requested that he return to you. I shall follow when I leave all here to my satisfaction. My dear husband, I have long placed duty before family, and now this is the right thing to do. A great future lies with Henry if he makes no further youthful miscalculation. God and his holy angels bless you all. And may the good Lord of all things keep my beloved family in good health . . .

As she dripped sealing wax onto the letter and stamped her seal upon it, she mused, After all, I am Normandy's Duchess and it is time I visited my family and our duchy. Let us pray Stephen will be so relieved to see the back of Henry, he will be glad to see him off.

Stephen — keen to appear benign to the nobles — paid up, just as she had predicted, and Henry was sent back to Normandy, supposedly in disgrace; but, all through summer, talk circulated about Henry's escapade, how the young Prince was entitled to claim his throne. He was, by this absurd exploit, fully recognised as his grandfather's heir and a youth with great courage. Henry was affectionately called 'Hal' about the counties. He was discussed in Devizes ale houses and within her court.

Maud did not mind Henry's popularity amongst her supporters, even though she found herself grumbling to Beatrice and Lenora, 'They have not accepted me in the same way they praise my son. The difference is that he is a man.' Bitterness leaked through her words.

Lenora flashed her dark Castilian eyes. 'Quite true, my lady, it is unfair, but one day it will all change. The time for us Amazons will come.'

'Amen to that. Still, I am concentrating my efforts on Henry, male as he is.' Maud sighed. 'And, Lenora, I do wonder if I should remove myself from England. The Pope has insisted I return Devizes to the Church.' She pointed to a letter lying on her table. 'I won't invite his wrath – or, worse, excommunication.' She shuddered as she said the fearful word and raised her chin. 'I can fight for our cause from Rouen, if I must, and help Henry raise a proper army, since I don't trust Geoffrey to do it. Robert and the others can do likewise here.'

Autumn 1147

During October, events pushed change forward more quickly than Maud had anticipated. On the last fine morning of autumn, she suggested her ladies gather windfalls in the orchard and dine under the trees at dawn. 'This will be the end of our late summer,' she remarked, as they spread a linen cloth with cheese, bread, pies and fruit. She peered up through branches at a sunrise sky the colour of butter. Although the trees had turned orange, there was still little leaf fall.

She had just tossed a napkin over her shoulder when a visitor hurried through the gate, wearing Earl Robert's gold and red colours, perspiring and out of breath.

'My lady,' he said, kneeling on a small pile of golden leaves that crackled under his knees, his face distressed.

Her ladies daintily raised napkins to their noses; he stank of horse and sweat, evidently the result of a hard ride. Maud frowned at them and the napkins lowered.

'My lord is gravely ill with a fever,' he gasped out.

She rose from her cushion as nimbly as a young woman.

The messenger's eyes were wet. 'My lord has a fever, my lady. Lady Mabel says he may yet recover, but his physicians fear for him, so she sends this message to you.'

As he spoke, Maud felt the blood drain from her face. The day lost all joy. *God, spare my brother.* She turned to her women. 'Pack all this away –' she waved at the food – 'it is not appropriate. We'll attend chapel and pray for my brother's recovery.' Her ladies obediently began packing pies and bread into the baskets. Turning to the messenger, she said quietly, 'Follow me into the hall and the servants will bring you food. I must write a letter and you will ride back to Bristol with it this evening.'

As if God mourned Robert's illness, dark ominous clouds gathered that afternoon, and a storm broke. The wet weather continued; Maud could not travel to Bristol, as the fastest routes quickly flooded. She hung on the reports of messengers, who could ride obscure ways through the muddy, windswept roads. It seemed that Robert had rallied, and she breathed more easily with relief. October dragged on, and All Saints' Day passed.

On the third morning of November, Maud received devastating news in a short but sorrowful letter from Mabel. As she read the words, *He is with God and at peace*, her heart felt as if a rock had lodged within. Robert had taken a turn for the worse and had passed from the world of men on the Night of All Souls. Maud closed herself away, would speak with no one, and her flood barricades opened. She wept, denied all food, and mourned her beloved brother's passing for two long days and nights. She could never replace Robert as a friend, advisor and the dearest brother any woman could have, always kind, loyal and steadfast.

'May Robert's soul rest in peace,' she whispered over her much-loved relic containing Christ's blood, her tears dropping onto the crystal reliquary. Robert had been a constant all her life. He had arranged her return to England – almost a decade ago, now. He had commanded her troops and fought relentlessly for her crown. Her heart felt as if shards of glass had pierced it.

During the days following Robert's death, Maud finally made her decision to organise her return to Normandy in the new year. With

Robert had died her youth, and her vain hopes for the stolen crown. Now, she must be the wise advisor that Robert had been to her. She must be certain others supported her plan to continue to fight for Prince Henry's inheritance after her return to Normandy. All her earls would gather for Robert's funeral in Bristol. She would call a conference before they returned to their own lands because, above all, they must agree to her departure – and agree to protect the kingdom in the west during her absence.

Maud wept inconsolably at her brother's funeral, glancing away from the bier and around the peaceful church, which he had built and so much loved. The wall paintings and the acanthus decorations on the pillars comforted her through their messages and stories as much as their beauty. Her eyes dwelled on the Wedding at Canaan, and for a moment she recollected how Robert and Brien had been approving when she was furious at being told to marry an imp so much younger than she and of a lesser status than the Empress of the German lands, Queen of the Romans. Well, the imp had grown into a fine warrior who cared as much about their children's inheritance as she. It was he who had won Normandy for them. Geoffrey also cared deeply about the Church, encouraging Henry to respect its teachings and protect its abbeys. Yet, it had been and still was impossible for her to love Geoffrey. They would never again share a bed, she thought, when she returned to Anjou. Her eyes filled with tears for a different reason, sliding almost involuntarily to Count Brien, who stood opposite her, on the other side of Robert's bier. If only it had all been different. But God had not willed it so.

She would return to Geoffrey – a friend, if not a lover – and to Normandy. She planned to visit abbeys, to found nunneries, to guide Henry's ambitions. The fight in England belonged to others, now. Ranulf of Chester, that arrogant son-in-law of Robert's, would not waver again – he despised Stephen for the latter's treatment of him. John Fitz Gilbert was solid as the rocks that fringed England's shores. Pious Patrick of Salisbury nevertheless showed loyalty and determination – he owed her his earldom, after all. William of Gloucester and Roger of Hereford had youth on their side and a future to embrace once Henry was crowned their king. But it was a great sorrow for Mabel, and for them all, that Philip, the son who had defected to Stephen, had died on his way to King Louis' Crusade, losing his life in a skirmish somewhere she had never heard of, deep in the pine forests of Hungary. Maud wondered if perhaps Robert, in the end, had lost the will to live, when he heard of his son's death.

Robert had been a loyal brother, and he had been the best of all the men she had known. She could almost see their faces – her hot-tempered father, Geoffrey the Imp, fashionable Brien, Miles, Robert. She loved them all, in a way, but Robert had been the one she trusted most, she could see now. She could not continue to live in England without him, though she was comforted by knowing her dearest brother and confidant would be at peace, placed amongst the finest of God's holy angels.

Wareham and the Narrow Sea
February 1148

On a chill February day, Maud, her ladies and household knights rode to Wareham over frozen roads and beneath a pale sun. Her coffers were packed and already waiting to be loaded onto the *Golden Lion*, the ship that, followed by her small fleet, would carry her to Normandy. Her ladies bubbled with anticipation. Many of them, like Lenora, had been with her for years and, at last, they would see their families in Anjou and Normandy again. She noticed Beatrice and Xander holding hands. They dropped their clasp when she glanced their way, which caused a smile to play about her lips. Alice and Jacques, their two children, their maids and nurses, stood together in a small windswept knot. There were five ships accompanying her small fleet, built with shelters for her ladies and deep holds for her horses.

She felt someone step up behind her as she waited to board the *Golden Lion*, and turned. Brien was smiling at her through his beautiful sad dark eyes. His hair was greying, these days, as was his neatly trimmed beard. But he wore a beautiful fur-lined cloak of blue wool, clasped at the shoulder with a pin on which was engraved her Queen of the Romans image, the same as was stamped on her coins. She instinctively reached out and touched it. 'You come to bid me farewell, my heart,' she said.

When he smiled at her, his eyes twinkled as ever, though the sorrow of this parting was sad and its pain reached deep into her heart. If only he could – would – come with her to Falaise. His mouth quirked and she caught her breath as, for a heartbeat, she hoped he might.

But he said nothing, only looked at her, and she knew it was not to be. Brien was an honourable man, who would not leave the Countess Tilda. How fortunate I have been, Maud thought to herself, to always be surrounded by such honourable men. The men who helped me make decisions have all been truly chivalrous knights.

Brien whispered into her ear. She nodded and they moved away from the others, along the quayside. Batted by wind, they spoke of Henry's future and of her own as Duchess of Normandy. He told her that he had decided to enter a monastery and Countess Tilda wished to end her days in a nunnery. Maud was unsurprised about Tilda, but wondered momentarily if Brien could be as elegant a monk as he had been a fashionable knight. Was he telling her all? Was Brien unwell?

'Are you sure this is what you really want, Brien?'

'Dearest Maud, I crave peace within the shelter of the cloisters.'

She studied him. It was true. He *was* tired, just like her. She could not ask him if he was unwell. She could not bear to know, if he did not wish to tell her. They had spent their youth now, and their love belonged to that time.

'I have the promise that William Boterell will safeguard Wallingford, for we have no heirs,' he continued. 'Wallingford Castle will be Henry's when he is King.'

There was little more to say. So many words of love had been left unsaid, but that was as well. One day, Count Brien would depart the world without leaving a trace. If she herself still lived, she would ensure the monks of Reading Abbey prayed many long years for the soul of Brien, whom she had loved all of her life.

Maud looked over her shoulder. Her ladies and knights were anxiously glancing her way. It was time to catch the tide and she must leave him. Realising this too, Brien bent over her hand, turned it around and kissed her palm. Then he kissed her gently on her lips.

'Dearest Maud, Empress of my heart and soul, God speed your sailing and may your seas ahead ever remain calm . . .' He trailed off and took a small leather-bound book from the folds of his cloak. Giving it to her, he said in a soft voice, 'Remember me, Maud, when you read these. I'll never forget how we used to read together. I wrote them for you myself, about Odysseus and Penelope. My artist has decorated them.'

She opened it and her breath caught at the beauty of the illustrations. 'Thank you, my lord Brien. I shall treasure this book all my days.' Tears clouded her eyes as she said, 'Farewell, dearest of knights.'

Her heart heavy, she boarded the *Golden Lion*. Standing by the ship's rail, she watched Brien shrink until he became another small figure on the wharf, absorbed into a crowd of people waving her farewell.

That night, the wind calmed, and as they rocked in the middle of the sea below a canopy of bright stars, the solemn Sir Jacques pointed up to the sky and said, 'Empress, the constellation up there is called the Great Bear.'

'Ah,' she said, with a small catch in her breath. 'The Great Bear. How the stars endure, ever present for us.' She had experienced much change in her life and yet God's lanterns remained a constant, gently twinkling up above in the heavens. 'They are watching over us,' she whispered. 'Thank you, Sir Jacques, for reminding me of their shining beauty.'

Rouen
September 1148

Geoffrey greeted her the following late summer, along with their sons, in Rouen. Until then, she had spent months secluded and resting in Falaise Castle.

She rode into the palace courtyard at Rouen, followed by her retinue, and Geoffrey took her hands as she dismounted. It was a warm early September afternoon, with a soft lilac sky above and the scent of cooking drifting from the kitchens. There would be a welcoming feast. Geoffrey, as solid and good-looking as he ever was, if more lined of face and grey of beard, embraced her. She found herself welling up with emotion.

He held her back and said, in a low voice only she was meant to hear, 'My dearest wife and Duchess, we have managed well together all these years apart, for the sake of our sons. You look well. The months in Falaise, whilst we were quelling a rebellion in Anjou, have allowed you time to reacquaint yourself with our abbeys, our Norman nobles and our subjects, but how it is good to see you!' He touched her veil. 'Though we have both grown grey hairs, God willing, we have years remaining ahead of us to plan further for our children's futures.' He laughed. 'And I have kept young Henry close under my supervision.'

She could not find words, but felt overcome with a desire to see them all. Tears coursed down her cheeks. Geoffrey took a small linen cloth from his cloak pocket and dabbed them away.

'I must see my boys now, this minute,' she croaked through her tears of joy.

'Come, they are waiting in the hall to greet you, all three of our handsome boys.' She noted kindness in his blue eyes, which were misting over too.

Theirs had been a long journey, a great adventure beset with dangers. Now, she was at home in Rouen, in the palace she had long loved. She and Geoffrey had, at long last, discovered an angle of repose and her boys were waiting for her.

Epilogue

Savernake
1149–53

In May of the year 1149, Alice and Jacques and their four children – three boys and Ami – sailed back to England with the Prince they affectionately called Harry. Prince Henry was to be knighted by his great uncle, King David. Jacques travelled north with Henry's troops, to Carlisle. The Prince was sixteen years old.

Alice was welcomed home to her estate on the edge of the Savernake Forest by her steward and his wife and the small collection of servants she had left behind when they crossed the sea to Normandy, eighteen months earlier. To her delight, during her absence, the interior walls of Middleton Manor had been whitewashed and painted as she had instructed. The hall's walls were decorated with woodland scenes suitable for such a handsome dwelling nestling at the edge of a great forest. As she walked through the hall and climbed the staircase to her own chamber and those of her children, she was met with further paintings which she had designed and commissioned. Her nurses, Gudrun and the children followed with wide-open eyes, peering into painted woods, acanthus tendrils, and looking at the small creatures depicted amongst the painted flowers. The smallest boy, Simon, only a year old, was carried by his nurse. Ami and her two little brothers gasped their delight at the Noah's Ark when they entered their nursery. It covered one wall of their chamber.

Alice turned to Gudrun. 'Ah, it is good to return. Much as I love Anjou, and was happy in Bellevue, I have missed England.' She peered from her window, which looked out towards the forest border, where trees had burst into leaf. 'There is nothing as lovely as springtime in England.'

'Mama, can we make flower perfumes? You promised me.' Seven-year-old Ami was tugging at her hand.

'Tomorrow, my love. Today, we must unpack and settle in,' Alice said gently, but firmly. 'But Gudrun will take you to visit the still room now. There is much to look at.'

Ami was mollified and slid her hand into the maid's.

Jacques returned from the north a month later. Their journey had been fraught with difficulties, as they were pursued by – and escaped from – Stephen's son Eustace and his larger army. Seated with Alice in the garden, enjoying twilight with its shade and shadows, Jacques stretched out his long legs and leaned back on a cushion set behind him on the stone bench he shared with her. 'We were fortunate to escape Eustace's ambushes,' he explained. 'His behaviour was despicable. He has no respect for the common people or the clergy. I doubt Harry need fear the competition. Eustace will never be accepted as Stephen's heir.' He glanced around the peaceful garden, where blackbirds and thrushes were roosting in pear trees. 'As well, Alice, we are tucked away here. We should be safe from clashing armies. Even so, we shall fortify the manor. I intend building a tower and a stout drawbridge over our moat before I depart to serve Sir John in Marlborough. I shall leave you with a guard well experienced with both crossbow and longbow.'

She dipped her head over a small garment she was stitching for their second son. Small John was already growing fast and, at three and a half, was a serious child who loved to draw pictures and collect small creatures as pets. She bit off her thread. 'So, we are to remain here after Harry returns to Normandy?'

'Yes, he must sail back, but I think you like it well here. I shall serve Sir John whilst Harry is away. Geoffrey has passed on the dukedom of Normandy to him – Anjou and Maine as well. They must travel to Paris to give homage to the French King Louis. And so, my dear heart, my own time will be divided between here, Marlborough and Lugershall.'

Alice made a quick stitch, looked up, leaned over and kissed him. 'I am so happy here.'

'I am glad of it, since I must spend time with Sir John.'

She nodded and grinned. 'It's a happy manor.'

'I have other news of interest, Alice.'

'You have?' She glanced up from her sewing once again.

'The Benedictine monk from the inn in Southwark appeared again.'

Alice felt her eyes open wide with surprise. She had almost totally forgotten the slippery monk, dishonest without doubt.

Jacques laughed. 'You won't believe it. We discovered him selling relics in a town not far from here – well, closer to the River Severn. I made Sir John aware of who and what we suspected him to be, so Sir John himself approached the false monk's stall and grabbed him by the scruff of the neck, intending to take him prisoner.'

Alice gasped. 'He's never in Marlborough Castle's cells!'

'No, he and his bag of relics are now at the bottom of the Severn. The creature drew a dagger from his boot and attempted to stab Sir John – unsuccessfully, I have to add, but he slashed Sir John's hand as Sir John tried to take the weapon off him. Sir John took the rogue prisoner, gave him a summary trial at our camp. The wretch squirmed and lied. Finally, he half-admitted he had spied and was selling false relics. Sir John had three of his troopers take him out on a skiff into the middle of the Severn. They tied him with rope, weighted him down with heavy stones and dropped him overboard, along with his relics. I doubt he survived.'

Alice crossed herself. It was a harsh punishment, but the Benedictine – who was no monk, but an imposter, a spy and a felon and crook – had long deserved his fate.

In the spring of 1152, Alice received a letter from Beatrice, who was now formally married to Xander, though she still spent some time at Maud's court in Rouen. They had one child, a small boy they called Hugh.

Beatrice wrote:

*. . . The Vexin, as you know, was ceded to King Louis. He divorced
his wife Queen Eleanor, his reason given being consanguinity, but we
believe the truth is that, after fifteen years of marriage, she only gave
him daughters and no sons . . . but events have taken a strange course.
Prince Henry, now Duke of Normandy, has married the very beautiful Eleanor. She is near enough nine years his senior . . .*

How events repeat themselves, Alice thought, with a laugh. How
ironic! I hope she loves him more than Maud did Geoffrey. She
returned to the letter:

*. . . Count Geoffrey has died and the Lady of Aquitaine is with child.
Of course, they pray for a son . . .*

And I am with child again, thought Alice, and I hope for a girl. She
touched her swelling belly. Ami wants a sister. Surely, this time,
we'll be blessed with another daughter.

The summer passed. Jacques, who travelled back and forth from
Marlborough, was at home helping gather in the apple harvest.

'What news?' Alice, heavy with child, asked as they filled baskets
with fruit.

'Stephen cannot command enough support to have his son, Eustace, crowned. Eustace has a poor reputation. The barons do not
consider him throne-worthy. Stephen's son is no noble knight and
he has had no respect for anyone's property. Stephen is furious, as
well as heartbroken following Queen Matilda's death. And, I have
further news: Stephen besieged Newbury, but, during a truce, to
guarantee good behaviour from Sir John, Stephen insisted on taking
hostage one of Sir John's sons. And so Sir John gave up his younger
son, William, as a hostage. Then, the King said, if Sir John did not
give Newbury Castle to him, he would hang the child. He's only six
years old.'

Alice sat her basket down and instinctively placed her hand on
her belly. She paled, despite the warmth of the autumn afternoon.

'Sweet Jesus. A little boy.' Her eyes followed her own boys, who were playing chase through the orchard.

'But Alice, Stephen did not hang William, even after John sent him a message saying, *I still have the hammer and anvil with which to forge more and better sons.* Sir John, by the way, still holds his fastness at Newbury. Stephen has moved away, towards Wallingford.'

Her relief was visible. She wiped sweat from her brow. 'I want a daughter, not more sons,' she said, with a shudder. 'Not this time. Not again. By the rood, Sir John is a hard man.'

'He can be.' Jacques drew her into his arms and added, 'It matters not whether our child is a boy or a girl, my love, as long as the child is healthy. God will give as God intends.'

In January, Alice gave birth to a boy. They named him Jacques, for his father.

Alice's longed-for second daughter, Matilda, was born on the sixth day of November, on the very day a treaty was signed at Winchester to finally end a seemingly endless war. Robert was dead and Maud had long lived in Normandy, but, with this treaty, all lands taken during the conflict were to be returned to their original owners. Henry, Maud's son, would be Stephen's heir. Stephen would remain King until he died.

During the first week of December 1153, Ingrid and Walter rode to Middleton for Alice's churching ceremony. As they sat around a blazing fire on the afternoon of their arrival, Ingrid produced a letter from Countess Tilda. The Countess was residing in a quiet priory close to Oxford, and Count Brien had become a lay monk of Reading Abbey. He passed the months left to him in contemplation and prayer, for the Count was dying of a wasting sickness.

'What memories he must revisit,' Alice said sadly, as she broke Countess Tilda's seal and opened her letter. 'Well, well,' she said, before reading aloud: '. . . *you have a claim to lands and a manor within the county of Leicestershire. They are to be returned to you, as your father's heir. I send you the deed confirming them.*'

Ingrid withdrew from her scrip a rolled deed, with ribbons and Robert de Beaumont's seal. 'It is here.'

Alice read on before examining it: '. . . *My cousin, your father, was the youngest son of a youngest son, and it gives me great pleasure to tell you this at last. May God and his angels protect you, Lady Alice.*' Alice took possession of the deed. 'At last, I have received my inheritance.'

'And,' remarked Ingrid, 'the child of Sir John, William Marshal, has been returned to his father.'

'So I hear, and that Harry one day will be England's King.' She drew a long deep breath. 'Ingrid, I have decided one thing.' She paused and drew breath again, for what she was about to say went against their deeply instilled beliefs. 'With four boys and two daughters, my childbearing years are over.'

'Do not say never, Alice. You are a wealthy woman, and you and Jacques are well able to provide for whatever number of children God grants you.'

Alice shrugged. Childbirth carried many dangers. She was into her fourth decade and six children were enough.

After her churching and the feast following it, Alice's visitors departed. The following morning, she climbed the new tower and peered out at the forest through an arrow-slit window. Out there, somewhere, is my father's home, she thought. When spring returns, we shall visit my inheritance.

Rouen
December 1154

Maud knelt before the Madonna in the Lady Chapel of Rouen Cathedral. It was a bitter day, with a layer of snow coating court-yards and cloisters. She did not notice the chill. The Virgin had spoken to her and helped her to make this difficult decision. She had decided not to attend her son's coronation, but to remain in Rouen as his Regent. Maud had discovered great serenity over the past years, founding new abbeys and making bequests to others. She now had a beloved grandson, and hoped for more. For the ceremony in Westminster Abbey, she had sent Henry a jewel-studded crown, which she had carried amongst her many other treasures from Germany, decades earlier.

At first, claiming his throne had not been easy for Henry, despite the Treaty of Winchester, a year earlier. Horror of horrors, Stephen wanted to adopt Henry as his own son to ensure the succession. Eustace had sought revenge after the Treaty and attacked Bury St Edmunds, sacking the town without quarter. It was God's judgement, she believed, that Eustace died of a seizure shortly after. When Henry had taken Warwick and Bedford castles, Robert de Beaumont came to an agreement with him over his English lands. Lady Alice, amongst others, received their inheritances.

Maud shivered inside her fur-lined mantle. She had been kneeling far too long. Her ladies prayed at a discreet distance, and one, noticing Maud shiver, removed her own mantle and placed it over Maud's shoulders. 'My gown is of warm scarlet wool. I do not have need of this,' the Lady Beatrice whispered into her ear. Maud murmured two further Pater Nosters, counting them off as she clicked her amber beads.

The stolen crown was Henry's, and Henry's alone. The glory was all his and Maud was content.

Author's Note

The story of Matilda, Empress Maud, is an extraordinary historical tale, as is England's twelfth-century Civil War, known to historians as 'The Anarchy'. It was a great pleasure to write this novel and in doing so I have kept closely to the historical record throughout. As a novelist I thoroughly enjoyed animating the personalities involved and dramatising the events. Any errors are my own.

I used both primary and secondary sources whilst researching Maud's fascinating narrative, trying to grasp hold of her possible personality and the personalities of characters close to her, in particular Brien Fitz Count, her half-brother, Robert of Gloucester and Miles of Gloucester. She was close to all three personalities and later put her trust in Sir John the Marshal. It is true that Sir John lost an eye defending Wherwell Priory and that he escaped to Lugershall. The events around Empress Maud's aborted coronation, her escape from Winchester and Robert's capture by Queen Matilda are recorded in the primary sources. It was written in the Histoire de Guillaume le Mareschal that the Empress was riding 'en seant' as women were accustomed to do. It's not practical riding side-saddle at speed and Maud did have lacerations on her thighs on reaching Lugershall. Therefore I put her on a charger and riding astride during her escape from Winchester. She may, in fact, have changed mounts after they crossed the River Test. The earlier eclipse is recorded in William of Malmesbury who lived at the time of these events. Sir John the Marshal was a chivalrous, honourable knight and he was tough. His son William, only six years old, was held hostage by Stephen at Newbury

Castle. Stephen threatened to hang the child but relented. William grew up to become 'The Greatest Knight', significant in English history during the reigns of Henry II, Richard I, King John and into the early reign of King John's son, the boy king, Henry III.

It is my belief that Henry I wanted a grandson to rule England and therefore by the end of Henry's life I believe that he perceived Maud as a regent. It would have been hard in England at that time for a woman to rule in her own right for many reasons that I gave in the novel. Maud was proud and experienced, politically astute, acting as a regent for her first husband, the Holy Roman Emperor, Henry V. Although she was politically aware, as the story says, she made mistakes. She ignored the advice of advisors before her coronation and was not accepted by the London burghers, who preferred Stephen as he facilitated English trading links to Boulogne through his wife, Matilda of Boulogne. Empress Maud was supposed to have been arrogant but if she had been male this accusation might not have been thrown her way. Maud did not attend her son Henry II's coronation, not wishing, I believe, to upstage him in any way, but also because after Geoffrey's death Henry was Duke of Normandy. Empress Maud acted as his regent during his absences from Normandy. She saw him married to Eleanor of Aquitaine, she saw grandchildren born, but Empress Maud never returned to England. I believe Empress Maud and Geoffrey of Anjou, after a turbulent beginning, found peace, an angle of repose, within their marriage, but it was Brien Fitz Count whom Maud loved dearly, though it is unlikely they were ever actual lovers. Their closeness is recorded in various primary sources.

I invented Alice and her brothers. They lived on the Shillingford farm and were musicians and puppeteers. Sir Jacques is also an invented character.

I intended Alice as a foil to Maud but, of course, no invented character really could match the Empress, or Lady of the English, as Maud was also known, in strength of personality and courage. I have long been interested in medieval drama, mummers, their stories, and puppetry during this age. Twelfth-century puppeteers may have used glove puppets, but after a bit of research I found it was more likely the puppets during this period were stick puppets. I felt these characters opened up the novel's scope, allowing a reader to see a little of twelfth-century life other than courtly life and conflict.

Of course, living close to Oxford, my favourite scenes to research and fictionalise were those depicting the Oxford Siege and Maud's escape from Oxford Castle during mid-winter. We do not know the names of the knights who escaped over the ice with Maud and slipped through Stephen's camp with her to Abingdon and Wallingford. It was a remarkable escape and it is recorded in the annals that she and her companions wore white cloaks concealing them when they (most likely) descended from a postern gate and slipped over the millstream as far as the River Isis, as the River Thames was then known at Oxford. The *Anglo-Saxon Chronicles* record that, during the period of The Anarchy, 'Christ and his saints slept.' The Anarchy was a bitter, fifteen-year-long conflict. Maud resided in England for nine years of that conflict.

Empress Maud concerned herself later with the administration of Normandy and supported the Church by founding Cistercian monasteries. She was buried under the High Altar at Bec Abbey after her death in 1167.

I hope you enjoyed reading this book as much as I enjoyed writing it. Reviews are valuable for other readers and for the author. If you could leave a few lines on Amazon or elsewhere I would be appreciative. If you have questions, you can contact me via my website www.carolcmcgrath.co.uk. I also put out a frequent newsletter which you might enjoy. You can subscribe free on my website home page drop-downs. Finally, thank you for reading *The Stolen Crown*. Without prospective readers, Maud's story, or rather my version of it, would never have been written.

If you are interested in further reading about The Anarchy, I recommend both *The Empress Matilda* by Marjorie Chibnall and *Matilda: Empress, Queen, Warrior* by Catherine Hanley.

Acknowledgements

An author never works in a vacuum. A number of people are involved in bringing a book to life and to readers. I would like to thank my publishers at Headline, especially Rosanna Hildyard who read the initial draft of *The Stolen Crown* and provided superb revision advice. My new editor at Headline, Imogen Taylor, is brilliantly supportive, as is her approachable assistant, Zara Baig. Thank you both. I also have a superb line and copy editor, Penelope, and a brilliant proof reader, Jill, who are simply gold. They both have a scary, very sharp and appreciated eye. Then, there's the cover designer and those map artists who all work behind the scenes. My agent, Lisa Eveleigh, is first rate. She also reads my novels closely before they ever see print. I owe Lisa much thanks and value her involvement and encouragement. I feel blessed to have such wonderful support.

I am fortunate to be part of a writer's group called The Vestas, namely Gail, Sue and Denise, all published and successful writers, who read and critique sections of my work that I have found tricky to fictionalise. We have been meeting in Cornwall and in Greece for years, discussing our work and enjoying all our writing retreats in such beautiful locations. I would like, too, to thank historian Sharon Bennett Connolly, who lent me her *Life of Stephen*, an invaluable primary source difficult to find translated from Latin. My Latin is school Latin and rusty. I have two other writers to acknowledge: Alexandra Walsh and Cathie Dunn both read my complete manuscript before anyone else other than Lisa saw it. These two author friends were exceptionally generous with their time and comments. Thank you, Alex and Cathie.

Finally, how does my husband, Patrick, put up with me forever buried away with writing whilst he cooks delicious meals and shops for us? Well, actually, he is also a brilliant wordsmith. My dearest Patrick is a support and helpmate and I owe him more thanks than I can ever express.